FROM
POTTER'S
FIELD

ALSO BY PATRICIA CORNWELL

Postmortem

Body of Evidence

All That Remains

Cruel and Unusual

The Body Farm

PATRICIA CORNWELL

FROM POTTER'S FIELD

LITTLE, BROWN AND COMPANY

A *Little, Brown* Book

First published in the United States in 1995 by Scribner

First published in Great Britain in 1995
by Little, Brown and Company

Copyright © by Patricia Daniels Cornwell 1995

The right of Patricia Cornwell to be identified as the Author
of this Work has been asserted by her in accordance
with the Copyright Designs and Patents Act 1988.

*All characters in this publication are fictitious
and any resemblance to real persons, living or dead,
is purely coincidental.*

A CIP catalogue record for this book
is available from the British Library.

HARDBACK ISBN 0 316 91414 2
C FORMAT ISBN 0 316 91415 0

Typeset by Palimpsest Book Production Limited,
Polmont, Stirlingshire
Printed and bound in Great Britain by
Clays Ltd, St Ives plc

Little, Brown and Company (UK)
Brettenham House
Lancaster Place
London WC2E 7EN

This book is for Dr. Erika Blanton
(Scarpetta would call you friend)

And he said, What hast thou done? the voice of thy
brother's blood crieth unto me from the ground.

FROM
POTTER'S
FIELD

'TWAS THE NIGHT BEFORE CHRISTMAS

He walked with sure steps through snow, which was deep in Central Park, and it was late now, but he was not certain how late. Toward the Ramble rocks were black beneath stars, and he could hear and see his breathing because he was not like anybody else. Temple Gault had always been magical, a god who wore a human body. He did not slip as he walked, for example, when he was quite certain others would, and he did not know fear. Beneath the bill of a baseball cap, his eyes scanned.

In the spot – and he knew precisely where it was – he squatted, moving the skirt of a long black coat out of the way. He set an old army knapsack in the snow and held his bare bloody hands in front of him, and though they were cold, they weren't impossibly cold. Gault did not like gloves unless they were made of latex, which was not warm, either. He washed his hands and face in soft new snow, then patted the used snow into a bloody snowball. This he placed next to the knapsack because he could not leave them.

He smiled his thin smile. He was a happy dog digging on the beach as he disrupted snow in the park, eradicating footprints, looking for the emergency door. Yes, it was where he thought, and he brushed aside more snow until he found the folded aluminum foil he had placed between the door and the frame. He gripped the ring that was the handle and opened the lid in the ground. Below were the dark bowels of the subway and the screaming of a train. He dropped the knapsack and snowball inside. His boots rang on a metal ladder as he went down.

1

Christmas Eve was cold and treacherous with black ice, and crime crackling on scanners. It was rare I was driven through Richmond's housing projects after dark. Usually, I drove. Usually, I was the lone pilot of the blue morgue van I took to scenes of violent and inexplicable death. But tonight I was in the passenger seat of a Crown Victoria, Christmas music drifting in and out of dispatchers and cops talking in codes.

'Sheriff Santa just took a right up there.' I pointed ahead. 'I think he's lost.'

'Yeah, well, I think he's fried,' said Captain Pete Marino, the commander of the violent precinct we were riding through. 'Next time we stop, take a look at his eyes.'

I wasn't surprised. Sheriff Lamont Brown drove a Cadillac for his personal car, wore heavy gold jewelry, and was beloved by the community for the role he was playing right now. Those of us who knew the truth did not dare say a word. After all, it is sacrilege to say that Santa doesn't exist, and in this case, Santa truly did not. Sheriff Brown snorted cocaine and probably stole half of what was donated to be delivered by him to the poor each year. He was a scumbag who recently had made certain I was summoned for jury duty because our dislike of each other was mutual.

Windshield wipers dragged across glass. Snowflakes brushed and swirled against Marino's car like dancing maidens, shy in white. They swarmed in sodium vapor lights and turned as black as the ice coating the streets. It was very cold. Most of the city was home with family, illuminated trees filling windows and fires lit. Karen Carpenter was dreaming of a white Christmas until Marino rudely changed the radio station.

'I got no respect for a woman who plays the drums.' He punched in the cigarette lighter.

'Karen Carpenter's dead,' I said, as if that granted her immunity from further slights. 'And she wasn't playing the drums just now.'

'Oh yeah.' He got out a cigarette. 'That's right. She had one of those eating problems. I forget what you call it.'

The Mormon Tabernacle Choir soared into the 'Hallelujah' chorus. I was supposed to fly to Miami in the morning to see my mother, sister and Lucy, my niece. Mother had been in the hospital for weeks. Once she had smoked as much as Marino did. I opened my window a little.

He was saying, 'Then her heart quit – in fact, that's really what got her in the end.'

'That's really what gets everybody in the end,' I said.

'Not around here. In this damn neighborhood it's lead poisoning.'

We were between two Richmond police cruisers with lights flashing red and blue in a motorcade carrying cops, reporters and television crews. At every stop, the media manifested its Christmas spirit by shoving past with notepads, microphones and cameras. Frenzied, they fought for sentimental coverage of Sheriff Santa beaming as he handed out presents and food to forgotten children of the projects and their shell-shocked mothers. Marino and I were in charge of blankets, for they had been my donation this year.

Around a corner, car doors opened along Magnolia Street in Whitcomb Court. Ahead, I caught a glimpse of blazing red as Santa passed through headlights, Richmond's chief of police and other top brass not far behind. Television cameras lit up and hovered in the air like UFOs, and flashguns flashed.

Marino complained beneath his stack of blankets, 'These things smell cheap. Where'd you get them, a pet store?'

'They're warm, washable, and won't give off toxic gases like cyanide in the event of a fire,' I said.

'Jesus. If that don't put you in a holiday mood.'

I wondered where we were as I looked out the window.

'I wouldn't use one in my doghouse,' he went on.

'You don't have a dog or a doghouse, and I didn't offer to give you one to use for anything. Why are we going into this apartment? It's not on the list.'

'That's a damn good question.'

Reporters and people from law enforcement agencies and social services were outside the front door of an apartment that looked like all the others in a complex reminiscent of cement barracks. Marino and I squeezed through as camera lights floated in the dark, headlights burned and Sheriff Santa bellowed, 'HO! HO! HO!'

We pushed our way inside as Santa sat a small black boy on his knee and gave him several wrapped toys. The boy's name, I overheard, was Trevi, and he wore a blue cap with a marijuana leaf over the bill. His eyes were huge and he looked bewildered on this man's red velvet knee near a silver tree strung with lights. The overheated small room was airless and smelled of old grease.

'Coming through, ma'am.' A television cameraman nudged me out of the way.

'You can just put it over here.'

'Who's got the rest of the toys?'

'Look, ma'am, you're going to have to step back.' The cameraman practically knocked me over. I felt my blood pressure going up.

'We need another box . . .'

'No we don't. Over there.'

'. . . of food? Oh, right. Gotcha.'

'If you're with social services,' the cameraman said to me, 'then how 'bout standing over there?'

'If you had half a brain you'd know she ain't with social services.' Marino glared at him.

An old woman in a baggy dress had started crying on the couch, and a major in white shirt and brass sat beside her to offer comfort. Marino moved close to me so he could whisper.

'Her daughter was whacked last month, last name King. You remember the case?' he said in my ear.

I shook my head. I did not remember. There were so many cases.

'The drone we think whacked her is a badass drug dealer named Jones,' he continued, to prod my memory.

I shook my head again. There were so many badass drug dealers, and Jones was not an uncommon name.

The cameraman was filming and I averted my face as Sheriff Santa gave me a contemptuous, glassy stare. The cameraman bumped hard into me again.

'I wouldn't do that one more time,' I warned him in a tone that made him know I meant it.

The press had turned their attention to the grandmother because this was the story of the night. Someone had been murdered, the victim's mother was crying, and Trevi was an orphan. Sheriff Santa, out of the limelight now, set the boy down.

'Captain Marino, I'll take one of those blankets,' a social worker said.

'I don't know why we're in this crib,' he said, handing her the stack. 'I wish someone would tell me.'

'There's just one child here,' the social worker went on. 'So we don't need all of these.' She acted as if Marino hadn't followed instructions as she took one folded blanket and handed the rest back.

'There's supposed to be four kids here. I'm telling you, this crib ain't on the list,' Marino grumbled.

A reporter came up to me. 'Excuse me, Dr. Scarpetta? So what brings you out this night? You waiting for someone to die?'

He was with the city newspaper, which had never treated me kindly. I pretended not to hear him. Sheriff Santa disappeared into the kitchen, and I thought this odd since he did not live here and had not asked permission. But the grandmother on the couch was in no frame of mind to see or care where he had gone.

I knelt beside Trevi, alone on the floor, lost in the wonder of new toys. 'That's quite a fire truck you've got there,' I said.

'It lights up.' He showed me a red light on the toy truck's roof that flashed when he turned a switch.

Marino got down beside him, too. 'They give you any extra batteries for that thing?' He tried to sound gruff, but couldn't disguise the smile in his voice. 'You gotta get the size right. See this little compartment here? They go in there, okay? And you got to use size C . . .'

The first gunshot sounded like a car backfire coming from the kitchen. Marino's eyes froze as he yanked his pistol from its holster and Trevi curled up on the floor like a centipede. I folded my body over the boy, gunshots exploding in rapid succession as the magazine of a semiautomatic was emptied somewhere near the back door.

'Get *down*! GET DOWN!'

'Oh my God!'

'Oh Jesus!'

Cameras, microphones crashed and fell as people screamed and fought for the door and got flat on the floor.

'EVERYBODY GET DOWN!'

Marino headed toward the kitchen in combat stance, nine-millimeter drawn. The gunfire stopped and the room fell completely still.

I scooped up Trevi, my heart hammering. I began shaking. Grandmother remained on the couch, bent over, arms covering her head as if her plane were about to crash. I sat next to her, holding the boy close. He was rigid, his grandmother sobbing in terror.

'Oh Jesus. Please no Jesus.' She moaned and rocked.

'It's all right,' I firmly told her.

'Not no more of this! I can't stand no more of this. *Sweet Jesus!*'

I held her hand. 'It's going to be all right. Listen to me. It's quiet now. It's stopped.'

She rocked and wept, Trevi hugging her neck.

Marino reappeared in the doorway between the living room and kitchen, face tense, eyes darting. 'Doc.' He motioned to me.

I followed him out to a paltry backyard strung with sagging clotheslines, where snow swirled around a dark heap on the frosted grass. The victim was young, black and on his back, eyes barely open as they stared blindly at the milky sky. His blue down vest bore tiny rips. One bullet had entered through his right cheek, and as I compressed his chest and blew air into his mouth, blood covered my hands and instantly turned cold on my face. I could not save him. Sirens wailed and whelped in the night like a posse of wild spirits protesting another death.

I sat up, breathing hard. Marino helped me to my feet as shapes moved in the corner of my eye. I turned to see three officers leading Sheriff Santa away in handcuffs. His stocking cap had come off and I spotted it not far from me in the yard where shell casings gleamed in the beam of Marino's flashlight.

'What in God's name?' I said, shocked.

'Seems Old Saint Nick pissed off Old Saint Crack and they had a little tussle out here in the yard,' Marino said, very agitated and out of breath. 'That's why the parade got diverted to this particular crib. The only schedule it was on was the sheriff's.'

I was numb. I tasted blood and thought of AIDS.

The chief of police appeared and asked questions.

Marino began to explain. 'It appears the sheriff thought he'd deliver more than Christmas in this neighborhood.'

'Drugs?'

'We're assuming.'

'I wondered why we stopped here,' said the chief. 'This address isn't on the list.'

'Well, that's why.' Marino stared blankly at the body.

'Do we have an identity?'

'Anthony Jones of the Jones Brothers fame. Seventeen years old, been in jail more'n the Doc there's been to the opera. His older brother got whacked last year by a Tec 9. That was in Fairfield Court, on Phaup Street. And last month we think Anthony murdered Trevi's mother, but you know how it goes around here. Nobody saw nothing. We had no case. Maybe now we can clear it.'

'Trevi? You mean the little boy in there?' The chief's expression did not change.

'Yo. Anthony's probably the kid's father. Or was.'

'What about a weapon?'

'In which case?'

'In this case.'

'Smith and Wesson thirty-eight, all five rounds fired. Jones hadn't dumped his brass yet and we found a speedloader in the grass.'

'He fired five times and missed,' said the chief, resplendent in dress uniform, snow dusting the top of his cap.

'Hard to say. Sheriff Brown's got on a vest.'

'He's got on a bulletproof vest beneath his Santa suit.' The chief continued repeating the facts as if he were taking notes.

'Yo.' Marino bent close to a tilting clothesline pole, the beam of light licking over rusting metal. With a gloved thumb, he rubbed a dimple made by a bullet. 'Well, well,' he said, 'looks like we got one black and one Pole shot tonight.'

The chief was silent for a moment, then said, 'My wife is Polish, Captain.'

Marino looked baffled as I inwardly cringed. 'Your last name ain't Polish,' he said.

'She took my name and I am not Polish,' said the chief, who was black. 'I suggest you refrain from ethnic and racial jokes, Captain,' he warned, jaw muscles bunching.

The ambulance arrived. I began to shiver.

'Look, I didn't mean . . .' Marino started to say.

The chief cut him off. 'I believe you are the perfect candidate for cultural diversity class.'

'I've already been.'

'You've already been, *sir*, and you'll go again, *Captain*.'

'I've been three times. It's not necessary to send me again,' said Marino, who would rather go to the proctologist than another cultural diversity class.

Doors slammed and a metal stretcher clanked.

'Marino, there's nothing more I can do here.' I wanted to shut him up before he talked himself into deeper trouble. 'And I need to get to the office.'

'What? You're posting him tonight?' Marino looked deflated.

'I think it's a good idea in light of the circumstances,' I said seriously. 'And I'm leaving town in the morning.'

'Christmas with the family?' said Chief Tucker, who was young to be ranked so high.

'Yes.'

'That's nice,' he said without smiling. 'Come with me, Dr. Scarpetta, I'll give you a lift to the morgue.'

Marino eyed me as he lit a cigarette. 'I'll stop by as soon as I clear up here,' he said.

2

Paul Tucker had been appointed Richmond's chief of police several months ago, but we had encountered each other only briefly at a social function. Tonight was the first time we had met at a crime scene, and what I knew about him I could fit on an index card.

He had been a basketball star at the University of Maryland and a finalist for a Rhodes scholarship. He was supremely fit, exceptionally bright and a graduate of the FBI's National Academy. I thought I liked him but wasn't sure.

'Marino doesn't mean any harm,' I said as we passed through a yellow light on East Broad Street.

I could feel Tucker's dark eyes on my face and sense their curiosity. 'The world is full of people who mean no harm and cause a great deal of it.' He had a rich, deep voice that reminded me of bronze and polished wood.

'I can't argue with that, Colonel Tucker.'

'You can call me Paul.'

I did not tell him he could call me Kay, because after many years of being a woman in a world such as this, I had learned.

'It will do no good to send him to another cultural diversity class,' I went on.

'Marino needs to learn discipline and respect.' He was staring ahead again.

'He has both in his own way.'

'He needs to have both in the proper way.'

'You will not change him, Colonel,' I said. 'He's difficult, aggravating, ill-mannered, and the best homicide detective I've ever worked with.'

Tucker was silent until we got to the outer limits of the Medical College of Virginia and turned right on Fourteenth Street.

'Tell me, Dr. Scarpetta,' he said. 'Do you think your friend Marino is a good precinct commander?'

The question startled me. I had been surprised when Marino had advanced to lieutenant and was stunned when he had become a captain. He had always hated the brass, and then he had become the thing he hated, and he still hated *them* as if he were not *them*.

'I think Marino is an excellent police officer. He's unimpeachably honest and has a good heart,' I said.

'Do you intend to answer my question or not?' Tucker's tone hinted of amusement.

'He is not a politician.'

'Clearly.'

The clock tower of Main Street Station announced the time from its lofty position high above the old domed train station with its terra-cotta roof and network of railroad tracks. Behind the Consolidated Laboratory building, we parked in a slot designated *Chief Medical Examiner*, an unimpressive slip of blacktop where my car spent most of its life.

'He gives too much time to the FBI,' Tucker then said.

'He gives an invaluable service,' I said.

'Yes, yes, I know, and you do, too. But in his case, it poses a serious difficulty. He is supposed to be commanding First

Precinct, not working other cities' crimes, and I am trying to run a police department.'

'When violence occurs anywhere, it is everybody's problem,' I said. 'No matter where your precinct or department is.'

Tucker stared thoughtfully ahead at the shut steel bay door. He said, 'I sure as hell couldn't do what you do when it's this late at night and there's nobody around except the people in the refrigerator.'

'It isn't them I fear,' I matter-of-factly stated.

'Irrational as it may be, I would fear them a great deal.'

Headlights bored into dingy stucco and steel all painted the same insipid beige. A red sign on a side door announced to visitors that whatever was inside was considered a biological hazard and went on to give instruction about the handling of dead bodies.

'I've got to ask you something,' Colonel Tucker said.

The wool fabric of his uniform whispered against upholstery as he shifted positions, leaning closer to me. I smelled Hermès cologne. He was handsome, with high cheekbones and strong white teeth, his body powerful beneath his skin as if its darkness were the markings of a leopard or a tiger.

'Why do you do it?' he asked.

'Why do I do what, Colonel?'

He leaned back in the seat. 'Look,' he said as lights danced across the scanner. 'You're a lawyer. You're a doctor. You're a chief and I'm a chief. That's why I'm asking. I don't mean disrespect.'

I could tell he didn't. 'I don't know why,' I confessed.

He was silent for a moment. Then he spoke again. 'My father was a yardman and my mother cleaned houses for rich people in Baltimore.' He paused. 'When I go to Baltimore now I stay in fine hotels and eat in restaurants at the harbor. I am saluted. I am addressed "The Honorable" in some mail I get. I have a house in Windsor Farms.

'I command more than six hundred people who wear guns

in this violent town of yours. I know why I do what I do, Dr. Scarpetta. I do it because I had no power when I was a boy. I lived with people who had no power and learned that all the evil I heard preached about in church was rooted in the abuse of this one thing I did not have.'

The tempo and choreography of the snow had not changed. I watched it slowly cover the hood of his car.

'Colonel Tucker,' I said, 'it is Christmas Eve and Sheriff Santa has allegedly just shot someone to death in Whitcomb Court. The media must be going crazy. What do you advise?'

'I will be up all night at headquarters. I will make sure your building is patrolled. Would you like an escort home?'

'I would imagine that Marino will give me a ride, but certainly I will call if I think an additional escort is necessary. You should be aware that this predicament is further complicated by the fact that Brown hates me, and now I will be an expert witness in his case.'

'If only all of us could be so lucky.'

'I do not feel lucky.'

'You're right.' He sighed. 'You shouldn't feel lucky, for luck has nothing to do with it.'

'My case is here,' I said as the ambulance pulled into the lot, lights and sirens silent, for there is no need to rush when transporting the dead.

'Merry Christmas, Chief Scarpetta,' Tucker said as I got out of his car.

I entered through a side door and pressed a button on the wall. The bay door slowly screeched open, and the ambulance rumbled inside. Paramedics flung open the tailgate. They lifted the stretcher and wheeled the body up a ramp as I unlocked a door that led inside the morgue.

Fluorescent lighting, pale cinder block and floors gave the corridor an antiseptic ambience that was deceptive. Nothing was sterile in this place. By normal medical standards, nothing was even clean.

'Do you want him in the fridge?' one of the squad members said to me.

'No. You can wheel him into the X-ray room.' I unlocked more doors, the stretcher clattering after me, leaving drips of blood on tile.

'You going solo tonight?' asked a paramedic who looked Latin.

'I'm afraid so.'

I opened a plastic apron and slipped it over my head, hoping Marino would show up soon. In the locker room, I fetched a green surgical gown off a shelf. I pulled on shoe covers and two pairs of gloves.

'Can we help you get him on the table?' a paramedic asked.

'That would be terrific.'

'Hey, guys, let's get him on the table for the Doc.'

'Sure thing.'

'Shoot, this pouch is leaking, too. We gotta get some new ones.'

'Which way do you want his head to go?'

'This end for the head.'

'On his back?'

'Yes,' I said. 'Thank you.'

'Okay. One-two-three *heave*.'

We lifted Anthony Jones from the stretcher to the table, and one of the paramedics started to unzip the pouch.

'No, no, leave him in,' I said. 'I'll X-ray him through it.'

'How long will it take?'

'Not long.'

'You're going to need some help moving him again.'

'I'll take all the help I can get,' I told them.

'We can hang around a few more minutes. Were you really going to do all this alone?'

'I'm expecting someone else.'

A little later, we moved the body into the autopsy suite and

I undressed it on top of the first steel table. The paramedics left, returning the morgue to its usual sounds of water running into sinks and steel instruments clattering against steel. I attached the victim's films to light boxes where the shadows and shapes of his organs and bones brightly bared their souls to me. Bullets and their multitude of ragged pieces were lethal snowstorms in liver, lungs, heart and brain. He had an old bullet in his left buttock and a healed fracture of his right humerus. Mr. Jones, like so many of my patients, had died the way he had lived.

I was making the Y-incision when the buzzer sounded in the bay. I did not pause. The security guard would take care of whoever it was. Moments later I heard heavy footsteps in the corridor, and Marino walked in.

'I would've got here sooner but all the neighbors decided to come out and watch the fun.'

'What neighbors?' I looked quizzically at him, scalpel poised midair.

'This drone's neighbors in Whitcomb Court. We were afraid there was going to be a friggin' riot. Word went down he was shot by a cop, and then it was Santa who whacked him, and next thing there's people crawling out of cracks in the sidewalk.'

Marino, still in dress uniform, took off his coat and draped it over a chair. 'They're all gathered around with their two-liter bottles of Pepsi, smiling at the television cameras. Friggin' unbelievable.' He slid a pack of Marlboros out of his shirt pocket.

'I thought you were doing better with your smoking,' I said.

'I am. I get better at it all the time.'

'Marino, it isn't something to joke about.' I thought of my mother and her tracheotomy. Emphysema had not cured her habit until she had gone into respiratory arrest.

'Okay.' He came closer to the table. 'I'll tell you the serious truth. I've cut it down by half a pack a day, Doc.'

I cut through ribs and removed the breastplate.

'Molly won't let me smoke in her car or house.'

'Good for Molly,' I said of the woman Marino began dating at Thanksgiving. 'How are the two of you doing?'

'Real good.'

'Are you spending Christmas together?'

'Oh yeah. We'll be with her family in Urbana. They do a big turkey, the whole nine yards.' He tapped an ash to the floor and fell silent.

'This is going to take a while,' I said. 'The bullets have fragmented as you can see from his films.'

Marino glanced around at the morbid chiaroscuro displayed on light boxes around the room.

'What was he using? Hydra-Shok?' I asked.

'All the cops around here are using Hydra-Shok these days. I guess you can see why. It does the trick.'

'His kidneys have a finely granular surface. He's very young for that.'

'What does that mean?' Marino looked on curiously.

'Probably an indication of hypertension.'

He was quiet, probably wondering if his kidneys looked the same, and I suspected they did.

'It really would help if you'd scribe,' I said.

'No problem, as long as you spell everything.'

He went to a counter and picked up clipboard and pen. He pulled on gloves. I had just begun dictating weights and measurements when his pager sounded.

Detaching it from his belt, he held it up to read the display. His face darkened.

Marino went to the phone at the other end of the autopsy suite and dialed. He talked with his back to me and I caught only words now and then. They drifted through the noise at my table, and I knew whatever he was being told was bad.

When he hung up, I was removing lead fragments from the brain and scribbling notes with a pencil on an empty, bloody glove packet. I stopped what I was doing and looked at him.

'What's going on?' I said, assuming the call was related to this case, for certainly what had happened tonight was bad enough.

Marino was perspiring, his face dark red. 'Benton sent me a 911 on my pager.'

'He sent you what?' I asked.

'That's the code we agreed to use if Gault hit again.'

'Oh God,' I barely said.

'I told Benton not to bother calling you since I'm here to tell you the news in person.'

I rested my hands on the edge of the table. 'Where?' I said tensely.

'They've found a body in Central Park. Female, white, maybe in her thirties. It looks like Gault decided to celebrate Christmas in New York.'

I had feared this day. I had hoped and prayed Gault's silence might last forever, that maybe he was sick or dead in some remote village where no one knew his name.

'The Bureau's sending a chopper for us,' Marino went on. 'As soon as you finish up this case, Doc. We gotta get out of here. Goddam son of a bitch!' He started pacing furiously. 'He had to do this Christmas Eve!' He glared. 'It's deliberate. His timing's deliberate.'

'Go call Molly,' I said, trying to remain calm and work more quickly.

'And wouldn't you know I'd have this thing on.' He referred to his dress uniform.

'You have a change of clothes?'

'I'll have to stop by my house real fast. I gotta leave my gun. What are you going to do?'

'I always keep things here. While you're out, would you mind calling my sister's house in Miami? Lucy should have gotten down there yesterday. Tell her what's happened, that I'm not going to make it down, at least not right now.' I gave him the number and he left.

*   *   *

20

At almost midnight, the snow had stopped and Marino was back. Anthony Jones had been locked inside the refrigerator, his every injury, old and new, documented for my eventual day in court.

We drove to the Aero Services International terminal, where we stood behind plate glass and watched Benton Wesley descend turbulently in a Belljet Ranger. The helicopter settled neatly on a small wooden platform as a fuel truck glided out of deep shadows. Clouds slid like veils over the full face of the moon.

I watched Wesley climb out and hurry away from flying blades. I recognized anger in his bearing and impatience in his stride. He was tall and straight and carried himself with a quiet power that made people afraid.

'Refueling will take about ten minutes,' he said when he got to us. 'Is there any coffee?'

'That sounds like a good idea,' I said. 'Marino, can we bring you some?'

'Nope.'

We left him and walked to a small lounge tucked between rest rooms.

'I'm sorry about this,' Wesley said softly to me.

'We have no choice.'

'He knows that, too. The timing is no accident.' He filled two Styrofoam cups. 'This is pretty strong.'

'The stronger the better. You look worn out.'

'I always look that way.'

'Are your children home for Christmas?'

'Yes. Everyone is there – except, of course, me.' He stared off for a moment. 'His games are escalating.'

'If it's Gault again, I agree.'

'I know it's him,' he said with an iron calm that belied his rage. Wesley hated Temple Brooks Gault. Wesley was incensed and bewildered by Gault's malignant genius.

The coffee was not very hot and we drank it fast. Wesley

made no show of our familiarity with each other except with his eyes, which I had learned to read quite well. He did not depend on words, and I had become skilled at listening to his silence.

'Come on,' he said, touching my elbow, and we caught up with Marino as he was heading out the door with our bags.

Our pilot was a member of the Bureau's Hostage Rescue Team, or HRT. In a black flight suit and watchful of what went on around him, he looked at us to acknowledge he was aware we existed. But he did not wave, smile or say a word as he opened the helicopter's doors. We ducked beneath blades, and I would forever associate the noise and wind caused by them with murder. Whenever Gault struck, it seemed, the FBI arrived in a maelstrom of beating air and gleaming metal and lifted me away.

We had chased him now for several years, and a complete inventory of the damage he had caused was impossible to take. We did not know how many people he had savaged, but there were at least five, including a pregnant woman who once had worked for me and a thirteen-year-old boy named Eddie Heath. We did not know how many lives he had poisoned with his machinations, but certainly mine was one of them.

Wesley was behind me with his headset on, and my seat back was too high for me to see him when I glanced around. Interior lights were extinguished and we began to slowly lift, sailing sideways and nosing northeast. The sky was scudded with clouds, and bodies of water shone like mirrors in the winter night.

'What kind of shape's she in?' Marino's voice sounded abruptly in my headset.

Wesley answered, 'She's frozen.'

'Meaning, she could've been out for days and not started decomposing. Right, Doc?'

'If she's been outside for days,' I said, 'you would think someone would have found her before now.'

Wesley said, 'We believe she was murdered last night. She was displayed, propped against . . .'

'Yo, the squirrel likes that. That's his thing.'

'He sits them up or kills them while they're sitting,' Wesley went on. 'Every one so far.'

'Every one we know about so far,' I reminded them.

'The victims we're aware of.'

'Right. Sitting up in cars, a chair, propped against a Dumpster.'

'The kid in London.'

'Yes, he wasn't.'

'Looks like he was just dumped near railroad tracks.'

'We don't know who did that one.' Wesley seemed certain. 'I don't believe it was Gault.'

'Why do you think it's important to him that the bodies are sitting?' I asked.

'It's his way of giving us the finger,' said Marino.

'Contempt, taunting,' Wesley said. 'It's his signature. I suspect there is a deeper meaning.'

I suspected there was, too. All of Gault's victims were sitting, heads bowed, hands in their laps or limply by their sides, as if they were dolls. The one exception was a woman prison guard named Helen. Though her body, dressed in uniform, was propped up in a chair, she was missing her head.

'Certainly the positioning . . .' I started to say, and the voice-activated microphones were never quite in sync with the tempo of conversation. It was an effort to talk.

'The bastard wants to rub our noses in it.'

'I don't think that's his only . . .'

'Right now, he *wants* us to know he's in New York . . .'

'Marino, let me finish. Benton? The symbolism?'

'He could display the bodies any number of ways. But so far he's always chosen the same position. *He sits them up*. It's part of his fantasy.'

'What fantasy?'

'If I knew that, Pete, maybe this trip wouldn't be happening.'

Sometime later our pilot took the air: 'The FAA's issued a SIGMET.'

'What the hell is that?' Marino asked.

'A warning about turbulence. It's windy in New York City, twenty-five knots gusting at thirty-seven.'

'So we can't land?' Marino, who hated to fly, sounded slightly panicky.

'We're going to be low and the winds are going to be much higher.'

'What do you mean *low*? You ever seen how *high* the buildings are in New York?'

I reached back between my seat and the door and patted Marino's knee. We were forty nautical miles from Manhattan, and I could just barely make out a light winking on top of the Empire State Building. The moon was swollen, planes moving in and away from La Guardia like floating stars, and from smokestacks steam rose in huge white plumes. Through the chin bubble at my feet I watched twelve lanes of traffic on the New Jersey Turnpike, and everywhere lights sparkled like jewels, as if Fabergé had crafted the city and its bridges.

We flew behind the Statue of Liberty's back, then passed Ellis Island, where my grandparents' first introduction to America was a crowded immigration station on a frigid winter day. They had left Verona, where there had been no future for my grandfather, born the fourth son of a railroad worker.

I came from a hearty, hardworking people who emigrated from Austria and Switzerland in the early eighteen hundreds, thus explaining my blond hair and blue eyes. Despite my mother's assertion that when Napoleon I ceded Verona to Austria, our ancestors managed to keep the Italian bloodline pure, I believed otherwise. I suspected there was genetic cause for some of my more Teutonic traits.

Macy's, billboards and the golden arches of McDonald's appeared, as New York slowly became concrete and parking lots and street sides banked high with snow that looked dirty even from the air. We circled the VIP Heliport on West Thirtieth Street, lighting up and ruffling the Hudson's murky waters as a bright wind sock stood on end. We swayed into a space near a gleaming Sikorsky S-76 that made all other birds seem common.

'Watch out for the tail rotor,' our pilot said.

Inside a small building that was only vaguely warm, we were greeted by a woman in her fifties with dark hair, a wise face and tired eyes. Bundled in a thick wool coat, slacks, lace-up boots and leather gloves, she introduced herself as Commander Frances Penn of the New York Transit Police.

'Thank you so much for coming,' she said, offering her hand to each of us. 'If we're ready, I have cars waiting.'

'We're ready,' Wesley said.

She led us back out into the bitter cold, where two police cruisers waited, two officers in each, engines running and heat on high. There was an awkward moment as we held doors open and decided who would ride with whom. As so often happens, we divided by gender, and Commander Penn and I rode together. I began to ask her about jurisdiction, because in a high-profile case like this one, there would be many people who thought they should be in charge.

'The Transit Police has an interest because we believe the victim met her assailant on the subway,' explained the commander, who was one of three command chiefs in the sixth-largest police department in America. 'This would have been late yesterday afternoon.'

'How do you know this?'

'It's really rather fascinating. One of our plainclothes officers was patrolling the subway station at Eighty-first and Central Park West, and at around five-thirty in the afternoon – this was yesterday – he noticed a peculiar couple emerge from

25

the Museum of Natural History exit that leads directly into the subway.'

We bumped over ice and potholes that shook the bones in my legs.

'The man immediately lit a cigarette while the woman held a pipe.'

'That's interesting,' I commented.

'Smoking is against the law in the subway, which is another reason the officer remembers them.'

'Were they given a summons?'

'The man was. The woman wasn't because she hadn't lit the pipe. The man showed the officer his driver's license, which we now believe was false.'

'You said the couple was strange looking,' I said. 'How so?'

'She was dressed in a man's topcoat and an Atlanta Braves baseball cap. Her head was shaved. In fact, the officer wasn't certain she was a she. At first he assumed this was a homosexual couple.'

'Describe the man she was with,' I said.

'Medium height, thin, with strange sharp features and very weird blue eyes. His hair was carrot red.'

'The first time I saw Gault his hair was platinum. When I saw him last October, it was shoe-polish black.'

'It was definitely carrot red yesterday.'

'And is probably yet another color today. He does have weird eyes. Very intense.'

'He's very clever.'

'There is no description for what he is.'

'Evil comes to mind, Dr. Scarpetta,' she said.

'Please call me Kay.'

'If you call me Frances.'

'So it appears they visited the Museum of Natural History yesterday afternoon,' I said. 'What is the exhibit?'

'Sharks.'

I looked over at her, and her face was quite serious as the young officer driving deftly handled New York traffic.

'The exhibit right now is sharks. I suppose every sort you can imagine from the beginning of time,' she said.

I was silent.

'As best we can reconstruct what happened to this woman,' Commander Penn went on, 'Gault – we may as well call him that since we believe this is who we're dealing with – took her to Central Park after leaving the subway. He led her to a section called Cherry Hill, shot her and left her nude body propped against the fountain.'

'Why would she have gone with him into Central Park after dark? Especially in this weather?'

'We think he may have enticed her into accompanying him into the Ramble.'

'Which is frequented by homosexuals.'

'Yes. It is a meeting place for them, a very overgrown, rocky area with twisting footpaths that don't seem to lead anywhere. Even NYPD's Central Park Precinct officers don't like to go in there. No matter how often you've been, you still get lost. It's high-crime. Probably twenty-five percent of all crime committed in the park occurs there. Mostly robberies.'

'Then Gault must be familiar with Central Park if he took her to the Ramble after dark.'

'He must be.'

This suggested that Gault may have been hiding out in New York for a while, and the thought frustrated me terribly. He had been virtually in our faces and we had not known.

Commander Penn said to me, 'The crime scene is being secured overnight. I assumed you would want to look before we get you safely to your hotel.'

'Absolutely,' I said. 'What about evidence?'

'We recovered a pistol shell from inside the fountain that bears a distinctive firing pin mark consistent with a Glock nine-millimeter. And we found hair.'

'Where was the hair?'

'Close to where her body was displayed, in the scrollwork of an ornate wrought iron structure inside the fountain. It may be that when he was positioning the body, a strand of his hair got caught.'

'What color?'

'Bright red.'

'Gault is too careful to leave a cartridge shell or hair,' I said.

'He wouldn't have been able to see where the shell went,' said Commander Penn. 'It was dark. The shell would have been very hot when it hit the snow. So you can see what would have happened.'

'Yes,' I said. 'I can see.'

3

Within minutes of each other, Marino, Wesley and I arrived at Cherry Hill, where lights had been set up to aid old post lamps at the periphery of a circular plaza. What once had been a carriage turnaround and watering hole for horses was now thick with snow and encircled with yellow crime scene tape.

Central to this eerie spectacle was a gilt and wrought iron ice-coated fountain that did not work any time of year, we were told. It was here a young woman's nude body had been propped. She had been mutilated, and I believed Gault's purpose this time was not to remove bite marks, but to leave his signature so we would instantly identify the artist.

As best we could tell, Gault had forced his latest victim to strip and walk barefoot to the fountain where her frozen body had been found this morning. He had shot her at close range in the right temple and excised areas of skin from her inner thighs and left shoulder. Two sets of footprints led to the fountain, and only one led away. The blood of this woman whose name we did not know brightly stained snow, and beyond the arena of her hideous death Central Park dissolved into thick, foreboding shadows.

I stood close to Wesley, our arms touching, as if we needed each other for warmth. He did not speak as he intensely studied footprints and the fountain and the distant darkness of the Ramble. I felt his shoulder lift as he took a deep breath, then settle more heavily against me.

'Jeez,' Marino muttered.

'Did you find her clothes?' I asked Commander Penn, though I knew the answer.

'Not a trace.' She was looking around. 'Her footprints are not shoeless until the edge of this plaza, right over here.' She pointed about five yards west of the fountain. 'You can clearly see where her bare footprints start. Before that she had on some sort of boot, I guess. Something with no tread and a heel, like a dingo or cowboy boot, maybe.'

'What about him?'

'We may have found his footprints as far west as the Ramble, but it's hard to say. There are so many footprints over there and a lot of churned-up snow.'

'So the two of them left the Museum of Natural History through the subway station, entered the west side of the park, possibly walked to the Ramble, then headed over here.' I tried to piece it together. 'Inside the plaza, he apparently forced her to disrobe and take off her shoes. She walked barefoot to the fountain, where he shot her in the head.'

'That's the way it appears at this time,' said a stocky NYPD detective who introduced himself as T. L. O'Donnell.

'What is the temperature?' asked Wesley. 'Or better put, what was it late last night?'

'It got down to eleven degrees last night,' said O'Donnell, who was young and angry, with thick black hair. 'The windchill was about ten below zero.'

'And she took off her clothes and shoes,' Wesley seemed to say to himself. 'That's bizarre.'

'Not if someone's got a gun stuck to your head.' O'Donnell lightly stomped his feet. His hands were burrowed deep inside the pockets of a dark blue police jacket, which was not warm enough for temperatures this low, even with body armor on.

'If you are forced to disrobe outside in this cold,' Wesley reasonably said, 'you know you are going to die.'

No one spoke.

'You wouldn't be forced to take off clothes and shoes otherwise. The very act of disrobing is to go against any survival instinct, because obviously, you could not survive naked out here long.'

Still, everyone was silent as we stared at the fountain's grisly display. It was filled with snow stained red, and I could see the indentations made by the victim's bare buttocks when her body was positioned. Her blood was as bright as when she had died because it was frozen.

Then Marino spoke. 'Why the hell didn't she run?'

Wesley abruptly moved away from me and squatted to look at what we assumed were Gault's footprints. 'That's the question of the day,' he said. 'Why didn't she?'

I got down beside him to look at the footprints, too. The tread pattern of the impression clearly left in snow was curious. Gault had been wearing some type of footwear with intricate raised diamond-shaped and wavy tread, and a manufacturer's mark in the instep, and a wreathed logo in the heel. I estimated he wore a size seven and a half or eight.

'How is this being preserved?' I asked Commander Penn.

Detective O'Donnell answered, 'We've photographed the shoe impressions, and over there' – he pointed to a cluster of police officers some distance away on the opposite side of the fountain – 'are some better ones. We're trying to make a cast.'

Casting footwear impressions in snow was rife with perils. If the liquid dental stone wasn't cool enough and the snow wasn't frozen hard enough, one ended up melting the evidence. Wesley and I got up. We walked in silence to where the detective had pointed, and as I glanced around I saw Gault's steps.

He did not care that he had left very distinctive footprints. He did not care that he had left a trail in the park that we would painstakingly follow until we reached its end. We were determined to know every place he had been, and yet it did not matter to him. He did not believe we would catch him.

The officers on the other side of the fountain were spraying two shoe impressions with Snow Print Wax, holding aerosol cans a safe distance away and at an angle so the blast of pressurized red wax would not eradicate delicate tread detail. Another officer was stirring liquid dental stone in a plastic bucket.

By the time several layers of wax had been applied to the shoe prints, the dental stone would be cool enough to pour and make casts. The conditions were actually good for what was ordinarily a risky procedure. There was neither sun nor wind, and apparently the NYPD crime scene technicians had properly stored the wax at room temperature, because it had not lost its pressure. Nozzles were not spitting or clogged as I had so often seen with attempts in the past.

'Maybe we'll be lucky this time,' I said to Wesley as Marino headed our way.

'We're going to need all the luck we can get,' he said, staring off into dark woods.

East of us was the outer limits of the thirty-seven acres known as the Ramble, the isolated area of Central Park famous for bird-watching and winding footpaths through dense, rocky terrain. Every guidebook I had ever seen warned tourists that the Ramble was not recommended for lone hikers at any season or time of day. I wondered how Gault had enticed his victim into the park. I wondered where he had met her and what it was that had set him into motion. Perhaps it was simply that she had been an opportunity and he had been in the mood.

'How does one get from the Ramble to here?' I asked anybody who would listen.

The officer stirring dental stone met my eyes. He was about Marino's age, cheeks fleshy and red from the cold.

'There's a path along the lake,' he said, breath smoking.

'What lake?'

'You can't see it real well. It's frozen and covered with snow.'

'Do you know if this path is the one they took?'

'This is a big park, ma'am. The snow's real messed up in most other places, like the Ramble, for example. Over there, nothing – not ten feet of snow – is going to keep away people after drugs or an encounter. Now here in Cherry Hill, you got another story. You got no cars allowed and for sure the horses aren't coming up here in weather like this. So we're lucky. We got a crime scene left.'

'Why are you thinking the perpetrator and the victim started in the Ramble?' asked Wesley, who was always direct and often terse when his profiler's mind was going through its convoluted subroutines and searching its scary database.

'One of the guys thinks he may have spotted her shoe prints over there,' said the officer, who liked to talk. 'Problem is, as you can see, hers aren't very distinctive.'

We looked around snow that was getting increasingly marred by law enforcement feet. The victim's footwear had no tread.

'Plus,' he went on, 'since there may be a homosexual component, we're considering the Ramble might have been a primary destination.'

'What homosexual component?' Wesley blandly asked.

'Based on earlier descriptions of both of them, they appeared to be a homosexual couple.'

'We're not talking about two men,' Wesley stated.

'At a glance, the victim did not look like a female.'

'At whose glance?'

'The Transit Police. You really need to talk to them.'

'Hey, Mossberg, you ready with the dental stone?'

'I'd do another layer.'

'We've done four. We got a really good shell, I mean, if your stuff is cool enough.'

The officer whose surname was Mossberg squatted and began to carefully pour viscous dental stone into a red wax-coated impression. The victim's footprints were near the ones we wanted to save, her foot about the same size as Gault's. I wondered if we would ever find her boots as my eyes followed the trail to an area some fifteen feet from the fountain, where impressions became those of bare feet. In fifteen steps, her bare footprints went straight to the fountain where Gault had shot her in the head.

As I looked around at shadows pushed back from the lighted plaza, as I felt the bite of intense cold, I could not understand this woman's mind-set. I could not understand her compliance last night.

'Why didn't she resist?' I said.

'Because Gault had her scared out of her mind,' said Marino, now by my side.

'Would you take off your clothes out here for any reason?' I asked him.

'I'm not her.' Anger flexed beneath his words.

'We do not know anything about her,' Wesley logically added.

'Except that she had shaved her head for some wacko reason,' Marino said.

'We don't know enough to get a handle on her behavior,' Wesley said. 'We don't even know who she is.'

'What do you think he did with her clothes?' Marino asked, looking around, hands in the pockets of a long camel's hair coat that he had begun to wear after several dates with Molly.

'Probably the same thing he did with Eddie Heath's clothes,' Wesley said, and he could no longer resist walking into the woods, just a little way.

Marino looked at me. 'We don't know what Gault did with Eddie Heath's clothes.'

'I suppose that's the point.' I watched Wesley with a heavy heart.

'Me, I personally don't think the squirrel keeps them for souvenirs. He don't want a lot of crap to haul around when he's on the move.'

'He disposes of them,' I said.

A Bic lighter sparked several times before begrudgingly offering Marino a small flame.

'She was completely under his control,' I thought aloud. 'He led her here and told her to undress, and she did. You can see where her shoe prints stop and her bare footprints begin. There was no struggle, no thought of running away. No resistance.'

He lit a cigarette. Wesley backed away from the woods, careful where he stepped. I felt him look at me.

'They had a relationship,' I said.

'Gault don't have relationships,' Marino said.

'He has his own type of them. Bent and warped as they may be. He had one with the warden of the penitentiary in Richmond and with Helen the guard.'

'Yeah, and he whacked both of them. He cut off Helen's head and left it in a friggin' bowling bag in a field. The farmer who found that little present still ain't right. I heard he started drinking like a fish and won't plant nothing in that field. He won't even let his cows go there.'

'I didn't say he didn't kill the people he has relationships with,' I replied. 'I just said that he has relationships.'

I stared at her footprints nearby. She had worn a size nine or ten shoe.

'I hope they're going to cast hers, too,' I said.

The officer named Mossberg was using a paint stirrer to deftly spread dental stone into every portion of the shoe print he was trying to cast. It had begun to snow again, hard small flakes that stung.

'They won't cast hers,' Marino said. 'They'll get pictures and that's it since she ain't going to be on any witness stand in this world.'

I was accustomed to witnesses who did not speak to anyone but me. 'I would like a cast of her shoe impression,' I said. 'We have to identify her. Her shoes might help.'

Marino went to Mossberg and his comrades, and they all began to talk as they periodically glanced my way. Wesley looked up at the overcast sky as snow fell harder.

'Christ,' he said. 'I hope this stops.'

Snow fell more furiously as Frances Penn drove us to the New York Athletic Club on Central Park South. There was nothing more anyone could do until the sun came up, and I feared by then Gault's homicidal trail would be covered.

Commander Penn was pensive as she drove on streets that were deserted for the city. It was almost half past two A.M. None of her officers were with us. I was in front, Marino and Wesley in the back.

'I will tell you frankly that I do not like multijurisdictional investigations,' I said to her.

'Then you have had much experience with them, Dr. Scarpetta. Anyone who has been through them doesn't like them.'

'They're a pain in the butt,' Marino offered as Wesley, typically, just listened.

'What should we expect?' I asked, and I was being as diplomatic as possible, but she knew what I wanted.

'NYPD will *officially* work this case, but it will be my officers out there digging, putting in the most hours, doing the dog work. That's always the way it is when we share a case that gets a lot of media attention.'

'My first job was with NYPD,' Marino said.

Commander Penn eyed him in the rearview mirror.

'I left this sewer because I wanted to,' he added with his usual diplomacy.

'Do you still know anybody?' she asked.

'Most of the guys I started with have probably either retired, left on disability, or else they've been promoted and are fat and chained to desks.'

I wondered if Marino considered that maybe his peers might say the latter about him.

Then Wesley spoke. 'It might not be a bad idea to see who's still around, Pete. Friends, I mean.'

'Yeah, well, don't hold your breath.'

'We don't want a problem here.'

'No way to totally avoid that,' Marino said. 'Cops are going to fight over this and be stingy with what they know. Everyone wants to be a hero.'

'We can't afford that,' Wesley went on without the slightest fluctuation of intensity or tone.

'No, we can't,' I agreed.

'Come to me whenever you wish,' Commander Penn said. 'I will do everything I can.'

'If they let you,' Marino said.

There were three commands in the Transit Police, and hers was Support and Development. She was in charge of education, training and crime analysis. The department's decentralized detectives fell under the Field Command and therefore did not answer to her.

'I am in charge of computers and, as you know, our department has one of the most sophisticated computer systems in the United States. It is because of our connection with CAIN that I was able to notify Quantico so quickly. I am involved in this investigation. Not to worry,' Commander Penn said calmly.

'Tell me more about CAIN's usefulness in this case,' Wesley spoke again.

'The minute I got details about the nature of the homicide, I thought there was something familiar. I entered what we knew on the VICAP terminal and got a hit. So I called you literally as CAIN was calling me.'

'You'd heard of Gault?' Wesley asked her.

'I can't say that I am intimately acquainted with his MO.'

'You are now,' Wesley said.

Commander Penn pulled in front of the Athletic Club and unlocked the doors.

'Yes,' she said grimly. 'I am now.'

We checked in at a deserted desk inside a lovely lobby of antiques and old wood, and Marino headed for the elevator. He did not wait for us, and I knew why. He wanted to call Molly, with whom he was still infatuated beyond good sense, and whatever Wesley and I might do was something he did not care to know about.

'I doubt the bar is open this late,' Wesley said to me as brass doors shut and Marino invisibly rose to his floor.

'I'm quite certain it isn't.'

We looked around for a moment, as if, if we stood here long enough, someone would magically appear with glasses and a bottle.

'Let's go.' He lightly touched my elbow and we headed upstairs.

On the twelfth floor, he walked me to my room and I was nervous as I tried to insert my plastic card, which at first I held upside down. Then I could not get the magnetized strip in the proper way, and the tiny light on the brass handle stayed red.

'Here,' Wesley said.

'I think I've got it.'

'Could we have a nightcap?' he asked as I opened my door and turned on a light.

'At this hour, we'd probably be better off with a sleeping pill.'

'That's sort of what a nightcap is.'

My quarters were modest but handsomely appointed, and I dropped my bag on the queen-size bed.

'Are you a member here because of your father?' I asked.

Wesley and I had never been to New York together, and it

bothered me that there was yet one more detail about him I did not know.

'He worked in New York. So yes, that's why. I used to come into the city a lot when I was growing up.'

'The minibar is under the TV,' I said.

'I need the key.'

'Of course you do.'

Amusement flickered in his eyes as he took the small steel key from my outstretched hand, his fingers touching my palm with a gentleness that reminded me of other times. Wesley had his way, and he was not like anyone else.

'Should I try to find ice?' He unscrewed the cap from a two-jigger bottle of Dewar's.

'Straight up and neat is fine.'

'You drink like a man.' He handed me my glass.

I watched him slip out of his dark wool overcoat and finely tailored jacket. His starched white shirt was wrinkled from the labors of this long day, and he removed his shoulder holster and pistol and placed them on a dresser.

'It's strange to be without a gun,' I said, for I often carried my .38 or, on more nerve-rattling occasions, the Browning High Power. But New York gun laws did not often bend for visiting police or people like me.

Wesley sat on the bed opposite the one I was on, and we sipped our drinks and looked at each other.

'We haven't been together much the last few months,' I said.

He nodded.

'I think we should try to talk about it,' I went on.

'Okay.' His gaze had not wavered from mine. 'Go ahead.'

'I see. So I have to start.'

'I could start, but you might not like what I would say.'

'I would like to hear whatever you want to say.'

He said, 'I'm thinking that it's Christmas morning and I'm inside your hotel room. Connie is home alone asleep in our

39

bed and unhappy because I'm not there. The kids are unhappy because I'm not there.'

'I should be in Miami. My mother is very ill,' I said.

He silently stared off, and I loved the sharp angles and shadows of his face.

'Lucy is there, and as usual I'm not. Do you have any idea how many holidays with my family I've missed?'

'Yes, I have a very good idea,' he said.

'In fact, I'm not sure there has ever been a holiday when my thoughts have not been darkened by some terrible case. So it almost doesn't matter whether I am with family or alone.'

'You have to learn to turn it off, Kay.'

'I've learned that as well as it can be learned.'

'You have to leave it outside the door like stinking crime scene clothes.'

But I could not. A day never went by when a memory wasn't triggered, when an image didn't flash. I would see a face bloated by injury and death, a body in bondage. I would see suffering and annihilation in unbearable detail, for nothing was hidden from me. I knew the victims too well. I closed my eyes and saw bare footprints in snow. I saw blood the bright red of Christmas.

'Benton, I do not want to spend Christmas here,' I said with deep depression.

I felt him sit next to me. He pulled me to him and we held each other for a while. We could not be close without touching.

'We should not be doing this,' I said as we continued doing it.

'I know.'

'And it's really difficult to talk about.'

'I know.' He reached for the lamp and turned it off.

'I find that ironical,' I said. 'When you think of what we share, what we have seen. Talking should not be difficult.'

'Those darker landscapes have nothing to do with intimacy,' he said.

'They do.'

'Then why are you not intimate with Marino? Or your deputy chief, Fielding?'

'Working the same horrors does not mean the next logical step is to go to bed. But I don't think I could be intimate with someone who does not understand what it's like for me.'

'I don't know.' His hands went still.

'Do you tell Connie?' I referred to his wife, who did not know that Wesley and I had become lovers last fall.

'I don't tell her everything.'

'How much does she know?'

'She knows nothing about some things.' He paused. 'She knows very little, really, about my work. I don't want her to know.'

I did not reply.

'I don't want her to know because of what it does to us. We change color, just as when cities become sooty, moths change color.'

'I don't want to take on the dingy shade of our habitat. I refuse.'

'You can refuse all you like.'

'Do you think it's fair you hold so much back from your wife?' I said quietly, and it was very hard to think because my flesh felt hot where he traced the contours of it.

'It isn't fair for her, and it isn't fair for me.'

'But you feel you have no choice.'

'I know I don't. She understands that there are places in me beyond her reach.'

'Is that the way she wants it?'

'Yes.' I felt him reach for his Scotch. 'You ready for another round?'

'Yes,' I said.

He got up and metal snapped in the dark as he broke screw

41

cap seals. He poured straight Scotch into our glasses and sat back down.

'That's all there is unless you want to switch to something else,' he said.

'I don't even need this much.'

'If you're asking me to say what we've done is right, I can't,' he said. 'I won't say that.'

'I know what we've done is not right.'

I took a swallow of my drink and as I reached to set the glass on the bedside table, his hands moved. We kissed again more deeply, and he did not waste time on buttons as his hands slid under and around whatever was in their way. We were frenzied, as if our clothes were on fire and we had to get them off.

Later, curtains began to glow with morning light and we floated between passion and sleep, mouths tasting like stale whiskey. I sat up, gathering covers around me.

'Benton, it's half past six.'

Groaning, he covered his eyes with an arm as if the sun were very rude to rouse him. He lay on his back, tangled in sheets, as I took a shower and began to dress. Hot water cleared my head, and this was the first Christmas morning in years when someone other than me had been in my bed. I felt I had stolen something.

'You can't go anywhere,' Wesley said, half asleep.

I buttoned my coat. 'I have to,' I said, sadly looking down at him.

'It's Christmas.'

'They're waiting for me at the morgue.'

'I'm sorry to hear it,' he mumbled into the pillow. 'I didn't know you felt that bad.'

4

New York's Office of the Chief Medical Examiner was on First Avenue, across from the Gothic red brick hospital called Bellevue, where the city's autopsies had been performed in earlier years. Winter-brown vines and graffiti marred walls and wrought iron, and fat black bags of trash awaited pickup on top of filthy snow. Christmas music played nonstop inside the beat-up yellow cab squeaking to a halt on a street almost never this still.

'I need a receipt,' I said to my Russian driver, who had spent the last ten minutes telling me what was wrong with the world.

'How much for?'

'Eight.' I was generous. It was Christmas morning.

He nodded, scribbling, as I watched a man on the sidewalk watching me, near Bellevue's fence. Unshaven, with wild long hair, he wore a blue jean jacket lined with fleece, the cuffs of stained army pants caught in the tops of battered cowboy boots. He began playing an imaginary guitar and singing as I got out of the cab.

'Jingle bells, jingle bells, jingle all the day. OHHH what fun it is to ride to Galveston today-AAAAAYYYYY . . .'

'You have admirer,' my amused driver said as I took the receipt through an open window.

He drove off in a swirl of exhaust. There was not another person or car in sight, and the horrendous serenading got louder. Then my mentally disfranchised admirer darted after me. I was appalled when he began screaming, 'Galveston!' as if it were my name or an accusation. I fled into the chief medical examiner's lobby.

'There's someone following me,' I said to a security guard decidedly lacking in Christmas spirit as she sat at her desk.

The deranged musician pressed his face against the front door, staring in, nose flattened, cheeks blanched. He opened his mouth wide, obscenely rolling his tongue over the glass and thrusting his pelvis back and forth as if he were having sex with the building. The guard, a sturdy woman with dreadlocks, strode over to the door and banged on it with her fist.

'Benny, cut it out,' she scolded him loudly. 'You quit that right now, Benny.' She rapped harder. *Don't you make me come out there.'*

Benny backed away from the glass. Suddenly he was Nureyev doing pirouettes across the empty street.

'I'm Dr. Kay Scarpetta,' I said to the guard. 'Dr. Horowitz is expecting me.'

'No way the chief's expecting you. It's Christmas.' She regarded me with dark eyes that had seen it all. 'Dr. Pinto's on call. Now, I can try to get hold of him, if you want.' She headed back to her station.

'I'm well aware it's Christmas' – I followed her – 'but Dr. Horowitz is supposed to meet me here.' I got out my wallet and displayed my chief medical examiner's gold shield.

She was not impressed. 'You been here before?'

'Many times.'

'Hmm. Well, I sure haven't seen the chief today. But I guess that don't mean he didn't come in through the bay and didn't tell me. Sometimes they're here half a day and

I don't know. Hmm. That's right, don't *nobody* bother to tell me.'

She reached for the phone. 'Hmm. No sir, I don't need to know.' She dialed. 'I don't need to know *nothing*, no not me. Dr. Horowitz? This is Bonita with security. I got a Dr. Scarlett.' She paused. 'I don't know.'

She looked at me. 'How you spell that?'

'S-c-a-r-p-e-t-t-a,' I patiently said.

She still didn't get it right but was close enough. 'Yes, sir, I sure will.' She hung up and announced, 'You can go on and have a seat over there.'

The waiting area was furnished and carpeted in gray, magazines arranged on black tables, a modest artificial Christmas tree in the center of the room. Inscribed on a marble wall was *Taceant Colloquia Effugiat Risus Hic Locus Est Ubi Mors Gaudet Succurrere Vitae*, which meant one would find little conversation or laughter in this place where death delighted to help the living. An Asian couple sat across from me on a couch, tightly holding hands. They did not speak or look up, Christmas for them forever wrapped in pain.

I wondered why they were here and whom they had lost, and I thought of all I knew. I wished I could somehow offer comfort, yet that gift did not seem meant for me. After all these years, the best I could say to the bereft was that death was quick and their loved one did not suffer. Most times when I offered such words, they weren't entirely true, for how does one measure the mental anguish of a woman made to strip in an isolated park on a bitterly cold night? How could any of us imagine what she felt when Gault marched her to that ice-filled fountain and cocked his gun?

Forcing her to disrobe was a reminder of the unlimited depths of his cruelty and his insatiable appetite for games. Her nudity had not been necessary. She had not needed it telegraphed to her that she was going to die alone at Christmas with no one knowing her name. Gault could have just shot her and been done with it. He could have pulled out his Glock and caught her unaware. *The bastard.*

'Mr. and Mrs. Li?' A white-haired woman appeared before the Asian couple.

'Yes.'

'I'll take you in now if you're ready.'

'Yes, yes,' said the man as his wife began to cry.

They were led in the direction of the viewing room, where the body of someone they loved would be carried up from the morgue by a special elevator. Many people could not accept death unless they saw or touched it first, and despite the many viewings I had arranged and witnessed over the years, I really could not imagine going through such a ritual. I did not think I could bear that last fleeting glance through glass. Feeling the beginning of a headache, I closed my eyes and began massaging my temples. I sat like this for a long time until I sensed a presence.

'Dr. Scarpetta?' Dr. Horowitz's secretary was standing over me, her face concerned. 'Are you all right?'

'Emily,' I said, surprised. 'Yes, I'm fine, but I certainly wasn't expecting to see you here today.' I got up.

'Would you like some Tylenol?'

'You're very kind, but I'm fine,' I said.

'I wasn't expecting to see you here today, either. But things aren't exactly normal right now. I'm surprised you managed to get in without being accosted by reporters.'

'I didn't see any reporters,' I said.

'They were everywhere last night. I assume you saw the morning *Times*?'

'I'm afraid I haven't had a chance,' I said uncomfortably. I wondered if Wesley was still in bed.

'Things are a mess,' said Emily, a young woman with long, dark hair who was always so demure and plainly dressed that she seemed to have stepped forth from another age. 'Even the mayor's called. This is not the sort of publicity the city wants or needs. I still can't believe a reporter just happened to find the body.'

I glanced sharply at her as we walked. 'A reporter?'

'Well, he's really a copy editor or some such with the *Times* – one of these nutcakes who jogs no matter the weather. So he happens to be out in the park yesterday morning and takes a turn through Cherry Hill. It was very cold and snowy and deserted. He nears the fountain and there the poor woman is. Needless to say, the description in the morning paper is very detailed and people are frightened out of their wits.'

We passed through several doorways, then she poked her head inside the chief's office to gently announce us so we would not startle him. Dr. Horowitz was getting on in years and was getting hard of hearing. His office was scented with the light perfume of many flowering plants, for he loved orchids, African violets and gardenias, and they thrived in his care.

'Good morning, Kay.' He got up from his desk. 'Did you bring someone with you?'

'Captain Marino is supposed to meet us.'

'Emily will make certain he is shown the way. Unless you'd rather wait.'

I knew Horowitz did not want to wait. There was not time. He commanded the largest medical examiner's office in the country, where eight thousand people a year – the population of a small city – were autopsied on his steel tables. A fourth of the victims were homicides, and many would never have a name. New York had such a problem with identifying their dead that the NYPD's detective division had a missing persons unit in Horowitz's building.

The chief picked up the phone and spoke to someone he did not name.

'Dr. Scarpetta's here. We're on our way down,' he said.

'I'll make sure I find Captain Marino,' Emily said. 'Seems like I know his name.'

'We've worked together for many years,' I told her. 'And he's been assisting the FBI's Investigative Support Unit at Quantico for as long as it has existed.'

'I thought it was called the Behavioral Science Unit, like in the movies.'

'The Bureau changed the name, but the purpose is the same,' I said of the small group of agents who had become famous for their psychological profiling and pursuit of violent sex offenders and killers. When I recently had become the consulting forensic pathologist for the unit, I had not believed there was much left that I had not seen. I had been wrong.

Sunlight filled windows in Horowitz's office and was caught in glass shelves of flowers and miniature trees. I knew that in the bathroom orchids grew in the steamy dark from perches around the sink and tub, and that at home he had a greenhouse. The first time I had met Horowitz he had reminded me of Lincoln. Both men had gaunt, benevolent faces shadowed by a war that was ripping society apart. They bore tragedy as if they had been chosen to, and had large, patient hands.

We went downstairs to what the N.Y. office called their mortuary, an oddly genteel appellation for a morgue set in one of the most violent cities in America. Air seeping in from the bay was very cold and smelled of stale cigarettes and death. Signs posted on aqua walls asked people not to throw bloody sheets, shrouds, loose rags or containers into Dumpsters.

Shoe covers were required, eating was prohibited and red biological hazard warnings were on many of the doors. Horowitz explained that one of his thirty deputy chiefs would be performing the autopsy on the unknown woman we believed was Gault's latest victim.

We turned into a locker room where Dr. Lewis Rader was dressed in scrubs and attaching a battery pack to his waist.

'Dr. Scarpetta,' Horowitz said, 'have you and Dr. Rader met?'

'We've known each other forever,' Rader said with a smile.

'Yes, we have,' I said warmly. 'But the last time we saw each other, I guess, was San Antonio.'

'Gee. Has it been that long?'

This had been at the American Academy of Forensic Sciences Bring Your Own Slide session, an evening once a year when people like us got together for show and tell. Rader had presented the case of a bizarre lightning death involving a young woman. Because the victim's clothing had been blown off and her head injured when she had fallen and struck concrete, she had come into the ME's office as a sexual assault. The cops were convinced until Rader showed them that the woman's belt buckle was magnetized and she had a small burn on the bottom of one foot.

I remembered after the presentation Rader had poured me a Jack Daniel's, neat and straight up in a paper cup, and we had reminisced about the old days when there were few forensic pathologists and I was the only woman. Rader was getting close to sixty and was much acclaimed by his peers. But he would not have made a good chief. He did not relish warfare with paperwork and politicians.

We looked like we were suiting up for outer space as we put on air packs, face shields and hoods. AIDS was a worry if one got a needle stick or cut while working on an infected body, but a bigger threat were infections borne on air, such as tuberculosis, hepatitis and meningitis. These days we double-gloved, breathed purified air and covered ourselves with greens and gowns that could be thrown away. Some medical examiners like Rader wore stainless steel mesh gloves reminiscent of chain mail.

I was pulling the hood over my head when O'Donnell, the detective I had met last night, walked in with Marino, who looked irritable and hungover. They put on surgical masks and gloves, no one meeting anybody's eyes or speaking. Our nameless case was in steel drawer 121, and as we filed out of the locker room, mortuary assistants hoisted the body out and set it on top of a gurney. The dead woman was nude and pitiful on her cold, steel tray.

Areas of flesh excised from her shoulder and inner thighs were ghastly patches of darkened blood. Her skin was bright pink from cold livor mortis, typical in frozen bodies or people who have died of exposure. The gunshot wound to her right temple was large caliber, and I could see at a glance the distinct muzzle mark stamped into her skin when Gault had pressed the pistol's barrel against her head and pulled the trigger.

Men in scrubs and masks rolled her into the X-ray room, where each of us was given a pair of orange-tinted plastic glasses to add to our armor. Rader set up a light energy source called a Luma-Lite, which was a simple black box with an enhanced blue fiber-optic cable. It was another set of eyes that could see what ours could not, a soft white light that turned fingerprints fluorescent and caused hairs, fibers and narcotic and semen stains to glare like fire.

'Someone hit the lights,' Rader said.

In the dark, he began going over the body with the Luma-Lite, and multiple fibers lit up like fine-gauge hot wire. With forceps, Rader collected evidence from pubic hair, feet, hands and the stubble on her scalp. Small areas of yellow got bright like the sun as he passed the light over the finger pads of her right hand.

'She's got some chemical here,' Rader said.

'Sometimes semen lights up like that.'

'I don't think that's it.'

'It could be street drugs,' I offered my opinion.

'Let's get it on a swab,' said Rader. 'Where's the hydrochloric acid?'

'Coming up.'

The evidence was recovered and Rader moved on. The small white light passed over the geography of the woman's body, into the dark recessed areas where her flesh had been removed, over the flat plain of her belly and gentle slopes of her breasts. Virtually no trace evidence clung to her wounds. This corroborated our theory that Gault had killed and maimed her where she was found, because had she been transported after the assault, debris would have adhered to drying blood. Indeed, her injuries were the cleanest areas of her body.

We worked in the dark for more than an hour, and she was revealed to me inches at a time. Her skin was fair and seemed a stranger to the sun. She was poorly muscled, thin, and five foot eight. Her left ear had been pierced three times, her right ear twice, and she wore studs and small loops, all in gold. She was dark blond with blue eyes and even features that may not have been so bland had she not shaved her head and were she not dead. Her fingernails were unpainted and chewed to the quick.

The only sign of old injuries were healed scars on her forehead and the top of her head over the left parietal bone. The scars were linear, one and a half to two inches long. The only visible gunshot residue on her hands was an ejector port mark on her right palm between her index finger and thumb, which I believed placed that hand in a defensive position when the pistol was fired. The residue most likely ruled out suicide even if all other evidence had pointed to it, which of course it did not.

'I guess we don't know which was her dominant hand.' Horowitz's voice sounded in the dark somewhere behind me.

'Her right arm is slightly more developed than her left,' I observed.

'Right-handed, then, my guess is. Her hygiene, nutrition were poor,' Horowitz said.

'Like a street person, a prostitute. That's going to be my guess,' offered O'Donnell.

'No hooker I know's gonna shave her head.' Marino's gruff voice sounded from darkness across the table.

'Depends on who she was trying to attract,' said O'Donnell. 'The plainclothes officer who spotted her in the subway thought at first she was a man.'

'This was when she was with Gault,' Marino said.

'When she was with the guy you think was Gault.'

'I don't think it,' Marino said. 'That's who she was with. I can almost smell the son of a bitch, like he leaves a bad odor everywhere he's been.'

'I think what you smell is her,' O'Donnell said.

'Move it down, right about here. Good, thanks.' Rader collected more fibers as disembodied voices continued to converse in a darkness as thick as velvet.

Finally, I confessed, 'I find this very unusual. Generally I associate so much trace with someone who has been wrapped in a dirty blanket or transported in the trunk of a car.'

'It's obvious she hasn't bathed lately, and it's winter,' Rader said as he moved the fiber-optic cable, illuminating a faint childhood scar from a smallpox inoculation. 'She may have been wearing the same clothing for days, and if she traveled on the subway or by bus, she could have collected a lot of debris.'

What this added up to was an indigent woman who had not been reported missing as far as we could tell because she had no home, no one who knew or cared she was gone. She was the tragically typical street person, we assumed, until we got her on table six in the autopsy room, where forensic dentist Dr. Graham waited to chart her teeth.

A broad-shouldered young man with an air of abstraction that I associated with medical school professors, he was an oral surgeon on Staten Island when he worked on the living. But today was his day to work on those who complained with silent tongues, which he did for a fee that probably would not cover his taxi fare and lunch. Rigor mortis was set, and like an obstinate child who hates the dentist, the dead woman would not cooperate. He finally pried her jaws open with a thin file.

'Well Merry Christmas,' he said, moving a bright light close. 'She's got a mouth full of gold.'

'Most curious,' Horowitz said, like a mathematician pondering a problem.

'These are gold foil restorations.' Graham began pointing out kidney bean-shaped gold fillings near the gum line of each front tooth. 'She has them here and here and here.' He pointed again and again. 'Six in all. This is just very rare. In fact, I've never seen it. Not in a morgue.'

'What the hell is gold foil?' Marino asked.

'It's a pain in the ass, is what it is,' said Graham. 'A very difficult, unattractive restoration.'

'I believe in the old days, they were required to pass your dental license exam,' I said.

'That's right.' Graham continued to work. 'The students hated them.'

He went on to explain that gold foil restorations required the dentist to pound gold pellets into a tooth, and the slightest bit of moisture would cause the filling to fall out. Although the restorations were very good, they were labor intensive, painful and expensive.

'And not many patients,' he added, 'want gold showing, especially on the facial surface of their front teeth.'

He continued charting various repairs, extractions, shapes and misshapes that made this woman who she was. She had a slightly open bite and a semicircular wear pattern to her front teeth possibly consistent with her biting down on a pipe, since it was reported to him that she had been seen with a pipe.

'If she was a chronic pipe smoker, wouldn't you expect her teeth to be stained from tobacco?' I said, for I saw no evidence of it.

'Possibly. But look at how eroded her tooth surfaces are – these scooped-out areas at the gum line that required the gold foil.' He showed us. 'The major damage to her teeth is consistent with obsessive overbrushing.'

'So if she brushed the hell out of her teeth ten times a day, she's not going to have tobacco stains,' Marino said.

'Brushing the hell out of her teeth doesn't fit with her poor hygiene,' I commented. 'In fact, her mouth seems inconsistent with everything else about her.'

'Can you tell when she had this work done?' Rader asked.

'Not really,' Graham said as he continued probing. 'But it is consistently good. I'd say it was probably the same dentist who did all of it, and about the only area in the country where you find gold foil restorations still being done is the West Coast.'

'I'm wondering how you can know that,' Detective O'Donnell said to him.

'You can only get these restorations done where there are dentists who still do them. I don't do them. I personally don't know anybody who does them. But there is an organization called the American Academy of Gold Foil Operators that has several hundred members – dentists who pride themselves on still doing this particular restoration. And the largest concentration of them is in Washington State.'

'Why would someone want a restoration like this?' O'Donnell then asked.

'Gold lasts a long time.' Graham glanced up at him. 'There are people who are nervous about what is put into their mouths. The chemicals in composite white fillings supposedly can cause nerve damage. They stain and wear out more quickly. Some people believe silver causes everything from cystic fibrosis to hair loss.'

Then Marino spoke. 'Yo, well, some squirrels just like the way gold looks.'

'Some do,' Graham agreed. 'She might be one of those.'

But I did not think so. This woman did not strike me as one who cared about her appearance. I suspected she had not shaved her head to make a statement or because she thought it looked trendy. As we began to explore her internally, I understood more, even as the mystery of her deepened.

She had undergone a hysterectomy that had removed her uterus vaginally and left her ovaries, and her feet were flat. She also had an old intracerebral hematoma in the frontal lobe of her brain from a coup injury that had fractured her skull beneath the scars we had found.

'She was the victim of an assault, possibly many years ago,' I said. 'And it's the sort of head injury you associate with personality change.' I thought of her wandering the world and of no one missing her. 'She probably was estranged from her family and had a seizure disorder.'

Horowitz turned to Rader. 'See if we can put a rush on tox. Let's check her for diphenylhydantoin.'

5

Little could be done the rest of the day. The city's mind was on Christmas, and laboratories and most offices were closed. Marino and I walked several blocks toward Central Park before stopping at a Greek coffee shop, where I drank coffee because I could not eat. Then we found a cab.

Wesley was not in his room. I returned to mine and for a long time stood before the window looking out at dark, tangled trees and black rocks amid snowy expanses of the park. The sky was gray and heavy. I could not see the ice-skating rink, nor the fountain where the murdered woman was found. Though I had not been on the scene when her body was, I had studied the photographs. What Gault had done was horrible, and I wondered where he was right now.

I could not count the violent deaths I had worked since my career began, yet I understood many of them better than I let on from the witness stand. It is not difficult to comprehend people being so enraged, drugged, frightened or crazy that they kill. Even psychopaths have their own twisted logic. But Temple Brooks Gault seemed beyond description or deciphering.

His first encounter with the criminal justice system had been less than five years ago when he was drinking White Russians in a bar in Abingdon, Virginia. An intoxicated truck driver, who did not like effeminate males, began to harass Gault, who had a black belt in karate. Without a word, Gault smiled his strange smile. He got up, spun around and kicked the man in the head. Half a dozen off-duty state troopers happened to be at a nearby table, which was perhaps the only reason Gault was caught and charged with manslaughter.

His career in Virginia's state penitentiary was brief and bizarre. He became the pet of a corrupt warden, who falsified Gault's identity, facilitating his escape. Gault had been out but a very short time before he happened upon a boy named Eddie Heath and killed him in much the same style he had butchered the woman in Central Park. He went on to murder my morgue supervisor, the prison warden and the prison guard named Helen. At the time, Gault was thirty-one years old.

Flakes of snow had begun to drift past my window and in the distance were caught like fog in trees. Hoofs rang against pavement as a horse-drawn carriage went by with two passengers bundled in plaid blankets. The white mare was old and not surefooted, and when she slipped the driver beat her savagely. Other horses looked on in sad relief against the weather, heads down, coats unkempt, and I felt rage rise in my throat like bile. My heart beat furiously. I suddenly swung around as someone knocked on my door.

'Who is it?' I demanded.

Wesley said, after a pause, 'Kay?'

I let him in. A baseball cap and the shoulders of his overcoat were wet from snow. He pulled off leather gloves and stuffed them in pockets, and removed his coat without taking his eyes off me.

'What is it?' he asked.

'I'll tell you exactly what it is.' My voice shook. 'Come right over here and look.' I grabbed his hand and pulled him to the window. 'Just look! Do you think those poor, pathetic horses ever get a day off? Do you think they are properly cared for? Do you think they're ever groomed or adequately shod? You know what happens when they stumble – when it's icy and they're old as hell and almost fall?'

'Kay . . .'

They're just beaten harder.'

'Kay . . .'

'So why don't you do something about it?' I railed on.

'What would you like me to do?'

'Just do something. The world is full of people who don't do anything and I'm goddam tired of it.'

'Would you like me to file a complaint with the SPCA?' he asked.

'Yes, I would,' I said. 'And I will, too.'

'Would it be okay if we did that tomorrow since I don't think anything's open today?'

I continued looking out the window as the driver beat his horse again. 'That's it,' I snapped.

'Where are you going?' He followed me out of the room.

He hurried after me as I headed to the elevator. I strode across the lobby and out the hotel's front door without a coat. By now, snow was falling hard, and the icy street was smooth with it. The object of my wrath was an old man in a hat hunched over in the driver's seat. He sat up straighter when he saw this middle-aged lady coming with a tall man in her wake.

'You like nice carriage ride?' he asked in a heavy accent.

The mare strained her neck toward me and cocked her ears as if she knew what was coming. She was scarred skin and bones with overgrown hoofs, her eyes dull and rimmed in pink.

'What is your horse's name?' I inquired.

'Snow White.' He looked as miserable as his pitiful mare as he started to cite his fares.

'I'm not interested in your fares,' I said as he looked wearily down at me.

He shrugged. 'So how long you want ride?'

'I don't know,' I said curtly. 'How long do I need to ride before you start beating Snow White again? And do you beat the shit out of her more or less when it's Christmas?'

'I am good to my horse,' he said stupidly.

'You are cruel to this horse and probably to everything alive and breathing,' I said.

'I have job to do,' he said as his eyes narrowed.

'I am a doctor and I am reporting you,' I said as my voice got tighter.

'What?' he chortled. 'You horse doctor?'

I stepped closer to the driver's box until I was inches from his blanket-covered legs. 'You whip this mare one more time, and I will see it,' I said with the iron calm I reserved for people I hated. 'And this man behind me will see it. From that window right up there—' I pointed. 'And one day you will wake up and find I have bought your company and fired you.'

'You do not buy company.' He glanced up curiously at the New York Athletic Club.

'You do not understand reality,' I said.

He tucked his chin into his collar and ignored me.

I was silent as I returned to my room, and Wesley did not speak, either. I took a deep breath and my hands would not stop shaking. He went to the minibar and poured us each a whiskey, then sat me on the bed, propped several pillows behind me, and took off his coat and spread it over my legs.

He turned lights off and sat next to me. For a while he rubbed my neck while I stared out the window. The snow-sky looked gray and wet, but not dreary as when it rained. I wondered about the difference, why snow seemed soft while rain felt hard and somehow colder.

It had been bitterly cold and raining in Richmond the Christmas when police discovered Eddie Heath's frail, naked body. He was propped against a Dumpster behind an abandoned building with windows boarded up, and though he would never regain consciousness, he was not yet dead. Gault had abducted him from a convenience store where Eddie had been sent by his mother to pick up a can of soup.

I would never forget the desolation of that filthy spot where the boy had been found or Gault's gratuitous cruelty of placing near the body the small bag containing the can of soup and candy bar Eddie had purchased before his death. The details made him so real that even the Henrico County officer wept. I envisioned Eddie's wounds and remembered the warm pressure of his hand when I examined him in pediatric intensive care before he was disconnected from life support.

'Oh God,' I muttered in this dim room. 'Oh God, I'm so tired of all this.'

Wesley did not reply. He had gotten up and was standing before the window, drink in hand.

'I'm so tired of cruelty. I'm so tired of people beating horses and killing little boys and head-injured women.'

Wesley did not turn around. He said, 'It's Christmas. You should call your family.'

'You're right. That's just what I need to cheer me up.' I blew my nose and reached for the phone.

At my sister's house in Miami, no one answered. I dug an address book out of my purse and called the hospital where my mother had been for weeks. A nurse in the intensive care unit said Dorothy was with my mother and she would get her.

'Hello?'

'Merry Christmas,' I said to my only sibling.

'I guess that's an irony when you consider where I am. There's certainly nothing merry about this place, not that you would know since you aren't here.'

'I'm quite familiar with intensive care,' I said. 'Where is Lucy and how is she?'

'She's out running errands with her friend. They dropped me off and will be back in an hour or so. Then we're going to Mass. Well, I don't know if the friend will since she's not Catholic.'

'Lucy's friend has a name. Her name is Janet, and she is very nice.'

'I'm not going to get into that.'

'How is Mother?'

'The same.'

'The same as what, Dorothy,' I said, and she was beginning to get to me.

'They've had to suction her a lot today. I don't know what the problem is, but you can't imagine what it's like to watch her try to cough and not make a sound because of that awful tube in her throat. She only made it five minutes off the ventilator today.'

'Does she know what day it is?'

'Oh yes,' Dorothy said ominously. 'Oh yes indeed. I put a little tree on her table. She's been crying a lot.'

A dull ache welled in my chest.

'When are you getting here?' she went on.

'I don't know. We can't leave New York right now.'

'Does it ever strike you, Katie, that you've spent most of your life worrying about dead people?' Her voice was getting sharp. 'I think all your relationships are with dead—'

'Dorothy, you tell Mother I love her and that I called. Please tell Lucy and Janet that I'll try again later tonight or tomorrow.'

I hung up.

Wesley was still standing before the window with his back to me. He was quite familiar with my family difficulties.

'I'm sorry,' he said kindly.

'She would be like that even if I were there.'

'I know. But the point is, you should be there and I should be home.'

When he talked about home I got uncomfortable, because his home and mine were different. I thought again about this case, and when I closed my eyes I saw the woman who looked like a manikin without clothing or wig. I envisioned her awful wounds.

I said, 'Benton, who is he really killing when he kills these people?'

'Himself,' he said. 'Gault is killing himself.'

'That can't be all of it.'

'No, but it is part of it.'

'It's a sport to him,' I said.

'That, too, is true.'

'What about his family? Do we know anything more?'

'No.' He did not turn around. 'Mother and father are healthy and in Beaufort, South Carolina.'

'They moved from Albany?'

'Remember the flood.'

'Oh yes. The storm.'

'South Georgia was almost washed away. Apparently the Gaults left and are in Beaufort now. I think they're also looking for privacy.'

'I can only imagine.'

'Right. Tour buses were rolling past their house in Georgia. Reporters were knocking on their door. They will not cooperate with the authorities. As you know, I have repeatedly requested interviews and have been denied.'

'I wish we knew more about his childhood,' I said.

'He grew up on the family plantation, which was basically a big white frame house set on hundreds of acres of pecan trees. Nearby was the factory that made nut logs and other candies you see in truck stops and restaurants, mostly in the South. As for what went on inside that house while Gault lived there, we don't know.'

'And his sister?'

'Still on the West Coast somewhere, I guess. We can't find her to talk to her. She probably wouldn't anyway.'

'What is the likelihood that Gault would contact her?'

'Hard to say. But we've not learned anything that would indicate the two of them have ever been close. It doesn't appear that Gault has been close – in the normal sense – to anyone his entire life.'

'Where have you been today?' My voice was gentler and I felt more relaxed.

'I talked to several detectives and did a lot of walking.'

'Walking for exercise or work?'

'Mostly the latter, but both. By the way, Snow White is gone. The driver just left with an empty carriage. And he didn't hit her.'

I opened my eyes. 'Please tell me more about your walk.'

'I walked through the area where Gault was seen in the subway station with the victim at Central Park West and Eighty-first. Depending on the weather and what route you take, that particular subway entrance is maybe a five-, ten-minute walk from the Ramble.'

'But we don't know that they went in there.'

'We don't know a damn thing,' he said, letting out a long, weary breath. 'Certainly, we have recovered footwear impressions. But there are so many other footprints, hoof prints, dog prints and God knows what. Or at least there were.' He paused as snow streaked past the glass.

'You're thinking he's been living around there.'

'That subway station's not a transfer station. It's a destination station. People who get off there either live on the Upper West Side or are going to one of the restaurants, the museum or events in the park.'

'Which is why I don't think Gault has been living in that neighborhood,' I said. 'In a station like the one at Eighty-first or others nearby, you probably see the same people over and over again. It seems that the transit officer who gave Gault a ticket would have recognized him if Gault was local and used the subway a lot.'

'That's a good point,' Wesley said. 'It appears Gault was

familiar with the area where he chose to commit the crime. Yet there's no indication he ever spent time in that area. So how could he be familiar with it?' He turned around to face me.

The lights were off in the room, and he was in the shadows before a marbled background of gray sky and snow. Wesley looked thin, dark trousers hanging from his hips, a belt pulled to a new notch.

'You've lost weight,' I said.

'I'm flattered you would notice,' he wryly said.

'I know your body well only when you have no clothes on,' I said matter-of-factly. 'And then you are beautiful.'

'Then is the only time it matters, I guess.'

'No it isn't. How much have you lost and why?'

'I don't know how much. I never weigh myself. Sometimes I forget to eat.'

'Have you eaten today?' I asked as if I were his primary care physician.

'No.'

'Get your coat on,' I said.

We walked hand in hand along the wall of the park, and I could not recall if we had shown affection before in public. But the few people out could not see our faces clearly, not that they would have cared. For a moment my heart was light, and snow hitting snow sounded like snow hitting glass.

We walked without talking for many blocks, and I thought about my family in Miami. I probably would call them again before the end of the day, and my reward would be more complaints. They were unhappy with me because I had not done what they wanted, and whenever that was the case, I furiously wanted to quit them as if they were a bad job or a vice. In truth, I worried most about Lucy, whom I had always loved as if she were my daughter. Mother I could not please, and Dorothy I did not like.

I moved closer to Benton and took his arm. He reached over

with his other hand to take mine as I pressed my body against him. Both of us wore caps, which made it difficult to kiss. So we stopped on the sidewalk in the gathering dark, turned our caps backward like hoodlums and resolved the problem. Then we laughed at each other because of how we looked.

'Damn, I wish I had a camera.' Wesley laughed some more.

'No, you don't.'

I returned the cap to its proper position as I thought of anyone taking a picture of us together. I was reminded that we were outlaws, and the merry moment vanished. We walked on.

'Benton, this can't go on forever,' I said.

He did not speak.

I went on, 'In your real world you are a committed husband and father, and then we go out of town.'

'How do you feel about it?' he said, tension returning to his voice.

'I suppose I feel the same way most people do when they're having an affair. Guilt, shame, fear, sadness. I get headaches and you lose weight.' I paused. 'Then we get around each other.'

'What about jealousy?' he asked.

I hesitated. 'I discipline myself not to feel that.'

'You can't discipline yourself not to feel.'

'Certainly you can. We both do it all the time when we're working cases like this one.'

'Are you jealous of Connie?' he persisted as we walked.

'I have always been fond of your wife and think she is a fine person.'

'But are you jealous of her relationship with me? It would be very understandable—'

I interrupted him. 'Why must you push this, Benton?'

'Because I want us to face the facts and sort through them, somehow.'

'All right, then you tell me something,' I said. 'When I was with Mark while he was your partner and best friend, were you ever jealous?'

'Of whom?' He tried to be funny.

'Were you ever jealous of my relationship with Mark?' I said.

He did not answer right away.

'I would be lying if I didn't admit that I've always been attracted to you. Strongly attracted,' he finally said.

I thought back to times when Mark, Wesley and I had been together. I searched for the faintest hint of what he had just said. I could not remember. But when I had been with Mark, I was focused only on him.

'I have been honest,' Wesley went on. 'Let's talk about you and Connie again. I need to know.'

'Why?'

'I need to know if all of us could ever be together,' he said. 'Like the old days when you had dinner with us, when you came to visit. My wife has begun to ask why you don't do that anymore.'

'You're saying that you fear she is suspicious.' I felt paranoid.

'I'm saying that the subject has come up. She likes you. Now that you and I work together, she wonders why that means she sees less of you rather than more.'

'I can see why she might wonder,' I said.

'What are we going to do?'

I had been in Benton's home and watched him with his children and his wife. I remembered the touching, the smiles and allusions to matters beyond my ken as they briefly shared their world with friends. But in those days it was different because I had been in love with Mark, who now was dead.

I let go of Wesley's hand. Yellow cabs rushed by in sprays of snow, and lights were warm in apartment building windows. The park glowed the whiteness of ghosts beneath tall iron lamps.

'I can't do it,' I said to him.

We turned onto Central Park West.

'I'm sorry, but I just don't think I can be around you and Connie,' I added.

'I thought you said you could discipline your emotions.'

'That's easy for you to say because I don't have someone else in my life.'

'You're going to have to do it at some point. Even if we break this off, you're going to have to deal with my family. If we are to continue working together, if we are to be friends.'

'So now you're giving me ultimatums.'

'You know I'm not.'

I quickened my pace. The first time we had made love I had made my life a hundred times more complicated. Certainly, I had known better. I had seen more than one poor fool on my autopsy table who had decided to get involved with someone married. People annihilated themselves and others. They became mentally ill and got sued.

I passed Tavern on the Green. I stared up at the Dakota on my left, where John Lennon was killed on a corner years ago. The subway station was very close to Cherry Hill, and I wondered if Gault might have left the park and come here. I stood and stared. That night, December 8, I was driving home from a court case when I heard on the radio that Lennon had been shot dead by a nobody carrying a copy of *Catcher in the Rye*.

'Benton,' I said, 'Lennon used to live there.'

'Yes,' he said. 'He was killed right over there by that entrance.'

'Is there any possibility Gault cared about that?'

He paused. 'I haven't thought about it.'

'Should we think about it?'

He was silent as he looked up at the Dakota with its sandblasted brick, wrought iron and copper trim.

'We probably should think about everything,' he said.

'Gault would have been a teenager when Lennon was murdered. As I recall from Gault's apartment in Richmond, he seemed to prefer classical music and jazz. I don't remember that he had any albums by Lennon or the Beatles.'

'If he's preoccupied with Lennon,' Wesley said, 'it's not for musical reasons. Gault would be fascinated by such a sensational crime.'

We walked on. 'There just aren't enough people to ask the questions we need answered,' I said.

'We would need an entire police department. Maybe the entire FBI.'

'Can we check to see if anyone fitting his description has been seen around the Dakota?' I asked.

'Hell, he could be staying there,' Wesley said bitterly. 'So far, money hasn't seemed to be his problem.'

Around the corner of the Museum of Natural History was the snowcapped pink awning of a restaurant called Scaletta, which I was surprised to find lit up and noisy. A couple in fur coats turned in and went downstairs, and I wondered if we shouldn't do the same. I was actually getting hungry, and Wesley didn't need to lose any more weight.

'Are you up for this?' I asked him.

'Absolutely. Is Scaletta a relative of yours?' he teased.

'I think not.'

We got as far as the door, where the maître d' informed us that the restaurant was closed.

'You certainly don't look closed,' I said, suddenly exhausted and unwilling to walk any more.

'But we are, signora.' He was short, balding and wearing a tuxedo with a bright red cummerbund. 'This is a private party.'

'Who is Scaletta?' Wesley asked him.

'Why you want to know?'

'It is an interesting name, much like mine,' I said.

'And what is yours?'

'Scarpetta.'

He looked carefully at Wesley and seemed puzzled. 'Yes, of course. But he is not with you this evening?'

I stared blankly at him. 'Who is not with me?'

'Signor Scarpetta. He was invited. I'm most sorry, I did not realize you were in his party . . .'

'Invited to what?' I had no idea what he was talking about. My name was rare. I had never encountered another Scarpetta, not even in Italy.

The maître d' hesitated. 'You are not related to the Scarpetta who comes here often?'

'What Scarpetta?' I said, getting uneasy.

'A man. He has been here many times recently. A very good customer. He was invited to our Christmas party. So you are not his guests?'

'Tell me more about him,' I said.

'A young man. He spends much money.' The maître d' smiled.

I could feel Wesley's interest pique. He said, 'Can you describe him?'

'I have many people inside. We reopen tomorrow . . .'

Wesley discreetly displayed his shield. The man regarded it calmly.

'Of course.' He was polite but unafraid. 'I find you a table.'

'No, no,' Wesley said. 'You don't have to do that. But we need to ask more about this man who said his last name was Scarpetta.'

'Come in.' He motioned us. 'We talk, we may as well sit. You sit, you may as well eat. My name is Eugenio.'

He led us to a pink-covered table in a corner far removed from guests in party clothes filling most of the dining room. They were toasting, eating, talking and laughing with the gestures and cadences of Italians.

'We do not have full menu tonight,' Eugenio apologized. 'I can bring you *costoletta di vitello alla griglia* or *pollo al limone* with maybe a little *cappellini primavera* or *rigatoni con broccolo*.'

We said yes to all and added a bottle of Dolcetto D'Alba, which was a favorite of mine and difficult to find.

Eugenio went to get our wine while my mind spun slowly and sick fear pulled at my heart.

'Don't even suggest it,' I said to Wesley.

'I'm not going to suggest anything yet.'

He didn't have to. The restaurant was so close to the subway station where Gault had been seen. He would have noticed Scaletta's because of the name. It would have made him think of me, and I was someone he probably thought about a lot.

Almost instantly, Eugenio was back with our bottle. He peeled off foil and twisted in the corkscrew as he talked. 'See, 1979, very light. More like a Beaujolais.' He pulled the cork out and poured a little for me to taste.

I nodded, and he filled our glasses.

'Have a seat, Eugenio,' Wesley said. 'Have some wine. Tell us about Scarpetta.'

He shrugged. 'All I can say is he first come in here several weeks ago. I know he had not been in before. To tell the truth, he was unusual.'

'In what way?' Wesley asked.

'Unusual looking. Very bright red hair, thin, dressed unusual. You know, long black leather coat and Italian trousers with maybe T-shirt.' He looked up at the ceiling and shrugged again. 'If you can imagine wearing nice trousers and shoes like Armani and then wearing T-shirt. It was not ironed, either.'

'Was he Italian?' I asked.

'Oh no. He could fool some people, but not me.' Eugenio shook his head and poured himself a glass of wine. 'He was American. But he maybe spoke Italian because he used the Italian part of the menu. He ordered that way, you know? He would not order in English. Actually, he was very good.'

'How did he pay?' Wesley asked.

'Always charge card.'

'And the name on the charge card was Scarpetta?' I asked.

'Yes, I'm certain. No first name, just the initial K. He said his name was Kirk. Not exactly Italian.' He smiled and shrugged.

'He was friendly, then,' Wesley said as my mind kept slamming into this information.

'He was very friendly sometimes and not so friendly other times. He always had something to read. Newspapers.'

'He was alone?' Wesley asked.

'Always.'

'What kind of charge card?' I said.

He thought. 'American Express. A gold card, I believe.'

I looked at Wesley.

'Do you have yours with you?' he asked me.

'I would assume so.'

I got out my billfold. The card wasn't there.

'I don't understand.' I felt the blood rise to the roots of my hair.

'Where did you have it last?' Wesley asked.

'I don't know.' I was stunned. 'I don't use it much. So many places won't take it.'

We were silent. Wesley sipped his wine and looked around the room. I was frightened and bewildered. I did not understand what any of this meant. Why would Gault come here and pretend to be me? If he had my gold card, how did he get it? And even as I asked that last question, a dark suspicion stirred. Quantico.

Eugenio had gotten up to see about our food.

'Benton,' I said as my blood roared. 'I let Lucy use that card last fall.'

'When she began her internship with us?' He frowned.

'Yes. I gave it to her after she left UVA and was on her way to the Academy. I knew she'd be back and forth to visit me. She'd be flying to Miami for the holidays and so on. I gave her my American Express card to use mostly for plane and Amtrak tickets.'

'And you haven't seen it since then?' He looked dubious.

'I haven't thought about it, to tell you the truth. I generally use MasterCard or Visa, and it seems to me that the Amex card

72

expires this February. So I must have figured Lucy could have it until then.'

'You'd better call her.'

'I will.'

'Because if she doesn't have it, Kay, then I'm going to suspect Gault stole it when the Engineering Research Facility was broken into last October.'

This was what I feared.

'What about your bills?' he asked. 'Have you noticed any strange charges over recent months?'

'No,' I said. 'I don't recall there being any charges at all during October or November.' I paused. 'Should we cancel the card or use it to track him?'

'Tracking him with it may be a problem.'

'Because of money.'

Wesley hesitated. 'I'll see what I can do.'

Eugenio returned with our pasta. He said he was trying to remember if there might be anything else.

'I think his last time here was Thursday night.' He counted his fingers. 'Four days ago. He likes the *bistecca*, the *carpaccio*. Uhhh, let me see. He got *funghi e carciofi* one time and *cappellini* plain. No sauce. Just a little butter. We invite him to the party. Every year we do this to show appreciation to friends and special customers.'

'Did he smoke?' Wesley asked.

'Yes, he did.'

'Do you remember what?'

'Yes, brown cigarettes. Nat Shermans.'

'What about drinking?'

'He like expensive Scotch and nice wine. Only he was' – he lifted his nose – 'snobbish. He think only the French make wine.' Eugenio laughed. 'So he usually got Château Carbonnieux or Château Olivier, and the vintage could be no earlier than 1989.'

'He only got white wine?' I said.

'No red, none. He would not touch red. I send him glass on the house once and he send it back.'

Eugenio and Wesley exchanged cards and other information, then our maître d' returned his attention to his party, which by now was going strong.

'Kay,' Wesley said, 'can you think of any other explanation for what we've just learned?'

'No,' I said. 'The description of the man sounds like Gault. Everything sounds like Gault. Why is he doing this to me?' My fear was turning to fury.

Wesley's gaze was steady. 'Think. Is there anything else of late that you should tell me about? Weird phone calls, weird mail, hang ups?'

'No weird phone calls or hang ups. I get some strange mail, but that's fairly routine in my business.'

'Nothing else? What about your burglar alarm? Has that gone off more than usual?'

I slowly shook my head. 'It's gone off a couple times this month, but there was no sign of anything out of order. And I really don't think Gault has been spending time in Richmond.'

'You've got to be very careful,' he said almost irritably, as if I had not been careful.

'I'm always very careful,' I said.

6

The next day, the city was at work again, and I took Marino to lunch at Tatou because I thought both of us needed an uplifting atmosphere before we went to Brooklyn Heights to meet Commander Penn.

A young man was playing the harp, and most tables were occupied by attractive, well-dressed men and women who probably knew little about life beyond the publishing houses and high-rise businesses that consumed their days.

I was struck by my sense of alienation. I felt lonely as I looked across the table at Marino's cheap tie and green corduroy jacket, at the nicotine stains on his broad furrowed nails. Although I was glad for his company, I could not share my deeper thoughts with him. He would not understand.

'Looks to me like you could use a glass of wine with lunch, Doc,' Marino said, eyeing me closely. 'Go ahead. I'm driving.'

'No, you're not. We're taking a taxi.'

'Point is, you're not driving so you may as well relax.'

'What you're really saying is that you'd like a glass of wine.'

'Don't mind if I do,' he said as the waitress appeared. 'What you got by the glass that's worth drinking?' he asked her.

75

She did a good job of not looking offended as she went through an impressive list that left Marino lost. I suggested he try a Beringer reserve cabernet that I knew was good, and then we ordered cups of lentil soup and spaghetti bolognese.

'This dead lady's driving me crazy,' Marino said after the waitress was gone.

I leaned closer to the table's edge and encouraged him to lower his voice.

He leaned closer, too, adding, 'There's a reason he picked her.'

'He probably picked her because she was there,' I said, pricked by anger. 'His victims are nothing to him.'

'Yeah, well, I think there's more to it than that. And I'd also like to know what brought his ass here to New York City. You think he met up with her in the museum?'

'He might have,' I said. 'Maybe we'll know more when we get there.'

'Don't it cost money to go in there?'

'If you look at the exhibits it does.'

'She may have a lot of gold in her mouth, but it don't look to me like she had much money when she died.'

'I would be surprised if she did. But she and Gault got in the museum somehow. They were seen leaving.'

'So maybe he met her earlier, took her there and paid her way.'

'I'm hoping it will be helpful when we look at what he was looking at,' I said.

'I know what the squirrel was looking at. Sharks.'

The food was wonderful, and it would have been easy to sit for hours. I was tired beyond explanation, as I sometimes got. My disposition was built upon many layers of pain and sadness that had started with my own when I was young. Then over the years, I had added. Every so often I got in moods that were dark, and I was in one now.

I paid the check because when Marino and I were together,

if I picked the restaurant, I picked up the bill. Marino really could not afford Tatou. He really could not afford New York. Looking at my MasterCard made me think of my American Express card, and my mood got worse.

To get to the shark exhibit in the Museum of Natural History, we had to pay five dollars each and go up to the third floor. Marino climbed stairs more slowly than I and tried to disguise his labored breathing.

'Damn, you would think they got an elevator in this joint,' he complained.

'They do,' I said. 'But stairs are good for you. Today this may be the only exercise we get.'

We entered the exhibit of reptiles and amphibians, passing a fourteen-foot American crocodile killed a hundred years ago in the Biscayne Bay. Marino couldn't help but linger at each display, and I got an eyeful of lizards, snakes, iguanas and Gila monsters.

'Come on,' I whispered.

'Look at the size of this thing,' Marino marveled before the twenty-three-foot reticulated python remains. 'Can you imagine stepping on that in the jungle?'

Museums always made me cold no matter how much I loved them. I blamed the phenomenon on hard marble floors and high ceilings. But I hated snakes and their pit organs. I despised spitting cobras, frilled lizards and alligators with bared teeth. A guide was giving a tour to a group of young people who were enthralled before a showcase populated with Komodo reptiles of Indonesia and leatherback sea turtles who would never traverse sand or water again.

'I beg of you, when you're at the beach and have plastic, shove it in the trash, because these fellows don't have Ph.D.'s,' the guide was saying with the passion of an evangelist. 'They think it's jellyfish . . .'

'Marino, let's move on.' I tugged his sleeve.

'You know, I haven't been to a museum since I was a kid.

Wait a minute.' He looked surprised. 'That's not true. Well, I'll be damned. Doris took me here once. I thought this joint looked familiar.'

Doris was his ex-wife.

'I'd just signed on with the NYPD and she was pregnant with Rocky. I remember looking at stuffed monkeys and gorillas and telling her it was bad luck. I told her the kid was going to end up swinging through trees and eating bananas.'

'I beg of you. Their numbers are dwindling and dwindling and dwindling!' The tour guide went on and on about the plight of sea turtles.

'So maybe that's what the hell happened to him,' Marino continued. 'It was coming in this joint.'

I had rarely heard him even allude to his only child. In fact, as well as I knew Marino, I knew nothing about his son.

'I didn't know your son's name was Rocky,' I quietly said as we started walking again.

'It's really Richard. When he was a kid we called him Ricky, which somehow turned into Rocky. Some people call him Rocco. He gets called a lot of things.'

'Do you have much contact with him?'

'There's a gift shop. Maybe I should get a shark key chain or something for Molly.'

'We can do that.'

He changed his mind. 'Maybe I'll just bring her some bagels.'

I did not want to push him about his son, but the topic was within reach, and I believed their estrangement from each other was the root of many of Marino's problems.

'Where is Rocky?' I cautiously asked.

'An armpit of a town called Darien.'

'Connecticut? And it's not an armpit of a town.'

'This Darien's in Georgia.'

'It surprises me I haven't known that before now.'

'He don't do anything you'd have any reason to know about.'

Marino bent over, his face against glass as he stared at two small nurse sharks swimming along the bottom of a tank outside the exhibit.

'They look like big catfish,' he said as the sharks stared with dead eyes, tails silently fanning water.

We wandered into the exhibit and did not have to wait in line, for few visitors were here in the middle of this workday. We drifted past Kiribati warriors in suits of woven coconut husks, and Winslow Homer's painting of the Gulf Stream. Shark images had been painted on airplanes, and it was explained that sharks can detect odors from the length of a football field and electric charges as weak as one-millionth of a volt. They have as many as fifteen rows of backup teeth, are shaped the way they are to more efficiently torpedo through water.

During a short film we were shown a great white battering a cage and lunging for a tuna on a rope. The narrator explained that sharks are legendary hunters of the deep, the perfect killing machine, the jaws of death, the master of the sea. They can smell one drop of blood in twenty-five gallons of water and feel the pressure waves of other animals passing by. They can outswim their prey, and no one is quite certain why some sharks attack humans.

'Let's get out of here,' I said to Marino as the movie ended.

I buttoned my coat and put on my gloves, imagining Gault watching monsters ripping flesh as blood spread darkly through water. I saw his cold stare and the twisted spirit behind his thin smile. In the most frightening reaches of my mind, I knew he smiled as he killed. He bared his cruelty in that strange smile I had seen on the several occasions I had been near him.

I believed he had sat in this dark theater with the woman whose name we did not know, and she unwittingly had watched her own death on screen. She had watched her own blood spilled, her own flesh sliced. Gault had given her a preview of what he had in store for her. The exhibit had been his foreplay.

We returned to the rotunda, where a barosaurus fossil was surrounded by schoolchildren. Her elongated neck bones rose to the lofty ceiling as she eternally tried to protect her baby from an attacking allosaurus. Voices carried, and the sounds of feet echoed off marble as I glanced around. People in uniforms were quiet behind their ticket counters as they guarded the entrances of exhibits from people who had not paid. I looked out glass front doors at dirty snow piled along the cold, crowded street.

'She came in here to get warm,' I said to Marino.

'What?' He was preoccupied with dinosaur bones.

'Maybe she came in here to get out of the cold,' I said. 'You can stand here all day looking at these fossils. As long as you don't go into the exhibits, it doesn't cost you anything.'

'So you're thinking this is where Gault met her for the first time?' He looked skeptical.

'I don't know if it was the first time,' I said.

Brick smokestacks were quiet, and beyond guardrails of the Queens Expressway were bleak edifices of concrete and steel.

Our taxi passed depressing apartments, and stores selling smoked and cured fish, marble and tile. Coils of razor wire topped chain-link fences, and trash was on roadsides and caught in trees as we headed into Brooklyn Heights, to the Transit Authority on Jay Street.

An officer in navy blue uniform pants and commando sweater escorted us to the second floor, where we were shown to the three-star command executive office of Frances Penn. She had been thoughtful enough to have coffee and Christmas cookies waiting for us at the small table where we were to confer about one of the most gruesome homicides in Central Park's history.

'Good afternoon,' she said, firmly shaking our hands. 'Please have a seat. And we did take the calories out of the cookies. We always do that. Captain, do you take cream and sugar?'

'Yeah.'

She smiled a little. 'I guess that means both. Dr. Scarpetta, I have a feeling you drink your coffee black.'

'I do,' I said, regarding her with growing curiosity.

'And you probably don't eat cookies.'

'I probably won't.' I removed my overcoat and took a chair.

Commander Penn was dressed in a dark blue skirt suit with pewter buttons and a high-collared white silk blouse. She needed no uniform to look imposing, yet she was neither severe nor cold. I would not have called her bearing militaristic, but dignified, and I thought I detected anxiety in her hazel eyes.

'It appears Mr. Gault may have met the victim in the museum versus the two of them having met prior to that,' she began.

'It's interesting you would say that,' I said. 'We were just at the museum.'

'According to one of the security guards, a woman fitting the victim's description was seen loitering in the rotunda area. At some point she was observed talking with a man who bought two tickets for the exhibits. In fact, they were observed by several museum employees because of their odd appearance.'

'What is your theory as to why she was inside the museum?' I asked.

'It was the impression of those who remember her that she was a homeless person. My guess is she went in to get warm.'

'Don't they run street people out?' said Marino.

'If they can.' She paused. 'Certainly if they're causing a disturbance.'

'Which she wasn't, I assume,' I said.

Commander Penn reached for her coffee. 'Apparently she was quiet and unobtrusive. She seemed to be interested in the dinosaur bones, walking round and around them.'

'Did she speak to anyone?' I asked.

'She did ask where the ladies' room was.'

'That would suggest to me she'd never been there before,' I said. 'Did she have an accent?'

'If she did, no one remembers.'

'Then it is unlikely she is foreign,' I said.

'Any description on her clothing?' Marino asked.

'A coat – maybe brown or black, short. An Atlanta Braves baseball cap, maybe navy or black. Possibly she was wearing jeans and boots. That's as much as anyone seems to remember.'

We were silent, lost in thought.

I cleared my throat. 'Then what?' I said.

'Then she was spotted talking with a man, and the description of his clothing is interesting. He's remembered as having worn a rather dramatic overcoat. It was black, cut like a long trench coat – the sort you associate with what the Gestapo wore during World War Two. Museum personnel also believe he had on boots.'

I thought of the unusual footwear impressions at the scene, and of the black leather coat mentioned by Eugenio at Scaletta.

'The two of them were spotted in several other areas of the museum, and they did go into the shark exhibit,' Commander Penn went on. 'In fact, the man bought a number of books in the gift shop.'

'You know what kind of books?' Marino asked.

'Books on sharks, including one containing graphic photographs of people who have been attacked by sharks.'

'Did he pay cash for the books?' I asked.

'I'm afraid so.'

'Then he leaves the museum and gets a summons in the subway station,' Marino said.

She nodded. 'I'm sure you're interested in the identification he produced.'

'Yo, lay it on.'

'The name on his driver's license was Frank Benelli, Italian male thirty-three years old from Verona.'

'Verona?' I asked. 'That's interesting, my ancestors are from there.'

Marino and the commander looked briefly at me.

'You saying this squirrel spoke with an Italian accent?' Marino asked.

'The officer recalled that his English was broken. He had a heavy Italian accent, and I'm assuming Gault does not?' Commander Penn said.

'Gault was born in Albany, Georgia,' I said. 'So no, he does not have an Italian accent, but that doesn't mean he didn't imitate one.'

I explained to her what Wesley and I had discovered last night at Scaletta.

'Has your niece confirmed that your charge card is stolen?' she asked.

'I have not been able to get hold of Lucy yet.'

She pinched off a small piece of a cookie and slipped it between her lips, then said, 'The officer who wrote the summons grew up in an Italian family here in New York, Dr. Scarpetta. He thought the man's accent seemed authentic. Gault must be very good.'

'I'm sure he is.'

'Did he ever take Italian in high school or college?'

'I don't know,' I said. 'But he didn't finish college.'

'Where did he go?'

'A private college in North Carolina called Davidson.'

'It's very expensive and difficult to get into,' she said.

'Yes. His family has money and Gault is extremely intelligent. From what I understand, he lasted about a year.'

'Kicked out?' I could tell she was fascinated by him.

'As I understand it.'

'Why?'

'I believe he violated the honor code.'

'I know it's hard to believe,' Marino said sarcastically.

'And then what? Another college?' Commander Penn inquired.

'I don't think so,' I said.

'Has anyone gone down to Davidson to ask about him?' She

looked skeptical, as if those who had been working this case had not done enough.

'I don't know if anyone has, but I doubt it, to be frank.'

'He's only in his early thirties. We're not talking that long ago. People there should remember him.'

Marino had begun picking apart his Styrofoam coffee cup. He looked up at the commander. 'You checked out this Benelli guy to see if he really exists?'

'We're in the process. So far we have no confirmation,' she replied. 'These things can be slow, especially this time of year.'

'The Bureau has a legal attaché at the American Embassy in Rome,' I said. 'That might expedite the matter.'

We talked a while longer, and then Commander Penn walked us to the door.

'Dr. Scarpetta,' she said, 'I wonder if I could have a quick word with you before you go.'

Marino glanced at both of us and said, as if the question had been posed to him, 'Sure. Go ahead, I'll be out here.'

Commander Penn shut her door.

'I'm wondering if we could get together later,' she said to me.

I hesitated. 'I suppose that would be possible. What did you have in mind?'

'Might you be free for dinner tonight, say around seven? I thought we could talk some more and relax.' She smiled.

I had hoped Wesley and I could have dinner together. I told her, 'That is very gracious of you. Of course I will come.'

She slipped a card from a pocket and handed it to me. 'My address,' she said. 'I'll see you then.'

Marino did not ask what Commander Penn had said to me, but it was clear he wondered and was bothered that he had been excluded from the communication.

'Everything all right?' he asked as we were shown to the elevator.

'No,' I said. 'Everything is not all right. If it were, we would not be in New York right now.'

'Hell,' he said sourly, 'I quit having holidays when I became a cop. Holidays aren't for people like us.'

'Well, they should be,' I said, waving at a cab that was already engaged.

'That's bullshit. How many times have you been called out on Christmas Eve, Christmas Day, Thanksgiving, Labor Day weekend?'

Another cab flew by.

'Holidays is when squirrels like Gault got no place to go and no one to see, so they entertain themselves the way he did the other night. And half the rest of the world gets depressed and leaves their husband, wife, blows their brains out or gets drunk and dies in a car wreck.'

'Darn,' I muttered, searching up and down the busy street. 'If you'd like to assist in this endeavor, it would be appreciated. Unless you'd like to walk across the Brooklyn Bridge.'

He stepped out into the street and waved his arms. Instantly, a cab veered toward us and halted. We got in. The driver was Iranian and Marino was not nice to him. When I returned to my room, I took a long hot bath and tried to call Lucy again. Dorothy, unfortunately, answered the phone.

'How is Mother?' I said right off.

'Lucy and I spent the morning with her at the hospital. She's very depressed and looks horrible. I think of all those years I told her not to smoke, and look at her. A machine breathes for her. She has a hole cut in her neck. And yesterday I caught Lucy smoking a cigarette in the backyard.'

'When did she start smoking?' I said, dismayed.

'I have no idea. You see her more than I do.'

'Is she there?'

'Hold on.'

The receiver bumped loudly against whatever Dorothy set it on.

'Merry Christmas, Aunt Kay,' Lucy's voice came over the line, and she did not sound merry.

'It hasn't been a very merry one for me, either,' I said. 'How was your visit with Grans?'

'She started crying and we couldn't understand what she was trying to tell us. Then Mother was in a hurry to leave because she had a tennis match.'

'Tennis?' I said. 'Since when?'

'She's on another one of her fitness kicks.'

'She says you're smoking.'

'I don't do it much.' Lucy dismissed my remark as if it were nothing.

'Lucy, we need to talk about this. You don't need another addiction.'

'I'm not going to get addicted.'

'That's what I thought when I started at your age. Quitting was the hardest thing I've ever done. It was absolute hell.'

'I know all about how hard it is to quit things. I have no intention of putting myself in a situation that I can't control.'

'Good.'

She added, 'I'm flying back to Washington tomorrow.'

'I thought you were going to stay in Miami at least a week.'

'I've got to get back to Quantico. Something's going on with CAIN. ERF paged me early this afternoon.'

The Engineering Research Facility was where the FBI worked on researching and designing highly classified technology ranging from surveillance devices to robots. It was here that Lucy had been developing the Crime Artificial Intelligence Network.

CAIN was a centralized computer system linking police departments and other investigative agencies to one massive database maintained by the FBI's Violent Criminal Apprehension Program, or VICAP. The point was to alert police that they might be dealing with a violent offender who has raped or murdered elsewhere before. Then, if requested, Wesley's unit could be called in, as we had been by New York City.

'Is there a problem?' I asked uneasily, for there had been a serious problem in the recent past.

'Not according to the audit log. There's no record of anyone being in the system who isn't supposed to be. But CAIN seems to be sending messages that he hasn't been instructed to send. Something strange has been going on for a while, but so far I've been unable to track it. It's as if he's thinking for himself.'

'I thought that was the point of artificial intelligence,' I said.

'Not quite,' said my niece, who had a genius IQ. 'These are not normal messages.'

'Can you give me an example?'

'Okay. Yesterday, the British Transport Police entered a case in their VICAP terminal. It was a rape that occurred in Central London in one of the subways. CAIN processed the information, ran details against its database and called back the terminal where the case had been entered. The investigating officer in London got the message that further information was requested on the description of the assailant. Specifically, CAIN wanted to know the color of the assailant's pubic hair and if the victim had had an orgasm.'

'You aren't serious,' I said.

'CAIN has never been programmed to ask anything remotely similar to that. Obviously, it's not part of VICAP's protocol. The officer in London was upset and reported what had happened to an assistant chief constable, who called the director at Quantico, who then called Benton Wesley.'

'Benton called you?' I asked.

'Well, he actually had someone from ERF call me. He's heading back to Quantico tomorrow, too.'

'I see.' My voice was steady and I did not show I cared that Wesley was leaving tomorrow or anytime without having told me first. 'Are we certain that the officer in London was telling the truth – that maybe he didn't make up something like this as a joke?'

'A printout was faxed, and according to ERF the message looks authentic. Only a programmer intimately familiar with CAIN could have gotten in and faked a transmission like that. And again, from what I've been told, there is no evidence in the audit log that anyone has tampered with anything.'

Lucy went on to explain again that CAIN was run on a UNIX platform with Local Area Networks connected to Greater Area Networks. She talked about gateways and ports and passwords that automatically changed every sixty days. Only the three superusers, of which she was one, could really tamper with the brains of the system. Users at remote sites, like the officer in London, could do nothing beyond entering their data on a dumb terminal or PC connected to the twenty-gigabyte server that resided at Quantico.

'CAIN is probably the most secure system I've ever heard of,' Lucy added. 'Keeping it airtight is our top priority.'

But it wasn't always airtight. Last fall ERF had been broken into, and we had reason to believe Gault was involved. I did not need to remind Lucy of this. She had been interning there at the time and now was responsible for undoing the damage.

'Look, Aunt Kay,' she said, reading my mind. 'I have turned CAIN inside out. I've been through every program and rewritten major portions of some to ensure there's no threat.'

'No threat from whom?' I asked. 'CAIN or Gault?'

'No one will get in,' she said flatly. 'No one will. No one can.'

Then I told her about my American Express card, and her silence was chilling.

'Oh no,' she said. 'It never even entered my mind.'

'You remember I gave it to you last fall when you started your internship at ERF,' I reminded her. 'I said you could use it for train and plane tickets.'

'But I never needed it because you ended up letting me use

your car. Then the wreck happened and I didn't go anywhere for a while.'

'Where did you keep the card? In your billfold?'

'No.' She confirmed my fears. 'At ERF, in my desk drawer in a letter from you. I figured that was as safe as any place.'

'And that's where it was when the break-in occurred?'

'Yes. It's gone, Aunt Kay. The more I think about it, the more I'm sure. I would have seen it since then,' she stammered. 'I would have come across it while digging in the drawer. I'll check when I get back, but I know it's not going to be there.'

'That's what I thought,' I said.

'I'm really sorry. Has someone rung up a lot of charges on it?'

'I don't think so.' I did not tell her who that someone was.

'You've canceled it by now, right?'

'It's being taken care of,' I said. 'Tell your mother I will be down to see Grans as soon as I can.'

'As soon as you can is never soon,' my niece said.

'I know. I'm a terrible daughter and a rotten aunt.'

'You're not always a rotten aunt.'

'Thank you very much,' I said.

7

Commander Frances Penn's private residence was on the west side of Manhattan where I could see the lights of New Jersey on the other side of the Hudson River. She lived fifteen floors up in a dingy building in a dirty part of the city that was instantly forgotten when she opened her white front door.

Her apartment was filled with light and art and the fragrances of fine foods. Walls were whitewashed and arranged with pen-and-ink drawings and abstracts in watercolor and pastel. A scan of books on shelves and tables told me that she loved Ayn Rand and Annie Leibovitz and read numerous biographies and histories, including Shelby Foote's magnificent volumes on that terrible, tragic war.

'Let me take your coat,' she said.

I relinquished it, gloves and a black cashmere scarf I was fond of because it had been a gift from Lucy.

'You know, I didn't think to ask if there's anything you can't eat,' she said from the hall closet near the front door. 'Can you eat shellfish? Because if you can't, I have chicken.'

'Shellfish would be wonderful,' I said.

'Good.' She showed me into the living room, which offered

a magnificent view of the George Washington Bridge spanning the river like a necklace of bright jewels caught in space. 'I understand you drink Scotch.'

'Something lighter would be better,' I said, sitting on a soft leather couch the color of honey.

'Wine?'

I said that would be fine, and she disappeared into the kitchen long enough to pour two glasses of a crisp chardonnay. Commander Penn was dressed in black jeans and a gray wool sweater with sleeves shoved up. I saw for the first time that her forearms were horribly scarred.

'From my younger, more reckless days.' She caught me looking. 'I was on the back of a motorcycle and ended up leaving quite a lot of my hide on the road.'

'Donorcycles, as we call them,' I said.

'It was my boyfriend's. I was seventeen and he was twenty.'

'What happened to him?'

'He slid into oncoming traffic and was killed,' she said with the matter-of-factness of someone who has freely talked about a loss for a long time. 'That was when I got interested in police work.' She sipped her wine. 'Don't ask me the connection because I'm not sure I know.'

'Sometimes when one is touched by tragedy he becomes its student.'

'Is that your explanation?' She watched me closely with eyes that missed little and revealed less.

'My father died when I was twelve,' I simply said.

'Where was this?'

'Miami. He owned a small grocery store, which my mother eventually ran because he was sick many years before he died.'

'If your mother ran the store, so to speak, then who ran your household while your father lingered?'

'I suppose I did.'

'I thought as much. I probably could have told you that before you said a word. And my guess is you are the oldest child, have no brothers, and have always been an overachiever who cannot accept failure.'

I listened.

'Therefore, personal relationships are your nemesis because you can't have a good one by overachieving. You can't earn a happy love affair or be promoted into a happy marriage. And if someone you care about has a problem, you think you should have prevented it and most certainly should fix it.'

'Why are you dissecting me?' I asked directly but without defensiveness. Mostly, I was fascinated.

'Your story is my story. There are many women like us. Yet we never seem to get together, have you ever noticed that?'

'I notice it all the time,' I said.

'Well' – she set down her wine – 'I really didn't invite you over to interview you. But I would be less than honest if I told you that I didn't want an opportunity for us to get better acquainted.'

'Thank you, Frances,' I said. 'I am pleased you feel that way.'

'Excuse me a minute.'

She got up and returned to the kitchen. I heard a refrigerator door shut, water run and pots and pans quietly bang. Momentarily, she was back with the bottle of chardonnay inside an ice bucket, which she set on the glass coffee table.

'The bread is in the oven, asparagus is in the steamer, and all that's left is to sauté the shrimp,' she announced, reseating herself.

'Frances,' I said, 'your police department has been on-line with CAIN for how long now?'

'Only for several months,' she replied. 'We were one of the first departments in the country to hook up with it.'

'What about NYPD?'

'They're getting around to it. The Transit Police have a

more sophisticated computer system and a great team of programmers and analysts. So we got on-line very early.'

'Thanks to you.'

She smiled.

I went on, 'I know the Richmond Police Department is on-line. So are Chicago, Dallas, Charlotte, the Virginia State Police, the British Transport Police. And quite a number of other departments both here and abroad are in the process.'

'What's on your mind?' she asked me.

'Tell me what happened when the body of the unidentified woman we believe Gault killed was found Christmas Eve. How was CAIN a factor?'

'The body was found in Central Park early in the morning, and of course I heard about it immediately. As I've already mentioned, the MO sounded familiar, so I entered details into CAIN to see what came back. This would have been by late afternoon.'

'And what came back?'

'Very quickly CAIN called our VICAP terminal with a request for more information.'

'Can you recall exactly what sort of information?'

She thought for a moment. 'Well, let's see. It was interested in the mutilation, wanting to know from which parts of the body skin had been excised and what class cutting instrument had been used. It wanted to know if there had been a sexual assault, and if so, was the penetration oral, vaginal, anal or other. Some of this we couldn't know since an autopsy had not yet been performed. However, we did manage to get other information by calling the morgue.'

'What about other questions?' I asked. 'Did CAIN ask anything that struck you as peculiar or inappropriate?'

'Not that I'm aware of.' She regarded me quizzically.

'Has CAIN ever sent any messages to the Transit Police terminal that have struck you as peculiar or confusing?'

She thought some more. 'We've entered, at the most, twenty

cases since going on-line in November. Rapes, assaults, homicides that I thought might be relevant to VICAP because the circumstances were unusual or the victims were unidentified.

'And the only messages from CAIN that I'm aware of have been routine requests for further information. There has been no sense of urgency until this Central Park case. Then CAIN sent an *Urgent mail waiting* message in flashing bold because the system had gotten a hit.'

'Should you get any messages that are out of the ordinary, Frances, please contact Benton Wesley immediately.'

'Would you mind telling me what it is you're looking for?'

'There was a breach of security at ERF in October. Someone broke in at three in the morning, and circumstances indicate Gault may have been behind it.'

'Gault?' Commander Penn was baffled. 'How could that have happened?'

'One of ERF's system analysts, as it turned out, was connected to a spy shop in northern Virginia that was frequented by Gault. We know this analyst – a woman – was involved in the break-in, and the fear is that Gault put her up to it.'

'Why?'

'What wouldn't he like better than to get inside CAIN and have at his disposal a database containing the details of the most horrendous crimes committed in the world?'

'Isn't there some way to keep him out?' she asked. 'To tighten security so there is no way he or anyone else can slip through the system?'

'We thought that had been taken care of,' I replied. 'In fact, my niece, who is their top programmer, was certain the system was secure.'

'Oh yes. I think I've heard about your niece. She's really CAIN's creator.'

'She has always been gifted with computers and would rather be around them than most people.'

'I'm not sure I blame her. What is her name?'

'Lucy.'

'And she's how old?'

'Twenty-one.'

She got up from the couch. 'Well, maybe there's just some glitch that is causing these weird messages you're speaking of. A bug. And Lucy will figure it out.'

'We can always hope.'

'Bring your wine and you can keep me company in the kitchen,' she said.

But we did not get that far before her telephone rang. Commander Penn answered it and I watched the pleasant evening drain from her face.

'Where?' she quietly said, and I knew the tone of voice quite well. I recognized the frozen stare.

I was already opening the hall closet door to fetch my coat when she said, 'I'll be right there.'

Snow had begun drifting down like ashes when we arrived at the Second Avenue subway station in the squalid section of lower Manhattan known as the Bowery.

Wind howled and blue and red lights throbbed as if the night were injured, and stairs leading into that hellhole had been cordoned off. Derelicts had been herded out, commuters had been detoured, and news vans and cars were arriving in droves because an officer with the Transit Police Homeless Unit was dead.

His name was Jimmy Davila. He was twenty-seven. He had been a cop one year.

'You better put these on.' An officer with an angry, pale face handed me a reflective vest and surgical mask and gloves.

Police were pulling flashlights and more vests out of the back of a van, and several officers with darting eyes and riot guns flashed past me down the stairs. Tension was palpable. It pulsed in the air like a dark pounding heart, and the voices of legions who had come to aid their gunned-down comrade blended with scuffing feet and the strange language radios speak. Somewhere far off a siren screamed.

Commander Penn handed me a high-powered flashlight as we were escorted down by four officers who were husky in Kevlar and coats and reflective vests. A train blew by in a stream of liquid steel, and we inched our way along a catwalk that led us into dark catacombs littered with crack vials, needles, garbage and filth. Lights licked over hobo camps set up on pallets and ledges within inches of rails, and the air was fetid with the stench of human waste.

Beneath the streets of Manhattan were forty-eight acres of tunnels where in the late eighties as many as five thousand homeless people had lived. Now the numbers were substantially smaller, but their presence was still found in filthy blankets piled with shoes, clothes and odds and ends.

Grimy stuffed animals and fuzzy fake insects had been hung like fetishes from walls. The squatters, many of whom the Homeless Unit knew by name, had vanished like shadows from their subterranean world, except for Freddie, who was roused from a drugged sleep. He sat up beneath an army blanket, looking about, dazed.

'Hey, Freddie, get up.' A flashlight shone on his face.

He raised a bandaged hand to his eyes, squinting as small suns probed the darkness of his tunnel.

'Come on, get up. What'd you do to your hand?'

'Frostbite,' he mumbled, staggering to his feet.

'You got to take care of yourself. You know you can't stay here. We got to walk you out. You want to go to a shelter?'

'No, man.'

'Freddie,' the officer went on in a loud voice, 'you know what's happened down here? You heard about Officer Davila?'

'I dunno nothing.' Freddie swayed and caught himself, squinting in the lights.

'I know you know Davila. You call him Jimbo.'

'Yeah, Jimbo. He's all right.'

'No, I'm afraid he's not all right, Freddie. He got shot down here tonight. Someone shot Jimbo and he's dead.'

Freddie's yellow eyes got wide. 'Oh no, man.' He cast about as if the killer might be looking on – as if someone might want to blame him for this.

'Freddie, you seen anybody down here tonight you didn't know? You seen anybody down here who might have done something like that?'

'No, I ain't seen nothing.' Freddie almost lost his balance and steadied himself against a concrete support. 'Not nobody or nothing, I swear.'

Another train burst out of the darkness and blew past on southbound tracks. Freddie was led away and we moved on, sidestepping rails and rodents moiling beneath trash. Thank God I had worn boots. We walked for at least ten minutes more, my face perspiring beneath my mask as I got increasingly disoriented. I could not tell if round bright lights far down the tracks were police flashlights or oncoming trains.

'Okay, we've got to step over the third rail,' Commander Penn said, and she had stayed close to me.

'How much farther?' I asked.

'Just down there, where those lights are. We're going to step over now. Do it sideways, slowly, one foot at a time, and don't touch.'

'Not unless you want the shock of your life,' an officer said.

'Yeah, six hundred volts that won't let go,' said another in the same hard tone.

We followed rails deeper into the tunnel as the ceiling got lower. Some men had to duck as we passed through an arch. On the other side, crime scene technicians were scouring the area while a medical examiner in hood and gloves examined the body. Lights had been set up, and needles, vials, and blood glistened harshly in them.

Officer Davila was on his back, his winter jacket unzipped,

revealing the stiff shape of a bulletproof vest beneath a navy blue commando sweater. He had been shot between the eyes with the .38 revolver on top of his chest.

'Is this exactly as he was found?' I asked, stepping close.

'Exactly as we found him,' said a detective with NYPD.

'His jacket was unzipped and the revolver was just like that?'

'Just like that.' The detective's face was flushed and sweating, and he would not meet my eyes.

The medical examiner looked up. I could not make out the face behind the plastic hood. 'We can't rule out suicide here,' she said.

I leaned closer and directed my light at the dead man's face. His eyes were open, head turned a little to the right. Blood pooled beneath him was bright red and getting thick. He was short, with the muscular neck and lean face of someone who was seriously fit. My light traveled to his hands, which were bare, and I squatted to take a closer look.

'I see no gunshot residue,' I said.

'You don't always,' said the medical examiner.

'The wound to his forehead is not contact and looks to me as if it's slightly angled.'

'I would expect it to be slightly angled if he shot himself,' the medical examiner replied.

'It's angled down. I wouldn't expect that,' I said. 'And how did his gun come to rest so neatly on his chest?'

'One of the street people in here might have moved it.'

I was beginning to get annoyed. 'Why?'

'Maybe someone picked it up and then had second thoughts about keeping it. So he put it where it is.'

'We really should bag his hands,' I said.

'One thing at a time.'

'He didn't wear gloves?' I squinted up in the circle of bright light. 'It's very cold down here.'

'We haven't finished going through his pockets, ma'am,' said the woman medical examiner, who was the young, rigid sort I associated with anal-retentive autopsies that took half a day.

'What is your name?' I asked her.

'I'm Dr. Jonas. And I'm going to have to ask you to back away, ma'am. We're trying to preserve a crime scene here and it's best you don't touch or disturb anything in any way.' She held up a thermometer.

'Dr. Jonas' – and it was Commander Penn who spoke – 'this is Dr. Kay Scarpetta, the chief medical examiner of Virginia and consulting forensic pathologist for the FBI. She is quite familiar with preserving crime scenes.'

Dr. Jonas looked up and I caught a glint of surprise behind her face shield. I detected embarrassment in the long moment it required her to read the chemical thermometer.

I leaned closer to the body, paying attention to the left side of his head.

'His left ear is lacerated,' I said.

'That probably happened when he fell,' said Dr. Jonas.

I scanned the surroundings. We were on a smooth concrete platform. There were no rails to strike. I shone my light over concrete supports and walls, scanning for blood on any structure that Davila might have hit.

Squatting near the body, I looked more closely at his injured ear and a reddish area below it. I began to see the class characteristics of a tread pattern that was wavy with small holes. Under his ear was the curve from the edge of a heel. I stood, sweat rolling down my face. Everyone was watching me as I stared down the dark corridor at a light getting closer.

'He was kicked in the side of the head,' I said.

'You don't know that he didn't hit his head,' Dr. Jonas said defensively.

I stared at her. 'I do know,' I asserted.

'How do we know he wasn't stomped?' an officer asked.

'His injuries are inconsistent with that,' I replied. 'People usually stomp more than once and in other areas of the body.

I would also expect there to be injury to the other side of his face, which would have been against the concrete when the stomping occurred.'

A train blew by in a rush of warm, screeching air. Lights floated in the distant dark, the figures attached to them shadows with voices that faintly carried.

'He was disabled by a kick, then shot with his own gun,' I said.

'We need to get him to the morgue,' the medical examiner said.

Commander Penn's eyes were wide, her face upset and angry.

'It's him, isn't it?' she said to me as we began to walk.

'He's kicked people before,' I said.

'But why? He has a gun, a Glock. Why didn't he use his own gun?'

'The worst thing that can happen to a cop is to be shot with his own gun,' I said.

'So Gault would have done that deliberately because of how it would make the police . . . make us feel?'

'He would have thought it was funny,' I said.

We walked back over rails and through trash alive with rats. I sensed Commander Penn was crying. Minutes passed.

She said, 'Davila was a good officer. He was so helpful, never complained, and his smile. He brightened a room.' Her voice was clenched in fury now. 'He was just a goddam kid.'

Her officers were around us but not too close, and as I looked down the tunnel and across the tracks, I thought of the subterranean acres of twists and turns of the subway system. The homeless had no flashlights, and I did not understand how they could see. We passed another squalid camp where a white man who looked vaguely familiar sat up smoking crack from a piece of car antenna as if there were no such thing as law and order in the land. When I noticed his baseball cap the meaning didn't register at first. Then I stared.

101

'Benny, Benny, Benny. Shame on you,' one of the officers impatiently said. 'Come on. You know you can't do this, man. How many times are we going to go through this, man?'

Benny had chased me into the medical examiner's office yesterday morning. I recognized his filthy army pants, cowboy boots and blue jean jacket.

'Then just go on and lock me up,' he said, lighting his rock again.

'Oh yeah, your ass is gonna be locked up, all right. I've had it with you.'

I quietly said to Commander Penn, 'His cap.'

It was a dark blue or black Atlanta Braves cap.

'Hold on,' she told her troops. She asked Benny, 'Where did you get your cap?'

'I don't know nothing,' he said, snatching it off a tuft of dirty gray hair. His nose looked as if something had chewed on it.

'Of course you do know,' the commander said.

He stared crazily at her.

'Benny, where did you get your cap?' she asked again.

Two officers lifted him up and cuffed him. Beneath a blanket were paperback books, magazines, butane lighters, small Ziploc bags. There were several energy bars, packages of sugarless gum, a tin whistle and a box of saxophone reeds. I looked at Commander Penn, and she met my eyes.

'Gather up everything,' she told her troops.

'You can't take my place.' Benny struggled against his captors. 'You can't take my motherfucking place.' He stomped his feet. 'You goddam son of a bitch . . .'

'You're just making this harder, Benny.' They tightened his cuffs, a cop on each arm.

'Don't touch anything without gloves,' Commander Penn ordered.

'Don't worry.'

They put Benny's worldly belongings in trash bags, which we carried out with their owner. I followed with my flashlight, the vast darkness a silent void that seemed to have eyes. Frequently, I turned back and saw nothing but a light I thought was a train, until it suddenly moved sideways. Then it became a flashlight illuminating a concrete arch Temple Gault was passing through. He was a sharp silhouette in a long dark coat, his face a white flash. I grabbed the commander's sleeve and screamed.

8

More than thirty police officers searched the Bowery and its subways throughout the overcast night. No one knew how Gault had gotten into the tunnels, unless he never left after murdering Jim Davila. We were clueless as to how he had gotten out after I spotted him, but he had.

The next morning, Wesley headed for La Guardia while Marino and I returned to the morgue. I did not encounter Dr. Jonas from the night before, nor was Dr. Horowitz in, but I was told Commander Penn was here with one of her detectives and we would find them in the X-ray room.

Marino and I slipped in with the silence of a couple arriving late for a movie, then we lost each other in the dark. I suspected he found a wall, since he had trouble with his balance in situations like this. It was easy to get almost mesmerized and begin to sway. I moved close to the steel table, where dark shapes surrounded Davila's body, a finger of light exploring his ruined head.

'I would like one of the casts for comparison,' someone was saying.

'We've got photos of the shoe prints. I've got some here.' I recognized Commander Penn's voice.

'That would be good.'

'The labs have the casts.'

'Yours?'

'No, not ours,' said Commander Penn. 'NYPD's.'

'This area of abrasion and patterned contusion right here is from the heel.' The light stopped below the left ear. 'The wavy lines are fairly clear and I see no trace embedded in the abrasion. There's also this pattern right here. I can't make it out. This contusion, uh, sort of a blotch with a little tail. I don't know what that is.'

'We can try image enhancement.'

'Right, right.'

'What about his ear itself? Any pattern?'

'It's hard to tell, but it's split versus cut. The jagged edges are nonabraded and connected by tissue bridges. And I would say based on this curved laceration right down here' – the latex-sheathed finger pointed – 'the heel smashed the ear.'

'That's why it's split.'

'A single blow delivered with great force.'

'Enough to kill him?'

'Maybe. We'll see. My guess is he's going to have fractures of the left temporal parietal skull and a big epidural hemorrhage.'

'That's what I bet.'

The gloved hands manipulated forceps and the light. A hair, black and about six inches long, clung to the bloody collar of Davila's commando sweater. The hair was collected and placed in an envelope as I worked my way through thick darkness, finding the door. Returning my tinted glasses to a cart, I slipped out. Marino was right behind me.

'If that hair's his,' he said in the corridor, 'then he's dyed it again.'

'I would expect him to have done that,' I said, envisioning the silhouette I had seen last night. Gault's face was very white but, I could not tell about his hair.

'So he's not a redhead anymore.'

'By now he may have purple hair, for all we know.'

'He keeps changing his hair like that, maybe it will fall out.'

'Not likely,' I said. 'But the hair may not be his. Dr. Jonas has dark hair about that long, and she was hovered over the body for a while last night.'

We were in gowns, gloves and masks and looked like a team of surgeons about to perform some remarkable procedure like a heart transplant. Men were carrying in a shipment of pitiful pine boxes destined for Potter's Field, and behind glass, the morning's autopsies had begun. There were only five cases so far, one of them a child who obviously had died violently. Marino averted his gaze.

'Shit,' he muttered, his face dark red. 'What a way to start your day.'

I did not respond.

'Davila'd only been married two months.'

There was nothing I could say.

'I talked to a couple guys who knew him.'

The personal effects of the crack addict named Benny had been unceremoniously heaped on table four, and I decided to move them farther away from the dead child.

'He always wanted to be a cop. I hear that all the damn time.'

The trash bags were heavy, a foul odor drifting from the top of them, where they were tied. I began carrying them over to table eight.

'You tell me why anybody wants to do this?' Marino was getting more furious as he grabbed a bag and followed me.

'We want to make a difference,' I said. 'We want to somehow make things better.'

'Right,' he said sarcastically. 'Davila sure as hell made a difference. He sure as hell made things better.'

'Don't take that away from him,' I said. 'The good he did and might have done is all he has left.'

A Stryker saw started, water drummed and X rays bared bullets and bones in this theater with its silent audience and actors that were dead. Momentarily, Commander Penn walked in, eyes exhausted above her mask. She was accompanied by a dark young man she introduced as Detective Maier. He showed us the photographs of tread patterns left in the snows of Central Park.

'They're pretty much to scale,' he explained. 'I will admit that the casts would be better if we could get them.'

But NYPD had those, and I was willing to bet that the Transit Police would never see them. Frances Penn almost did not look like the same woman I had visited last night, and I wondered why she really had invited me to her apartment. What might she have confided had we not been summoned to the Bowery?

We began untying bags and placing items on the table, except for the fetid wool blankets that had been Benny's home. These we folded and stacked on the floor. The inventory was an odd one that could be explained in only two ways. Either Benny had been living with someone who owned a pair of size seven and a half men's boots. Or he had somehow acquired the possessions of someone who owned a pair of size seven and a half men's boots. Benny's shoe size, we were told, was eleven.

'What's Benny got to say this morning?' Marino asked.

Detective Maier answered, 'He says the stuff in that pile just showed up on his blankets. He went up on the street, came back and there it was, inside the knapsack.' He pointed to a soiled green canvas knapsack that had many stories to tell.

'When was this?' I asked.

'Well now, Benny isn't real clear on that. In fact, he's not real clear on just about anything. But he thinks it was in the last few days.'

'Did he see who left the knapsack?' Marino asked.

'He says he didn't.'

I held a photograph close to the bottom of one of the boots to compare the sole, and the size and stitching were the same.

Benny had somehow acquired the belongings of the woman we believed Gault had savaged in Central Park. The four of us were silent for a while as we began going through each item we believed was hers. I felt lightheaded and weary as we began reconstructing a life from a tin whistle and rags.

'Can't we call her something?' Marino said. 'It's bugging me she's got no name.'

'What would you like to call her?' Commander Penn asked.

'Jane.'

Detective Maier glanced up at Marino. 'That's very original. What's her last name, Doe?'

'Any possibility the saxophone reeds are Benny's?' I asked.

'I don't think so,' Maier said. 'He said all this stuff was in the knapsack. And I'm not aware Benny's musically inclined.'

'He plays an invisible guitar sometimes,' I said.

'So would you if you smoked crack. And that's all he does. He begs and smokes crack.'

'He used to do something before he did that,' I said.

'He was an electrician and his wife left him.'

'That's no reason to move into a sewer,' said Marino, whose wife also had left him. 'There's gotta be something else.'

'Drugs. He ended up across the street in Bellevue. Then he'd sober up and they'd let him out. Same old thing, over and over.'

'Might there have been a saxophone that went with the reeds, and perhaps Benny hocked it?' I asked.

'I got no way to know,' Maier answered. 'Benny said this is all there was.'

I thought of the mouth of this woman we now called Jane, of the cupping of the front teeth that the forensic dentist blamed on smoking a pipe.

'If she has a long history of playing a clarinet or saxophone,' I said, 'that could explain the damage to her front teeth.'

'What about the tin whistle?' Commander Penn asked.

She bent closer to a gold metal whistle with a red mouthpiece.

The brand was Generation, it was British made and did not look new.

'If she played it a lot, then that probably just added to the damage to her front teeth,' I said. 'It's also interesting that it's an alto whistle and the reeds are for an alto sax. So she may have played an alto sax at some point in her life.'

'Maybe before her head injury,' Marino said.

'Maybe,' I said.

We continued sifting through her belongings and reading them like tea leaves. She liked sugarless gum and Sensodyne toothpaste, which made sense in light of her dental problems. She had one pair of men's black jeans, size thirty-two in the waist and thirty-four in length. They were old and rolled up at the cuffs, suggesting they were hand-me-downs or she had gotten them in a secondhand clothing store. Certainly they were much too big for the size she was when she died.

'Are we certain these don't belong to Benny?' I asked.

'He says they don't,' Maier replied. 'The stuff he says belongs to him is in that bag.' He pointed to a bulging bag on the floor.

When I slipped a gloved hand into a back pocket of the jeans, I found a red-and-white paper tag that was identical to the ones Marino and I had been given when we visited the American Museum of Natural History. It was round, the size of a silver dollar and attached to a loop of string. Printed on one side was *Contributor*, with the museum's logo on the other.

'This should be processed for prints,' I said, placing the tag in an evidence bag. 'She should have touched it. Or Gault may have touched it if he paid for admission into the exhibits.'

'Why would she save something like that?' Marino said. 'Usually you take it off your shirt button and drop it in the trash on your way out.'

'Perhaps she put it in her pocket and forgot,' Commander Penn said.

'It could be a souvenir,' suggested Maier.

'It doesn't look like she collects souvenirs,' I said. 'In fact, she seems very deliberate about what she kept and what she didn't.'

'Are you suggesting she might have kept the tag so someone would eventually find it?'

'I don't know,' I said.

Marino lit a cigarette.

'That makes me wonder if she knew Gault,' Maier said.

I replied, 'If she did, and if she knew she was in danger, then why did she go with him into the park at night?'

'See, that's what don't add up.' Marino exhaled a large cloud of smoke, his mask pulled down.

'It doesn't if she was a complete stranger to him,' I said.

'So maybe she knew him,' Maier said.

'Maybe she did,' I agreed.

I slid my hand into other pockets of the same black pants and found eighty-two cents, a saxophone reed that had been chewed and several neatly folded Kleenex tissues. An inside-out blue sweatshirt was size medium, and whatever had been written on the front of it was too faded to read.

She also had owned two pairs of gray sweatpants and three pairs of athletic socks with different-colored stripes. In a compartment of the knapsack was a framed photograph of a spotted hound sitting in the dappled shadows of trees. The dog seemed to be grinning at whoever was taking the picture while a figure in the far background looked on.

'This needs to be processed for prints,' I said. 'In fact, if you hold it obliquely you can see latents on the glass.'

'I bet that's her dog,' Maier said.

Commander Penn said, 'Can we tell what part of the world it was taken in?'

I studied the photograph more closely. 'It looks flat. It's sunny. I don't see any tropical foliage. It doesn't look like a desert.'

'In other words, it could be almost anywhere,' Marino said.

'Almost,' I said. 'I can't tell anything about the figure in the background.'

Commander Penn examined the photograph. 'A man, maybe?'

'It could be a woman,' I said.

'Yeah, I think it is,' said Maier. 'A real thin one.'

'So maybe it's Jane,' Marino said. 'She liked baseball caps, and this person has on some kind of cap.'

I looked at Commander Penn. 'I'd appreciate copies of any photographs, including this one.'

'I'll get them to you ASAP.'

We continued our excavation of this woman who seemed to be in the room with us. I felt her personality in her paltry possessions and believed she had left us clues. Apparently, she had worn men's undershirts instead of bras, and we found three pairs of ladies' panties and several bandannas.

All of her belongings were worn and dirty, but there was a suggestion of order and care in neatly mended tears, and the needles, thread and extra buttons she had kept in a plastic box. Only the black jeans and faded sweatshirt had been rudely wadded or were inside out, and we suspected this was because she had been wearing them when Gault forced her to disrobe in the dark.

By late morning, we had gone through every item with no success in getting closer to identifying the victim we had begun to call Jane. We could only assume that Gault got rid of any identification she might have carried, or else Benny had taken what little money she might have owned and disposed of what she had kept it in. I didn't understand the chronology of when Gault might have left the knapsack on Benny's blanket, if that was, in fact, what Gault had done.

'How much of this stuff are we checking for prints?' Maier said.

'In addition to the items we've already gotten,' I suggested, 'the tin whistle has a good surface for prints. You might try an

112

alternate light source on the knapsack. Especially the inside of the flap, since it's leather.'

'The problem's still her,' Marino said. 'Nothing here's going to tell us who she is.'

'Well, I got news for you,' said Maier. 'I don't think identifying *Jane's* gonna help us catch the guy who killed her.'

I looked at him and watched his interest in her fade. The light went out of his eyes, and I had seen this before in deaths where the victim was no one. Jane had gotten as much time as she was going to get. Ironically, she would have gotten even less had her killer not been notorious.

'Do you think Gault shot her in the park, then went from there to the tunnel where her knapsack was found?' I asked.

'He might have,' Maier said. 'All he had to do was leave Cherry Hill and catch the subway at, say, Eighty-sixth or Seventy-seventh Streets. It would take him straight to the Bowery.'

'Or he could have taken a taxi, for that matter,' Commander Penn said. 'What he couldn't have done was walk. It's quite a distance.'

'What if the knapsack was left at the scene, right out there by the fountain?' Marino then asked. 'Possible Benny might have found it?'

'Why would he be in Cherry Hill at that hour? Remember what the weather was like,' Commander Penn said.

A door opened and several attendants wheeled in a gurney carrying Davila's body.

'I don't know why,' Maier said. 'Did she have her knapsack with her at the museum?' he asked Commander Penn.

'I believe it was mentioned that she had some sort of bag slung over one shoulder.'

'That could have been the knapsack.'

'It could have.'

'Does Benny sell drugs?' I asked.

'After a while you gotta sell if you're gonna buy,' Maier said.

'There may be a connection between Davila and the murdered woman,' I said.

Commander Penn watched me with interest.

'We shouldn't discount that possibility,' I went on. 'At a glance, it seems unlikely. But Gault and Davila were both down in that tunnel at the same time. Why?'

'Luck of the draw.' Maier stared off.

Marino didn't comment. His attention had drifted to autopsy table five, where two medical examiners were photographing the slain officer from different angles. An attendant with a wet towel scrubbed blood off the face in a manner that would have been rough could Davila feel. Marino was unaware anyone was watching him, and for a moment his vulnerability showed. I saw the ravages from years of storms, and the weight pressing his shoulders.

'And Benny was in that same tunnel, too,' I said. 'He either got the knapsack from the murder scene or from someone, or it was dropped on his blankets as he claims.'

'Frankly, I don't think it just turned up on his blankets,' Maier said.

'Why?' Commander Penn asked him.

'Why would Gault want to carry it from Cherry Hill? Why not just leave it and be on his way?' he said.

'Maybe there was something in it,' I said.

'Like what?' Marino asked.

'Like anything that might identify her,' I said. 'Maybe he didn't want her identified and needed a chance to go through her effects.'

'That could be,' Commander Penn said. 'Certainly we have found nothing among her belongings that would seem to identify her.'

'But in the past Gault hasn't seemed to care whether we identified his victims,' I said. 'Why care now? Why would he care about this head-injured, homeless woman?'

Commander Penn did not seem to hear me, and no one

else answered. The medical examiners had begun undressing Davila, who did not want their help. He held his arms rigidly folded across his torso, as if blocking blows in football. The doctors were having a terrible time getting the commando sweater free of limbs and over his head when a pager went off. We involuntarily touched our waistbands, then stared toward Davila's table as the beeping continued.

'It's not mine,' one of the doctors said.

'Damn,' the other doctor said. 'It's his.'

A chill swept through me as he removed a pager from Davila's belt. Everyone was silent. We could not take our eyes off table five or Commander Penn, who walked there because this was her murdered officer and someone had just tried to call him. The doctor handed her the pager and she held it up to read the display. Her face colored. I could see her swallow.

'It's a code,' she said.

Neither she nor the doctor had thought not to touch the pager. They did not know it might matter.

'A code?' Maier looked mystified.

'A police code.' Her voice was tight with fury. 'Ten-dash-seven.'

Ten-dash-seven meant *End of tour.*

'Fuck,' Maier said.

Marino took an involuntary step, as if he were about to engage in a foot pursuit. But there was no one to chase that he could see.

'Gault,' he said, incredulous. He raised his voice. 'The son of a bitch must've got his pager number after he blew his brains all over the subway. You understand what that means?' He glared at us. 'It means he's watching us! He knows we're here doing this.'

Maier looked around.

'We don't know who sent the message,' said the doctor, who was completely disconcerted.

But I knew. I had no doubt.

'Even if Gault did it, he didn't have to see what was going on this morning to know what's going on,' Maier said. 'He would know the body was here, that we would be here.'

Gault would know that I would be here, I thought. He wouldn't have necessarily known the others would.

'He's somewhere where he just used a phone.' Marino glanced wildly around. He could not stand still.

Commander Penn ordered Maier, 'Put it on the air, an all-units broadcast. Send a teletype, too.'

Maier pulled his gloves off and angrily slammed them into a trash can as he ran from the room.

'Put the pager in an evidence bag. It needs to be processed for prints,' I said. 'I know we've touched it, but we can still try. That's why his coat was unzipped.'

'Huh?' Marino looked stunned.

'Davila's coat was unzipped and there was no reason for that.'

'Yeah, there was a reason. Gault wanted Davila's gun.'

'It wasn't necessary to unzip his coat to get his gun,' I said. 'There's a slit in the jacket's side where the holster is. I think Gault unzipped Davila's coat to find the pager. Then he got the number off it.'

The doctors had returned their efforts to the body. They pulled off boots and socks and unfastened an ankle holster holding a Walther .380 that Davila shouldn't have been carrying and had never had a chance to use. They took off his Kevlar vest, a navy police T-shirt, and a silver crucifix on a long chain. On his right shoulder was a small tattoo of a rose entwining a cross. In his wallet was a dollar.

9

I left New York that afternoon on a USAir shuttle and got into Washington National at three. Lucy could not meet me at the airport because she had not driven since her accident, and there was no appropriate reason for me to find Wesley waiting at my gate.

Outside the airport I suddenly felt sorry for myself as I struggled alone with briefcase and bag. I was tired and my clothes felt dirty. I was hopelessly overwhelmed and ashamed to admit it. I couldn't even seem to get a taxi.

Eventually, I arrived at Quantico in a dented cab painted robin's-egg blue with glass tinted purple. My window in back would not roll down, and it was impossible for my Vietnamese driver to communicate who I was to the guard at the FBI Academy entrance.

'Lady doctor,' the driver said again, and I could tell he was unnerved by the security, the tire shredders, the many antennae on tops of buildings. 'She okay.'

'No,' I said to the back of his head. 'My *name* is Kay. Kay Scarpetta.'

I tried to get out, but doors were locked, the buttons removed. The guard reached for his radio.

'Please let me out,' I said to the driver, who was staring at the nine-millimeter pistol on the guard's belt. 'I need for you to let me out.'

He turned around, frightened. 'Out here?'

'No,' I said as the guard emerged from the booth.

The driver's eyes widened.

'I mean, I do want out here, but just for a minute. So I can explain to the guard.' I pointed and spoke very slowly. 'He doesn't know who I am because I can't open the window and he can't see through the glass.'

The driver nodded some more.

'I must get out,' I said firmly and with emphasis. 'You must open the doors.'

The locks went up.

I got out and squinted in the sun. I showed my identification to the guard, who was young and militaristic.

'The glass is tinted and I couldn't see you,' he said. 'Next time just roll your window down.'

The driver had started taking my luggage out of the trunk and setting it on the road. He glanced about frantically as artillery fire cracked and gunshots popped from Marine Corps and FBI firing ranges.

'No, no, no.' I motioned him to put the luggage back in the trunk. 'Drive me there, please.' I pointed toward Jefferson, a tall tan brick building on the other side of a parking lot.

It was clear he did not want to drive me anywhere, but I got back in the car before he could get away. The trunk slammed and the guard waved us through. The air was cold, the sky bright blue.

Inside Jefferson's lobby a video display above the reception desk welcomed me to Quantico and wished me a happy and safe holiday. A young woman with freckles signed me in and gave me a magnetic card to open doors around the Academy.

'Was Santa good to you, Dr. Scarpetta?' she cheerfully asked, sorting through room keys.

'I must have been bad this year,' I said. 'I mostly got switches.'

'I can't imagine that. You're always so sweet,' she said. 'We've got you on the security floor, as usual.'

'Thank you.' I could not recall her name and had a feeling she knew it.

'How many nights will you be with us?'

'Just one.' I thought her name might be Sarah, and for some reason it seemed very important that I remember it.

She handed me two keys, one plastic, one metal.

'You're Sarah, aren't you?' I took a risk and asked.

'No, I'm Sally.' She looked hurt.

'I meant Sally,' I said, dismayed. 'Of course. I'm sorry. You always take such good care of me, and I thank you.'

She gave me an uncertain look. 'By the way. Your niece walked through maybe thirty minutes ago.'

'Which way was she headed?'

She pointed toward glass doors leading from the lobby into the heart of the building and clicked the lock free before I had a chance to insert my card. Lucy could have been en route to the PX, post office, Boardroom, ERF. She could have been heading toward her dormitory room, which was in this building but on a different wing.

I tried to imagine where my niece might be at this hour of the afternoon, but where I found her was the last place I would have looked. She was in my suite.

'Lucy!' I exclaimed when I opened the door and she was standing on the other side. 'How did you get in?'

'The same way you did,' she said none too warmly. 'I have a key.'

I carried my bags into the living room and set them down. 'Why?' I studied her face.

'My room's on this side, yours is on that.'

The security floor was for protected witnesses, spies or any other person the Department of Justice decided needed extra

119

protection. To get into rooms, one had to pass through two sets of doors, the first requiring a code entered on a digital keypad that was reconfigured each time it was used. The second needed a magnetized card that was also often changed. I'd always suspected the telephones were monitored.

I was assigned these quarters more than a year ago because Gault was not the only worry in my life. I was baffled that Lucy had now been assigned here, too.

'I thought you were in Washington dorm,' I said.

She went into the living room and sat down. 'I was,' she said. 'And as of this afternoon, I'm here.'

I took the couch across from her. Silk flowers had been arranged, curtains drawn back from a window filled with sky. My niece wore sweatpants, running shoes, and a dark FBI sweatshirt with a hood. Her auburn hair was short, her sharp-featured face flawless except for the bright scar on her forehead. Lucy was a senior at UVA. She was beautiful and brilliant, and our relationship had always been one of extremes.

'Did they put you here because I'm here?' I was still trying to understand.

'No.'

'You didn't hug me when I came in.' It occurred to me as I got up. I kissed her cheek, and she stiffened, pulling away from my arms. 'You've been smoking.' I sat back down.

'Who told you that?'

'No one needs to tell me. I can smell it in your hair.'

'You hugged me because you wanted to see if I smell like cigarettes.'

'And you didn't hug me because you know you smell like cigarettes.'

'You're nagging me.'

'I most certainly am not,' I said.

'You are. You're worse than Grans,' she said.

'Who is in the hospital because she smoked,' I said, holding her intense green gaze.

'Since you know my secret, I may as well light up now.'

'This is a nonsmoking room. In fact, nothing is allowed in this room,' I said.

'Nothing?' She did not blink.

'Absolutely nothing.'

'You drink coffee in here. I know. I've heard you zap it in the microwave when we've been on the phone.'

'Coffee is all right.'

'You said *nothing*. To many people on this planet, coffee is a vice. I bet you drink alcohol in here, too.'

'Lucy, please don't smoke.'

She slipped a pack of Virginia Slim menthols out of a pocket. 'I'll go outside,' she said.

I opened windows so she could smoke, unable to believe she had taken up a habit I had shed much blood to quit. Lucy was athletic and superbly fit. I told her I did not understand.

'I'm flirting with it. I don't do it much.'

'Who moved you into my suite? Let's get back to that,' I asked as she puffed away.

'They moved me.'

'Who is they?'

'Apparently, the order came from the top.'

'Burgess?' I referred to the assistant director in charge of the Academy.

She nodded. 'Yes.'

'What would his purpose be?' I frowned.

She tapped an ash into her palm. 'No one's told me a reason. I can only suppose it's related to ERF, to CAIN.' She paused. 'You know, the weird messages, et cetera.'

'Lucy,' I said, 'what exactly is going on?'

'We don't know,' she spoke levelly. 'But something is.'

'Gault?'

'There's no evidence that anyone's been in the system – no one who isn't supposed to be.'

'But you believe someone has.'

She inhaled deeply, like veteran smokers do. 'CAIN is not doing what we're telling him to do. He's doing something else, getting his instruction from somewhere else.'

'There's got to be a way to track that,' I said.

Her eyes sparked. 'Believe me, I'm trying.'

'I'm not questioning your efforts or ability.'

'There's no trail,' she went on. 'If someone is in there, he's leaving no tracks. And that's not possible. You can't just go into the system and tell it to send messages or do anything else without the audit log reflecting it. And we have a printer running morning, noon and night that prints every keystroke made by anybody for any reason.'

'Why are you getting angry?' I said.

'Because I'm tired of being blamed for the problems over there. The break-in wasn't my fault. I had no idea that someone who worked right next to me . . .' She took another drag. 'Well, I only said I'd fix it because I was asked to. Because the senator asked me to. Or asked you, really . . .'

'Lucy, I'm not aware that anyone is blaming you for problems with CAIN,' I said gently.

Anger burned brighter in her eyes. 'If I'm not being blamed, I wouldn't have been assigned to a room up here. What this constitutes is house arrest.'

'Nonsense. I stay here every time I come to Quantico, and I'm certainly not under house arrest.'

'They put you here for security and privacy,' she said. 'But that's not why I'm here. I'm being blamed again. I'm being watched. I can tell it in the way certain people are treating me over there.' She nodded in the direction of ERF, which was across the street from the Academy.

'What happened today?' I asked.

She went into the kitchen, ran water over the cigarette butt and dropped it into the disposal. She sat back down and didn't say anything. I studied her and got more unsettled. I did not know why she was this angry, and whenever she acted in a way that could not be explained, I was frightened again.

Lucy's car accident could have been fatal. Her head injury could have ruined her most remarkable gift, and I was assaulted by images of hematomas and a skull fractured like a hard-boiled egg. I thought of the woman we called Jane with her shaved head and scars, and I imagined Lucy in places where no one knew her name.

'Have you been feeling all right?' I asked my niece.

She shrugged.

'What about the headaches?'

'I still get them.' Suspicion shadowed her eyes. 'Sometimes the Midrin helps. Sometimes it just makes me throw up. The only thing that really works is Fiorinal. But I don't have any of that.'

'You don't need any of that.'

'You're not the one who gets the headaches.'

'I get plenty of headaches. You don't need to be on barbiturates,' I answered. 'You're sleeping and eating all right, and getting exercise?'

'What is this, a doctor's appointment?'

'In a matter of speaking, since it just so happens I'm a doctor. Only you didn't make an appointment but I'm nice enough to see you anyway.'

A smile tugged at the corner of her mouth. 'I'm doing fine,' she said less defensively.

'Something happened today,' I said again.

'I guess you haven't talked to Commander Penn.'

'Not since this morning. I didn't know you knew her.'

'Her department's on-line with us, with CAIN. At twelve noon CAIN called the Transit Police VICAP terminal. I guess you had already left for the airport.'

I nodded, my stomach tightening as I thought of Davila's

beeper going off in the morgue. 'What was the message this time?' I asked.

'I have it if you want to see it.'

'Yes,' I said.

Lucy went into her room and returned carrying a briefcase. She unzipped it and pulled out a stack of papers, handing me one that was a printout from the VICAP terminal located in the Communications Unit, which was under Frances Penn's command. It read:

- - -MESSAGE PQ21 96701 001145 BEGINS- - -
FROM: – CAIN
TO: – ALL UNITS & COMMANDS
SUBJECT: – DEAD COPS
TO ALL COMMANDS CONCERNED:
   MEMBERS WILL, FOR THE PURPOSE OF SAFETY WHEN
   RESPONDING TO OR BEING ON PATROL IN THE SUBWAY
   TUNNELS, WEAR HELMETS.
- - -MESSAGE PQ21 96701 001145 ENDS- - -

I stared at the printout for a while, unnerved and inflamed. Then I asked, 'Is there a username associated with whoever logged on to type this?'

'No.'

'And there's absolutely no way to trace this?'

'Not by conventional means.'

'What do you think?'

'I think when ERF was broken into, whoever got into CAIN planted a program.'

'Like a virus?' I asked.

'It is a virus, and it has been attached to a file that we just haven't thought of. It's allowing someone to move inside our system without leaving tracks.'

I thought of Gault backlit by his flashlight in the tunnel last night, of endless rails leading deeper into darkness and disease.

Gault moved freely through spaces most people could not see. He nimbly stepped over greasy steel, needles and the fetid nests of humans and rats. He was a virus. He had somehow gotten into our bodies and our buildings and our technology.

'CAIN is infected by a virus,' I said. 'In summary.'

'An unusual one. This isn't a virus oriented toward crashing the hard disk or trashing data. This virus isn't generic. It is specific for the Crime Artificial Intelligence Network because its purpose is to allow someone access to CAIN and the VICAP database. This virus is like a master key. It opens up every room in the house.'

'And it's attached to an existing program.'

'You might say it has a host,' she said. 'Yes. Some program routinely used. A virus can't cause its damage unless the computer goes through a routine or subroutine which causes a host program – like autoexec.bat in DOS – to be read.'

'I see. And this virus is not embedded in any files that are read when the computer is booted, for example.'

Lucy shook her head.

'How many program files are there in CAIN?'

'Oh my God,' she said. Thousands. And some of them are long enough to wrap around this building. The virus could be attached anywhere, and the situation is further complicated because I didn't do all of the programming. I'm not as familiar with files others wrote.'

Others meant Carrie Grethen, who had been Lucy's programming partner and intimate friend. Carrie had also known Gault and was responsible for the ERF break-in. Lucy would not talk about her and avoided saying her name.

'Is there any possibility this virus might be attached only to programs Carrie wrote?' I asked.

The expression did not change on Lucy's face. 'It might be attached to one of the programs I didn't write. It might also be attached to one I did. I don't know. I'm looking. It may take a long time.'

The telephone rang.

'That's probably Jan.' She got up and went into the kitchen.

I glanced at my watch. I was due down in the unit in half an hour. Lucy placed her hand over the receiver. 'Do you care if Jan drops by? We're going running.'

'I don't mind in the least,' I said.

'She wants to know if you want to run with us.'

I smiled and shook my head. I couldn't keep up with Lucy even if she smoked two packs a day, and Janet could pass for a professional athlete. The two of them gave me the vague sensation of being old and left in the wrong drawer.

'How about something to drink?' Lucy was off the phone and inside the refrigerator.

'What are you offering?' I watched her slight figure bent over, one arm holding open the door while the other slid cans around on shelves.

'Diet Pepsi, Zima, Gatorade and Perrier.'

'Zima?'

'You haven't had it?'

'I don't drink beer.'

'It's not like beer. You'll like it.'

'I didn't know they had room service here,' I said with a smile.

'I got some stuff at the PX.'

'I'll have Perrier.'

She came over with our drinks.

'Aren't there antivirus programs?' I said.

'Antivirus programs only find known viruses like Friday the Thirteenth, the Maltese Amoeba, the Stoned virus, Michelangelo. What we're dealing with inside CAIN was created specifically for CAIN. It was an inside job. There is no antivirus program unless I write one.'

'Which you can't do until you find the virus first.'

She took a big swallow of Gatorade.

'Lucy, should CAIN be shut down?'

She got up. 'Let me check on Jan. She can't get through those outer doors and I doubt we'll hear her knocking.'

I got up too and carried my bags into my bedroom with its plain decor and simple pine wardrobe. Unlike other rooms, the security suite had private baths. Through windows I had an unspoiled view of snow-patched fields unrolling into endless woods. The sun was so bright it felt like spring, and I wished there were time to bathe. I wanted to scrub New York away.

'Aunt Kay? We're out of here,' Lucy called as I brushed my teeth.

I quickly rinsed my mouth and returned to the living room. Lucy had slipped on a pair of Oakleys and was stretching by the door. Her friend had one foot propped up on a chair as she tightened a shoelace.

'Good afternoon, Dr. Scarpetta,' Janet said to me, quickly straightening up. 'I hope you don't mind my stopping by. I didn't mean to disturb you.'

Despite my efforts at putting her at ease, she always acted like a corporal startled by Patton walking in. She was a new agent, and I had first noticed her when I was a guest lecturer here last month. I remembered showing slides about violent death and crime scene preservation while she kept her eyes on me from the back of the room. In the dark I could feel her studying me from her chair, and it made me curious that during breaks she did not speak to anyone. She would disappear downstairs.

Later I learned she and Lucy were friends, and perhaps that and shyness explained Janet's demeanor toward me. Well built from hours in the gym, she had shoulder-length blond hair and blue eyes that were almost violet. If all went well, she would graduate from the Academy in less than two months.

'If you'd ever like to run with us, Dr. Scarpetta, you'd be welcome,' Janet politely repeated her invitation.

'You are very kind.' I smiled. 'And I am flattered that you would think I could.'

'Of course you could.'

'No, she couldn't.' Lucy finished her Gatorade and set the empty bottle on the counter. 'She hates running. She thinks negative thoughts the whole time she's doing it.'

I returned to the bathroom as they went out the door, and I washed my face and stared in the mirror. My blond hair seemed grayer than it had this morning and the cut had somehow gotten worse. I wore no makeup, and my face looked like it had just come out of the dryer and needed to be pressed. Lucy and Janet were unblemished, taut and bright, as if nature took joy in sculpting and polishing only the young. I brushed my teeth again and that made me think of Jane.

Benton Wesley's unit had changed names many times and was now part of HRT. But its location remained sixty feet below the Academy in a windowless area that once had been Hoover's bomb shelter. I found Wesley in his office talking on the phone. He glanced at me as he flipped through paperwork in a thick file.

Spread out in front of him were scene photographs from a recent consultation that had nothing to do with Gault. This victim was a man who had been stabbed and slashed 122 times. He had been strangled with a ligature, his body found facedown on a bed in a motel room in Florida.

'It's a signature crime. Well, the blatant overkill and the unusual configuration of the bindings,' Wesley was saying. 'Right. A loop around each wrist, handcuff style.'

I sat down. Wesley had reading glasses on and I could tell he had been running his fingers through his hair. He looked tired. My eyes rested on fine oil paintings on his walls and autographed books behind glass. He was often contacted by people writing novels and scripts, but he did not flaunt celebrity connections. I think he found them embarrassing and in poor taste. I did not believe he would talk to anyone if the decision were left completely up to him.

'Yes, it was a very bloody method of attack, to say the

least. The others were, too. We're talking about a theme of domination, a ritual driven by rage.'

I noticed he had several pale blue FBI manuals on his desk that were from ERF. One of them was an instruction manual for CAIN that Lucy had helped write, and pages were marked in numerous places with paper clips. I wondered if she had marked them or if he had, and my intuition answered the question as my chest got tight. My heart hurt the way it always did when Lucy was in trouble.

'That threatened his sense of domination.' Wesley met my eyes. 'Yes, the reaction's going to be anger. Always, with someone like this.'

His tie was black with pale gold stripes, and typically his shirt was white and starched. He wore Department of Justice cuff links, his wedding band and an understated gold watch with a black leather band that Connie had given him for their twenty-fifth wedding anniversary. He and his wife came from money, and the Wesleys lived quietly well.

He hung up the phone and took off his glasses.

'What's the problem?' I asked, and I hated the way he made my pulse pick up.

He gathered photographs and dropped them inside a manilla envelope. 'Another victim in Florida.'

'The Orlando area again?'

'Yes. I'll get you reports as soon as we get them.'

I nodded and changed the subject to Gault. 'I'm assuming you know what happened in New York,' I said.

'The pager.'

I nodded again.

'I'm afraid I know.' He winced. 'He's taunting us, showing his contempt. He's playing his games, only it's getting worse.'

'It's getting much worse. But we shouldn't focus only on him,' I said.

He listened, eyes locked on mine, hands folded on the case file of the murdered man he had just been discussing on the phone.

'It would be all too easy to become so obsessed with Gault that we don't really work the cases. For example, it is very important to identify this woman we think he murdered in Central Park.'

'I would assume everyone thinks that's important, Kay.'

'Everyone will say they think it is important,' I replied, and anger began quietly stirring. 'But in fact, the cops, the Bureau want to catch Gault, and identifying this homeless lady isn't a priority. She's just another poor, nameless person prisoners will bury in Potter's Field.'

'Obviously, she is a priority to you.'

'Absolutely.'

'Why?'

'I think she has something yet to say to us.'

'About Gault?'

'Yes.'

'On what are you basing this?'

'Instinct,' I said. 'And she's a priority because we are bound morally and professionally to do everything we can for her. She has a right to be buried with her name.'

'Of course she does. NYPD, the Transit Police, the Bureau – we all want her identified.'

But I did not believe him. 'We really don't care,' I flatly said. 'Not the cops, not the medical examiners, and not this unit. We already know who killed her, so who she is no longer matters. That's the black and white of it when you're talking about a jurisdiction as overwhelmed by violence as New York is.'

Wesley stared off, running his tapered fingers over a Mont Blanc pen. 'I'm afraid there's some truth in what you're saying.' He looked back at me. 'We don't care because we can't. It isn't because we don't want to. I want Gault caught before he kills again. That's my bottom line.'

'As it should be. And we don't know that this dead woman can't help with that. Maybe she will.'

I saw depression and felt it in the weariness of his voice.

'It would seem her only link to Gault is that they met in the museum,' he said. 'We've been through her personal effects, and nothing among them might lead us to him. So my question is, what else might you learn from her that would help us catch him?'

'I don't know,' I said. 'But when I have unidentified cases in Virginia, I don't rest until I've done all I can to solve them. This case is in New York, but I'm involved because I work with your unit and you have been invited into the investigation.'

I talked with conviction, as if the case of Jane's vicious murder were being tried in this room. 'If I am not allowed to uphold my own standards,' I went on, 'then I cannot serve as a consultant for the Bureau any longer.'

Wesley listened to all this with troubled patience. I knew he felt much of the same frustration that I did, but there was a difference. He had not grown up poor, and when we had our worst fights, I held that against him.

'If she were an important person,' I said, 'everyone would care.'

He remained silent.

'There is no justice if you're poor,' I said, 'unless the issue is forced.'

He stared at me.

'Benton, I'm forcing the issue.'

'Explain to me what you want to do,' he said.

'I want to do whatever it takes to find out who she is. I want you to support me.'

He studied me for a moment. He was analyzing. 'Why this victim?' he asked.

'I thought I'd just explained that.'

'Be careful,' he said. 'Be careful that your motivation isn't subjective.'

'What are you suggesting?'

'Lucy.'

I felt a rush of irritation.

131

'Lucy could have been as badly head injured as this woman was,' he said. 'Lucy's always been an orphan, of sorts, and not so long ago she was missing, wandering around in New England, and you had to go find her.'

'You're accusing me of projecting.'

'I'm not accusing you. I'm exploring the possibility with you.'

'I'm simply attempting to do my job,' I said. 'And I have no desire to be psychoanalyzed.'

'I understand.' He paused. 'Do whatever you need to do. I'll help in any way I can. And I'm sure Pete will, too.'

Then we switched to the more treacherous subject of Lucy and CAIN, and this Wesley did not want to talk about. He got up for coffee as the phone in the outer office rang, and his secretary took another message. The phone had not stopped ringing since my arrival, and I knew it was always like this. His office was like mine. The world was full of desperate people who had our numbers and no one else to call.

'Just tell me what you think she did,' I said when he got back.

He set my coffee before me. 'You're speaking like her aunt,' he said.

'No. Now I'm speaking like her mother.'

'I would rather you and I talk about this like two professionals,' he said.

'Fine. You can start by filling me in.'

'The espionage that began last October when ERF was broken into is still going on,' he said. 'Someone is inside CAIN.'

'That much I know.'

'We don't know who is doing it,' he said.

'We assume it's Gault, I suppose,' I said.

Wesley reached for his coffee. He met my eyes. 'I'm certainly no expert in computers. But there's something you need to see.'

He opened a thin file folder and withdrew a sheet of paper.

As he handed it to me I recognized it as a printout from a computer screen.

'That's a page of CAIN's audit log for the exact time that the most recent message was sent to the VICAP terminal in the Transit Police Department's Communications Unit,' he said. 'Do you notice anything unusual?'

I thought of the printout Lucy had shown me, of the evil message about 'Dead Cops.' I had to stare for a minute at the log-ins and log-outs, the IDs, dates and times before I realized the problem. I felt fear.

Lucy's user ID was not traditional in that it was not comprised of the initial of her first name and first seven letters of her surname. Instead, she called herself LUCYTALK, and according to this audit trail she had been signed on as the superuser when CAIN had sent the message to New York.

'Have you questioned her about this?' I asked Wesley.

'She's been questioned and wasn't concerned because as you can see from the printout, she's on and off the system all day long, and sometimes after hours, as well.'

'She is concerned. I don't care what she said to you, Benton. She feels she's been moved to the security floor so she can be watched.'

'She is being watched.'

'Just because she was signed on at the same time the message was sent to New York doesn't mean she sent it,' I persisted.

'I realize that. There's nothing else in the audit log to indicate she sent it. There's nothing to indicate anybody sent it, for that matter.'

'Who brought this to your attention?' I then asked, for I knew Wesley did not routinely look at audit logs.

'Burgess.'

'Then, someone from ERF brought it to his attention first.'

'Obviously.'

'There are still people over there who don't trust Lucy, because of what happened last fall.'

His gaze was steady. 'I can't do anything about that, Kay. She has to prove herself. We can't do that for her. You can't do that for her.'

'I'm not trying to do anything for her,' I said hotly. 'All I ask is fairness. Lucy is not to blame for the virus in CAIN. She did not put it there. She's trying to do something about it, and frankly, if she can't, I don't think anyone will be able to help. The entire system will be corrupted.'

He picked up his coffee but changed his mind and set it back down.

'And I don't believe she's been put on the security floor because some people think she's sabotaging CAIN. If you really thought that, you'd send her packing. The last thing you'd do is keep her here.'

'Not necessarily,' he said, but he could not fool me.

'Tell me the truth.'

He was thinking, looking for a way out.

'You assigned Lucy to the security floor, didn't you?' I went on. 'It wasn't Burgess. It wasn't because of this log-in time you just showed me. That's flimsy.'

'Not to some people it isn't,' he said. 'Someone over there raised a red flag and asked me to get rid of her. I said not now. We would watch her first.'

'Are you telling me you think Lucy *is* the virus?' I was incredulous.

'No.' He leaned forward in his chair. 'I think Gault is the virus. And I want Lucy to help us track him.'

I looked at him as if he had just pulled out a gun and shot it into the air. 'No,' I said with feeling.

'Kay, listen to me . . .'

'Absolutely not. Leave her out of this. She's not a goddam FBI agent.'

'You're overreacting . . .'

But I would not let him talk. 'She's *a college student*, for God's sake. She has no business—' My voice caught. 'I know her. She'll

134

try to communicate with him. Don't you see?' I looked fiercely at him. 'You don't know her, Benton!'

'I think I do.'

'I won't let you use her like this.'

'Let me explain.'

'You should shut CAIN down,' I said.

'I can't do that. It might be the only trail Gault leaves.' He paused as I continued to glare at him. 'Lives are at stake. Gault hasn't finished killing.'

I blurted, 'That's exactly why I don't want Lucy even thinking about him!'

Wesley was silent. He looked toward the shut door, then back at me. 'He already knows who she is,' he said.

'He doesn't know much about her.'

'We don't know how much he knows about her. But at the very least he probably knows what she looks like.'

I could not think. 'How?'

'From when your American Express gold card was stolen,' he said. 'Hasn't Lucy told you?'

'Told me what?'

'The things she kept in her desk.' When he could see I did not know what he was talking about, he abruptly caught himself. I sensed he had brushed against details he would not tell me.

'What things?' I asked.

'Well,' he went on, 'she kept a letter in her desk at ERF – a letter from you. The one that had the credit card in it.'

'I know about that.'

'Right. Also inside this letter was a photograph of you and Lucy together in Miami. You were sitting in your mother's backyard, apparently.'

I shut my eyes for a moment and took a deep breath as he grimly went on.

'Gault also knows Lucy is your point of greatest vulnerability. I don't want him fixing on her, either. But what I'm trying to suggest to you is that he probably already has. He's broken into a world where she is god. He has taken over CAIN.'

'So that's why you moved her,' I said.

Wesley watched me as he struggled for a way to help. I saw the hell behind his cool reserve and sensed his terrible pain. He, too, had children.

'You moved her on the security floor with me,' I said. 'You're afraid Gault might come after her.'

Still he did not speak.

'I want her to return to UVA, to Charlottesville. I want her back there tomorrow,' I said with a ferocity I did not feel. What I really wanted was for Lucy not to know my world at all, and that would never be possible.

'She can't,' he simply said. 'And she can't stay with you in Richmond. To tell you the truth, she really can't stay anywhere right now but here. This is where she's safest.'

'She can't stay here the rest of her life,' I said.

'Until he's caught . . .'

'He may never be caught, Benton!'

He looked wearily at me. 'Then both of you may end up in our Protected Witness Program.'

'I will not give up my identity. My life. How is that any better than being dead?'

'It is better,' he said quietly, and I knew he was seeing bodies kicked, decapitated, and with bullet wounds.

I got up. 'What do I do about my stolen credit card?' I numbly asked.

'Cancel it,' he said. 'I was hoping we could use money from seized assets, from drug raids. But we can't.' He paused as I shook my head in disbelief. 'It's not my choice. You know the budget problems. You have them, too.'

'Lord,' I said. 'I thought you wanted to trail him.'

'Your credit card isn't likely to show us where he is, only where he's been.'

'I can't believe this.'

'Blame it on the politicians.'

'I don't want to hear about *budget problems or politicians*,' I exclaimed.

'Kay, the Bureau can barely afford ammunition for the ranges these days. And you know our staffing problems. I'm personally working a hundred and thirty-nine cases even as we speak. Last month two of my best people retired.

'Now my unit's down to nine. *Nine.* That's a total of ten of us trying to cover the entire United States plus any cases submitted from abroad. Hell, the only reason we have you is we don't pay you.'

'I don't do this for money.'

'You can cancel your Amex card,' he said wearily. 'I'd do it immediately.'

I looked a long time at him and left.

10

Lucy had finished her run and showered by the time I returned to the room. Dinner was being served in the cafeteria, but she was at ERF working.

'I'm going back to Richmond tonight,' I said to her on the phone.

'I thought you were spending the night,' she said, and I detected disappointment.

'Marino's coming to get me,' I said.

'When?'

'He's on his way. We could have dinner before I go.'

'Okay. I'd like Jan to come.'

'That's fine,' I said. 'We should include Marino, though. He's already on the road.'

Lucy was silent.

'Why don't you and I visit alone first?' I suggested.

'Over here?'

'Yes. I'm cleared as long as you let me through all those scanners, locked doors, X-ray machines and heat-seeking missiles.'

'Well, I'll have to check with the attorney general. She hates it when I call her at home.'

'I'm on my way.'

The Engineering Research Facility was three concrete-and-glass pods surrounded by trees, and one could not get into the parking lot without stopping at a guard booth that was no more than a hundred feet from the one at the Academy's entrance. ERF was the FBI's most classified division, its employees required to scan their fingerprints into biometric locks before Plexiglas doors would let them in. Lucy was waiting for me in front. It was almost eight P.M.

'Hi,' she said.

'There are at least a dozen cars in the parking lot,' I said. 'Do people usually work this late?'

'They drift in and out at all hours. Most of the time I never see them.'

We walked through a vast space of beige carpet and walls, passing shut doors leading into laboratories where scientists and engineers worked on projects they could not discuss. I had only vague notions of what went on here beyond Lucy's work with CAIN. But I knew the mission was to technically enhance whatever job a special agent might have, whether it was surveillance, or shooting or rappelling from a helicopter, or using a robot in a raid. For Gault to have gotten inside here was the equivalent of him wandering freely through NASA or a nuclear power plant. It was unthinkable.

'Benton told me about the photograph that was in your desk,' I said to Lucy as we boarded an elevator.

She keyed us up to the second floor. 'Gault already knows what you look like, if that's what you're worried about. He's seen you before – at least twice.'

'I don't like that he might now know what you look like,' I said pointedly.

'You're assuming he has the photograph.'

We entered a gray rabbit warren of cubicles with workstations and printers and stacks of paper. CAIN himself was behind glass in an air-conditioned space filled with monitors, modems and miles of cable hidden beneath a raised floor.

'I've got to check something,' she said, scanning her fingerprint to unlock CAIN's door.

I followed her into chilled air tense with the static of invisible traffic moving at incredible speeds. Modem lights blinked red and green, and an eighteen-inch video display announced CAIN in bold bright letters that looped and whorled like the fingerprint of the person who was just scanned in.

'The photograph was in the envelope with the American Express card he apparently now has,' I said. 'Logic would tell you that he may have both.'

'Someone else could have it.' She was intensely watching the modems, then glancing at the time on her screen and making notes. 'It depends on who actually went through my desk.'

We had always assumed it was Carrie alone who had broken in and taken whatever she wanted. Now I was not so sure.

'Carrie may not have been by herself,' I said.

Lucy did not reply.

'In fact, I don't believe Gault could have resisted the opportunity to come in here. I think he was with her.'

'That's awfully risky when you're wanted for murder.'

'Lucy, it's awfully risky to break into here to begin with.'

She continued making notes while CAIN's colors swirled on the screen and lights glowed on and off. CAIN was a space-age squid with tentacles connecting law enforcement entities here and abroad, his head an upright beige box with various buttons and slots. As cold air whirred, I almost wondered if he knew what we were saying.

'What else might have disappeared from your office?' I then said. 'Is there anything else missing?'

She was studying a modem's flashing light, her face perplexed. She glanced up at me. 'It's got to be coming in through one of these modems.'

'What is?' I asked, puzzled.

141

She sat before a keyboard, struck the space bar and the CAIN screen saver vanished. She logged on and began typing UNIX commands that made no sense to me. Next she pulled up the System Administrator Menu and got into the audit log.

'I've been coming in here routinely and checking the traffic on the modems,' she said, scanning. 'Unless this person is physically located in this building and hardwired into the system, he's got to be dialing in by modem.'

'There's no other way,' I said.

'Well' – she took a deep breath – 'theoretically you could use a receiver to pick up keyboard input via Van Eck radiation. Some Soviet agents were doing that not so long ago.'

'But that wouldn't actually get you inside the system,' I said.

'It could get you passwords and other information that might get you in if you had the dial-in number.'

'Were those changed after the break-in?'

'Of course. I changed everything I could think of, and in fact, the dial-in numbers have been changed again since. Plus we have callback modems. You call CAIN and he calls you back to make certain you're legit.' She looked discouraged and angry.

'If you attached a virus to a program,' I said, trying to help, 'wouldn't it change the size of the file? Couldn't that be a way to find out where the virus is?'

'Yes, it would change the file size,' she said. 'But the problem is that the UNIX program used to scan files for something like that is called *checksum*, and it's not cryptographically secure. I'm sure who ever did this included a balancing *checksum* to cause the bytes in the virus program to disappear.'

'So the virus is invisible.'

She nodded, distracted, and I knew she was thinking about Carrie. Then Lucy typed a *who* command to see what law enforcement agencies were logged on, if any. New York was. So were Charlotte and Richmond, and Lucy pointed out their modems to me. Lights danced across the front of them as data was transmitted over telephone lines.

'We should go eat dinner,' I said gently to my niece.

She typed more commands. 'I'm not hungry now.'

'Lucy, you can't let this take over your life.'

'You're one to talk.'

She was right.

'War has been declared,' she added. 'This is war.'

'This is not Carrie,' I said of the woman who, I suspected, had been more than Lucy's friend.

'It doesn't matter who it is.' She continued typing.

But it did. Carrie Grethen did not murder people and mutilate their bodies. Temple Gault did.

'Was anything else of yours taken during the break-in?' I tried again.

She stopped what she was doing and looked at me, her eyes glinting. 'Yes, if you must know,' she said. 'I had a big manilla envelope that I didn't want to leave in my dorm rooms at UVA or here because of roommates and other people in and out. It was personal. I thought it was safer in my desk up here.'

'What was in this envelope?'

'Letters, notes, different things. Some of them were from you, including the letter with the photograph and charge card. Most were from her.' Her face colored. 'There were a few notes from Grans.'

'Letters from Carrie?' I did not understand. 'Why would she write you? Both of you were here at Quantico and you didn't know each other before last fall.'

'We sort of did,' she said, her face turning a brighter red.

'How?' I asked, baffled.

'We met through a computer bulletin board, through Prodigy over the summer. I saved all the printouts of the notes we sent.'

'Did you deliberately try to arrange it so you could be at ERF together?' I said as my disbelief grew.

143

'She was already in the process of getting hired by the Bureau,' Lucy answered. 'She encouraged me to try to get an internship here.'

My silence was heavy.

'Look,' she demanded. 'How could I have known?'

'I guess you couldn't have,' I said. 'But she set you up, Lucy. She wanted you here. This was planned long before she met you through Prodigy. She probably had already met Gault in that northern Virginia spy shop, then they decided she should meet you.'

She angrily stared off.

'God,' I said with a loud sigh. 'You were lured right into it.' I stared off, almost sick. 'It's not just because of how good you are at what you do. It's also because of me.'

'Don't try to turn this into your fault. I hate it when you do that.'

'You are my niece. Gault has probably known that for a while.'

'I am also well known in the computer world.' She looked defiantly at me. 'Other people in the computer world have heard of me. Everything doesn't have to be because of you.'

'Does Benton know how you met Carrie?'

'I told him a long time ago.'

'Why didn't you tell me?'

'I didn't want to. I feel bad enough. It's personal.' She wouldn't look at me. 'It was between Mr. Wesley and me. And more to the point, I didn't do anything wrong.'

'Are you telling me that this large manilla envelope was missing after the break-in?'

'Yes.'

'Why would someone want it?'

'She would,' she said bitterly. 'It had things in it that she'd written to me.'

'Has she tried to contact you since then?'

'No,' she said as if she hated Carrie Grethen.

'Come on,' I said in the firm tone of a mother. 'Let's go find Marino.'

He was in the Boardroom, where I tried a Zima and he ordered another beer. Lucy was off to find Janet, and this gave Marino and me a few minutes to talk.

'I don't know how you stand that stuff,' he said, disdainfully eyeing my drink.

'I don't know how I'll stand it either since I've never had one before.' I took a sip. It was actually quite good, and I said so.

'Maybe you should try something before you judge it,' I added.

'I don't drink queer beer. And I don't have to try a lot of things to know they ain't for me.'

'I guess one of the major differences between us, Marino, is I am not constantly worried about whether people think I'm gay.'

'Some people think you are,' he said.

I was amused. 'Well, rest assured nobody thinks you are,' I said. 'The only thing most people assume about you is that you are a bigot.'

Marino yawned without covering his mouth. He was smoking and drinking Budweiser from the bottle. He had dark circles under his eyes, and though he had yet to divulge intimate details about his relationship with Molly, I recognized the symptoms of someone in lust. There were times when he looked as if he had been up and athletic for weeks on end.

'Are you all right?' I inquired.

He set down his bottle and looked around. The Boardroom was busy with new agents and cops drinking beer and eating popcorn while a television blared.

'I'm beat,' he said, and he seemed very distracted.

'I appreciate your coming to get me.'

'Just poke me if I start falling asleep at the wheel,' he said.

'Or you can drive. Those things you're drinking probably don't have any booze in them anyway.'

'They have enough. I won't be driving, and if you're that tired, perhaps we should stay here.'

He got up to get another beer. I followed him with my eyes. Marino was going to be difficult tonight. I could sense his storm fronts better than any meteorologist.

'We got a lab report back from New York that you might find interesting,' he said as he sat back down. 'It's got to do with Gault's hair.'

'The hair found in the fountain?' I asked with interest.

'Yeah. And I don't got the sort of scientific detail I know you want, okay? So you'll have to call up there yourself for that. But the bottom line is they found drugs in his hair. They said he had to be drinking and doing coke for this stuff to have shown up in his hair.'

'They found cocaethylene,' I said.

'I think that's the name. It was all through his hair, from the roots to the ends, meaning he's been drinking and drugging for a while.'

'Actually, we can't be certain how long he's been doing it,' I said.

'The guy I talked to said we're looking at five months of growth,' Marino said.

'Testing hair for drugs is controversial,' I explained. 'It's not certain that some positive results for cocaine in hair aren't due to external contamination. Say, smoke in crack houses that gets absorbed by the hair just like cigarette smoke does. It's not always easy to distinguish between what has been absorbed and what has been ingested.'

'You mean he could be contaminated.' Marino pondered this.

'Yes, he could be. But that doesn't mean he isn't drinking and drugging, too. In fact, he has to be. Cocaethylene is produced in the liver.'

Marino thoughtfully lit another cigarette. 'What about him dyeing his hair all the time?'

'That can affect test results, too,' I said. 'Some oxidizing agents might destroy some of the drug.'

'Oxidizing?'

'As in peroxides, for example.'

'Then it's possible some of this cocaethylene's been destroyed,' Marino reasoned. 'Meaning it's also possible his drug level was really higher than it looks.'

'It could be.'

'He has to be getting drugs somewhere.' Marino stared off.

'In New York that certainly wouldn't be hard,' I said.

'Hell, it's not hard anywhere.' The expression on his face was getting more tense.

'What are you thinking?' I asked.

'I'll tell you what I'm thinking,' he started in. 'This drug connection ain't working out so hot for Jimmy Davila.'

'Why? Do we know his toxicology results?' I asked.

'They're negative.' He paused. 'Benny's started singing. He's saying Davila dealt.'

'I should think people might consider the source on that one,' I said. 'Benny doesn't exactly strike me as a reliable narrator.'

'I agree with you,' Marino said. 'But some people are trying to paint Davila as a bad cop. There's a rumor they want to pin Jane's murder on him.'

'That's crazy,' I said, surprised. 'That makes absolutely no sense.'

'You remember the stuff on Jane's hand that glowed in the Luma-Lite?'

'Yes.'

'Cocaine,' he said.

'And her toxicology?'

'Negative. And that's weird.' Marino looked frustrated. 'But the other thing Benny's saying now is that it was Davila who gave the knapsack to him.'

'Oh come on,' I said with irritation.

'I'm just telling you.'

'It wasn't Davila's hair found in the fountain.'

'We can't prove how long that had been there. And we don't know it's Gault's,' he said.

'DNA will verify it's Gault's,' I said with conviction. 'And Davila carried a .380 and a .38. Jane was shot with a Glock.'

'Look' – Marino leaned forward, resting his arms on the table – 'I'm not here to argue with you, Doc. I'm just telling you that things aren't looking good. New York politicians want this case cleared, and a good way to do that is to pin the crime on a dead man. So what do you do? You turn Davila into a dirtbag and nobody feels sorry for him. Nobody cares.'

'And what about what happened to Davila?'

'That dumbshit medical examiner who went to the scene still thinks it's possible he committed suicide.'

I looked at Marino as if he'd lost his mind. 'He kicked himself in the head?' I said. 'Then shot himself between the eyes?'

'He was standing up when he shot himself with his own gun, and when he fell he hit concrete or something.'

'His vital reaction to his injuries shows he received the blow to his head first,' I said, getting angrier. 'And please explain how his revolver ended up so neatly on his chest.'

'It's not your case, Doc.' Marino looked me in the eye. 'That's the bottom line. You and me are both guests. We got invited.'

'Davila did not commit suicide,' I said. 'And Dr. Horowitz is not going to allow such a thing to come out of his office.'

'Maybe he won't. Maybe they'll just say that Davila was a dirtbag who got whacked by another drug dealer. Jane ends up in a pine box in Potter's Field. End of story. Central Park and the subway are safe again.'

I thought of Commander Penn and felt uneasy. I asked Marino about her.

'I don't know what she's got to do with any of this,' he said. 'I've just been talking to some of the guys. But she's jammed.

On the one hand, she wouldn't want anyone to think she had a bad cop. On the other, she don't want the public to think there's a crazed serial killer running through the subway.'

'I see,' I said as I thought of the enormous pressure she must be under, for it was her department's mandate to take the subway back from the criminals. New York City had allocated the Transit Police tens of millions of dollars to do that.

'Plus,' he added, 'it was a friggin' reporter who found Jane's body in Central Park. And this guy's relentless as a jackhammer from what I've heard. He wants to win a Nobel Prize.'

'Not likely,' I said irritably.

'You never know,' said Marino, who often made predictions about who would win a Nobel Prize. By now, according to him, I had won several.

'I wish we knew whether Gault is still in New York,' I said.

Marino drained his second beer and looked at his watch. 'Where's Lucy?' he asked.

'Looking for Janet, last I heard.'

'What's she like?'

I knew what he was wondering. 'She's a lovely young woman,' I said. 'Bright but very quiet.'

He was silent.

'Marino, they've put my niece on the security floor.'

He turned toward the counter as if he were thinking about another beer. 'Who did? Benton?'

'Yes.'

'Because of the computer mess?'

'Yes.'

'You want another Zima?'

'No, thank you. And you shouldn't have another beer, since you're driving. In fact, you're probably driving a police car and shouldn't have had the first one.'

'I've got my truck tonight.'

I was not at all happy to hear that, and he could tell.

'Look, so it don't have a damn air bag. I'm sorry, okay?

But a taxi or limo service wouldn't have had an air bag, either.'

'Marino . . .'

'I'm just going to buy you this huge air bag. And you can drag it around with you everywhere you go like your own personal hot-air balloon.'

'A file was stolen from Lucy's desk when ERF was broken into last fall,' I said.

'What sort of file?' he asked.

'A manilla envelope containing personal correspondence.' I told him about Prodigy and how Lucy and Carrie had met.

'They knew each other before Quantico?' he said.

'Yes. And I think Lucy believes it was Carrie who went into her desk drawer.'

Marino glanced around as he restlessly moved his empty beer bottle in small circles on the table.

'She seems obsessed with Carrie and can't see anything else,' I went on. 'I'm worried.'

'Where is Carrie these days?' he asked.

'I have no earthly idea,' I said.

Because it could not be proven that she had broken into ERF or had stolen Bureau property, she had been fired but not prosecuted. Carrie had never been locked up, not even for a day.

Marino thought for a moment. 'Well, that bitch isn't what Lucy should be worried about. It's him.'

'Certainly, I am more concerned about him.'

'You think he's got her envelope?'

'That's what I'm afraid of.' I felt a hand on my shoulder and turned around.

'We sitting here or moving on?' Lucy asked, and she had changed into khaki slacks and a denim shirt with the FBI logo embroidered on it. She wore hiking boots and a sturdy leather belt. All that was missing was a cap and a gun.

Marino was more interested in Janet, who could fill a polo shirt in a manner that was riveting. 'So, let's talk about what was in this envelope,' he said to me, unable to shift his eyes from Janet's chest.

'Let's don't do it here,' I said.

Marino's truck was a big blue Ford he kept much cleaner than his police car. His truck had a CB radio and a gun rack, and other than cigarette butts filling the ashtray, there was no trash to be seen. I sat in front, where air fresheners suspended from the rearview mirror gave the darkness a potent scent of pine.

'Tell me exactly what was in the envelope,' Marino said to Lucy, who was in back with her friend.

'I can't tell you *exactly*,' Lucy said, scooting forward and resting a hand on top of my seat.

Marino crept past the guard booth, then shifted gears as his truck loudly got interested in being alive.

'Think.' He raised his voice.

Janet quietly spoke to Lucy, and for a moment they conversed in murmurs. The narrow road was black, firing ranges unusually still. I had never ridden in Marino's truck, and it struck me as a bold symbol of his male pride.

Lucy started talking. 'I had some letters from Grans, Aunt Kay, and E-mail from Prodigy.'

'From Carrie, you mean,' Marino said.

She hesitated. 'Yes.'

'What else?'

'Birthday cards.'

'From who?' Marino asked.

'The same people.'

'What about your mother?'

'No.'

'What about your dad?'

'I don't have anything from him.'

'Her father died when she was very small,' I reminded Marino.

'When you wrote Lucy did you use a return address?' he asked me.

'Yes. My stationery would have that.'

'A post office box?'

'No. My personal mail is delivered to my house. Everything else goes to the office.'

'What are you trying to find out?' Lucy said with a trace of resentment.

'Okay,' Marino said as he drove through dark countryside, 'let me tell you what your thief knows so far. He knows where you go to school, where your aunt Kay lives in Richmond, where your grandmother in Florida lives. He knows what you look like and when you were born.

'Plus he knows about your friendship with Carrie because of the E-mail thing.' He glanced into the rearview mirror. 'And that's just the minimum of what this toad knows about you. I haven't read the letters and notes to see what else he's found out.'

'She knew most of all that anyway,' Lucy said angrily.

'*She?*' Marino pointedly asked.

Lucy was silent.

It was Janet who gently spoke. 'Lucy, you've got to get over it. You've got to give it up.'

'What else?' Marino asked my niece. 'Try to remember the smallest thing. What else was in the envelope?'

'A few autographs and a few old coins. Just things from when I was a kid. Things that would have no value to anyone but me. Like a shell from the beach I picked up when I was with Aunt Kay one time when I was little.'

She thought for a moment. 'My passport. And there were a few papers I did in high school.'

The pain in her voice tugged at my heart, and I wanted to hug her. But when Lucy was sad she pushed everyone away. She fought.

'Why did you keep them in the envelope?' Marino was asking.

'I had to keep them somewhere,' she snapped. 'It was my

damn stuff, okay? And if I'd left it in Miami my mother probably would have thrown it in the trash.'

'The papers you did in high school,' I said. 'What were they about, Lucy?'

The truck got quiet, filled with no voice but its own. The sound of its engine rose and fell with acceleration and the shifting of gears as Marino drove into the tiny town of Triangle. Roadside diners were lit up, and I suspected many of the cars out were driven by marines.

Lucy said, 'Well, it's sort of ironical now. One of the papers I did back then was a practical tutorial on UNIX security. My focus was basically passwords, you know, what could happen if users chose poor passwords. So I talked about the encryption subroutine in C libraries that—'

'What was the other paper about?' Marino interrupted her. 'Brain surgery?'

'How did you guess?' she said just as snootily.

'What was it on?' I asked.

'Wordsworth,' she said.

We ate at the Globe and Laurel, and as I looked around at Highland plaid, police patches and beer steins hanging over the bar, I thought of my life. Mark and I used to eat here, and then in London a bomb detonated as he walked past. Wesley and I once came here often. Then we began knowing each other too well, and we no longer went out in public much.

Everyone had French onion soup and tenderloin. Janet was typically quiet, and Marino would not stop staring at her and making provocative comments. Lucy was getting increasingly infuriated with him, and I was surprised at his behavior. He was no fool. He knew what he was doing.

'Aunt Kay,' Lucy said, 'I want to spend the weekend with you.'

'In Richmond?' I asked.

'That's where you still live, isn't it?' She did not smile.

I hesitated. 'I think you need to stay where you are right now.'

'I'm not in prison. I can do what I want.'

'Of course you're not in prison,' I said quietly. 'Let me talk to Benton, all right?'

She was silent.

'So tell me what you think of the Sig-nine,' Marino was saying to Janet's bosom.

She boldly looked him in the eye and said, 'I'd rather have a Colt Python with a six-inch barrel. Wouldn't you?'

Dinner continued to deteriorate, and the ride back to the Academy was tensely silent except for Marino's unrelenting attempts to engage Janet in a dialogue. After we let her and Lucy out of the truck, I turned to him and boiled over.

'For God's sake,' I exploded. 'What has gotten into you?'

'I don't know what you're talking about.'

'You were obnoxious. Absolutely obnoxious, and you know exactly what I'm talking about.'

He sped through the darkness along J. Edgar Hoover Road, heading toward the interstate as he fumbled for a cigarette.

'Janet will probably never want to be around you again,' I went on. 'I wouldn't blame Lucy for avoiding you, either. And that's a shame. The two of you had become friends.'

'Just because I've given her shooting lessons don't mean we're friends,' he said. 'As far as I'm concerned she's a spoiled brat just like she's always been, and a smart-ass. Not to mention, I don't like her type and I sure as hell don't understand why you let her do the things she does.'

'What *things*?' I said, getting more put out with him.

'Has she ever dated a guy?' He glanced over at me. 'I mean, even once?'

'Her private life is none of your concern,' I replied. 'It is not relevant to how you behaved this evening.'

'Bullshit. If Carrie hadn't been Lucy's girlfriend, ERF probably never would have been broken into, and we wouldn't have Gault running around inside the computer.'

'That's a ridiculous statement not based on a single fact,' I said. 'I suspect Carrie would have completed her mission whether Lucy was part of the scenario or not.'

'I tell you' – he blew smoke toward his slightly opened window – 'queers are ruining this planet.'

'God help us,' I said with disgust. 'You sound like my sister.'

'I think you need to send Lucy someplace. Get her some help.'

'Marino, you simply must stop this. Your opinions are based on ignorance. They are hateful. If my niece prefers women instead of men, please tell me why that is so threatening to you.'

'It don't threaten me in the least. It's just unnatural.' He tossed the cigarette butt out the window, a tiny missile extinguished by the night. 'But hey, it's not that I don't understand it. It's a known fact that a lot of women go for each other because it's the best they can do.'

'I see,' I said. 'A known fact.' I paused. 'So tell me, would that be the case with Lucy and Janet?'

'That's why I recommend them getting help, because there's hope. They could get guys easy. Especially Janet could with the way she's built. If I wasn't so tied up, I'd have half a mind to ask her out.'

'Marino,' I said, and he was making me tired, 'leave them alone. You're just setting yourself up to be disliked and snubbed. You're setting yourself up to look like a damn fool. The Janets of the world are not going to date you.'

'Her loss. If she had the right experience, it might straighten her out. What women do with each other's not what I consider the real thing. They have no idea what they're missing.'

The thought that Marino might consider himself an expert on what women needed in bed was so absurd that I forgot to be annoyed. I laughed.

'I feel protective of Lucy, okay?' he went on. 'I sort of feel like an uncle, and see, the problem is she's never been around men. Her dad died. You're divorced. She's got no brothers and her mother is in and out of bed with goofballs.'

'That much is true,' I said. 'I wish Lucy could have had a positive male influence.'

'I guarantee if she had she wouldn't have turned out queer.'

'That's not a kind word,' I said. 'And we really don't know why people turn out the way they do.'

'Then you tell me.' He glanced my way. 'You explain what went wrong.'

'In the first place, I'm not going to say that anything went wrong. There may be a genetic component to one's sexual orientation. Maybe there isn't. But what's important is that it doesn't matter.'

'So you don't care.'

I thought about this for a minute. 'I care because it is a harder way to live,' I said.

'And that's it?' he said skeptically. 'You mean you wouldn't rather she was with a man?'

Again, I hesitated. 'I guess at this point, I just want her with good people.'

He got quiet as he drove. Then he said, 'I'm sorry about tonight. I know I was a jerk.'

'Thank you for apologizing,' I said.

'Well, the truth is, things aren't going so good for me personally right now. Molly and me were doing fine until about a week ago when Doris called.'

I wasn't terribly surprised. Old spouses and lovers have a way of resurfacing.

'Seems she found out about Molly because Rocky said something. Now all of a sudden she wants to come home. She wants to get back with me.'

When Doris had left, Marino was devastated. But at this stage in my life I somewhat cynically believed that fractured relationships could not be set and healed like bones. He lit another cigarette as a truck bore down on our rear and swung past. A vehicle rushed up behind us, its high beams in our eyes.

'Molly wasn't happy about it,' he went on with difficulty. 'Truth is, we hadn't been getting along so hot since and it's just as well we didn't spend Christmas together. I think she's started going out on me, too. This sergeant she met. Wouldn't you know. I introduced them at the FOP one night.'

'I'm very sorry.' I looked over at his face and thought he might cry. 'Do you still love Doris?' I gently asked.

'Hell, I don't know. I don't know nothing. Women may as well be from another planet. You know? It's just like tonight. Everything I do is wrong.'

'That's not true. You and I have been friends for years. You must be doing something right.'

'You're the only woman friend I got,' he said. 'But you're more like a guy.'

'Why, thank you.'

'I can talk to you like a guy. And you know what you're doing. You didn't get where you are because you're a woman. Goddam it' – he squinted into the rearview mirror, then adjusted it to diminish the glare – 'you got where you are in spite of your being one.'

He glanced again in the mirrors. I turned around. A car was practically touching our bumper, high beams blinding. We were going seventy miles an hour.

'That's weird,' I said. 'He has plenty of room to go around us.'

Traffic on I-95 was light. There was no reason for anyone to tailgate, and I thought of the accident last fall when Lucy had flipped my Mercedes. Someone had been on her rear bumper, too. Fear ran along my nerves.

'Can you see what kind of car it is?' I asked.

'Looks like a Z. Maybe an old 280 Z, something like that.'

He reached inside his coat and slid a pistol from its holster. He placed the gun in his lap as he continued to watch the mirrors. I turned around again and saw a dark shape of a head that looked male. The driver was staring straight at us.

'All right,' Marino growled. 'This is pissing me off.' He firmly tapped the brakes.

The car shot around us with a long, angry blare of the horn. It was a Porsche and the driver was black.

I said to Marino, 'You don't still have that Confederate flag bumper sticker on your truck, do you? The one that glows when headlights hit it?'

'Yeah, I do.' He returned the gun to its holster.

'Maybe you ought to consider removing it.'

The Porsche was tiny taillights far ahead. I thought of Chief Tucker threatening to send Marino to cultural diversity class. Marino could go the rest of his life and I wasn't sure it would cure him.

'Tomorrow's Thursday,' he said. 'I've got to go to First Precinct and see if anyone remembers that I still work for the city.'

'What's happening with Sheriff Santa?'

'He's scheduled for a preliminary hearing next week.'

'He's locked up, I presume,' I said.

'Nope. Out on bond. When do you start jury duty?'

'Monday.'

'Maybe you can get cut loose.'

'I can't ask for that,' I said. 'Somebody would make a big deal of it, and even if they didn't, it would be hypocritical. I'm supposed to care about justice.'

'Do you think I should see Doris?' We were in Richmond now, the downtown skyline in view.

I looked over at his profile, his thinning hair, big ears and face, and the way his huge hands made the steering wheel disappear. He could not remember his life before his wife. Their relationship had long ago left the froth and fire of sex and moved into an orbit of safe but boring stability. I believed they had parted because they were afraid of growing old.

'I think you should see her,' I said to him.

'So I should go up to New Jersey.'

'No,' I said. 'Doris is the one who left. She should come here.'

11

Windsor Farms was dark when we turned into it from Cary Street, and Marino did not want me entering my house alone. He pulled into my brick driveway and stared ahead at the shut garage door illuminated by his headlights.

'Do you have the opener?' he asked.

'It's in my car.'

'A lot of friggin' good that does when your car's inside the garage with the door shut.'

'If you would drop me off in front as I requested I could unlock my front door,' I said.

'Nope. You're not walking down that long sidewalk anymore, Doc.' He was very authoritative, and I knew when he got this way there was no point in arguing.

I handed him my keys. 'Then you go on in through the front and open the garage door. I'll wait right here.'

He opened his door. 'I got a shotgun between the seats.'

He reached down to show me a black Benelli twelve-gauge with an eight-round magazine extension. It occurred to me that Benelli, a manufacturer of fine Italian shotguns, was also the name on Gault's false driver's license.

'The safety's right there.' Marino showed me. 'All you do is push it in, pump it and fire.'

'Is there a riot about to happen that I've not been told about?'

He got out of the truck and locked the doors.

I cranked open the window. 'It might help if you knew my burglar alarm code,' I said.

'Already do.' He started walking across frosted grass. 'You're DOB.'

'How did you know that?' I demanded.

'You're predictable,' I heard him say before disappearing around a hedge.

Several minutes later the garage door began to lift and a light went on inside, illuminating yard and garden tools neatly arranged on walls, a bicycle I rarely rode, and my car. I could not see my new Mercedes without thinking of the one Lucy had wrecked.

My former 500E was sleek and fast with an engine partially designed by Porsche. Now I just wanted something big. I had a black S500 that probably would hold its own with a cement truck or a tractor trailer. Marino stood near my car, looking at me as if he wished I would hurry up. I honked the horn to remind him I was locked inside his truck.

'Why do people keep trying to lock me inside their vehicles?' I said as he let me out. 'A taxi this morning, now you.'

'Because it's not safe when you're loose. I want to look around your house before I leave,' he said.

'It's not necessary.'

'I'm not asking. I'm telling you I'm going to look,' he said.

'All right. Help yourself.'

He followed me inside, and I went straight to the living room and turned on the gas fire. Next I opened the front door and brought in the mail and several newspapers that one of my neighbors had forgotten to pick up. To anybody watching my gracious brick house, it would have been obvious that I was gone over Christmas.

I glanced around as I returned to the living room, looking for anything even slightly out of order. I wondered if anyone had thought about breaking in. I wondered what eyes had turned this way, what dark thoughts had enveloped this place where I lived.

My neighborhood was one of the wealthiest in Richmond, and certainly there had been problems before, mostly with gypsies who tended to walk in during the day when people were home. I was not as worried about them, for I never left doors unlocked, and the alarm was activated constantly. It was an entirely different breed of criminal I feared, and he was not as interested in what I owned as in who and what I was. I kept many guns in the house in places where I could get to them easily.

I seated myself on the couch, the shadow from flames moving on oil paintings on the walls. My furniture was contemporary European, and during the day the house was filled with light. As I sorted mail, I came across a pink envelope similar to several I had seen before. It was note size and not a good grade of paper, the stationery the sort one might buy in a drugstore. The postmark this time was Charlottesville, December 23. I slit it open with a scalpel. The note, like the others, was handwritten in black fountain ink.

Dear Dr. Scarpetta,
I hope you have a very special Christmas!
CAIN

I carefully set the letter on my coffee table.

'Marino?' I called out.

Gault had written the note before he had murdered Jane. But the mail was slow. I was just getting it now.

'Marino!' I got up.

I heard his feet moving loudly and quickly on stairs. He rushed into the living room, gun in hand.

'What?' he said, breathing hard as he looked around. 'Are you all right?'

I pointed to the note. His eyes fell to the pink envelope and matching paper.

'Who's it from?'

'Look,' I said.

He sat beside me, then got right back up. 'I'm going to set the alarm first.'

'Good idea.'

He came back and sat down again. 'Let me have a couple pens. Thanks.'

He used the pens to keep the notepaper unfolded so he could read without jeopardizing any fingerprints I hadn't already destroyed. When he was finished, he studied the handwriting and postmark on the envelope.

'Is this the first time you've gotten one of these?' he asked.

'No.'

He looked accusingly at me. 'And you didn't say nothing?'

'It's not the first note, but it's the first one signed *CAIN*,' I said.

'What have the rest of them been signed?'

'There's only been two others on this pink stationery, and they weren't signed.'

'Do you have them?'

'No. I didn't think they were important. The postmarks were Richmond, the notes kooky but not alarming. I frequently get peculiar mail.'

'Sent to your house?'

'Generally to the office. My home address isn't listed.'

'Shit, Doc!' Marino got up and started pacing. 'Didn't it disturb you when you got notes delivered to your home address when it's not listed?'

'The location of my home certainly isn't a secret. You know

how often we've asked the media not to film or photograph it, and they do it anyway.'

'Tell me what the other notes said.'

'Like this one, they were short. One asked me how I was and if I was still working too hard. It seems to me the other was more along the lines of missing me.'

'Missing you?'

I searched my memory. 'Something like, "It's been too long. We really must see each other."'

'You're certain it's the same person.' He glanced down at the pink note on the table.

'I think so. Obviously, Gault has my address, as you predicted he would.'

'He's probably been by your crib.' He stopped pacing and looked at me. 'You realize that?'

I did not answer.

'I'm telling you that Gault has seen where you live.' Marino ran his fingers through his hair. 'You understand what I'm saying?' he demanded.

'This needs to go to the lab first thing in the morning,' I said.

I thought of the first two notes. If they, too, were from Gault, he had mailed them in Richmond. He had been here.

'You can't stay here, Doc.'

'They can analyze the postage stamp. If he licked it, he left saliva on it. We can use PCR and get DNA.'

'You can't stay here,' he said again.

'Of course I can.'

'I'm telling you, you can't.'

'I have to, Marino,' I said stubbornly. 'This is where I live.'

He was shaking his head. 'No. It's out of the question. Or else I'm moving in.'

I was devoted to Marino but could not bear the thought of him in my house. I could see him wiping his feet on my oriental rugs and leaving rings on yew wood and mahogany. He would watch wrestling in front of the fire and drink Budweiser out of the can.

'I'm going to call Benton right now,' he went on. 'He's going to tell you the same thing.' He walked toward the phone.

'Marino,' I said. 'Leave Benton out of this.'

He walked over to the fire and sat on the sandstone hearth instead. He put his head in his hands, and when he looked up at me his face was exhausted. 'You know how I'll feel if something happens to you?'

'Not very good,' I said, ill at ease.

'It will kill me. It will, I swear.'

'You're getting maudlin.'

'I don't know what that word means. But I do know Gault's going to have to waste my ass first, you hear me?' He stared intensely at me.

I looked away. I felt the blood rise to my cheeks.

'You know, you can get whacked like anybody else. Like Eddie, like Susan, like Jane, like Jimmy Davila. Gault's fixed on you, goddam it. And he's probably the worst killer in this friggin' century.' He paused, watching me. '*Are you listening?*'

I lifted my eyes to his. 'Yes,' I said. 'I'm listening. I'm hearing every word.'

'You got to leave for Lucy's sake, too. She can't come see you here ever. And if something happens to you, just what do you think is going to happen to her?'

I shut my eyes. I loved my home. I had worked so hard for it. I had labored intensely and tried to be a good business-woman. What Wesley had predicted was happening. Protection was to be at the expense of who I was and all that I had.

'So I'm supposed to move somewhere and spend my savings?' I asked. 'I'm supposed to just give all of this up?' I swept my hand around the room. 'I'm supposed to give that monster that much power?'

'You can't drive your ride, either,' he went on, thinking aloud.

'You got to drive something he won't recognize. You can take my truck, if you want.'

'Hell no,' I said.

Marino looked hurt. 'It's a big thing for me to let someone use my truck. I never let anybody.'

'That's not it. I want my life. I want to feel Lucy is safe. I want to live in my house and drive my car.'

He got up and brought me his handkerchief.

'I'm not crying,' I said.

'You're about to.'

'No, I'm not.'

'You want a drink?' he asked.

'Scotch.'

'I think I'll have a little bourbon.'

'You can't. You're driving.'

'No, I'm not,' he said as he stepped behind the bar. 'I'm camping on your couch.'

Close to midnight, I carried in a pillow and blanket and helped him get settled. He could have slept in a guest room, but he wanted to be right where he was with the fire turned low.

I retreated upstairs and read until my eyes would no longer focus. I was grateful Marino was in my house. I did not know when I had ever been this frightened. So far Gault had always gotten his way. So far he had not failed in a single evil task he had set out to accomplish. If he wanted me to die, I had no confidence I could evade him. If he wanted Lucy to die, I believed that would happen, too.

It was the latter I feared most. I had seen his work. I knew what he did. I could diagram every piece of bone and ragged excision of skin. I looked at the black metal nine-millimeter pistol on the table by my bed, and I wondered what I always did. Would I reach for it in time? Would I save my life or someone else? As I surveyed my bedroom and adjoining study, I knew Marino was right. I could not stay here alone.

I drifted to sleep pondering this and had a disturbing dream.

A figure with a long dark robe and a face like a white balloon was smiling insipidly at me from an antique mirror. Every time I passed the mirror the figure in it was watching with its chilly smile. It was both dead and alive and seemed to have no gender. I suddenly woke up at one A.M. I listened for noises in the dark. I went downstairs and heard Marino snoring.

Quietly, I called his name.

The rhythm of his snoring did not alter.

'Marino?' I whispered as I drew closer.

He sat up, loudly fumbling for his gun.

'For God's sake don't shoot me.'

'Huh?' He looked around, his face pale in the low firelight. He realized where he was and put the gun back on the table. 'Don't sneak up on me like that.'

'I wasn't sneaking.'

I sat next to him on the couch. It occurred to me that I had a nightgown on and he had never seen me like this, but I did not care.

'Is something wrong?' he asked.

I laughed ruefully. 'I don't think there's much that isn't.'

His eyes began to wander, and I could feel the battle inside him. I had always known Marino had an interest in me that I could not gratify. Tonight the situation was more difficult, for I could not hide behind walls of lab coats, scrubs, business suits and titles. I was in a low-cut gown made of soft flannel the color of sand. It was after midnight and he was sleeping in my house.

'I can't sleep,' I went on.

'I was sleeping just fine.' He lay back down and put his hands behind his head, watching me.

'I start jury duty next week.'

He made no comment.

'I have several court cases coming up and an office to run. I can't just pack up and leave town.'

'Jury duty's no problem,' he said. 'We'll get you out of it.'

'I don't want to do that.'

'You're going to get struck anyway,' he said. 'No defense attorney alive is going to want you on his jury.'

I was silent.

'You may as well go on leave. The court cases can be continued. Hey, maybe head off skiing for a couple weeks. Out west someplace.'

The more he talked the more upset I got.

'You'll have to use an alias,' he went on. 'And you got to have security. You can't be off at some ski resort all by yourself.'

'Well,' I snapped, 'no one is going to assign an FBI or Secret Service agent to me, if that's what you're thinking. Rights are honored only in the breach. Most people don't get agents or cops assigned to them until they're already raped or dead.'

'You can hire someone. He can drive, too, but you shouldn't be in your own ride.'

'I am not hiring anybody and I insist on driving my own car.'

He thought for a minute, staring up at the vaulted ceiling. 'How long have you had it?'

'Not even two months.'

'You got it from McGeorge, right?' He referred to the Mercedes dealership in town.

'Yes.'

'I'll talk to them and see if they'll let you borrow something less conspicuous than that big black Nazimobile of yours.'

Furious, I got up from the couch and moved closer to the fire.

'And just what else should I give up?' I said bitterly as I stared at flames wrapping around artificial logs.

Marino did not answer.

'I won't let him turn me into Jane.' I launched into a diatribe. 'It's as if he's prepping me so he can do the same thing to me he did to her. He's trying to take away everything I have.

'Even my name. I'm supposed to have an alias. I'm supposed

to be less conspicuous. Or generic. I'm not to live anywhere or drive anything and can't tell people where to find me. Hotels, private security are very expensive.

'So, eventually, I will go through my savings. I'm the chief medical examiner of Virginia and hardly in the office anymore. The governor may fire me. Little by little I will lose all that I have and all that I've been. Because of him.'

Still, Marino did not answer, and I realized he was asleep. A tear slid down my cheek as I pulled the covers to his chin and went back upstairs.

12

I parked behind my building at a quarter after seven and for a while sat in my car, staring at cracked blacktop, dingy stucco and the sagging chain-link fence around the parking lot.

Behind me were railroad trestles and the I-95 overpass, then the outer limits of a downtown boarded up and battered by crime. There were no trees or plantings and very little grass. My appointment to this position certainly had never included a view, but right now I did not care. I missed my office and my staff, and all that I looked at was comforting.

Inside the morgue, I stopped by the office to check on the day's cases. A suicide needed to be viewed along with an eighty-year-old woman who had died at home from untreated carcinoma of the breast. An entire family had been killed yesterday afternoon when their car was struck by a train, and my heart was heavy as I read their names. Deciding to take care of the views while I waited for my assistant chiefs, I unlocked the walk-in refrigerator and doors leading into the autopsy suite.

The three tables were polished bright, the tile floor very clean. I scanned cubbyholes stacked with forms, carts neatly lined with instruments and test tubes, steel shelves arranged with camera equipment and film. In the locker room I checked linens and starchy lab coats as I put on plastic apron and gown, then went out in the hall to a cart of surgical masks, shoe covers, face shields.

Pulling on gloves, I continued my inspection as I went inside the refrigerator to retrieve the first case. Bodies were in black pouches on top of gurneys, the air properly chilled to thirty-four degrees and adequately deodorized considering we had a full house. I checked toe tags until I found the right one, and I wheeled the gurney out.

No one else would be in for another hour, and I cherished the silence. I did not even need to lock the autopsy suite doors because it was too early for the elevator across the hall to be busy with forensic scientists going upstairs. I couldn't find any paperwork on the suicide and checked the office again. The report of sudden death had been placed in the wrong box. The date scribbled on it was incorrect by two days, and much of the form had not been completed. The only other information it offered was the name of the decedent and that the body had been delivered at three o'clock this morning by Sauls Mortuary, which made no sense.

My office used three removal services for the pickup and delivery of dead bodies. These three local funeral homes were on call twenty-four hours a day, and any medical examiner case in central Virginia should be handled by one of them. I did not understand why the suicide had been delivered by a funeral home we had no contract with, and why the driver had not signed his name. I felt a rush of irritation. I had been gone but a few days and the system was falling apart. I went to the phone and called the night-time security guard, whose shift did not end for another half hour.

'This is Dr. Scarpetta,' I said when he answered.

'Yes, ma'am.'

'To whom am I speaking, please?'

'Evans.'

'Mr. Evans, an alleged suicide was delivered at three o'clock this morning.'

'Yes, ma'am. I let him in.'

'Who delivered him?'

He paused. 'Uh, I think it was Sauls.'

'We don't use Sauls.'

He got quiet.

'I think you'd better come over here,' I said to him.

He hesitated. 'To the morgue?'

'That's where I am.'

He stalled again. I could feel his strong resistance. Many people who worked in the building could not deal with the morgue. They did not want to come near it, and I had yet to employ a security guard who would so much as poke his head inside the refrigerator. Many guards and most cleaning crews did not work for me long.

While I waited for this fearless guard named Evans, I unzipped the black pouch, which looked new. The victim's head was covered by a black plastic garbage bag that had been tied around the neck with a shoelace. He was clothed in blood-soaked pajamas and wore a thick gold bracelet and Rolex watch. Peeking out of the breast pocket of his pajama top was what appeared to be a pink envelope. I took a step back, getting weak in the knees.

I ran to the doors, slammed them shut and turned dead bolt locks as I fumbled inside my pocketbook for my revolver. Lipsticks and hairbrush clattered to the floor. I thought of the locker room, of places one could hide as I dialed the telephone, my hands trembling. Depending on how warmly he was dressed, he could hide inside the refrigerator, I frantically thought as I envisioned the many gurneys and black body bags on top of them. I hurried to the great steel door and snapped the padlock on the handle while I waited for Marino to return my page.

The phone rang in five minutes just as Evans began tentatively knocking on the locked autopsy suite doors.

'Hold on,' I called out to him. 'Stay right there.' I picked up the phone.

'Yo,' Marino said over the line.

'Get here right now,' I said, fighting to hold my voice steady as I tightly gripped the gun.

'What is it?' He got alarmed.

'Hurry!' I said.

I hung up and dialed 911. Then I spoke through the door to Evans.

'The police are coming,' I said loudly.

'The police?' His voice went up.

'We've got a terrible problem in here.' My heart would not slow down. 'You go on upstairs and wait in the conference room, is that clear?'

'Yes, ma'am. I'm on my way there now.'

A Formica counter ran half the length of the wall and I climbed on top of it, positioning myself in such a way that I was sitting near the telephone and could see every door. I held the Smith & Wesson .38 and wished I had my Browning or Marino's Benelli shotgun. I watched the black pouch on the gurney as if it might move.

The telephone rang and I jumped. I grabbed the receiver.

'Morgue.' My voice trembled.

Silence.

'Hello?' I asked more strongly.

No one spoke.

I hung up and got off the counter as anger began pumping through me and quickly turned to rage. It dispelled my fear like sun burning off mist. I unlocked the double doors leading into the corridor and stepped inside the morgue office again. Above the telephone were four strips of Scotch tape and corners of torn paper left when someone had ripped the in-house telephone list off the wall. On that list was the morgue's number and my direct line upstairs.

'Dammit!' I exclaimed under my breath. 'Dammit, dammit, dammit!'

The buzzer sounded in the bay as I wondered what else had been tampered with or taken. I thought about my office upstairs as I went out and pushed a button on the wall. The great door screeched open. Marino, in uniform, stood on its other side with two patrolmen and a detective. They ran past me to the autopsy suite, holsters unsnapped. I followed them and set my revolver on the counter because I did not think I would need it now.

'What the hell's going on?' Marino asked as he looked blankly at the body in its unzipped pouch.

The other officers looked on, not seeing anything wrong. Then they looked at me and the revolver I had just set down.

'Dr. Scarpetta? What seems to be the problem?' asked the detective, whose name I did not know.

I explained about the removal service while they listened with no expression on their faces.

'And he came in with what appears to be a note in his pocket. What police investigator would allow that? What police department is working this, for that matter? There's no mention of one,' I said, next pointing out that the head was bagged with a garbage bag tied with a shoelace.

'What does the note say?' asked the detective, who wore a belted dark coat, cowboy boots, and a gold Rolex that I was certain was counterfeit.

'I haven't touched it,' I said. 'I thought it wise to wait until you got here.'

'I think we'd better look,' he said.

With gloved hands, I slid the envelope out of the pocket, touching as little of the paper as I could. I was startled to see my name and home address neatly written on the front of it in black fountain ink. The letter also was affixed with a stamp. Carrying it to the counter, I carefully slit it open with a scalpel and unfolded a single sheet of stationery that by now was chillingly familiar. The note read:

HO! HO! HO!
CAIN

'Who's CAIN?' an officer asked as I untied the shoelace and removed the trash bag from the dead man's head.

'Oh shit,' the detective said, taking a step back.

'Holy Christ,' Marino exclaimed.

Sheriff Santa had been shot between the eyes, a nine-millimeter shell stuck in his left ear. The firing pin impression was distinctly Glock. I sat down in a chair and looked around. No one seemed quite sure what to do. This had never happened before. People didn't commit homicides and then deliver their victims to the morgue.

'The night-shift security guard is upstairs,' I said, trying to catch my breath.

'He was here when this was delivered?' Marino lit a cigarette, eyes darting.

'Apparently.'

'I'm gonna go talk to him,' said Marino, who was in command, for we were in his precinct. He looked at his officers. 'You guys poke around down here and out in the bay. See what you find. Put something out over the air without tipping off the media. Gault's been here. He may still be in the area.' He glanced at his watch, then looked at me. 'What's the guy's name upstairs?'

'Evans.'

'You know him?'

'Vaguely.'

'Come on,' he said.

'Is someone going to secure this room?' I looked at the detective and two uniformed men.

'I will,' one of them said. 'But you might not want to leave your gun sitting there.'

I returned my revolver to my purse, which I carried with me. Marino stabbed the cigarette in an ash can, and we boarded the elevator across the hall. The instant the doors shut his face turned red. He lost his captain's composure.

'I'm not believing this!' He looked at me, eyes filled with fury. 'This can't happen, it just can't happen!'

Doors opened and he angrily strode down the hall on the floor where I had spent so much of my life.

'He should be in the conference room,' I said.

We passed my office and I barely glanced inside. I did not have time now to see if Gault had been in there. All he had to do was get on the elevator or climb the stairs, and he could have walked into my office. At three o'clock in the morning, who was going to check?

Inside the conference room, Evans sat stiffly in a chair about halfway between the head and foot of the table. Around the room many photographs of former chiefs gazed at me as I sat across from this security guard who had just allowed my workplace to be turned into a crime scene. Evans was an older black man who needed his job. He wore a khaki uniform with brown flaps over the pockets and carried a gun that I wondered if he knew how to use.

'Do you know what's going on?' Marino pulled out a chair and asked him.

'No, sir. I sure don't.' His eyes were scared.

'Someone made a delivery they wasn't supposed to make.' Marino got out his cigarettes again. 'It was while you was on.'

Evans frowned. He looked genuinely clueless. 'You mean a body?'

'Listen.' I stepped in. 'I know what the SOP is. We all do. You know about the suicide case. We just talked about it on the phone . . .'

Evans interrupted, 'Like I said, I let him in.'

'What time?' Marino asked.

He looked up at the ceiling. 'I guess it would've been around three in the morning. I was next door at the desk where I always sit and this hearse pulls up.'

'Pulls up where?' Marino asked.

'Behind the building.'

'If it was behind the building, how could you see it? The lobby where you sit's in front of the building,' Marino bluntly said.

'I didn't see it,' the guard went on. 'But this man walks up and I see him through the glass. I go out to ask what he wants, and he says he has a delivery.'

'What about paperwork?' I asked. 'He didn't show you anything?'

'He says the police hadn't finished their report and told him to go on. He says they'll bring it by later.'

'I see,' I said.

'He says his hearse is parked out back,' Evans continued. 'He says a wheel on his stretcher's stuck and asks if he can use one of ours.'

'Did you know him?' I asked, containing my anger.

He shook his head.

'Can you describe him?' I then asked.

Evans thought for a minute. 'To tell you the truth, I didn't look close. But it seems like he was light skinned with white hair.'

'His hair was white?'

'Yes, ma'am. I'm sure of that.'

'He was old?'

Evans frowned again. 'No, ma'am.'

'How was he dressed?'

'Seems like he had on a dark suit and tie. You know, the way most funeral home folks dress.'

'Fat, thin, tall, short?'

'Thin. Medium height.'

'Then what happened?' Marino said.

'Then I told him to pull up to the bay and I'd let him in. I cut through the building like I always do and open the bay door. He come in and there's a stretcher in the hall. So he takes it, gets the body and comes back. He signs him in and all that.' Evans's eyes drifted. 'And he put the body in the fridge and went on.' He wouldn't look at us.

I took a deep, quiet breath and Marino blew out smoke.

'Mr. Evans,' I said, 'I just want the truth.'

He glanced at me.

'You've got to tell us what happened when you let him in,' I said. 'That's all I want. Really.'

Evans looked at me and his eyes got bright. 'Dr. Scarpetta, I don't know what's happened, but I can tell it's bad. Please don't be getting mad at me. I don't like it down there at night. I'd be a liar if I said I did. I try to do a good job.'

'Just tell the truth.' I measured my words. 'That's all we want.'

'I take care of my mama.' He was about to cry. 'I'm all she's got and she's got terrible heart trouble. I been going over there every day and doing her shopping since my wife passed on. I got a daughter raising three young'uns on her own.'

'Mr. Evans, you are not going to lose your job,' I said, even though he deserved to.

He briefly met my eyes. 'Thank you, ma'am. I believe what you're saying. But it's what other people will say that worries me.'

'Mr. Evans.' I waited until he held my gaze. 'I'm the only other people you should worry about.'

He wiped away a tear. 'I'm sorry about whatever it is I done. If I caused somebody to be hurt, I don't know what I'm gonna do.'

'You didn't cause anything,' Marino said. 'That son of a bitch with white hair did.'

'Tell us about him,' I said. 'What exactly did he do when you let him in?'

'He rolled the body in like I said, and left it parked in the hall in front of the refrigerator. I had to unlock it, you know, and I said he could roll the body on in there. Which he did. Then I took him in the morgue office and showed him what he needed to fill out. I told him he needed to put in for his mileage so he could get reimbursed. But he didn't pay no attention to that.'

'Did you escort him back out?' I asked.

Evans sighed. 'No, ma'am. I'm not going to lie to you.'

'What did you do?' Marino asked.

'I left him down there filling out paperwork. I'd locked the fridge back up and wasn't worried about shutting the bay door after him. He didn't pull into the bay 'cause there's one of your vans in there.'

I thought for a minute. 'What van?' I asked.

'That blue one.'

'There's no van in the bay,' Marino said.

Evans's face went slack. 'There sure was at three this morning. I saw it sitting right in there when I held open the door so he could roll the body in.'

'Wait a minute,' I said. 'What was the man with white hair driving?'

'A hearse.'

I could tell he did not know that for a fact. 'You saw it,' I said.

He exhaled in frustration. 'No, I didn't. He said he had one, and I just assumed it was parked in the back lot near the bay door.'

'So when you pushed the button to open the bay door, you didn't actually wait and watch what drove in.'

He looked down at the tabletop.

'Was there a van parked in the bay when you originally went out to push the button on the wall? Before the body was wheeled in?' I asked.

Evans thought for a minute, the expression on his face getting more miserable. 'Damn,' he said, eyes cast down. 'I don't remember. I didn't look. I just opened the door in the hallway, hit the button on the wall and went back inside. I didn't look.' He paused. 'It may be that nothing was in there then.'

'So the bay could have been empty at that time.'

'Yes, ma'am. I guess it could have been.'

'And when you held the door open a few minutes later so the body could be rolled in, you didn't notice a van in the bay?'

'That's when I did notice it,' he said. 'I just thought it belonged to your office. It looked like one of your vans. You know, dark blue with no windows except in front.'

'Let's get back to the man rolling the body inside the refrigerator and your locking up,' Marino said. 'Then what?'

'I figured he'd leave after he finished his paperwork,' Evans said. 'I went back to the other side of the building.'

'Before he'd left the morgue.'

Evans hung his head again.

'Do you have any idea at all when he finally left?' Marino then asked.

'No, sir,' the security guard quietly said. 'I guess I can't swear he ever did.'

Everyone was silent, as if Gault might this minute walk in. Marino pushed his chair back and looked at the empty doorway.

It was Evans who next spoke. 'If that was his van, I guess he shut the bay door himself. I know it was shut at five because I walked around the building.'

'Well, it don't exactly require a rocket scientist to do that,' Marino said unkindly. 'You just drive out, go back inside and hit the damn button. Then you walk out through the side door.'

'The van certainly isn't in there now,' I said. 'Someone drove it out.'

'Are both vans outside?' Marino asked.

'They were when I got here,' I said.

Marino asked Evans, 'If you saw him in a lineup, could you pick him out?'

He looked up, terrified. 'What did he do?'

'Could you pick him out?' Marino said again.

'I think I could. Yes, sir. I sure would try.'

I got up and quickly walked down the hall. At my office I stopped in the doorway and looked around the same way I had last night when I had walked inside my house. I tried to sense the slightest shift in the environment – a rug disturbed, an object out of place, a lamp on that shouldn't be.

My desk was neatly stacked with paperwork waiting for my review, and the computer screen on the return told me I had mail waiting. The in basket was full, the out basket empty, and my microscope was shrouded in plastic because when I had last looked at slides I was about to fly to Miami for a week.

That seemed incredibly long ago, and it shocked me to think Sheriff Santa had been arrested Christmas Eve, and since then the world had changed. Gault had savaged a woman named Jane. He had murdered a young police officer. He had killed Sheriff Santa and broken into my morgue. In four days he had done all that. I moved closer to my desk, scanning, and as I got near my computer terminal I could almost smell a presence, or feel it, like an electrical field.

I did not have to touch my keyboard to know he had. I watched the mail-waiting message quietly flash green. I hit several keys to go into a menu that would show me my messages. But the menu did not come up, a screen saver did. It was a black background with CAIN in bright red letters that dripped as if they were bleeding. I walked back down the hall.

'Marino,' I said. 'Please come here.'

He left Evans and followed me to my office. I pointed to my computer. Marino stared stonily at it. There were wet rings under the arms of his white uniform shirt, and I could smell his sweat. Stiff black leather creaked when he moved. He was constantly rearranging the fully loaded belt beneath his full belly as if everything he'd amounted to in life was in his way.

'How hard would that be to do?' he asked, mopping his face with a soiled handkerchief.

'Not hard if you have a program ready to load.'

'Where the hell did he get the program?'

'That's what worries me,' I said, thinking of a question we didn't ask.

We returned to the conference room. Evans was standing, numbly looking at photographs on the wall.

'Mr. Evans,' I said. 'Did the man from the funeral home speak to you?'

He turned around, startled. 'No, ma'am. Not much.'

'Not much?' I puzzled.

'No, ma'am.'

'Then how did he convey what he wanted?'

'He said what he had to say.' He paused. 'He was a real quiet type. He spoke in a real quiet voice.' Evans was rubbing his face. 'The more I think about it, the stranger it is. He was wearing tinted glasses. And to tell you the truth' – he stopped – 'well, I had my impressions.'

'What impressions?' I asked.

Evans said, after a pause, 'I thought he might be homo-sexual.'

'Marino,' I said. 'Let's take a walk.'

We escorted Evans out of the building and waited until he'd rounded a corner because I did not want him to see what we did next. Both vans were parked in their usual spaces not far from my Mercedes. Without touching door or glass, I looked through the driver's window of the one nearest the bay and could plainly see the plastic on the steering column was gone, wires exposed.

'It's been hot-wired,' I said.

Marino snapped up his portable radio and held it close to his mouth.

'Unit eight hundred.'

'Eight hundred,' the dispatcher came back.

'Ten-five 711.'

The radio called the detective inside my building whose unit number was 711, and then Marino was saying, 'Ten-twenty-five me out back.'

'Ten-four.'

Marino next radioed for a tow truck. The van was to be processed for prints on the door handles. It was to be impounded and carefully processed inside and out after that. Unit 711 had yet to walk out the back door fifteen minutes later.

'He's dumb as a bag of hammers,' Marino complained, walking around the van, radio in hand. 'Lazy son of a bitch. That's why they called him *Detective 711*. Because he's so *quick*. Shit.' He glanced irritably at his watch. 'What'd he do? Get lost in the men's room?'

I waited on the tarmac, getting unbearably cold, for I had not changed out of my greens and was without a coat. I walked around the van several times, too, desperate to look in the back of it. Five more minutes passed and Marino got the dispatcher to call the other officers inside my building. Their response was immediate.

'Where's Jakes?' Marino growled at them the instant they came out the door.

'He said he was going to look around,' one of the officers replied.

'I raised him twenty damn minutes ago and told him to ten-twenty-five me out here. I thought he was with one of you.'

'No, sir. Not for the past half hour, at least.'

Marino again tried 711 on the radio and got no answer. Fear shone in his eyes.

'Maybe he's in some part of the building where he can't copy,' an officer suggested, looking up at windows. His partner had his hand near his gun and was looking around, too.

Marino radioed for backups. People had begun pulling into the parking lot and letting themselves into the building. Many of the scientists with their topcoats and briefcases were braced against the raw, cold day and paid no attention to us. After all, police cars and those who drove them were a common sight. Marino tried to raise Detective Jakes on the air. Still he did not answer.

'Where did you see him last?' Marino asked the officers.

'He got on the elevator.'

'Where?'

'On the second floor.'

Marino turned to me. 'He couldn't have gone up, could he?'

'No,' I said. 'The elevator requires a security key for any floor above two.'

'Did he go down to the morgue again?' Marino was getting increasingly agitated.

'I went down there a few minutes later and didn't see him,' an officer said.

'The crematorium,' I suggested. 'He could have gone down to that level.'

'All right. You check the morgue,' Marino said to the officers. 'And I want you staying together. The doc and I will look around the crematorium.'

Inside the bay, left of the loading dock, was an old elevator that serviced a lower level where at one time bodies donated to science were embalmed and stored and cremated after medical students were through with them. It was possible Jakes might have gone there to look. I pushed the down button. The elevator slowly rose with much clanking and complaining. I pulled a handle and shoved open heavy, paint-chipped doors. We ducked inside.

'Damn, I don't like this already,' Marino said, releasing the thumb snap on his holster as we descended.

He slipped out his pistol as the elevator bumped to a halt and doors opened onto my least favorite area of the building. I did not like this dimly lit windowless space even though I appreciated its importance. After I moved the Anatomical Division to MCV, we began using the oven to dispose of biological hazardous waste. I got out my revolver.

'Stay behind me,' Marino said, intensely looking around.

The large room was silent save for the roar of the oven behind a shut door midway along the wall. We stood silently scanning abandoned gurneys draped with empty body bags, and hollow blue drums that once contained the formalin used to fill vats in floors where bodies were stored. I saw Marino's eyes fix on tracks in the ceiling, on heavy chains and hooks that in a former time had lifted the vats' massive lids and the people stored beneath them.

He was breathing hard and sweating profusely as he moved closer to an embalming room and ducked inside. I stayed nearby as he checked abandoned offices. He looked at me and wiped his face on his sleeve.

'It must be ninety degrees,' he muttered, detaching his radio from his belt.

Startled, I stared at him.

'What?' he said.

'The oven's not supposed to be on,' I said, looking at the crematorium room's shut door.

I started walking toward it.

'There's no waste to be disposed of that I know of, and it's strictly against policy for the oven to run unattended,' I said.

Outside that door, we could hear the inferno on the other side. I placed my hand on the knob. It was very hot.

Marino stepped in front of me, turned the knob and shoved the door open with his foot. His pistol was combat ready in both hands as if the oven were a brute he might have to shoot.

'Jesus,' he said.

Flames showed in spaces around the monstrous old iron door,

and the floor was littered with bits and chunks of chalky burned bone. A gurney was parked nearby. I picked up a long iron tool with a crook at one end and hooked it through a ring on the oven door.

'Stand back,' I said.

We were hit with a blast of enormous heat, and the roar sounded like a hateful wind. Hell was through that square mouth, and the body burning on the tray inside had not been there long. The clothes had incinerated, but not the leather cowboy boots. They smoked on Detective Jakes's feet as flames licked the skin off his bones and inhaled his hair. I shoved the door shut.

I ran out and found towels in the embalming room while Marino got sick near a pile of metal drums. Wrapping my hands, I held my breath and went past the oven, throwing the switch that turned off the gas. Flames died immediately, and I ran back out of the room. I grabbed Marino's radio as he gagged.

'Mayday!' I yelled to the dispatcher. 'Mayday!'

13

I spent the rest of the morning working on two homicide cases I had not counted on while a SWAT team swarmed my building. Police were on the lookout for the hot-wired blue van. It had vanished while everyone was looking for Detective Jakes.

X rays revealed he had received a crushing blow to the chest prior to death. Ribs and sternum were fractured, his aorta torn, and a STAT carbon monoxide showed he was no longer breathing when he was set on fire.

It seemed Gault had delivered one of his karate blows, but we did not know where the assault had occurred. Nor could we come up with a reasonable scenario that might explain how one person could have lifted the body onto a gurney. Jakes weighed 185 pounds and was five foot eleven, and Temple Brooks Gault was not a big man.

'I don't see how he could do it,' Marino said.

'I don't either,' I agreed.

'Maybe he forced him at gunpoint to lie down on the gurney.'

'If he was lying down, Gault could not have kicked him like that.'

'Maybe he gave him a chop.'

'It was a very powerful blow.'

Marino paused. 'Well, it's more likely he wasn't alone.'

'I'm afraid so,' I said.

It was almost noon, and we were driving to the house of Lamont Brown, also known as Sheriff Santa, in the quiet neighborhood of Hampton Hills. It was across Cary Street from the Country Club of Virginia, which would not have wanted Mr. Brown for a member.

'I guess sheriffs get paid a whole lot more than I do,' Marino said ironically as he parked his police car.

'This is the first time you've seen his house?' I asked.

'I've been by it when I've been back here on patrol. But I've never been inside.'

Hampton Hills was a mixture of mansions and modest homes tucked in woods. Sheriff Brown's brick house was two stories with a slate roof, a garage and a swimming pool. His Cadillac and Porsche 911 were still parked in the drive, as were a number of police vehicles. I stared at the Porsche. It was dark green, old, but well maintained.

'Do you think it's possible?' I started to say to Marino.

'That's bizarre,' he said.

'Do you remember the tag?'

'No. Dammit.'

'It could have been him,' I went on as I thought about the black man tailing us last night.

'Hell, I don't know.' Marino got out of the car.

'Would he recognize your truck?'

'He sure could know about it if he wanted to.'

'If he recognized you he might have been harassing you,' I said as we followed a brick sidewalk. 'That might be all there was to it.'

'I got no idea.'

'Or it simply could have been your racist bumper sticker. A coincidence. What else do we know about him?'

'Divorced, kids grown.'

A Richmond officer neat and trim in dark blue opened the front door and we stepped into a hardwood foyer.

'Is Neils Vander here?' I asked.

'Not yet. ID's upstairs,' the officer said, referring to the police department's Identification Unit, which was responsible for collecting evidence.

'I want the alternate light source,' I explained.

'Yes, ma'am.'

Marino spoke gruffly, for he had worked homicide far too many years to be patient with other people's standards. 'We need more backups than this. When the press catches wind, all hell's gonna break loose. I want more cars out front and I want a wider perimeter secured. The tape's got to be moved back to the foot of the driveway. I don't want anybody walking or driving on the driveway. And tape's got to go around the backyard. This whole friggin' property's got to be treated like a crime scene.'

'Yes, sir, Captain.' He snapped up his radio.

The police had been working out here for hours. It had not taken them long to determine that Lamont Brown was shot in bed in the master suite upstairs. I followed Marino up a narrow staircase covered with a machine-made Chinese rug, and voices drew us down a hallway. Two detectives were inside a bedroom paneled in dark-stained knotty pine, the window treatments and bedding reminiscent of a brothel. The sheriff was fond of maroon and gold, tassels and velvet, and mirrors on the ceiling.

Marino did not voice an opinion as he looked around. His judgment of this man had been made before now. I stepped closer to the king-size bed.

'Has this been rearranged in any way?' I asked one of the detectives as Marino and I put on gloves.

'Not really. We've photographed everything and looked under the covers. But what you see is pretty much how we found it.'

'Were the doors locked when you got here?' Marino asked.

'Yeah. We had to break the glass out of the one in back.'

'So there was no sign of forced entry whatsoever.'

'Nothing. We found traces of coke downstairs on a mirror in the living room. But that could have been there for a while.'

'What else have you found?'

'A white silk handkerchief with some blood on it,' said the detective, who was dressed in tweed, and chewing gum. 'It was right there on the floor, about three feet from the bed. And looks like the shoelace used to tie the trash bag around Brown's head came from a running shoe there in the closet.' He paused. 'I heard about Jakes.'

'It's real bad.' Marino was distracted.

'He wasn't alive when . . .'

'Nope. His chest was crushed.'

The detective stopped chewing.

'Did you recover a weapon?' I asked as I scanned the bed.

'No. We're definitely not dealing with a suicide.'

'Yeah,' said the other detective. 'It'd be a little hard to commit suicide and then drive yourself to the morgue.'

The pillow was soaked with reddish-brown blood that had clotted and separated from serum at the margins. Blood dripped down the side of the mattress, but I saw none on the floor. I thought of the gunshot wound to Brown's forehead. It was a quarter of an inch with a burned, lacerated and abraded margin. I had found smoke and soot in the wound and burned and unburned powder in the underlying tissue, bone and dura. The gunshot wound was contact, and the body had no other injuries that might indicate a defensive gesture or struggle.

'I believe he was lying on his back in bed when he was shot,' I said to Marino. 'In fact, it's almost as if he were asleep.'

He came closer to the bed. 'Well, it'd be kind of hard to stick a gun between the eyes of somebody awake and not have them react.'

'There's no evidence he reacted at all. The wound is perfectly centered. The pistol was placed snugly against his skin and it doesn't seem he moved.'

'Maybe he was passed out,' Marino said.

'His blood alcohol was .16. He could have been passed out but not necessarily. We need to go over the room with the Luma-Lite to see if we find blood we might be missing,' I said.

'But it would appear he was moved from the bed directly into the body pouch.' I showed Marino the drips on the side of the mattress. 'If he had been carried very far, there would be more blood throughout the house.'

'Right.'

We walked around the bedroom, looking. Marino began opening drawers that had already been gone through. Sheriff Brown had a taste for pornography. He especially liked women in degrading situations involving bondage and violence. In a study down the hall we found two racks filled with shotguns, rifles and several assault weapons.

A cabinet underneath had been pried open, and it was difficult to determine how many handguns or boxes of ammunition were missing since we did not know what had been there originally. Remaining were nine-millimeters, ten-millimeters, and several .44 and .357 Magnums. Sheriff Brown owned a variety of holsters, extra magazines, handcuffs, and a Kevlar vest.

'He was into this big time,' Marino said. 'He's got to have had heavy connections in DC, New York, maybe Miami.'

'Maybe there were drugs in those cabinets,' I said. 'Maybe the guns weren't what Gault was after.'

'I'm thinking *they*,' Marino said as feet sounded on the stairs. 'Unless you think Gault could have handled that body pouch all by himself. What did Brown weigh?'

'Almost two hundred pounds,' I replied as Neils Vander rounded the corner, holding the Luma-Lite by its handle. An assistant followed with cameras and other equipment.

Vander wore an oversize lab coat and white cotton gloves that looked ridiculously incongruous with his wool trousers and snow boots. He had a way of looking at me as if we had never met. He was the mad scientist, as bald as a lightbulb, always in a rush and always right. I was terribly fond of him.

'Where do you want me to set up this thing?' he asked nobody in particular.

'The bedroom,' I said. 'Then the study.'

We returned to the sheriff's bedroom to watch Vander shine his magic wand around. Lights out and glasses on, and blood dully lit up, but nothing else important did until several minutes later. The Luma-Lite was set to its widest beam and looked like a flashlight shining through deep water as it worked its way around the room. A spot on a wall, high above a chest of drawers, luminesced like a small, irregular moon. Vander got close and looked.

'Someone get the lights, please,' he said.

Lights went on and we took our tinted glasses off. Vander was standing on his tiptoes, staring at a knothole.

'What the hell is it?' Marino asked.

'This is very interesting,' said Vander, who rarely got excited about anything. 'There's something on the other side.'

'The other side of what?' Marino moved next to him and stared up, frowning. 'I don't see anything.'

'Oh yes. There's something,' Vander said. 'And somebody touched this area of paneling while they had some type of residue on their hands.'

'Drugs?' I inquired.

'It certainly could be drugs.'

All of us stared at the paneling, which looked quite normal when the Luma-Lite wasn't shining on it. But when I pulled a chair closer, I could see what Vander was talking about. The tiny hole in the center of the knothole was perfectly round. It had been drilled. On the other side of the wall was the sheriff's study, and we had just searched it.

'That's weird,' Marino said as he and I went back out the bedroom door.

Vander, oblivious to adventure, resumed what he was doing while Marino and I walked inside the study and went straight to the wall where the knothole should be. It was covered by an entertainment center that we had gone through once. Marino opened the doors again and slid out the television. He pulled books off shelves overhead, not seeing anything.

'Hmmm,' he said, studying the entertainment center. 'Interesting that it's out about six inches from the wall.'

'Yes,' I said. 'Let's move it.'

We pulled it out more, and directly in line with the knothole was a tiny video camera with a wide-angle lens. It was simply situated on a shallow ledge, a cord running from it into the base of the entertainment center, where it could be activated by a remote control that looked like it belonged to the television set. By doing a little bit of experimentation, we discovered that the camera was completely invisible from Brown's bedroom, unless one put his eye right up to the knothole and the camera was on, a red light glowing.

'Maybe he was doing a few lines of coke and decided to have sex with somebody,' Marino said. 'And at some point he got up close to look through the hole to make sure the camera was going.'

'Maybe,' I said. 'How fast can we look at the tape?'

'I don't want to do it here.'

'I don't blame you. The camera's so small we couldn't see much anyway.'

'I'll take it to the Intelligence Division as soon as we finish up.'

There was little left for us to do at the scene. As he suspected, Vander found significant residues in the gun cabinet, but no blood anywhere else in the house. The neighbors on either side of Sheriff Brown's property were cloistered amid trees and had not heard or seen any activity late last night or early this morning.

'If you'll just drop me by my car,' I said as we drove away.

Marino glanced suspiciously at me. 'Where are you going?'

'Petersburg.'

'What the hell for?' he said.

'I've got to talk to a friend about boots.'

There were many trucks and much construction along a stretch of I-95 South that I always found bleak. Even the Philip Morris plant with its building-high pack of Merits was stressful, for the fragrance of fresh tobacco bothered me. I desperately missed smoking, especially when I was driving alone on a day like this. My mind streaked, eyes constantly on mirrors as I looked for a dark blue van.

The wind flailed trees and swamps, and snowflakes were flying. As I got closer to Ft. Lee I began to see barracks and warehouses where breastworks once had been built upon dead bodies during this nation's cruelest hour. That war seemed close when I thought of Virginia swamps and woods and missing dead. Not a year passed when I didn't examine old buttons and bones, and Minié balls turned into the labs. I had touched the fabrics and faces of old violence, too, and it felt different from what I put my hands on now. Evil, I believed, had mutated to a new extreme.

The US Army Quartermaster Museum was located in Ft. Lee, just past Kenner Army Hospital. I slowly drove past offices and classrooms housed in rows of white trailers, and squads of young men and women in camouflage and athletic clothes. The building I wanted was brick with a blue roof and columns and the heraldry of an eagle, crossed sword and key just left of the door. I parked and went inside, looking for John Gruber.

The museum was the attic for the Quartermaster Corps, which since the American Revolution had been the army's innkeeper. Troops were clothed, fed and sheltered by the QMC, which also had supplied Buffalo soldiers with spurs and saddles, and General Patton with bullhorns for his jeep. I was familiar with the museum because the corps was also responsible for collecting, identifying and burying the army's dead. Ft. Lee had the only Graves Registration Division in the country, and its officers rotated through my office regularly.

I walked past displays of field dress, mess kits, and a World War II trench scene with sandbags and grenades. I stopped at Civil War uniforms that I knew were real and wondered if tears in cloth were from shrapnel or age. I wondered about the men who had worn them.

'Dr. Scarpetta?'

I turned around.

'Dr. Gruber,' I said warmly. 'I was just looking for you. Tell me about the whistle.' I pointed at a showcase filled with musical instruments.

'That's a Civil War pennywhistle,' he said. 'Music was very important. They used it to tell the time of day.'

Dr. Gruber was the museum's curator, an older man with bushy gray hair and a face carved of granite. He liked baggy trousers and bow ties. He called me when an exhibit was related to war dead, and I visited him whenever unusual military objects turned up with a body. He could identify virtually any buckle, button or bayonet at a glance.

'I take it you've got something for me to look at?' he asked, nodding at my briefcase.

'The photographs I mentioned to you over the phone.'

'Let's go to the office. Unless you'd like to look around a bit.' He smiled like a bashful grandfather talking about his grandchildren. 'We have quite an exhibit on Desert Storm. And General Eisenhower's mess uniform. I don't believe that was here when you were here last.'

'Dr. Gruber, please let me do it another time.' I did not put up any pretenses. My face showed him how I felt.

He patted my shoulder and led me through a back door that took us out of the museum into a loading area where an old trailer painted army green was parked.

'Belonged to Eisenhower,' Dr. Gruber said as we walked. 'He

lived in there at times, and it wasn't too bad unless Churchill visited. Then the cigars. You can imagine.'

We crossed a narrow street, and the snow was blowing harder. My eyes began to water as I again envisioned the pennywhistle in the showcase and thought about the woman we called Jane. I wondered if Gault had ever come here. He seemed to like museums, especially those displaying artifacts of violence. We followed a sidewalk to a small beige building I had visited before. During World War II it had been a filling station for the army. Now it was the repository for the Quartermaster archives.

Dr. Gruber unlocked a door and we entered a room crowded with tables and manikins wearing uniforms from antiquity. Tables were covered with the paperwork necessary to catalog acquisitions. In back was a large storage area where the heat was turned low and aisles were lined with large metal cabinets containing clothing, parachutes, mess kits, goggles, glasses. What we were interested in was found in large wooden cabinets against a wall.

'May I see what you've got?' Dr. Gruber asked, turning on more lights. 'I apologize about the temperature, but we've got to keep it cold.'

I opened my briefcase and pulled out an envelope, from which I slid several eight-by-ten black-and-white photographs of the footprints found in Central Park. Mainly, I cared about those we believed had been left by Gault. I showed the photographs to Dr. Gruber, and he moved them closer to a light.

'I realize it's rather difficult to see since they were left in snow,' I said. 'I wish there were a little more shadow for contrast.'

'This is quite all right. I'm getting a very good idea. This is definitely military, and it's the logotype that fascinates me.'

I looked on as he pointed to a circular area on the heel that had a tail on one side.

'Plus you've got this area of raised diamonds down here and two holes, see?' He showed me. 'Those could be shoe grip holes for climbing trees.' He handed the photographs to me. 'This looks very familiar.'

He went to a cabinet and opened its double doors, revealing rows of army boots on shelves. One by one he picked up boots and turned them over to look at the soles. Then he went to the second cabinet, opened its doors and started again. Toward the back he pulled out a boot with green canvas uppers, brown leather reinforcements and two brown leather straps with buckles at the top. He turned it over.

'May I see the photographs again, please?'

I held them close to the boot. The sole was black rubber with a variety of patterns. There were nail holes, stitching, wavy tread and pebble grain. A large oval at the ball of the foot was raised diamond tread with the shoe grip holes that were so clear in the photographs. On the heel was a wreath with a ribbon that seemed to match the tail barely visible in the snow and also on the side of Davila's head where we believed Gault's heel had struck him.

'What can you tell me about this boot?' I said.

He was turning it this way and that, looking. 'It's World War Two and was tested right here at Ft. Lee. A lot of tread patterns were developed and tested here.'

'World War Two was a long time ago,' I said. 'How would someone have a boot like this now? Could someone even be wearing a boot like this now?'

'Oh sure. These things hold up forever. You might find a pair in an Army Surplus store somewhere. Or it could have been in someone's family.'

He returned the boot to its crowded locker, where I suspected it would be neglected again for a very long time. As we left the building and he locked it behind us, I stood on a sidewalk turning soft with snow. I looked up at skies solid gray and at the slow traffic on streets. People had turned their headlights on, and the day was still. I knew what kind of boots Gault had but wasn't sure it mattered.

'Can I buy you coffee, my dear?' Dr. Gruber said, slipping a little. I grabbed his arm. 'Oh my, it's going to be bad again,' he said. 'They're predicting five inches.'

'I've got to get back to the morgue,' I said, tucking his arm in mine. 'I can't thank you enough.'

He patted my hand.

'I want to describe a man to you and ask if you might have seen him here in the past.'

He listened as I described Gault and his many shades of hair. I described his sharp features and eyes as pale blue as a malamute's. I mentioned his odd attire, and that it was becoming clear he enjoyed military clothing or designs suggestive of it, such as the boots and the long black leather coat he was seen wearing in New York.

'Well, we get types like that, you know,' he said, reaching the museum's back door. 'But I'm afraid he doesn't ring a bell.'

Snow frosted the top of Eisenhower's mobile home. My hair and hands were getting wet, and my feet were cold. 'How hard would it be to run down a name for me?' I said. 'I'd like to know if a Peyton Gault was ever in the Quartermaster Corps.'

Dr. Gruber hesitated. 'I'm assuming you believe he was in the army.'

'I'm not assuming anything,' I said. 'But I suspect he's old enough to have served in World War Two. The only other thing I can tell you is at one time he lived in Albany, Georgia, on a pecan plantation.'

'Records can't be obtained unless you're a relative or have power of attorney. That would be St. Louis you'd call, and I'm sorry to say records A through J were destroyed in a fire in the early eighties.'

'Great,' I said dismally.

He hesitated again. 'We do have our own computerized list of veterans here at the museum.'

I felt a surge of hope.

'The veteran who wants to pull his record can do so for a twenty-dollar donation,' Dr. Gruber said.

'What if you want to pull the record of someone else?'

'Can't do it.'

'Dr. Gruber' – I pushed wet hair back – 'please. We're talking about a man who has viciously murdered at least nine people. He will murder many more if we don't stop him.'

He looked up at snow coming down. 'Why on earth are we having this conversation out here, my dear?' he said. 'We're both going to catch pneumonia. I assume Peyton Gault is this awful person's father.'

I kissed his cheek. 'You've got my pager number,' I said, walking off to find my car.

As I navigated through the snowstorm, the radio was nonstop about the murders at the morgue. When I reached my office I found television vans and news crews surrounding the building, and I tried to figure out what to do. I needed to go inside.

'The hell with it,' I muttered under my breath as I turned into the parking lot.

Instantly, a school of reporters darted toward me as I got out of my black Mercedes. Cameras flashed as I walked with purpose, eyes straight ahead. Microphones appeared from every angle. People yelled my name as I hurried to unlock the back door and slam it shut behind me. I was alone in the quiet, empty bay, and I realized everyone else probably had gone home for the day because of the weather.

As I suspected, the autopsy suite was locked, and when I took the elevator upstairs, the offices of my assistant chiefs were empty, and the receptionists and clerks were gone. I was completely alone on the second floor, and I started feeling frightened. When I entered my office and saw CAIN's dripping red name on my computer screen, I felt worse.

'All right,' I said to myself. 'No one is here right now. There's no reason to be afraid.'

I sat behind my desk and placed my .38 within reach.

'What happened earlier is the past,' I went on. 'You've got to get control of yourself. You're decompensating.' I took another deep breath.

I could not believe I was talking to myself. That wasn't in character, either, and I worried as I began dictating the morning's cases. The hearts, livers and lungs of the dead policemen were normal. Their arteries were normal. Their bones and brains and builds were normal.

'Within normal limits,' I said into the tape recorder. 'Within normal limits.' I said it again and again.

It was only what had been done to them that was not normal, for Gault was not normal. He had no limits.

At a quarter of five I called the American Express office and was fortunate that Brent had not left for the day.

'You should head home soon,' I said. 'Roads are getting bad.'

'I have a Range Rover.'

'People in Richmond do not know how to drive in the snow,' I said.

'Dr. Scarpetta, what can I help you with?' asked Brent, who was young and quite capable and had helped me with many problems in the past.

'I need you to monitor my American Express bill,' I said. 'Can you do that?'

He hesitated.

'I want to be notified about every charge. As it comes in, I'm saying, versus waiting until I get the statement.'

'Is there a problem?'

'Yes,' I said. 'But I can't discuss it with you. All I need from you this moment is what I just requested.'

'Hold on.'

I heard keys click.

'Okay. I've got your account number. You realize your card expires in February.'

'Hopefully, I won't need to do this by then.'

'There are very few charges since October,' he said. 'Almost none, actually.'

'I'm interested in the most recent charges.'

'There are five for the twelfth through the twenty-first. A place in New York called Scaletta. Do you want the amounts?'

'What's the average?'

'Uh, average is, let's see, I guess about eighty bucks a pop. What is that, a restaurant?'

'Keep going.'

'Most recent.' He paused. 'Most recent is Richmond.'

'When?' My pulse picked up.

'Two for Friday the twenty-second.'

That was two days before Marino and I delivered blankets to the poor and Sheriff Santa shot Anthony Jones. I was shocked to think Gault might have been in town, too.

'Please tell me about the Richmond charges,' I then said to Brent.

'Two hundred and forty-three dollars at a gallery in Shockhoe Slip.'

'A gallery?' I puzzled. 'You mean an art gallery?'

Shockhoe Slip was just around the corner from my office. I couldn't believe Gault would be so brazen as to use my credit card there. Most merchants knew who I was.

'Yes, an art gallery.' He gave me the name and address.

'Can you tell what was purchased?'

There was a pause. 'Dr. Scarpetta, are you *certain* there isn't a problem here that I can help you with?'

'You are helping me. You're helping me a great deal.'

'Let's see. No, it doesn't say what was purchased. I'm sorry.' He sounded more disappointed than I was.

'And the other charge?'

'To USAir. A plane ticket for five hundred and fourteen dollars. This was round trip from La Guardia to Richmond.'

'Do we have dates?'

'Only of the transaction. You'd have to get the actual departure and return dates from the airline. Here's the ticket number.'

I asked him to contact me immediately if further charges showed up on the bank's computer. Glancing up at the clock, I flipped through the telephone directory. When I dialed the number of the gallery, the phone rang a long time before I gave up.

Then I tried USAir and gave them the ticket number Brent had given me. Gault, using my American Express card, had flown out of La Guardia at 7:00 A.M. on Friday, December 22. He had returned on the 6:50 flight that night. I was dumbfounded. He was in Richmond an entire day. What did he do during that time besides visit an art gallery?

'I'll be damned,' I muttered as I thought about New York laws.

I wondered if Gault had come here to buy a gun, and I called the airline again.

'Excuse me,' I said, identifying myself one more time. 'Is this Rita?'

'Yes.'

'We just spoke. This is Dr. Scarpetta.'

'Yes, ma'am. What can I do for you?'

'The ticket we were just discussing. Can you tell if bags were checked?'

'Please hold on.' Keys rapidly clicked. 'Yes, ma'am. On the return flight to La Guardia one bag was checked.'

'But not on the original flight out of La Guardia.'

'No. No bags were checked on the La Guardia to Richmond leg of the trip.'

Gault had served time in a penitentiary that once was located in this city. There was no telling who he knew, but I was certain if he wanted to buy a Glock nine-millimeter pistol in Richmond, he could. Criminals in New York commonly came here for guns. Gault may have placed the Glock in the bag he checked and the next night he shot Jane.

What this suggested was premeditation, and that had never been part of the equation. All of us had supposed Jane was someone Gault chanced upon and decided to murder, much as he had his other victims.

I made myself a mug of hot tea and tried to calm down. It was only the middle of the afternoon in Seattle, and I pulled my National Academy of Medical Examiners directory off a shelf. I flipped through it and found the name and number of Seattle's chief.

'Dr. Menendez? It's Dr. Kay Scarpetta in Richmond,' I said when I got him on the phone.

'Oh,' he said, surprised. 'How are you? Merry Christmas.'

'Thank you. I'm sorry to bother you, but I need your help.'

He hesitated. 'Is everything all right? You sound very stressed.'

'I have a very difficult situation. A serial killer who is out of control.' I took a deep breath. 'One of the cases involves an unidentified young woman with a lot of gold foil restorations.'

'That's most curious,' he said thoughtfully. 'You know, there are still some dentists out here who do those.'

'That's why I'm calling. I need to talk to someone. Maybe the head of their organization.'

'Would you like me to make some calls?'

'What I'd like you to do is find out if by some small miracle their group is on a computer system. It sounds like a small and unusual society. They might be connected through E-mail or a bulletin board. Maybe something like Prodigy. Who knows? But I've got to have a way to get information to them instantly.'

'I'll put several of my staffers on it immediately,' he said. 'What's the best way for me to reach you?'

I gave him my numbers and hung up. I thought of Gault and the missing dark blue van. I wondered where he had gotten the body pouch he zipped Sheriff Brown in, and then I remembered. We always kept a new one in each van as a backup. So he had come here first and stolen the van. Then he had gone to Brown's house. I thumbed through the telephone directory again to see if the sheriff's residence was listed. It was not.

I picked up the phone and called directory assistance. I asked for Lamont Brown's number. The operator gave it to me and I dialed it to see what would happen.

'I can't get to the phone right now because I'm out delivering presents in my sleigh . . . ,' the dead sheriff's voice sounded strong and healthy from his answering machine. 'Ho! Ho! Ho! Merrrrrrry Christmas!'

Unnerved, I got up to go to the ladies' room, revolver in hand. I was walking around my office armed because Gault had ruined this place where I had always felt safe. I stopped in the hall and looked up and down it. Gray floors had a buildup of wax and walls were eggshell white. I listened for any sound. He had gotten in here once. He could get in again.

Fear gripped me strongly, and when I washed my hands in the bathroom sink, they were trembling. I was perspiring and breathing hard. I walked swiftly to the other end of the corridor and looked out a window. I could see my car covered in snow, and just one van. The other van remained missing. I returned to my office and resumed dictating.

A telephone rang somewhere and I started. The creaking of my chair made me jump. When I heard the elevator across the hall open, I reached for the revolver and sat very still, watching the doorway as my heart hammered. Quick, firm footsteps sounded, getting louder as they got nearer. I raised the gun, both hands on the rubber grips.

Lucy walked in.

'Jesus,' I exclaimed, my finger on the trigger. 'Lucy, my God.'

I set the gun on my desk. 'What are you doing here? Why didn't you call first? How did you get in?'

She looked oddly at me and the .38. 'Jan drove me down, and I've got a key. You gave me a key to your building a long time ago. I did call, but you weren't here.'

'What time did you call?' I was light-headed.

'A couple hours ago. You almost shot me.'

'No.' I tried to fill my lungs with air. 'I didn't almost shoot you.'

'Your finger wasn't on the side of the trigger guard, where it was supposed to be. It was on the trigger. I'm just glad you didn't have your Browning right now. I'm just glad you didn't have anything that's single action.'

'Please stop it,' I quietly said, and my chest hurt.

'The snow's more than two inches, Aunt Kay.'

Lucy was standing by the door, as if she were unsure about something. She was typically dressed in range pants, boots and a ski jacket.

An iron hand was squeezing my heart, my breathing labored. I sat motionless, looking at my niece as my face got colder.

'Jan's in the parking lot,' she was saying.

'The press is back there.'

'I didn't notice any reporters. But anyway, we're in the pay lot across the street.'

'They've had several muggings there,' I said. 'There was a shooting, too. About four months ago.'

Lucy was watching my face. She looked at my hands as I tucked the revolver in my pocketbook.

'You've got the shakes,' she said, alarmed. 'Aunt Kay, you're white as a sheet.' She stepped closer to my desk. 'I'm getting you home.'

Pain skewered my chest, and I involuntarily pressed a hand there.

'I can't.' I could barely talk.

The pain was so sharp and I could not catch my breath.

207

Lucy tried to help me up, but I was too weak. My hands were going numb, fingers cramping, and I leaned forward in the chair and shut my eyes as I broke out in a profuse cold sweat. I was breathing rapid, shallow breaths.

She panicked.

I was vaguely aware of her yelling into the phone. I tried to tell her I was all right, that I needed a paper bag, but I could not talk. I knew what was happening, but I could not tell her. Then she was wiping my face with a cool, wet cloth. She was massaging my shoulders, soothing me as I blearily stared down at my hands curled in my lap like claws. I knew what was going to happen, but I was too exhausted to fight it.

'Call Dr. Zenner,' I managed to say as pain stabbed my chest again. 'Tell her to meet us there.'

'Where is there?' Terrified, Lucy dabbed my face again.

'MCV.'

'You're going to be all right,' she said.

I did not speak.

'Don't you worry.'

I could not straighten my hands, and I was so cold I was shivering.

'I love you, Aunt Kay,' Lucy cried.

14

The Medical College of Virginia had saved my niece's life last year, for no hospital in the area was more adept at guiding the badly injured through their golden hour. She had been medflighted here after flipping my car, and I was convinced the damage to her brain would have been permanent had the Trauma Unit not been so skilled. I had been in the MCV emergency room many times, but never as a patient before this night.

By nine-thirty, I was resting quietly in a small, private room on the hospital's fourth floor. Marino and Janet were outside the door, Lucy at my bedside holding my hand.

'Has anything else happened with CAIN?' I asked.

'Don't think about that right now,' she ordered. 'You need to rest and be quiet.'

'They've already given me something to be quiet. I am being quiet.'

'You're a wreck,' she said.

'I'm not a wreck.'

'You almost had a heart attack.'

'I had muscle spasms and hyperventilated,' I said. 'I know

exactly what I had. I reviewed the cardiogram. I had nothing that a paper bag over my head and a hot bath wouldn't have fixed.'

'Well, they're not going to let you out of here until they're sure you don't have any more spasms. You don't fool around with chest pain.'

'My heart is fine. They will let me out when I say so.'

'You're noncompliant.'

'Most doctors are,' I said.

Lucy stared stonily at the wall. She had not been gentle since coming into my room. I was not sure why she was angry.

'What are you thinking about?' I asked.

'They're setting up a command post,' she said. 'They were talking about it in the hall.'

'A command post?'

'At police headquarters,' she said. 'Marino's been back and forth to the pay phone, talking to Mr. Wesley.'

'Where is he?' I asked.

'Mr. Wesley or Marino?'

'Benton.'

'He's coming here.'

'He knows I'm here,' I said.

Lucy looked at me. She was no fool. 'He's on his way here,' she said as a tall woman with short gray hair and piercing eyes walked in.

'My, my, Kay,' Dr. Anna Zenner said, leaning over to hug me. 'So now I must make house calls.'

'This doesn't exactly constitute a house call,' I said. 'This is a hospital. You remember Lucy?'

'Of course.' Dr. Zenner smiled at my niece.

'I'll be outside the door,' Lucy said.

'You forget I do not come downtown unless I have to,' Dr. Zenner went on. 'Especially when it snows.'

'Thank you, Anna. I know you don't make house calls,

hospital calls or any other kinds of calls,' I said sincerely as the door shut. 'I'm so glad you're here.'

Dr. Zenner sat by my bed. I instantly felt her energy, for she dominated a room without trying. She was remarkably fit for someone in her early seventies and was one of the finest people I knew.

'What have you done to yourself?' she asked in a German accent that had not lessened much with time.

'I fear it is finally getting to me,' I said. 'These cases.'

She nodded. 'It is all I hear about. Every time I pick up a newspaper or turn on TV.'

'I almost shot Lucy tonight.' I looked into her eyes.

'Tell me how that happened?'

I told her.

'But you did not fire the gun?'

'I came close.'

'No bullets were fired?'

'No,' I said.

'Then you did not come so close.'

'That would have been the end of my life.' I shut my eyes as they welled up with tears.

'Kay, it would also have been the end of your life had someone else been coming down that hall. Someone you had reason to fear, you know what I mean? You reacted as best you could.'

I took a deep, tremulous breath.

'And the result is not so bad. Lucy is fine. I just saw her and she is healthy and beautiful.'

I wept as I hadn't in a very long time, covering my face with my hands. Dr. Zenner rubbed my back and pulled tissues from a box, but she did not try to talk me out of my depression. She quietly let me cry.

'I'm so ashamed of myself,' I finally said between sobs.

'You mustn't be ashamed,' she said. 'Sometimes you have to let it out. You don't do that enough and I know what you see.'

211

'My mother is very ill and I have not been down to Miami to see her. Not once.' I was incapable of being consoled. 'I am a stranger at my office. I can no longer stay in my house – or anywhere else for that matter – without security.'

'I noticed many police outside your room,' she observed.

I opened my eyes and looked at her. 'He's decompensating,' I said.

Her eyes were fastened to mine.

'And that's good. He's more daring, meaning he's taking greater risks. That's what Bundy did in the end.'

Dr. Zenner offered what she did best. She listened.

I went on, 'The more he decompensates, the greater the likelihood he'll make a mistake and we'll get him.'

'I would also assume he is at his most dangerous right now,' she said. 'He has no boundaries. He even killed Santa Claus.'

'He killed a sheriff who plays Santa once a year. And this sheriff also was heavily involved in drugs. Maybe drugs were the connection between the two of them.'

'Tell me about you.'

I looked away from her and took another deep breath. At last I was calmer. Anna was one of the few people in this world who made me feel I did not need to be in charge. She was a psychiatrist. I had known her since my move to Richmond, and she had helped me through my breakup with Mark, then through his death. She had the heart and hands of a musician.

'Like him, I am decompensating,' I confessed in frustration.

'I must know more.'

'That's why I'm here.' I looked at her. 'That's why I'm in this gown, in this bed. It's why I almost shot my niece. It's why people are outside my door worried about me. People are driving the streets and watching my house, worrying about me. Everywhere, people are worrying about me.'

'Sometimes we have to call in the troops.'

'I don't want troops,' I said impatiently. 'I want to be left alone.'

'Ha. I personally think you need an entire army. No one can fight this man alone.'

'You're a psychiatrist,' I said. 'Why don't you dissect him?'

'I don't treat character disorders,' she said. 'Of course he is sociopathic.'

She walked to the window, parted curtains and looked out. 'It is still snowing. Do you believe that? I may have to stay here with you tonight. I have had patients over the years who were almost not of this world, and I did try to disengage from them quickly.

'That's the thing with these criminals who become the subject of legend. They go to dentists, psychiatrists, hairstylists. We cannot help but encounter them just like we encounter anyone. In Germany once I treated a man for a year until I realized he had drowned three women in the bathtub.

'That was his thing. He would pour them wine and wash them. When he would get to their feet, he would suddenly grab their ankles and yank. In those big tubs, you cannot get out if someone is holding your feet up in the air.' She paused. 'I am not a forensic psychiatrist.'

'I know that.'

'I could have been,' Dr. Zenner went on. 'I considered it many times. Did you know?'

'No, I didn't.'

'So I will tell you why I avoided that specialty. I cannot spend so much time with monsters. It is bad enough for people like you who take care of their victims. But I think to sit in the same room with the Gaults of the world would poison my soul.' She paused. 'You see, I have a terrible confession to make.'

She turned around and looked at me.

'I don't give a damn why any of them do it,' she said, eyes flashing. 'I think they should all be hanged.'

'I won't disagree with you,' I said.

'But this does not mean I don't have an instinct about him. I would call it a woman's instinct, actually.'

'About Gault?'

'Yes. You have met my cat, Chester,' she said.

'Oh, yes. He is the fattest cat I have ever seen.'

She did not smile. 'He will go out and catch a mouse. And he will play with it to death. It is really quite sadistic. Then he finally kills it and what does he do? He brings it in the house. He carries it up on the bed and leaves it on my pillow. This is his present to me.'

'What are you suggesting, Anna?' I was chilled again.

'I believe this man has a weird significant relationship with you. As if you are mother, and he brings you what he kills.'

'That is unthinkable,' I said.

'It excites him to get your attention, it is my guess. He wants to impress you. When he murders someone, it is his gift to you. And he knows you will study it very carefully and try to discover his every stroke, almost like a mother looking at her little boy's drawings he brings home from school. You see, his evil work is his art.'

I thought of the charge made at the gallery in Shockhoe Slip. I wondered what art Gault had bought.

'He knows you will analyze and think of him all the time, Kay.'

'Anna, you're suggesting these deaths might be my fault.'

'Nonsense. If you start believing that then I need to start seeing you in my office. Regularly.'

'How much danger am I in?'

'I must be careful here.' She stopped to think. 'I know what others must say. That's why there are many police.'

'What do you say?'

'I personally do not feel you are in great physical danger from him. Not this minute. But I think everyone around you is. You see, he is making his reality yours.'

'Please explain.'

'He has no one. He would like for you to have no one.'

'He has no one because of what he does,' I said angrily.

'All I can say is every time he kills, he is more isolated. And these days, so are you. There is a pattern. Do you see it?'

She had moved next to me. She placed her hand on my forehead.

'I'm not sure.'

'You have no fever,' she said.

'Sheriff Brown hated me.'

'See, another present. Gault thought you would be pleased. He killed the mouse for you and dragged it into your morgue.'

The thought made me sick.

She withdrew a stethoscope from a jacket pocket and put it around her neck. Rearranging my gown, she listened to my heart and lungs, her face serious.

'Breathe deeply for me, please.' She moved the head of the stethoscope around my back. 'Again.'

She took my blood pressure and felt my neck. She was a rare, old-world physician. Anna Zenner treated the whole person, not just the mind.

'Your pressure's low,' she said.

'So what else is new.'

'What do they give you here?'

'Ativan.'

The cuff made a ripping sound as she removed it from my arm. 'Ativan is okay. It has no appreciable effect on the respiratory or cardiovascular systems. It is fine for you. I can write a prescription.'

'No,' I said.

'An antianxiety agent is a good idea just now, I think.'

'Anna,' I said. 'Drugs are not what I need just now.'

She patted my hand. 'You are not decompensating.'

She got up and put on her coat.

'Anna,' I said, 'I have a favor to ask. How is your house at Hilton Head?'

She smiled. 'It is still the best antianxiety agent I know. And I've told you so how many times?'

'Maybe this time I will listen,' I said. 'I may have to take a trip near there, and I would like to be as private as possible.'

Dr. Zenner dug keys from her pocketbook and took one off the ring. Next she dashed off something on a blank prescription and set it and the key on a table by my bed.

'No need to do anything,' she said simply. 'But I leave for you the key and instructions. Should you get the urge in the middle of the night, you don't even need to let me know.'

'That is so kind of you,' I said. 'I doubt I'll need it long.'

'But you should need it long. It is on the ocean in Palmetto Dunes, a small, modest house near the Hyatt. I will not be using it anytime soon and don't think you will be bothered there. In fact, you can just be Dr. Zenner.' She chuckled. 'No one knows me there anyway.'

'Dr. Zenner,' I mused dryly. 'So now I'm German.'

'Oh, you are always German.' She opened the door. 'I don't care what you have been told.'

She left and I sat up straighter, energetic and alert. I got out of bed and was in the closet when I heard my door open. I walked out, expecting Lucy. Instead, Paul Tucker was inside my room. I was too surprised to be embarrassed as I stood barefoot with nothing on but a gown that barely covered anything.

He averted his gaze as I returned to bed and pulled up the covers.

'I apologize. Captain Marino said it was all right to come in,' said Richmond's chief of police, who did not seem particularly sorry, no matter what he claimed.

'He should have told me first,' I stated, looking him straight in the eye.

'Well, we all know about Captain Marino's manners. Do you mind?' He nodded at the chair.

'Please. I'm clearly a captive audience.'

'You are a captive audience because I have half my police

department looking out for you right now.' His face was hard.

I watched him carefully.

'I'm very aware of what happened in your morgue this morning.' Anger glinted in his eyes. 'You are in grave danger, Dr. Scarpetta. I'm here to plead with you. I want you to take this seriously.'

'How could you possibly assume I'm not taking this seriously?' I said with indignation.

'We'll start with this. You should not have returned to your office this afternoon. Two law enforcement officers were just murdered, one of them there while you were in the building.'

'I had no choice but to return to my office, Colonel Tucker. Just who do you think did those officers' autopsies?'

He was silent. Then he asked, 'Do you think Gault has left town?'

'No.'

'Why?'

'I don't know why, but I don't think he has.'

'How are you feeling?'

I could tell he was fishing for something, but I could not imagine what.

'I'm feeling fine. In fact, as soon as you leave, I'm going to get dressed and then I'm going to leave,' I replied.

He started to speak but didn't.

I watched him for a moment. He was dressed in dark blue FBI National Academy sweats and high-top leather cross-training shoes. I wondered if he had been working out in the gym when someone had called him about me. It suddenly struck me that we were neighbors. He and his wife lived in Windsor Farms just a few blocks from me.

'Marino's told me to evacuate my house,' I said in an almost accusatory tone. 'Are you aware of that?'

'I'm aware.'

'How much of a hand have you had in his suggestion to me?'

'Why would you think I've had anything to do with what Marino suggests to you?' he asked calmly.

'You and I are neighbors. You probably drive past my house every day.'

'I don't. But I know where you live, Kay.'

'Please don't call me Kay.'

'If I were white would you let me call you Kay?' he said with ease.

'No, I would not.'

He did not seem offended. He knew I did not trust him. He knew I was slightly afraid of him and probably of most people right now. I was getting paranoid.

'Dr. Scarpetta.' He got up. 'I've had your house under surveillance for weeks.' He paused, looking down at me.

'Why?' I asked.

'Sheriff Brown.'

'What are you talking about?' My mouth was getting dry.

'He was very involved in an intricate drug network that stretches from New York to Miami. Some of your patients were involved in it. At least eight that we know of at this time.'

'Drug shootings.'

He nodded, staring toward the window. 'Brown hated you.'

'That was clear. The reason was not.'

'Let's just say that you did your job too well. Several of his comrades were locked up for a very long time because of you.' He paused. 'We had reason to fear he planned to have you taken care of.'

I stared at him, stunned. 'What? What reason?'

'Snitches.'

'More than one?'

Tucker said, 'Brown had already offered money to somebody we had to take very seriously.'

I reached for my water glass.

'This was earlier in the month. Maybe three weeks ago.' His eyes wandered around the room.

'Who did he hire?' I asked.

'Anthony Jones.' Tucker looked at me.

My astonishment grew and I was shocked by what he told me next.

'The person who was supposed to get shot Christmas Eve was not Anthony Jones but you.'

I was speechless.

'That entire scenario of going to the wrong apartment in Whitcomb Court was for the purpose of taking you out. But when the sheriff went through the kitchen and into the backyard, he and Jones got into an argument. You know what happened.'

He got up. 'Now the sheriff is dead too and, frankly, you're lucky.'

'Colonel Tucker,' I said.

He stood by my bed.

'Did you know about this before it happened?'

'Are you asking me if I'm clairvoyant?' His face was grim.

'I think you know what I'm asking.'

'We had our eye on you. But no, we did not know until after the fact that Christmas Eve was when you were supposed to be killed. Obviously, had we known, you never would have been out riding around, delivering blankets.'

He looked down at the floor, thinking, before he spoke again. 'You're sure you're ready to check out of here.'

'Yes.'

'Where do you plan to go tonight?'

'Home.'

He shook his head. 'Out of the question. Nor do I recommend a local hotel.'

'Marino has agreed to stay with me.'

'Oh, now I bet that's safe,' he said wryly as he opened the door. 'Get dressed, Dr. Scarpetta. We have a meeting to attend.'

* * *

When I emerged from my hospital room not much later, I was met by stares and few words. Lucy and Janet were with Marino, and Paul Tucker was alone, a Gortex jacket on.

'Dr. Scarpetta, you ride with me.' He nodded at Marino. 'You follow with the young ladies.'

We walked along a polished white hallway toward elevators and headed down. Uniformed officers were everywhere, and when glass doors slid open outside the emergency room, three of them appeared to escort us to our cars. Marino and the chief had parked in police slots, and when I saw Tucker's personal car, I felt another spasm in my chest. He drove a black Porsche 911. It was not new, but it was in excellent condition.

Marino saw the car, too. He remained silent as he unlocked his Crown Victoria.

'Were you on 95 South last night?' I asked Tucker as soon as we were inside his car.

He pulled his shoulder harness across his chest and started the engine. 'Why would you ask me that?' He did not sound defensive, only curious.

'I was coming home from Quantico and a car similar to this one was tailgating us.'

'Who is us?'

'I was with Marino.'

'I see.' He turned right outside the parking deck, toward headquarters. 'So you were with the Grand Dragon.'

'Then it was you,' I said as wipers pushed away snow.

Streets were slick and I felt the car slip as Tucker slowed at a traffic light.

'I did see a Confederate flag bumper sticker last night,' he said. 'And I did express my lack of appreciation for it.'

'The truck it was on is Marino's.'

'I did not care whose truck it was.'

I looked over at him.

'Serves the captain right.' He laughed.

220

'Do you always act so aggressively?' I asked. 'Because it's a good way to get shot.'

'One is always welcome to try.'

'I don't recommend tailgating and taunting rednecks.'

'At least you admit he is a redneck.'

'I meant the comment in general,' I said.

'You are an intelligent, refined woman, Dr. Scarpetta. I fail to understand what you see in him.'

'There is a lot to see in him if one takes the trouble to look.'

'He is racist. He is homophobic and chauvinistic. He's one of the most ignorant human beings I've ever met, and I wish he were some other person's problem.'

'He doesn't trust anything or anyone,' I said. 'He's cynical, and not without reason, I'm sure.'

Tucker was quiet.

'You don't know him,' I added.

'I don't want to know him. What I'd like is for him to disappear.'

'Please don't do anything that wrong,' I said with feeling. 'You would be making such a mistake.'

'He is a political nightmare,' the chief said. 'He should never have been placed in charge of First Precinct.'

'Then transfer him back to the detective division, to A Squad. That's really where he belongs.'

Tucker quietly drove. He did not wish to discuss Marino anymore.

'Why was I never told someone wanted to kill me?' I asked, and the words sounded weird, and I really could not accept their meaning. 'I want to know why you did not tell me I was under surveillance.'

'I did what I thought was best.'

'You should have told me.'

He looked in his rearview mirror to make sure Marino was still behind us as he drove around the back of Richmond police department headquarters.

'I believed telling you what snitches had divulged would only place you in more danger. I was afraid you might become . . .' He paused. 'Well, aggressive, anxious. I did not want your demeanor substantially changing. I did not want you going on the offense and perhaps escalating the situation.'

'I do not think you had a right to be so secretive,' I said with feeling.

'Dr. Scarpetta.' He stared straight ahead. 'I honestly did not care what you thought and still don't. I only care about saving your life.'

At the police entrance to the parking lot, two officers with pump shotguns stood guard, their uniforms black against snow. Tucker stopped and rolled his window down.

'How's it going?' he asked.

A sergeant was stern, shotgun pointing at the planets. 'It's quiet, sir.'

'Well, you guys be careful.'

'Yes, sir. We will.'

Tucker shut his window and drove on. He parked in a space to the left of double glass doors that led into the lobby and lockup of the large concrete complex he commanded. I noticed few cruisers or unmarked cars in the lot. I supposed there were accidents to be worked this slippery night, and everyone else was out looking for Gault. To law enforcement, he had earned a new rank. He was a cop killer now.

'You and Sheriff Brown have similar cars,' I said, unfastening my seat belt.

'And there the similarity ends,' Tucker said, getting out.

His office was along a dreary hallway, several doors from A Squad, where the homicide detectives lived. The chief's quarters were surprisingly simple, furniture sturdy but utilitarian. He had no nice lamps or rugs, and walls were absent the expected photographs of himself with politicians or celebrities. I saw no certificates or diplomas that might tell where he had gone to school or what commendations he had won.

Tucker looked at his watch and showed us into a small adjoining conference room. Windowless, and carpeted in deep blue, it was furnished with a round table and eight chairs, a television and a VCR.

'What about Lucy and Janet?' I asked, expecting the chief to exclude them from the discussion.

'I already know about them,' he said, getting comfortable in a swivel chair as if he were about to watch the Super Bowl. 'They're agents.'

'I'm not an agent,' Lucy respectfully corrected him.

He looked at her. 'You wrote CAIN.'

'Not entirely.'

'Well, CAIN's a factor in all this, so you may as well stay.'

'Your department's on-line.' She held his gaze. 'In fact, yours was the first to be on-line.'

We turned as the door opened and Benton Wesley walked in. He was wearing corduroys and a sweater. He had the raw look of one too exhausted to sleep.

'Benton, I trust you know everyone,' Tucker said as if he knew Wesley quite well.

'Right.' Wesley was all business as he took a chair. 'I'm late because you're doing a good job.'

Tucker seemed perplexed.

'I got stopped at two checkpoints.'

'Ah.' The chief seemed pleased. 'We have everybody out. We're lucky as hell with the weather.'

He wasn't joking.

Marino explained to Lucy and Janet, 'The snow keeps most people home. The fewer people out, the easier for us.'

'Unless Gault's not out, either,' Lucy said.

'He's got to be somewhere,' Marino said. 'The toad don't exactly have a vacation home here.'

'We don't know what he has,' Wesley said. 'He could know someone in the area.'

'Where do you predict he might have gone after leaving the morgue this morning?' Tucker asked Wesley.

'I don't think he's left the area.'

'Why?' Tucker asked.

Wesley looked at me. 'I think he wants to be where we are.'

'What about his family?' Tucker then asked.

'They are near Beaufort, South Carolina, where they recently bought a sizable pecan plantation on an island. I don't think Gault will go there.'

'I don't think we can assume anything,' Tucker said.

'He's estranged from his family.'

'Not entirely. He's getting money from somewhere.'

'Yes,' Wesley said. 'They may give him money so he will stay away. They are in a dilemma. If they don't help him, he may come home. If they help him, he stays out there killing people.'

'They sound like fine upstanding citizens,' Tucker said sardonically.

'They won't help us,' Wesley said. 'We've tried. What else are you doing here in Richmond?'

Tucker answered, 'Everything we can. This asshole's killing cops.'

'I don't think cops are his primary target,' Wesley stated matter-of-factly. 'I don't think he cares about cops.'

'Well,' Tucker said hotly, 'he fired the first shot and we'll fire the next.'

Wesley just looked at him.

'We've got two-person patrol cars,' Tucker went on. 'We've got guards in the parking lot, primarily for shift change. Every car's got a photo of Gault, and we've been handing them out to local businesses – those we can find open.'

'What about surveillance?'

'Yes. Places he might be. They're being watched.' He looked at me. 'Including your house and mine. And the medical examiner's office.' He turned back to Wesley. 'If there are other places he might be, I wish you'd tell me.'

Wesley said, 'There can't be many. He has a nasty little habit of murdering his friends.' He stared off. 'What about State Police helicopters and fixed-wing aircraft?'

'When the snow stops,' Tucker said. 'Absolutely.'

'I don't understand how he can sneak around so easily,' said Janet, who most likely would spend the rest of her working life asking questions like that. 'He doesn't look normal. Why don't people notice him?'

'He's extremely cunning,' I said to her.

Tucker turned to Marino. 'You have the tape.'

'Yes, sir, but I'm not sure . . .' He stopped.

'You're not sure of what, Captain?' Tucker lifted his chin a little.

'I'm not sure they should see it.' He looked at Janet and Lucy.

'Please proceed, Captain,' the chief said curtly.

Marino inserted the tape into the VCR and cut the lights.

'It's about half an hour long,' his voice sounded as numbers and lines went by on the television screen. 'Anybody mind if I smoke?'

'I definitely mind,' Tucker said. 'Apparently, this was what we found in the video camera inside Sheriff Brown's house. I have not seen it yet.'

The tape started.

'Okay, what we got here is Lamont Brown's upstairs bedroom,' Marino began to narrate.

The bed I had looked at earlier today was neatly made, and in the background we could hear the sound of someone moving.

'I think this was when he was making sure his camera was working,' Marino said. 'Maybe it's when the white residue got on the wall. See. Now it's jumping ahead.'

He hit the pause button and we stared at a blurred image of the empty bedroom.

'Do we know if Brown was positive for cocaine?' the chief asked in the dark.

'It's too early to know if he had cocaine or it's metabolite, benzoyleconine, on board,' I said. 'All we have right now is his alcohol level.'

Marino resumed, 'It's like he turned the camera on and then off and then back on. You can tell because the time's different. First it was ten-oh-six last night. Now it's suddenly ten-twenty.'

'Clearly, he was expecting somebody,' Tucker spoke.

'Or else they was already there. Maybe doing a few lines of coke downstairs. Here we go.' Marino hit the play button. 'This is where the good stuff starts.'

The darkness in Tucker's conference room was absolutely silent save for the creaking of a bed and groaning that sounded more like pain than passion. Sheriff Brown was nude and on his back. From the rear we watched Temple Gault, wearing surgical gloves and nothing else. Dark clothes were laid out on the bed nearby. Marino got quiet. I could see the profiles of Lucy and Janet. Their faces were without expression, and Tucker seemed very calm. Wesley was beside me, coolly analyzing.

Gault was unhealthily pale, every vertebra and rib clearly defined. Apparently, he had lost a lot of weight and muscle tone, and I thought about the cocaine in his hair, which now was white, and as he shifted his position I saw his full breasts.

My eyes shot across the table as Lucy stiffened.

I felt Marino look at me as Carrie Grethen worked to give her client ecstasy. It seemed drugs had interfered, and no matter what she did, Sheriff Brown could not rise to receive what would prove to be the most he ever paid for pleasure. Lucy bravely kept her eyes on the television screen. She stared, shocked, as her former lover performed one lewd act after another on this big-bellied, intoxicated man.

The ending seemed predictable. Carrie would produce a gun and blow him away. But not so. Eighteen minutes into the video, footsteps sounded in Brown's bedroom, and her accomplice walked in. Temple Gault was dressed in a black suit and also wearing gloves. He seemed to have no clue that his every blink and sniffle were on camera. He stopped at the foot of the bed and watched. Brown had his eyes shut. I wasn't sure if he was conscious.

'Time's up,' Gault said impatiently.

His intense blue eyes seemed to penetrate the screen. They looked right into our conference room. He had not dyed his hair. It was still carrot red, long and slicked back from his forehead and behind his ears. He unbuttoned his jacket and withdrew a Glock nine-millimeter pistol. Nonchalantly, he walked toward the head of the bed.

Carrie looked on as Gault placed the barrel of the pistol between the sheriff's eyes. She placed her hands over her ears. My stomach tightened and I clenched my fists as Gault depressed the trigger, and the gun recoiled as if horrified by what it had just done. We sat in shock as the sheriff's agonal jerks and twitches stopped. Carrie dismounted.

'Oh damn,' Gault said, looking down at his chest. 'I got splashed.'

She snatched the handkerchief out of the breast pocket of his suit jacket and dabbed his neck and lapels.

'It won't show. It's a good thing you wore black.'

'Go put something on,' he said as if her nudity disgusted him. His voice was adolescent and uneven, and he was not loud.

He went to the foot of the bed and picked up the dark clothing.

'What about his watch?' She looked down at the bed. 'It's a Rolex. It's real, baby, and it's gold. The bracelet's real, too.'

Gault snapped, 'Get dressed now.'

'I don't want to get dirty,' she said.

She dropped the bloody handkerchief on the floor where the police would later find it.

'Then bring the bags in,' he ordered.

He seemed to be fooling with the clothing as he placed it on the dresser, but the angle of the camera made it impossible for us to see him well. She came back with the bags.

Together they disposed of Brown's body in a way that seemed careful and well planned. First, they dressed him in pajamas, for reasons we did not understand. Blood spilled on the pajama top as Gault pulled the garbage bag over the sheriff's head and tied it with a shoelace that came from a running shoe in the closet.

They lowered the body from the bed into the black pouch on the floor, Gault holding Brown under the arms while Carrie got his ankles. They tucked him in and zipped it up. We saw them carry Lamont Brown out and heard them on the stairs. Minutes later, Carrie ducked back in, got the clothing and left. Then the bedroom was empty.

Tucker tensely said, 'Certainly we can't ask for better evidence. Did the gloves come from the morgue?'

'Most likely from the van they stole,' I answered. 'We keep a box of gloves in each van.'

'It's not quite over,' Marino said.

He began advancing the film, speeding past scene after scene of the empty bedroom, until suddenly a figure was there. Marino rewound and the figure quickly walked backward out of the room.

Marino said, 'Look what happens exactly an hour and eleven minutes later.' He hit the play button again.

Carrie Grethen walked into the bedroom, dressed like Gault. Were it not for her white hair, I might have thought she was him.

'What? She's got on his suit?' Tucker asked, amazed.

'Not his suit,' I said. 'She's got on one like it, but it's not the suit Gault was wearing.'

'How can you tell?' Tucker said.

'There's a handkerchief in the pocket. She took Gault's handkerchief to wipe blood off him. And if you go back you'll see his jacket had no flaps on the pockets, but hers does.'

'Yeah,' Marino said. 'That's right.'

Carrie looked around the room, on the floor, on the bed, as if she had lost something. She was agitated and angry, and I was certain she was on the wrong side of a cocaine high. She looked around a minute longer, then left.

'I wonder what that was about,' Tucker said.

'Hold on,' Marino told us.

He advanced the film and Carrie was back. She searched some more, scowling, pulling covers back from the bed and looking under the bloody pillow. She got down on the floor and looked under the bed. She spewed a stream of profanities, eyes casting about.

'Hurry up,' Gault's impatient voice sounded from somewhere beyond the room.

She looked in the dresser mirror and smoothed her hair. For an instant, she was staring straight into the camera at close range, and I was startled by her deterioration. I once had thought her beautiful, with her clean complexion, perfect features and long brown hair. The creature standing before us now was gaunt and glassy eyed, with harsh white hair. She buttoned the suit jacket and walked off.

'What do you make of that?' Tucker asked Marino.

'I don't know. I've looked at it a dozen times and can't figure it out.'

'She's misplaced something,' Wesley said. 'That seems obvious.'

'Maybe it was just a last check,' Marino said. 'To make certain nothing was overlooked.'

'Like a video camera,' Tucker wryly said.

'She didn't care if something was overlooked,' Wesley said. 'She left Gault's bloody handkerchief on the floor.'

'But both of them was wearing gloves,' Marino said. 'I'd say they were pretty careful.'

'Was any money stolen from the house?' Wesley asked.

Marino said, 'We don't know how much. But Brown's wallet was cleaned out. He was probably missing guns, drugs, cash.'

'Wait a minute,' I said. 'The envelope.'

'What envelope?' Tucker asked.

'They didn't put it in his pocket. We watched them dress him and zip him up inside the pouch, but no envelope. Rewind it,' I said. 'Go back to that part to make certain I'm right.'

Marino rewound the tape and replayed the footage of Carrie and Gault moving the body out of the room. Brown was definitely zipped inside the pouch without the pink note that I had found in the breast pocket of his pajamas. I thought of other notes I had gotten and of all the problems Lucy was having with CAIN. The envelope had been addressed to me and fixed with a stamp as if the author's intention were to mail it.

'That may be what Carrie couldn't find,' I said. 'Maybe she's been the one sending me the letters. She intended to mail this most recent one, too, explaining why it was addressed and stamped. Then, unbeknownst to her, Gault put it in Brown's pajama pocket.'

Wesley asked, 'Why would Gault do that?'

'Perhaps because he knew the effect it would have,' I replied. 'I would see it in the morgue and instantly know that Brown was murdered and Gault was involved.'

'But what you're saying is that Gault isn't CAIN. You're saying that Carrie Grethen is,' Marino said.

It was Lucy who spoke. 'Neither of them is CAIN. They are spies.'

We were silent for a moment.

'Obviously,' I said, 'Carrie has continued helping Gault with the FBI computer. They are a team. But I think he took the note she wrote to me and did not tell her. I think that's what she was looking for.'

'Why would she look for it in Brown's bedroom?' Tucker wondered. 'Is there a reason she might have had it in there?'

'Certainly,' I said. 'She took her clothes off in there. Perhaps it was in a pocket. Play that part, Marino. When Gault is moving the dark clothing off the bed.'

He went back to that segment, and though we could not specifically see Gault remove the letter from a pocket, he did tamper with Carrie's clothing. He certainly could have gotten her letter at that time. He could have placed it in Brown's pocket later, in the back of the van or perhaps in the morgue.

'So you're really thinking she's the one who's been sending the notes to you?' Marino asked skeptically.

'I think it's probable.'

'But why?' Tucker was confounded. 'Why would *she* do this to you, Dr. Scarpetta? Do you know her?'

'I do not,' I said. 'I've only met her, but our last encounter was quite confrontational. And the notes don't seem like something Gault would do. They never have.'

'She would like to destroy you,' Wesley calmly said. 'She would like to destroy both Lucy and you.'

'Why?' Janet asked.

'Because Carrie Grethen is a psychopath,' Wesley said. 'She and Gault are twins. It's interesting that they are now dressing alike. They look alike.'

'I don't understand what he did with the letter,' Tucker said. 'Why not just ask Carrie for it instead of taking it without telling her?'

'You're asking me to tell you how Gault's mind works,' Wesley said.

'Indeed I am.'

'I don't know why.'

'But it must mean something.'

'It does,' Wesley said.

'What?' Tucker asked.

'It means she thinks she has a relationship with him. She thinks she can trust him, and she's wrong. It means he will eventually kill her, if he can,' Wesley said as Marino turned on lights.

Everybody squinted. I looked at Lucy, who had nothing to say, and sensed her anguish in one small way. She had put her glasses on when she did not need them to see unless she was sitting at a computer.

'Obviously, they're working tag team,' Marino said.

Janet spoke again. 'Who's in charge?'

'Gault is,' Marino said. 'That's why he's the one with the gun and she's the one giving the blow job.'

Tucker pushed back his chair. 'They somehow met Brown. They didn't just show up at his house.'

'Would he have recognized Gault?' Lucy asked.

'Maybe not,' Wesley said.

'I'm thinking they got in touch with him – or she did, anyway – to get drugs.'

'His phone number is unpublished but not unlisted,' I said.

'There weren't any significant messages on his answering machine,' Marino added.

'Well, I want to know the link,' Tucker said. 'How did these two know him?'

'Drugs would be my guess,' Wesley said. 'It may also be that Gault got interested in the sheriff because of Dr. Scarpetta. Brown shot someone Christmas Eve, and the media covered it ad infinitum. It was no secret that Dr. Scarpetta was there and would end up testifying. In fact, she might have ended up in the jury pool since, ironically, Brown summoned her for jury duty.'

I thought of what Anna Zenner said about Gault bringing gifts to me.

'And Gault would have been aware of all this,' Tucker said.

Wesley said, 'Possibly. If we ever find where he lives, we may discover that he gets the Richmond newspaper by mail.'

Tucker thought for a while and looked at me. 'Then who

killed the officer in New York? Was it this woman with white hair?'

'No,' I said. 'She could not have kicked him like that. Unless she is a black belt in karate.'

'And were they working together that night in the tunnel?' Tucker asked.

'I don't know that she was there,' I said.

'Well, you were there.'

'I was,' I said. 'I saw one person.'

'A person with white hair or red hair?'

I thought of the figure illuminated in the arch. I remembered the long dark coat and pale face. I had not been able to see the hair.

'I suspect it was Gault down there that night,' I said. 'I can't prove it. But there is nothing to suggest that he had an accomplice when Jane was killed.'

'Jane?' Tucker asked.

Marino said, 'That's what we call the lady he killed in Central Park.'

'Then the implication is he did not form a violent partnership with this Carrie Grethen until he returned to Virginia, after New York.' Tucker continued trying to fit the pieces together.

'We really don't know,' Wesley said. 'It's never going to be an exact science, Paul. Especially when we're dealing with violent offenders rotting their brains with drugs. The more they decompensate, the more bizarre the behavior.'

The chief of police leaned forward, looking hard at him. 'Please tell me what the hell you make of all this.'

'They were connected before. I suspect they met through a spy shop in northern Virginia,' Wesley said. 'That is how CAIN was compromised – is compromised. Now it appears the connection has moved to a different level.'

'Yeah,' Marino said. 'Bonnie's found Clyde.'

15

We drove to my home on streets barely touched by traffic. The late night was perfectly still, snow covering the earth like cotton and absorbing sound. Bare trees were black against white, the moon an indistinct face behind fog. I wanted to go for a walk, but Wesley would not let me.

'It's late and you've had a traumatic day,' he said as we sat in his BMW, which was parked behind Marino's car in front of my house. 'You don't need to be walking around out here.'

'You could walk with me.' I felt vulnerable and very tired, and did not want him to leave.

'Neither of us needs to be walking around out here,' he said as Marino, Janet and Lucy disappeared inside my house. 'You need to go inside and get some sleep.'

'What will you do?'

'I have a room.'

'Where?' I asked as if I had a right to know.

'Linden Row. Downtown. Go to bed, Kay. Please.' He paused, staring out the windshield. 'I wish I could do more, but I can't.'

'I know you can't and I'm not asking you to. Of course,

you can't any more than I could if you needed comfort. If you needed someone. That's when I hate loving you. I hate it so much. I hate it so much when I need you. Like now.' I struggled. 'Oh damn.'

He put his arms around me and dried my tears. He touched my hair and held my hand as if he loved it with all his heart. 'I could take you downtown with me tonight if that's what you really want.'

He knew I did not want that because it was impossible. 'No,' I said with a deep breath. 'No, Benton.'

I got out of his car and scooped up a handful of snow. I scrubbed my face with it as I walked around to the front door. I did not want anyone to know I had been crying in the dark with Benton Wesley.

He did not drive off until I had barricaded myself inside my house with Marino, Janet and Lucy. Tucker had ordered an around-the-clock surveillance, and Marino was in charge. He would not entrust our safety to uniformed men parked somewhere in a cruiser or van. He rallied us like Green Berets or guerrillas.

'All right,' he said as we walked into my kitchen. 'I know Lucy can shoot. Janet, you sure as hell better be able to if you're ever gonna graduate from the Academy.'

'I could shoot before the Academy,' she said in her quiet, unflappable way.

'Doc?'

I was looking inside the refrigerator.

'I can make pasta with a little olive oil, Parmesan and onion. I've got cheese if anybody wants sandwiches. Or if you give me a chance to thaw it, I've got *le piccagge col pesto di ricotta* or *tortellini verdi*. I think there's enough for four if I warm up both.'

Nobody cared.

I wanted so much to do something normal.

'I'm sorry,' I said in despair. 'I haven't been to the store lately.'

'I need to get into your safe, Doc,' Marino said.

'I've got bagels.'

'Hey. Anybody hungry?' Marino asked.

No one was. I closed the freezer. The gun safe was in the garage.

'Come on,' I told him.

He followed me out and I opened it for him.

'Do you mind telling me what you're doing?' I asked.

'I'm arming us,' he said as he picked up one handgun after another and looked at my stash of ammunition. 'Damn, you must own stock in Green Top.'

Green Top was an area gun shop that catered not to felons, but to normal citizens who enjoyed sports and home security. I reminded Marino of this, although I could not deny that by normal standards I owned too many guns and too much ammunition.

'I didn't know you had all this,' Marino went on, half inside my large, heavy safe. 'When the hell did you get all this? I wasn't with you.'

'I do shop alone now and then,' I said sharply. 'Believe it or not, I am perfectly capable of buying groceries, clothing and guns all by myself. And I'm very tired, Marino. Let's wind this up.'

'Where are your shotguns?'

'What do you want?'

'What do you have?'

'Remingtons. A Marine Magnum. An 870 Express Security.'

'That'll do.'

'Would you like me to see if I can round up some plastic explosives?' I said. 'Maybe I can put my hands on a grenade launcher.'

He pulled out a Glock nine-millimeter. 'So you're into combat Tupperware, too.'

'I've used it in the indoor range for test fires,' I said. 'That's what I've used most of these guns for. I've got several papers to present at various meetings. This is making me crazy. Are you going into my dresser drawers next?'

Marino tucked the Glock in the back of his pants. 'Let's see. And I'm gonna swipe your stainless steel Smith and Wesson nine-mil and your Colt. Janet likes Colts.'

I closed the safe and angrily spun the dial. Marino and I returned to the house and I went upstairs because I did not want to see him pass out ammunition and guns. I could not cope with the thought of Lucy downstairs with a pump shotgun, and I wondered if anything would faze or frighten Gault. I was to the point of thinking he was the living dead and no weapon known to us could stop him.

In my bedroom I turned out lights and stood before the window. My breath condensed on glass as I stared at a night lit up by snow. I remembered occasions when I had not been in Richmond long and woke up to a world quiet and white like this. Several times, the city was paralyzed and I could not go to work. I remembered walking my neighborhood, kicking snow up in the air and throwing snowballs at trees. I remembered watching children pull sleds along streets.

I wiped fog off the glass and was too sad to tell anyone my feelings. Across the street, holiday candles glowed in every window of every house but mine. The street was bright but empty. Not a single car went by. I knew Marino would stay up half the night with his female SWAT team. They would be disappointed. Gault would not come here. I was beginning to have an instinct about him. What Anna had said about him was probably right.

In bed I read until I fell to sleep, and I woke up at five. Quietly, I went downstairs, thinking it would be my luck to die from a shotgun blast inside my own home. But the door to one guest bedroom was shut, and Marino was snoring on the couch. I sneaked into the garage and backed my Mercedes out. It did wonderfully on the soft, dry snow. I felt like a bird and I flew.

I drove fast on Cary Street and thought it was fun when I fishtailed. No one else was out. I shifted the car into low gear and plowed through drifts in International Safeway's parking lot. The grocery store was always open, and I went in for fresh orange juice, cream cheese, bacon and eggs. I was wearing a hat and no one paid me any mind.

By the time I returned to my car, I was the happiest I had been in weeks. I sang with the radio all the way home and skidded when I safely could. I drove into the garage, and Marino was there with his flat black Benelli shotgun.

'What the hell do you think you're doing!' he exclaimed as I shut the garage door.

'I'm getting groceries.' My euphoria fled.

'Je-sus Christ. I can't believe you just did that,' he yelled at me.

'What do you think this is?' I lost my temper. 'Patty Hearst? Am I kidnapped now? Should we just lock me inside a closet?'

'Get in the house.' Marino was very upset.

I stared coldly at him. 'This is my house. Not your house. Not Tucker's house. Not Benton's house. This, goddam it, is my house. And I will get in it when I please.'

'Good. And you can die in it just like you can die anywhere else.'

I followed him into the kitchen. I yanked items out of the grocery bag and slammed them on the counter. I cracked eggs into a bowl and shoved shells down the disposal. I snapped on the gas burner and beat the hell out of omelets with onions and fontina cheese. I made coffee and swore because I had forgotten low-fat Cremora. I tore off squares of paper towel because I had no napkins, either.

'You can set the table in the living room and start the fire,' I said, grinding fresh pepper into frothy eggs.

'The fire's been started since last night.'

'Are Lucy and Janet awake?' I was beginning to feel better.

'I got no idea.'

I rubbed olive oil into a frying pan. 'Then go knock on their door.'

'They're in the same bedroom,' he said.

'Oh for God's sake, Marino.' I turned around and looked at him in exasperation.

We ate breakfast at seven-thirty and read the newspaper, which was wet.

'What are you going to do today?' Lucy asked me as if we were on vacation, perhaps at some lovely resort in the Alps.

She was dressed in her same fatigues, sitting on an ottoman before the fire. The nickel-plated Remington was nearby on the floor. It was loaded with seven rounds.

'I have errands to run and phone calls to make,' I said.

Marino had put on blue jeans and a sweatshirt. He watched me suspiciously as he slurped coffee.

I met his eyes. 'I'm going downtown.'

He did not respond. 'Benton's already headed out.'

I felt my cheeks get hot.

'I already tried to call him and he already checked out of the hotel.' Marino glanced at his watch. 'That would have been about two hours ago, around six.'

'When I mentioned downtown,' I said evenly, 'I was referring to my office.'

'What you need to do, Doc, is drive north to Quantico and check into their security floor for a while. Seriously. At least for the weekend.'

'I agree,' I said. 'But not until I've taken care of a few matters here.'

'Then take Lucy and Janet with you.'

Lucy was looking out the sliding glass doors now, and Janet was still reading the paper.

'No,' I said. 'They can stay here until we head out to Quantico.'

'It's not a good idea.'

240

'Marino, unless I've been arrested for something I know nothing about, I'm leaving here in less than thirty minutes and going to my office. And I'm going there *alone.*'

Janet lowered the paper and said to Marino, 'There comes a point when you've got to go on with your life.'

'This is a security matter,' Marino dismissed her.

Janet's expression did not change. 'No, it isn't. This is a matter of your acting like a man.'

Marino looked puzzled.

'You're being overly protective,' she added reasonably. 'And you want to be in charge and control everything.'

Marino did not seem angry because she was soft-spoken. 'You got a better idea?' he asked.

'Dr. Scarpetta can take care of herself,' Janet said. 'But she shouldn't be alone in this house at night.'

'He won't come here,' I said.

Janet got up and stretched. 'He probably won't,' she said. 'But Carrie would.'

Lucy turned away from the glass doors. Outside, the morning was blinding, and water dripped from eaves.

'Why can't I go into the office with you?' my niece wanted to know.

'There's nothing for you to do,' I said. 'You'd be bored.'

'I can work on the computer.'

Later, I drove Lucy and Janet to work with me and left them at the office with Fielding, my deputy chief. At eleven A.M., roads were slushy in the Slip, and businesses were opening late. Dressed in waterproof boots and a long jacket, I waited on a sidewalk to cross Franklin Street. Road crews were spreading salt, and traffic was sporadic this Friday before New Year's Eve.

James Galleries occupied the upper floor in a former tobacco warehouse near Laura Ashley and a record store. I entered a side door, followed a dim hallway and got on an elevator too small to carry more than three people my size. I pushed the button for the third floor, and soon the elevator opened onto another dimly lit hallway, at the end of which were glass doors with the name of the gallery painted on them in black calligraphy.

James had opened his gallery after moving to Richmond from New York. I had purchased a monoprint and a carved bird from him once, and the art glass in my dining room had come from him as well. Then I quit shopping here about a year ago after a local artist came up with inappropriate silk-screened lab coats in honor of me. They included blood and bones, cartoons and crime scenes, and when I asked James not to carry them, he increased his order.

I could see him behind a showcase, rearranging a tray of what looked like bracelets. He looked up when I rang the bell. He shook his head and mouthed that he was not open. I removed hat and sunglasses and knocked on the glass. He stared blankly until I pulled out my credentials and showed him my shield.

He was startled, then confused when he realized it was me. James, who insisted the world call him James because his first name was Elmer, came to the door. He took another look at my face and bells rattled against glass as he turned a key.

'What in the world?' he said, letting me in.

'You and I must talk,' I said, unzipping my coat.

'I'm all out of lab coats.'

'I'm delighted to hear it.'

'Me too,' he said in his petty way. 'Sold every one of them for Christmas. I sell more of those silly lab coats than anything in the gallery. We're thinking of silk-screened scrubs next, the same style you folks wear when you're doing autopsies.'

'You're not disrespectful of me,' I said. 'You're disrespectful of the dead. You will never be me, but you will someday be dead. Maybe you should think about that.'

'The problem with you is you don't have a sense of humor.'

'I'm not here to talk about what you perceive the problem with me is,' I calmly said.

242

A tall, fussy man with short gray hair and a mustache, he specialized in minimalist paintings, bronzes and furniture, and unusual jewelry and kaleidoscopes. Of course, he had a penchant for the irreverent and bizarre, and nothing was a bargain. He treated customers as if they were lucky to be spending money in his gallery. I wasn't sure James treated anyone well.

'What are you doing here?' he asked me. 'I know what happened around the corner, at your office.'

'I'm sure you do,' I said. 'I can't imagine how anybody could not know.'

'Is it true that one of the cops was put in . . .'

I gave him a stony stare.

He returned behind the counter, where I could now see he had been tying tiny price tags on gold and silver bracelets fashioned to look like serpents, soda can flip tops, braided hair, even handcuffs.

'Special, aren't they?' He smiled.

'They are different.'

'This is my favorite.' He held up one. It was a chain wrought of rose-gold hands.

'Several days ago someone came into your gallery and used my charge card,' I said.

'Yes. Your son.' He returned the bracelet to the tray.

'My *what*?' I said.

He looked up at me. 'Your son. Let's see. I believe his name is Kirk.'

'I do not have a son,' I told him. 'I have no children. And my American Express gold card was stolen several months ago.'

James chided me, 'Well, for crummy sake, why haven't you canceled it?'

'I didn't realize it was stolen until very recently. And I'm not here to talk to you about that,' I said. 'I need you to tell me exactly what happened.'

James pulled out a stool and sat down. He did not offer me

243

a chair. 'He came in the Friday before Christmas,' he said. 'I guess about four o'clock in the afternoon.'

'This was a man?'

James gave me a disgusted look. 'I *do* know the difference. Yes. He was a man.'

'Please describe him.'

'Five-ten, thin, sharp features. His cheeks were a little sunken. But I actually found him rather striking.'

'What about his hair?'

'He was wearing a baseball cap, so I didn't see much of it. But I got the impression it was a really terrible red. A Raggedy Andy red. I can't imagine who got hold of him, but he ought to sue for malpractice.'

'And his eyes?'

'He was wearing dark-tinted glasses. Sort of Armani-ish.' He got amused. 'I was so surprised you had a son like that. I would have figured your boy wore khakis, skinny ties and went to MIT . . .'

'James, there is nothing lighthearted about this conversation,' I abruptly said.

His face lit up and his eyes got wide as the meaning became clear. 'Oh my God. The man I've been reading about? That's who . . . My God. *He* was in my gallery?'

I made no comment.

James was ecstatic. 'Do you realize what this will do?' he said. 'When people find out he shopped here?'

I said nothing.

'It will be fabulous for my business. People from all over will come here. My gallery will be on the tour routes.'

'That's right. Be certain to advertise something like that,' I said. 'And character disorders from everywhere will stand in line. They'll touch your expensive paintings, bronzes, tapestries, and ask you endless questions. And they won't buy a thing.'

He got quiet.

'When he came in,' I said, 'what did he do?'

'He looked around. He said he was looking for a last-minute gift.'

'What was his voice like?'

'Quiet. Kind of high-pitched. I asked who the present was for, and he said his mother. He said she was a doctor. That's when I showed him the pin he ended up buying. It's a caduceus. Two white gold serpents twined around a yellow gold winged staff. The serpents have ruby eyes. It's handmade and absolutely spectacular.'

'That's what he bought for two hundred and fifty dollars?' I asked.

'Yes.' He was appraising me, crooked finger under his chin. 'Actually, it's you. The pin is really you. Would you like for me to have the artist make another one?'

'What happened after he bought the pin?'

'I asked if he wanted it gift wrapped, and he didn't. He pulled out the charge card. And I said, "Well, small, small world. Your mother works right around the corner." He didn't say anything. So I asked if he was home for the holidays, and he smiled.'

'He didn't talk,' I said.

'Not at all. It was like pulling hens' teeth. I wouldn't call him friendly. But he was polite.'

'Do you remember how he was dressed?'

'A long black leather coat. It was belted, so I don't know what he had on under it. But I thought he looked sharp.'

'Shoes?'

'It seems he had on boots.'

'Did you notice anything else about him?'

He thought for a while, looking past me at the door. He said, 'Now that you mention it, he had what looked like burns on his fingers. I thought that was a little scary.'

'What about his hygiene?' I then asked, for the more addicted a crack user got, the less he cared about clothing or cleanliness.

'He seemed clean to me. But I really didn't get close to him.'

'And he bought nothing else while he was here?'

'Unfortunately not.'

Elmer James propped an elbow on the showcase and rested his cheek on his fist. He sighed. 'I wonder how he found me.'

I walked back, avoiding slushy puddles on streets and the cars that drove through them heedlessly. I got splashed once. I returned to my office, where Janet was in the library watching a teaching videotape of an autopsy while Lucy worked in the computer room. I left them alone and went down to the morgue to check on my staff.

Fielding was at the first table, working on a young woman found dead in the snow below her bedroom window. I noted the pinkness of the body and could smell alcohol in the blood. On her right arm was a cast scribbled with messages and autographs.

'How are we doing?' I asked.

'She's got a STAT alcohol of .23,' he replied, examining a section of aorta. 'So that didn't get her. I think she's going to be an exposure death.'

'What are the circumstances?' I could not help but think of Jane.

'Apparently, she was out drinking with friends and by the time they took her home around eleven P.M. it was snowing pretty hard. They let her out and didn't wait to see her in. The police think her keys fell in the snow and she was too drunk to find them.'

He dropped the section of aorta into a jar of formalin. 'So she tried to get in a window by breaking it with her cast.'

He lifted the brain out of the scale. 'But that didn't work. The window was too high up, and with one arm she couldn't have climbed in it anyway. Eventually she passed out.'

'Nice friends,' I said, walking off.

Dr. Anderson, who was new, was photographing a ninety-one-year-old woman with a hip fracture. I collected paperwork from a nearby desk and quickly reviewed the case.

'Is this an autopsy?' I asked.

'Yes,' Dr. Anderson said.

'Why?'

She stopped what she was doing and looked at me through her face shield. I could see intimidation in her eyes. 'The fracture was two weeks ago. The medical examiner in Albemarle was concerned her death could be due to complications of that accident.'

'What are the circumstances of her death?'

'She presented with pleural effusion and shortness of breath.'

'I don't see any direct relationship between that and a hip fracture,' I said.

Dr. Anderson rested her gloved hands on the edge of the steel table.

'An act of God can take you at any time,' I said. 'You can release her. She's not a medical examiner's case.'

'Dr. Scarpetta,' Fielding spoke above the whining of the Stryker saw. 'Did you know that the Transplant Council meeting is Thursday?'

'I've got jury duty.' I turned to Dr. Anderson. 'Do you have court on Thursday?'

'Well, it's been continued. They keep sending me subpoenas even though they've stipulated my testimony.'

'Ask Rose to take care of it. If you're free and we don't have a full house on Thursday, you can go with Fielding to the council meeting.'

I checked carts and cupboards, wondering if any other boxes of gloves were gone. But it seemed Gault had taken only those that were in the van. I wondered what else he might find in my office, and my thoughts darkened.

I went directly to my office without speaking to anyone I passed and opened a cabinet door beneath my microscope. In back I had tucked a very fine set of dissecting knives Lucy had given to me for Christmas. German made, they were stainless steel with smooth light handles. They were expensive and incredibly sharp. I moved aside cardboard files of slides, journals, microscope lightbulbs and batteries and reams of printer paper. The knives were gone.

Rose was on the phone in her office adjoining mine, and I walked in and stood by her desk.

'But you've already stipulated her testimony,' she was saying. 'If you've stipulated her testimony, then you obviously don't need to subpoena her to appear so she can give you her testimony . . .'

She looked at me and rolled her eyes. Rose was getting on in years, but she was ever vigilant and forceful. Snow or shine she was always here, the headmistress of *Les Misérables*.

'Yes, yes. Now we're getting somewhere.' She scribbled something on a message pad. 'I can promise you Dr. Anderson will be very grateful. Of course. Good day.'

My secretary hung up and looked at me. 'You're gone entirely too much.'

'Tell me about it,' I said.

'You'd better watch out. One of these days you may find me with someone else.'

I was too worn out to joke. 'I wouldn't blame you,' I said.

She regarded me like a shrewd mother who knew I had been drinking or making out or sneaking cigarettes. 'What is it, Dr. Scarpetta?' she said.

'Have you seen my dissecting knives?'

She did not know what I was talking about.

'The ones Lucy gave me. A set of three in a hard plastic box. Three different sizes.'

Recognition registered on her face. 'Oh yes. I remember now. I thought you kept them in your cabinet.'

'They're not there.'

'Shoot. Not the cleaning crew, I hope. When was the last time you saw them?'

'Probably right after Lucy gave them to me, which was actually before Christmas because she didn't want to take them down to Miami. I showed the set to you, remember? And then I put them in my cabinet because I didn't want to keep them downstairs.'

Rose was grim. 'I know what you must be thinking. Uh.' She shivered. 'What a gruesome thought.'

I pulled up a chair and sat. 'The thought of him doing something like that with my—'

'You can't think about it,' she interrupted me. 'You have no control over what he does.'

I stared off.

'I'm worried about Jennifer,' my secretary then said.

Jennifer was one of the clerks in the front office. Her major responsibility was sorting photographs, answering the phones, and entering cases into our database.

'She's traumatized.'

'By what's just happened,' I assumed.

Rose nodded. 'She's been in the bathroom crying quite a lot today. Needless to say, what happened is awful and there are many tales circulating. But she's so much more upset than anyone else. I've tried to talk to her. I'm afraid she's going to quit.' She pointed the mouse at the WordPerfect icon and clicked a button. 'I'll print out the autopsy protocols for your review.'

'You've already typed both of them?'

'I came in early this morning. I've got four-wheel drive.'

'I'll talk to Jennifer,' I said.

I walked down the corridor and glanced into the computer room. Lucy was mesmerized by the monitor, and I did not bother her. Up front, Tamara was answering one line while two others rang and someone else was unhappily flashing on hold. Cleta made photocopies while Jo entered death certificates at a workstation.

I walked back down the hall and pushed open the door to the ladies' room. Jennifer was at one of the sinks, splashing cold water on her face.

'Oh!' she exclaimed when she saw me in the mirror. 'Hello, Dr. Scarpetta,' she said, unnerved and embarrassed.

She was a homely young woman who would forever struggle with calories and the clothes that might hide them. Her eyes were puffy and she had protruding teeth and flyaway hair. She wore too much makeup even at times like this when her appearance should not matter.

'Please sit down,' I said kindly, motioning to a red plastic chair near lockers.

'I'm sorry,' she said. 'I know I've not done right today.'

I pulled up another chair and sat so I would not tower over her.

'You're upset,' I said.

She bit her bottom lip to stop it from quivering as her eyes filled with tears.

'What can I do to help you?' I asked.

She shook her head and began to sob.

'I can't stop,' she said. 'I can't stop crying. And if someone even scrapes their chair across the floor I jump.' She wiped tears with a paper towel, hands shaking. 'I feel like I'm going crazy.'

'When did this all start?'

She blew her nose. 'Yesterday. After the sheriff and the policeman were found. I heard about the one downstairs. They said even his boots was on fire.'

'Jennifer, do you remember the pamphlets I passed out about Post Traumatic Stress Syndrome?'

'Yes, ma'am.'

'It's something everybody's got to worry about in a place like this. Every single one of us. I have to worry about it, too.'

'You do?' Her mouth fell open.

'Certainly. I have to worry about it more than anyone.'

250

'I just thought you was used to it.'

'God forbid that any of us should get used to it.'

'I mean' – she lowered her voice as if we were talking about sex – 'do you get like I am right now?' She quickly added, 'I mean, I'm sure you don't.'

'I'm sure I do,' I said. 'I get very upset sometimes.'

Her eyes brimmed with tears again and she took a deep breath. 'That makes me feel a whole lot better. You know, when I was little my daddy always was telling me how stupid and fat I was. I didn't figure someone like you would ever feel like I do.'

'No one should have ever said such a thing to you,' I replied with feeling. 'You are a lovely person, Jennifer, and we are very fortunate to have you here.'

'Thank you,' she said quietly, eyes cast down.

I got up. 'I think you should go home for the rest of the day and have a nice long weekend. How about it?'

She continued looking down at the floor. 'I think I saw him,' she said, biting her bottom lip.

'Who did you see?'

'I saw that man.' She glanced at my eyes. 'When I saw the pictures on TV, I couldn't believe it. I keep thinking if only I had told somebody.'

'Where is it you think you saw him?'

'Rumors.'

'The bar?' I asked.

She nodded.

'When was this?'

'Tuesday.'

I looked closely at her. 'This past Tuesday? The day after Christmas?'

That night Gault had been in New York. I had seen him in the subway tunnel, or at least I thought I had.

'Yes, ma'am,' Jennifer said. 'I guess it was about ten. I was dancing with Tommy.'

I did not know who Tommy was.

'I seen him hanging back from everyone. I couldn't help but notice because of his white hair. I'm not used to seeing anybody his age with hair that white. He was in a real cool black suit with a black T-shirt under it. I remember that. I figured he was from out of town. Maybe from a big place like Los Angeles or something.'

'Did he dance with anyone?'

'Yes, ma'am, he danced with a girl or two. You know, he'd buy them a drink. Then next thing I know he was gone.'

'Did he leave alone?'

'It looked to me like one girl went with him.'

'Do you know who?' I asked with dread. I hoped the woman, whoever she was, had lived.

'It wasn't anybody I knew,' Jennifer said. 'I just remember he was dancing with this one girl. He must've danced with her three times and then they walked off the floor together, holding hands.'

'Describe her,' I said.

'She was black. She was real pretty in this little red dress. It was low cut and kind of short. I remember she had bright red lipstick and all these little braids with little lights winking in them.' She paused.

'And you're certain they left the club together?' I asked.

'As far as I could tell. I never saw either one of them again that night, and me and Tommy stayed till two.'

I said to her, 'I want you to call Captain Marino and tell him what you just told me.'

Jennifer got out of the chair and felt important. 'I'll get started right this minute.'

I returned to my office as Rose was walking through the door.

'You need to call Dr. Gruber,' she said.

I dialed the number for the Quartermaster Museum, and he had stepped out. He called me back two hours later.

'Is the snow bad in Petersburg?' I asked him.

'Oh, it's just wet and messy.'

'How are things?'

'I've got something for you,' Dr. Gruber said. 'I feel real bad about it.'

I waited. When he offered nothing more, I said, 'What do you feel bad about, exactly?'

'I went into the computer and ran the name you wanted. I shouldn't have.' He got quiet again.

'Dr. Gruber, I'm dealing with a serial killer.'

'He was never in the army.'

'You mean his father wasn't,' I said, disappointed.

'Neither of them was,' Dr. Gruber said. 'Not Temple or Peyton Gault.'

'Oh,' I said. 'So the boots probably came from a surplus store.'

'Might have, but he may have an uncle.'

'Who has an uncle?'

'Temple Gault. That's what I'm wondering. There's a Gault in the computer, only his name is Luther. Luther Gault. He served in the Quartermaster Corps during World War Two.' He paused. 'In fact, he was right here at Ft. Lee a lot of the time.'

I had never heard of Luther Gault.

'Is he still alive?' I asked.

'He died in Seattle about five years ago.'

'What makes you suspicious this man might be Temple Gault's uncle?' I asked. 'Seattle's on the other side of the country from Georgia, which is where the Gaults are from.'

'The only real connection I can make is the last name and Ft. Lee.'

I then asked, 'Do you think it's possible the jungle boots once belonged to him?'

'Well, they're World War Two, and were tested here at Ft. Lee, which is where Luther Gault was stationed for most of his career. What would typically happen is soldiers, even some officers, would be asked to try out boots and other gear before any of it was sent to the boys in the trenches.'

'What did Luther Gault do after the army?'

'I don't have any information on him after the army except that he died at the age of seventy-eight.' He paused. 'But it might interest you to know he was a career man. He retired with the rank of major general.'

'And you had never heard of him before this?'

'I didn't say I've never heard of him.' He paused. 'I'm sure the army has quite a file on him if you could get your hands on it.'

'Would it be possible for me to get a photograph?'

'I have one on the computer – just your run-of-the-mill file photo.'

'Can you fax it?'

He hesitated again. 'Sure.'

I hung up as Rose walked in with yesterday's autopsy protocols. I reviewed them and made corrections while I waited for the fax machine to ring. Momentarily, it did, and the black-and-white image of Luther Gault materialized in my office. He stood proudly in dark mess jacket and pants with gold piping and buttons, and satin lapels. The resemblance was there. Temple Gault had his eyes.

I called Wesley.

'Temple Gault may have had an uncle in Seattle,' I said. 'He was a major general in the army.'

'How did you find that out?' he asked.

I did not like his coolness. 'It doesn't matter. What does is that I think we need to find out all we can about it.'

Wesley maintained his reserve. 'How is it germane?'

I lost my temper. 'How is anything germane when you're trying to stop somebody like this? When you've got nothing, you look at everything.'

'Sure, sure,' he said. 'It's no problem, but we can't schedule it just now. You too.' He hung up.

I sat there stunned, my heart gripped by pain. Someone must have been in his office. Wesley had never hung up on me before. My paranoia got more inflamed as I went to find Lucy.

'Hi,' she said before I spoke from the doorway.

She could see my reflection in the monitor.

'We've got to go,' I said.

'Why? Is it snowing again?'

'No. The sun's out.'

'I'm almost finished here,' she said, typing as she talked.

'I need to get you and Janet back to Quantico.'

'You need to call Grans,' she said. 'She's feeling neglected.'

'She is neglected and I feel guilty,' I said.

Lucy turned around and looked at me as my pager went off.

'Where is Janet?' I asked.

'I think she went downstairs.'

I pressed the display button and recognized Marino's home number. 'Well, you round her up and I'll meet you downstairs in a minute.'

I returned to my office and this time shut the doors. When I called Marino, he sounded as if he were on amphetamines.

'They're gone,' he said.

'Who is?'

'We found out where they was staying. The Hacienda Motel on US 1, that roach trap not too far from where you buy all your guns and ammo. That's where that bitch took her girlfriend.'

'What girlfriend?' I still did not know what he was talking about. Then I remembered Jennifer. 'Oh. The woman Carrie picked up at Rumors.'

'Yo.' He was so excited he sounded as if he had been on a Mayday. 'Her name's Apollonia and—'

'She's alive?' I interrupted.

'Oh yeah. Carrie took her back to the motel and they partied.'

'Who drove?'

'Apollonia did.'

'Did you find my van in the motel parking lot?'

'Not when we hit the joint a little while ago. And the rooms were cleared out. It's like they was never there.'

'Then Carrie wasn't in New York this past Tuesday,' I said.

'Nope. She was here partying while Gault was up there whacking Jimmy Davila. Then I'm thinking she got a place ready for him and probably helped intercept him wherever he was.'

'I doubt he flew from New York to Richmond,' I said. 'That would have been too risky.'

'I personally think he flew to DC on Wednesday . . .'

'Marino,' I said. 'I flew to DC on Wednesday.'

'I know you did. Maybe you and him was on the same plane.'

'I didn't see him.'

'You don't know that you didn't. But the point is, if you were on the same plane, you can bet he saw you.'

I remembered leaving the terminal and getting into that old, beat-up taxi with the windows and locks that didn't work. I wondered if Gault had been watching.

'Does Carrie have a car?' I asked.

'She's got a Saab convertible registered to her. But she sure as hell isn't driving it these days.'

'I'm not certain why she picked up this Apollonia woman,' I said. 'And how did you find her?'

'Easy. She works at Rumors. I'm not sure what all she sells, but it isn't just cigarettes.'

'Damn,' I muttered.

'I'm assuming the connection is coke,' Marino said. 'And it might interest you to know that Apollonia was acquainted with Sheriff Brown. In fact, they dated, you might say.'

'Do you think she could have had anything to do with his murder?' I asked.

'Yeah, I do. She probably helped lead Gault and Carrie to

him. I'm beginning to think the sheriff was pretty much a last-minute thing. I think Carrie asked Apollonia where she could score some coke, and Brown's name came up. Then Carrie tells Gault and he orchestrates another one of his impetuous nightmares.'

'That could very well be,' I said. 'Did Apollonia know Carrie was a woman?'

'Yeah. It didn't matter.'

'Damn,' I said again. 'We were so close.'

'I know. I just can't believe they slipped through the net like that. We got everything but the National Guard looking for them. We got choppers out, the whole nine yards. But in my gut I feel they've left the area.'

'I just called Benton and he hung up on me,' I said.

'What? You guys have a fight?'

'Marino, something is very wrong. I had a sense that someone was in his office and he didn't want this person to know he was talking to me.'

'Maybe it was his wife.'

'I'm heading up there now with Lucy and Janet.'

'You staying the night?'

'That all depends.'

'Well, I wish you wouldn't be driving around. And if anybody tries to pull you over for any reason, don't you stop. Not for lights or sirens or nothing. Don't stop for anything but a marked patrol car.' He gave me one of his lectures. 'And keep your Remington between the front seats.'

'Gault's not going to stop killing,' I said.

Marino got quiet on the line.

'When he was in my office he stole my set of dissecting knives.'

'You sure someone from the cleaning crew didn't do it? Those knives would be good for fileting fish.'

'I know Gault did it,' I said.

16

We returned to Quantico shortly after three, and when I tried to reach Wesley, he was not in. I left a message for him to find me at ERF, where I planned to spend the next few hours with my niece.

No engineers or scientists were on her floor because it was a holiday weekend, and we were able to work alone and in quiet.

'I could definitely get global mail out,' Lucy said, sitting at her desk. She glanced at her watch. 'Look, why not just throw something out there and see who bites?'

'Let me try the chief from Seattle again.'

I had his number on a slip of paper and called it. I was told he had left for the day.

'It's very important that I reach him,' I explained to the answering service. 'Perhaps he can be reached at home?'

'I'm not at liberty to give that out. But if you'll give me your phone number, when he calls in for his messages . . .'

'I can't do that,' I said as my frustration grew. 'I'm not at a number he can call.' I told her who I was, adding, 'What I'm going to do is give you my pager number. Please have him call me and then I'll call him.'

That didn't work. An hour later my pager remained silent.

'She probably didn't get it straight about putting pound signs after everything,' Lucy said as she cruised around inside CAIN.

'Any strange messages anywhere?' I asked.

'No. It's a Friday afternoon and a lot of people are on holiday. I think we should send something out over Prodigy and see what comes back.'

I sat next to her.

'What's the name of the group?'

'American Academy of Gold Foil Operators.'

'And their highest concentration is Washington State?'

'Yes. But it can't hurt to include the entire West Coast.'

'Well, this will include the entire United States,' Lucy said as she typed *Prodigy* and entered her service ID and password. 'I think the best way to do this is through the mail.' She pulled up a Jump Window. 'What do you want me to say?' She looked over at me.

'How about this? *To all American Academy of Gold Foil Operators. Forensic pathologist desperately needs your help ASAP.* And then give them the information to contact us.'

'All right. I'll give them a mailbox here and carbon copy it to your mailbox in Richmond.' She resumed typing. 'The replies may come in for a while. You may find you get a lot of dentists for pen pals.'

She tapped a key as if it were a coda and pushed back her chair. 'There. It's gone,' she said. 'Even as we speak, every Prodigy subscriber should have a *New Mail* message. Let's just hope someone out there is playing with their computer and can help.'

Even as she spoke, her screen suddenly went black, and bright green letters started flowing across it. A printer turned on.

'That was quick,' I started to stay.

But Lucy was out of her chair. She ran to the room where CAIN lived and scanned her fingerprint to get in. Glass doors unlocked with a firm click and I followed her inside. The same writing was flowing across the system monitor, and Lucy snatched a small beige remote control off the desk and pressed a button. She glanced at her Breitling and activated the stopwatch.

'Come on, come on, come on!' she said.

She sat before CAIN, staring into the screen as the message flowed. It was one brief paragraph repeated numerous times. It said:

```
- - -MESSAGE PQ43 76301 001732 BEGINS- - -
TO: - All COPS
FROM: - CAIN
    IF CAIN KILLED HIS BROTHER, WHAT DO YOU THINK HE'D
    DO TO YOU?
    IF YOUR PAGER GOES OFF IN THE MORGUE, IT'S JESUS
    CALLING.
- - -MESSAGE PQ43 76301 001732 ENDS- - -
```

I looked at the shelves of modems filling one wall, at lights flashing. Though I was not a computer expert, I saw no correlation between their activity and what was occurring on screen. I looked around some more and noticed a telephone jack below the desk. A cord that was plugged into it disappeared beneath the raised floor, and I found that odd.

Why would a device plugged into a telephone jack be stored beneath a floor? Telephones were on tables and desks. Modems were on shelves. I got down and lifted a panel that covered a third of the floor inside CAIN's room.

'What are you doing?' Lucy exclaimed, unable to take her eyes off the screen.

The modem beneath the floor looked like a small cube puzzle with rapid flashing lights.

'Shit!' Lucy said.

I looked up. She stared at her watch and wrote something

down. The activity on the screen had stopped. The lights on the modem quit flashing.

'Did I do something?' I asked in dismay.

'You bastard!' She pounded her fist on the desk, and the keyboard jumped. 'I almost had you. One more time and I would have had your ass!'

I got up. 'I didn't disconnect anything, I hope?' I said.

'No. Dammit! He logged off. I had him,' she said, still staring at her monitor as if the green words might begin to flow again.

'Gault?'

'CAIN's imposter.' She blew out a big breath of air and looked down at the naked guts of the creation she had named after the world's first murderer. 'You found it,' she blandly said. 'That's pretty good.'

'That's how he's been getting in,' I said.

'Yes. It's so obvious no one noticed.'

'You noticed.'

'Not at first.'

'Carrie put it there before she left last fall,' I said.

Lucy nodded. 'Like everybody else, I was looking for something more technologically recondite. But it was brilliant in its simplicity. She hid her own private modem and the dial-in is the number of a diagnostics line almost never used.'

'How long have you known?'

'As soon as the weird messages started, I knew.'

'So you just had to play the game with him,' I said, upset. 'Do you realize how dangerous this game is?' I asked.

She began typing. 'He tried it four times. God, we were close.'

'For a while you thought Carrie was doing this,' I said.

'She set it up, but I don't think she's the one getting in.'

'Why not?'

'Because I've been following this intruder day and night. This is someone unskilled.' For the first time in months, she spoke her former friend's name. 'I know how Carrie's mind works. And Gault's too narcissistic to let anyone be CAIN except him.'

'I got a note, possibly from Carrie, that was signed CAIN,' I said.

'And I'll bet Gault didn't know she mailed it. And I'll also bet that if he found out, he took that little pleasure away from her.'

I thought of the pink note we suspected Gault had spirited away from Carrie at Sheriff Brown's house. When Gault placed it in the pocket of the bloody pajama top, the act certainly served to reassert his dominance. Gault would use Carrie. In a sense, she always waited in the car except when he needed her help to move a body or perform a degrading act.

'What just happened here?' I said.

Lucy did not look at me when she answered, 'I found the virus and have planted my own. Every time he tries to send a message to any terminal connected to CAIN, I have the message replicate itself on his screen – like it's bouncing back in his face instead of going out anywhere. And he gets a prompt that says *Please Try Again*. So he tries again. The first time this happened to him, the system icon gave him a thumbs-up after two tries, so he thought the message was sent.

'But when he tried the next time, the same thing happened, but I made him try one additional time. The point is to keep him on the line long enough for us to trace the call.'

'Us?'

Lucy picked up the small beige remote control I had seen her grab earlier. 'My panic button,' she said. 'It goes via radio signal straight to HRT.'

'I assume Wesley has known about this hidden modem since you discovered it.'

'Right.'

'Explain something to me,' I said.

'Sure.' She gave me her eyes.

'Even if Gault or Carrie had this secret modem and its secret number, what about your password? How could either of them log on as a superuser? And aren't there UNIX commands you could type that would tell you if another user or device was logged on?'

'Carrie programmed the virus to capture my username and password whenever I changed them. The encrypted forms were reversed and sent to Gault via E-mail. Then he could log on as me, and the virus wouldn't let him log on unless I was logged on, too.'

'So he hides behind you.'

'Like a shadow. He's used my device name. My same username and password. I figured out what was going on when I did a WHO command one day and my username was there twice.'

'If CAIN calls users back to verify their legitimacy, why hasn't Gault's telephone number shown up on ERF's monthly bill?'

'That's part of the virus. It instructs the system on callbacks to bill the call to an AT&T credit card. So the calls never showed up on the Bureau's bills. They show up on the bills of Gault's father.'

'Amazing,' I said.

'Apparently, Gault has his father's phone card number and PIN.'

'Does he know his son has been using it?'

A telephone rang. She picked it up.

'Yes, sir,' she said. 'I know. We were close. Certainly, I will bring you the printouts immediately.' She hung up.

'I don't think anyone's told him,' Lucy said.

'No one here has told Peyton Gault.'

'Right. That was Mr. Wesley.'

'I must talk to him,' I said. 'Do you trust me to take him the printouts?'

Lucy was staring at the monitor again. The screen saver

had come back on, and brilliant triangles were slowly slipping through and around each other like geometry making love.

'You can take it to him,' she said, and she typed *Prodigy*. 'Before you go . . . Wow, you've got new mail waiting.'

'How much?' I moved closer to her.

'Oops. Just one so far.' She opened it.

It read: *What is gold foil?*

Lucy said, 'We're probably going to get a lot of that.'

Sally was working the front desk again when I walked into the Academy lobby, and she let me through without the bother of registration and a visitors' pass. I walked with purpose down the long tan corridor, around the post office and through the gun cleaning room. I will always love the smell of Hoppes Number 9.

A lone man in fatigues was blasting compressed air into the barrel of a rifle. Rows of long black countertops were bare and perfectly clean, and I thought of years of classes, of the men and women I had seen, and of the times I had stood at a counter cleaning my own handgun. I had watched new agents come and go. I had watched them run, fight, shoot and sweat. I had taught them and cared.

I pressed the elevator button, boarded and went down to the lower level. Several profilers were in their offices, and they nodded at me as I walked by. Wesley's secretary was on vacation, and I passed her desk and knocked on the shut door. I heard Wesley's voice. A chair moved and he walked to the door and pulled it open.

'Hello,' he said, surprised.

'These are the printouts you wanted from Lucy.' I handed them over.

'Thank you. Please come in.' He slipped on reading glasses, reviewing the message Gault had sent.

His jacket was off, a white shirt wrinkled around woven

leather suspenders. Wesley had been perspiring and he needed to shave.

'Have you lost more weight?' I asked.

'I never weigh myself.' He glanced at me over the top of his glasses as he seated himself behind his desk.

'You don't look healthy.'

'He's decompensating more,' he said. 'You can see that from this message. He's getting more reckless, more brazen. I would predict that by the end of the weekend, we will nail his location.'

'Then what?' I was not convinced.

'We deploy HRT.'

'I see,' I said dryly. 'They will rappel from helicopters and blow up the building.'

Wesley glanced at me again. He placed the paperwork on the desk. 'You're angry,' he said.

'No, Benton. I'm angry with you, versus being angry in general.'

'Why?'

'I asked you not to involve Lucy.'

'We have no choice,' he said.

'There are always choices. I don't care what anybody says.'

'In terms of locating Gault, she's really our only hope right now.' He paused, looking directly at me. 'She has a mind of her own.'

'Yes, she does. That's my point. Lucy doesn't have an off button. She doesn't always understand limits.'

'We won't let her do anything that might place her at risk,' he said.

'She's already been placed at risk.'

'You've got to let her grow up, Kay.'

I stared at him.

'She's going to graduate from the university this spring. She's a grown woman.'

'I don't want her coming back here,' I said.

He smiled a little, but his eyes were exhausted and sad. 'I hope she'll be back here. We need agents like her and Janet. We need all we can get.'

'She keeps many secrets from me. It seems the two of you conspire against me and I'm left in the dark. It's bad enough that . . .' I caught myself.

Wesley looked into my eyes. 'Kay, this has nothing to do with my relationship with you.'

'I would certainly hope not.'

'You want to know everything Lucy is doing,' he said.

'Of course.'

'Do you tell her everything you're doing when you're working a case?'

'Absolutely not.'

'I see.'

'Why did you hang up on me?'

'You got me at a bad time,' he answered.

'You've never hung up on me before, no matter how bad the time.'

He took his glasses off and carefully folded them. He reached for his coffee mug, looked inside and saw it was empty. He held it in both hands.

'I had someone in my office, and I didn't want this individual to know you were on the line,' he said.

'Who was it?' I said.

'Someone from the Pentagon. I won't tell you his name.'

'The Pentagon?' I said, mystified.

He was quiet.

'Why would you be concerned that someone from the Pentagon might know I was calling you?' I then asked.

'It seems you've created a problem,' Wesley simply said, setting the coffee mug down. 'I wish you hadn't started poking around Ft. Lee.'

I was astonished.

'Your friend Dr. Gruber may be fired. I would advise you

to refrain from contacting him further.'

'This is about Luther Gault?' I asked.

'Yes, General Gault.'

'They can't do anything to Dr. Gruber,' I protested.

'I'm afraid they can,' Wesley said. 'Dr. Gruber conducted an unauthorized search in a military database. He got you classified information.'

'Classified?' I said. 'That's absurd. It's one page of routine information that you can pay twenty dollars to see while you're visiting the Quartermaster Museum. It's not like I asked for a damn Pentagon file.'

'You can't pay the twenty dollars unless you are the individual or have power of attorney to access that individual's file.'

'Benton, we're talking about a serial killer. Has everybody lost their minds? Who the hell cares about a generic computer file?'

'The army does.'

'Are we dealing with national security?'

Wesley did not answer me.

When he offered nothing more, I said, 'Fine. You guys can have your little secret. I'm sick and tired of your little secrets. My only agenda is to prevent more deaths. I'm no longer certain what your agenda is.' My stare was unforgiving and hurt.

'Please,' Wesley snapped. 'You know, some days I wish I smoked like Marino does.' He blew out in exasperation. 'General Gault is not important in this investigation. He does not need to be dragged into it.'

'I think anything we know about Temple Gault's family could be important. And I can't believe you don't feel that way. Background information is vital to profiling and predicting behavior.'

'I'm telling you, General Gault is off limits.'

'Why?'

'Respect.'

'My God, Benton.' I leaned forward in my chair. 'Gault may

have killed two people with a pair of his uncle's damn jungle boots. And just how is the army going to like it when that hits *Time* magazine and *Newsweek*?'

'Don't threaten.'

'I most certainly will. I will do more than threaten if people don't do the right thing. Tell me about the general. I already know his nephew inherited his eyes. And the general was a bit of a peacock, since it seems he preferred being photographed in a splendid mess uniform like Eisenhower would have worn.'

'He may have had an ego but was a magnificent man, by all accounts,' Wesley said.

'Was he Gault's uncle, then? Are you admitting it?'

Wesley hesitated. 'Luther Gault is Temple Gault's uncle.'

'Tell me more.'

'He was born in Albany and graduated from the Citadel in 1942. Two years later, when he was a captain, his division moved to France, where he became a hero in the Battle of the Bulge. He won the Medal of Honor and was promoted again. After the war, he was sent to Ft. Lee as officer in charge of the uniform research division of the Quartermaster Corps.'

'Then the boots were his,' I said.

'They certainly could have been.'

'Was he a big man?'

'I am told that he and his nephew would have been the same size when General Gault was younger.'

I thought of the photograph of the general in the dress mess jacket. He was slender and not particularly tall. His face was strong, eyes unwavering, but he did not look unkind.

'Luther Gault also served in Korea,' Wesley went on. 'For a while he was assigned to the Pentagon as the assistant chief of staff, then it was back to Ft. Lee as the deputy commander. He finished his career in MAC-V.'

'I don't know what that is,' I said.

'Military Assistance Command – Vietnam.'

'After which he retired to Seattle?' I said.

'He and his wife moved there.'

'Children?'

'Two boys.'

'What about the general's interaction with his brother?'

'I don't know. The general is deceased and his brother will not talk to us.'

'So we don't know how Gault might have wound up with his uncle's boots.'

'Kay, there is a code with Medal of Honor winners. They are in their own class. The army gives them a special status and they are stringently protected.'

'That's what all this secrecy is about?' I said.

'The army isn't keen on having the world know that their Medal of Honor-winning two-star general is the uncle of one of the most notorious psychopaths our country has seen. The Pentagon is not exactly keen on having it known that this killer – as you have already pointed out – may have kicked several people to death with General Gault's boots.'

I got up from my chair. 'I'm tired of boys and their codes of honor. I'm tired of male bonding and secrecy. We are not kids playing cowboys and Indians. We're not neighborhood children playing *war*.' I was drained. 'I thought you were more highly evolved than that.'

He stood up, too, as my pager went off. 'You're taking this the wrong way,' he said.

I looked at the display. The area code was Seattle, and without asking Wesley's permission I used his phone.

'Hello,' said a voice I did not know.

'This number just paged me.' I was confused.

'I didn't page anybody. Where are you calling from?'

'Virginia.' I was about to hang up.

'I just called Virginia. Wait a minute. Are you calling about Prodigy?'

'Oh. Perhaps you talked to Lucy?'

'LUCYTALK?'

'Yes.'

'We just this minute sent mail to each other. I'm responding to the gold foil query. I'm a dentist in Seattle and a member of the Academy of Gold Foil Operators. Are you the forensic pathologist?'

'Yes,' I said. 'Thank you so much for responding. I'm trying to identify a dead young woman with extensive gold foil restorations.'

'Please describe them.'

I told him about Jane's dental work and the damage to her teeth. 'It's possible she was a musician,' I added. 'She may have played the saxophone.'

'There was a lady from out here who sounds a lot like that.'

'She was in Seattle?'

'Right. Everyone in our academy knew about her because she had such an incredible mouth. Her gold foil restorations and dental anomalies were used in slide presentations at a number of our meetings.'

'Do you recall her name?'

'Sorry. She wasn't my patient. But it seems I remember hearing she was a professional musician until she was in some terrible accident. That was when her dental problems began.'

'The lady I'm talking about has a lot of enamel loss,' I said. 'Probably from overbrushing.'

'Oh absolutely. The lady out here did, too.'

'It doesn't sound to me as if the lady out there was a street person,' I said.

'Couldn't be. Someone paid for that mouth.'

'My lady was a street person when she died in New York,' I said.

'Geez, that makes me sad. I guess whoever she was, she really couldn't care for herself.'

271

'What is your name?' I asked.

'I'm Jay Bennett.'

'Dr. Bennett? Do you remember anything else that might have been said during one of these slide presentations?'

A long silence followed. 'Okay, yes. This is very vague.' He hesitated again. 'Oh, I know,' he said. 'The lady out here was related to someone important. In fact, that might be who she lived with out here before she disappeared.'

I gave him further information so he could call me again. I hung up the phone and met Wesley's stare.

'I think Jane is Gault's sister,' I said.

'What?' He was genuinely shocked.

'I think Temple Gault murdered his sister,' I repeated. 'Please tell me you didn't already know that.'

He got upset.

'I've got to verify her identity,' I said, and I had no emotion left in me right now.

'Won't her dental records do that?'

'If we find them. If she still has X rays left. If the army stays out of my way.'

'The army doesn't know about her.' He paused, and for an instant his eyes were bright with tears. He looked away from me. 'He just told us what he did when he sent the message from CAIN today.'

'Yes,' I said. 'He said CAIN killed his brother. The description of Gault with her in New York sounded more like two men than a woman and a man.' I paused. 'Are there other siblings?'

'Just a sister. We've known she lived on the West Coast but have never been able to locate her because apparently she doesn't drive. DMV has no record of a valid license. Truth is, we've never been certain she is alive.'

I said to him, 'She's not.'

He flinched and looked away.

'She hadn't lived anywhere – at least not in recent years,' I said, thinking of her pitiful belongings and malnourished body.

'She'd been on the street for a while. In fact, I'd say she survived out there all right until her brother came to town.'

His voice caught and he looked wrecked as he said, 'How could anyone do something like that?'

I put my arms around him. I did not care who walked in. I hugged him as a friend.

'Benton,' I said. 'Go home.'

17

I spent the weekend and the New Year at Quantico, and though there was considerable mail on Prodigy, verifying Jane's identity was not promising.

Her dentist had retired last year and her Panorex X-rays had been reclaimed for silver. The missing films, of course, were the biggest disappointment, for they might have shown old fractures, sinus configurations, bony anomalies, that could have effected a positive identification. As for her charts, when I touched upon that subject, her dentist, who was retired and now living in Los Angeles, got evasive.

'You do have them, don't you?' I asked him point-blank on Tuesday afternoon.

'I've got a million boxes in my garage.'

'I doubt you have a million.'

'I have a lot.'

'Please. We're talking about a woman we're unable to identify. All human beings have a right to be buried with their name.'

'I'm going to look, okay?'

Minutes later, I said to Marino on the phone, 'We're going to have to try for DNA or a visual ID.'

'Yo,' he said drolly. 'And just what are you going to do? Show Gault a photograph and ask if the woman he did this to looks like his sister?'

'I think her dentist took advantage of her. I've seen it before.'

'What are you talking about?'

'Occasionally, someone takes advantage. They chart work they didn't do so they can collect from Medicare or the insurance company.'

'But she had a hell of a lot of work done.'

'He could have charted a hell of a lot more. Trust me. Twice as many gold foil restorations, for example. That would have meant thousands of dollars. He says he did them when he didn't. She's mentally impaired, living with an elderly uncle. What do they know?'

'I hate assholes.'

'If I could get hold of his charts, I would report him. But he's not going to give them up. In fact, they probably no longer exist.'

'You got jury duty at eight in the morning,' Marino said. 'Rose called to let me know.'

'I guess that means I leave here very early tomorrow.'

'Go straight to your house and I'll pick you up.'

'I'll just go straight to the courthouse.'

'No you won't. You ain't driving downtown by yourself right now.'

'We know Gault's not in Richmond,' I said. 'He's back wherever he usually hides out, an apartment or room where he has a computer.'

'Chief Tucker hasn't rescinded his order for security for you.'

'He can't order anything for me. Not even lunch.'

'Oh yeah he can. All he does is assign certain cops to you. You either accept the situation or try to outrun them. If he wants to order your damn lunch, you'll get that, too.'

The next morning, I called the New York Medical Examiner's

Office and left a message for Dr. Horowitz that suggested he begin DNA analysis on Jane's blood. Then Marino picked me up at my house while neighbors looked out windows and opened handsome front doors to collect their newspapers. Three cruisers were parked in front, Marino's unmarked Ford in the brick drive. Windsor Farms woke up, went to work and watched me squired away by cops. Perfect lawns were white with frost and the sky was almost blue.

When I arrived at the John Marshall Courthouse, it was as I had done so many times in the past. But the deputy at the scanner did not understand why I was here.

'Good morning, Dr. Scarpetta,' he said with a broad smile. 'How about that snow? Don't it just make you feel like you're living in the middle of a Hallmark card? And Captain, a nice day to you, sir,' he said to Marino.

I set off the X-ray machine. A female deputy appeared to search me while the deputy who enjoyed snow went through my bag. Marino and I walked downstairs to an orange-carpeted room filled with rows of sparsely populated orange chairs. We sat in the back, where we listened to people dozing, crackling paper, coughing and blowing their noses. A man in a leather jacket with shirt-tail hanging out prowled for magazines while a man in cashmere read a novel. Next door a vacuum cleaner roared. It butted into the orange room's door and quit.

Including Marino, I had three uniformed officers around me in this deadly dull room. Then at eight-fifty A.M. the jury officer walked in late and went to a podium to orient us.

'I have two changes,' she said, looking directly at me. 'The sheriff on the videotape you're about to see is no longer the sheriff.'

Marino whispered in my ear, 'That's because he's no longer alive.'

'And,' the jury officer went on, 'the tape will tell you the fee for jury duty is thirty dollars, but it's still twenty dollars.'

'Nuts.' Marino was in my ear again. 'Do you need a loan?'

We watched the video and I learned much about my important civic duty and its privileges. I watched Sheriff Brown on tape as he thanked me again for performing this important service. He told me I had been called up to decide the fate of another person and then showed the computer he had used to select me.

'Names called are then drawn from a jury ballot box,' he recited with a smile. 'Our system of justice depends on our careful consideration of the evidence. Our system depends on us.'

He gave a phone number I could call and reminded all of us that coffee was twenty-five cents a cup and no change was available.

After the video, the jury officer, a handsome black woman, came over to me.

'Are you police?' she whispered.

'No,' I said, explaining who I was as she looked at Marino and the other two officers.

'We need to excuse you now,' she whispered. 'You shouldn't be here. You should have called and told us. I don't know why you're here at all.'

The other draftees were staring. They had been staring since we walked in, and the reason crystallized. They were ignorant of the judicial system, and I was surrounded by police. Now the jury officer was over here, too. I was the defendant. They probably did not know that defendants don't read magazines in the same room with the jury pool.

By lunchtime I was gone and wondering if I would ever be allowed to serve on a jury even once in my life. Marino let me out at the front door of my building and I went into my office. I called New York again and Dr. Horowitz got on the phone.

'She was buried yesterday,' he said of Jane.

I felt a great sadness. 'I thought you usually wait a little longer than that,' I said.

'Ten days. It's been about that, Kay. You know the problem we have with storage space.'

'We can identify her with DNA,' I said.

'Why not dental records?'

I explained the problem.

'That's a real shame.' Dr. Horowitz paused and was reluctant when he spoke next. 'I'm very sorry to tell you that we've had a terrible snafu here.' He paused again. 'Frankly, I wish we hadn't buried her. But we have.'

'What happened?'

'No one seems to know. We saved a blood sample on filter paper for DNA purposes, just like we typically do. And of course we kept a stock jar with sections of all major organs, et cetera. The blood sample seems to have been misplaced, and it appears the stock jar was accidentally thrown out.'

'That can't have happened,' I said.

Dr. Horowitz was quiet.

'What about tissue in paraffin blocks for histology?' I then asked, for fixed tissue could also be tested for DNA, if all else failed.

'We don't take tissue for micros when the cause of death is clear,' he said.

I did not know what to say. Either Dr. Horowitz ran a frighteningly inept office, or these mistakes were not mistakes. I had always believed the chief was an impeccably scrupulous man. Maybe I had been wrong. I knew how it was in New York City. The politicians could not stay out of the morgue.

'She needs to be brought back up,' I said to him. 'I see no other way. Was she embalmed?'

'We rarely embalm bodies destined for Hart Island,' he said of the island in the East River where Potter's Field was located. 'Her identification number needs to be located and then she'll be dug up and brought back by ferry. We can do that. That's all we can do, really. It might take a few days.'

'Dr. Horowitz?' I carefully said. 'What is going on here?'

His voice was steady but disappointed when he answered, 'I have no earthly idea.'

I sat at my desk for a while, trying to figure out what to do. The more I thought, the less sense anything made. Why would the army care if Jane was identified? If she was General Gault's niece and the army knew she was dead, one would think they would want her identified and buried in a proper grave.

'Dr. Scarpetta.' Rose was in the doorway adjoining her office to mine. 'It's Brent from the Amex.'

She transferred the call.

'I've got another charge,' Brent said.

'Okay.' I tensed.

'Yesterday. A place called Fino in New York. I checked it out. It's on East Thirty-sixth Street. The amount is $104.13.'

Fino had wonderful northern Italian food. My ancestors were from northern Italy, and Gault had posed as a northern Italian named Benelli. I tried Wesley, but he was not in. Then I tried Lucy, and she was not at ERF, nor was she in her room. Marino was the only person I could tell that Gault was in New York again.

'He's just playing more games,' Marino said in disgust. 'He knows you're monitoring his charges, Doc. He's not doing anything he doesn't want you to know about.'

'I realize that.'

'We're not going to catch him through American Express. You ought to just cancel your card.'

But I couldn't. My card was like the modem Lucy knew was under the floor. Both were tenuous lines leading to Gault. He was playing games, but one day he might overstep himself. He might get too reckless and high on cocaine and make a mistake.

'Doc,' Marino went on, 'you're getting too wound up with this. You need to chill out.'

Gault might want me to find him, I thought. Every time he used my card he was sending a message to me. He was telling me more about himself. I knew what he liked to eat and that he did not drink red wine. I knew about the cigarettes he smoked, the clothes he wore, and I thought of his boots.

'Are you listening to me?' Marino was asking.

We had always assumed that the jungle boots were Gault's.

'The boots belonged to his sister,' I thought out loud.

'What are you talking about?' Marino said impatiently.

'She must have gotten them from her uncle years ago, and then Gault took them from her.'

'When? He didn't do it at Cherry Hill in the snow.'

'I don't know when. It may have been shortly before she died. It could have been inside the Museum of Natural History. They basically wore the same shoe size. They could have traded boots. It could be anything. But I doubt she gave them up willingly. For one thing, the jungle boots would be very good in snow. She would have been better off with them than the ones we found in Benny's hobo camp.'

Marino was silent a moment longer. Then he said, 'Why would he take her boots?'

'That's easy,' I said. 'Because he wanted them.'

That afternoon, I drove to the Richmond airport with a briefcase packed full and an overnight bag. I had not called my travel agent because I did not want anyone to know where I was going. At the USAir desk, I purchased a ticket to Hilton Head, South Carolina.

'I hear it's nice down there,' said the gregarious attendant. 'A lot of people play golf and tennis down there.' She checked my one small bag.

'You need to tag it.' I lowered my voice. 'It has a firearm in it.'

She nodded and handed me a blaze orange tag that proclaimed I was carrying an unloaded firearm.

'I'll let you put it inside,' the woman said to me. 'Does your bag lock?'

I locked the zipper and watched her set the bag on the conveyor belt. She handed me my ticket and I headed upstairs to the gate, which was very crowded with people who did not look happy to be going home or back to work after the holidays.

The flight to Charlotte seemed longer than an hour because I could not use my cellular phone and my pager went off twice. I went through the *Wall Street Journal* and the *Washington Post* while my thoughts slalomed through a treacherous course. I contemplated what I would say to the parents of Temple Gault and the slain woman we called Jane.

I could not even be sure the Gaults would see me because I had not called. Their number and address were unlisted. But I believed it could not be so hard to find the place they had bought near Beaufort. Live Oaks Plantation was one of the oldest in South Carolina, and the local people would know about this couple whose homestead in Albany had recently washed away in a flood.

There was enough time in the Charlotte airport for me to return my calls. Both were from Rose, who wanted me to verify void dates because several subpoenas had just come in.

'And Lucy tried to get you,' she said.

'She has my pager number,' I puzzled.

'I asked her if she had that,' my secretary said. 'She said she'd try you another time.'

'Did she say where she was calling from?'

'No. I assume she was calling from Quantico.'

I had no time to question further because Terminal D was a long walk, and the plane to Hilton Head left in fifteen minutes. I ran the entire way and had time for a soft pretzel without salt. I grabbed several packages of mustard and carried on board the only meal I'd had this day. The businessman I sat beside stared at my snack as if it told him I were a rude housewife who knew nothing about traveling on planes.

When we were in the air, I got into the mustard and ordered Scotch on the rocks.

'Would you by chance have change for a twenty?' I asked the man next to me, because I had overheard the flight attendant complaining about not having adequate change.

He got his wallet out as I opened the *New York Times*. He gave me a ten and two fives, so I paid for his drink. 'Quid pro quo,' I said.

'That's mighty nice,' he said in a syrupy southern accent. 'I guess you must be from New York.'

'Yes,' I lied.

'You by chance going to Hilton Head for the Carolina Convenience Store convention? It's at the Hyatt.'

'No. The funeral home convention,' I lied again. 'It's at the Holiday Inn.'

'Oh.' He shut up.

The Hilton Head airport was parked with private planes and Learjets belonging to the very wealthy who had homes on the island. The terminal was not much more than a hut, and baggage was stacked outside on a wooden deck. The weather was cool with volatile dark skies, and as passengers hurried to awaiting cars and shuttles, I overheard their complaints.

'Oh shit,' exclaimed the man who had been seated beside me. He was hauling golf clubs when thunder crashed and lightning lit up parts of the sky as if a war had begun.

I rented a silver Lincoln and spent some time ensconced inside it at the airport parking lot. Rain drummed the roof, and I could not see out the windshield as I studied the map Hertz had given to me. Anna Zenner's house was in Palmetto Dunes, not far from the Hyatt, where the man on the plane was headed. I looked in vain to see if his car might still be in the parking lot, but as far as I could tell, he and his golf clubs were gone.

The rain eased and I followed the airport exits to the William Hilton Parkway, which took me to Queens Folly Road. I just wandered for a while after that until I found the house. I had expected something smaller. Anna's hideaway was not a bungalow. It was a splendid rustic manor of weathered wood and glass. The yard in back where I parked was dense with tall palmettos and water oaks draped in Spanish moss. A squirrel ran down a tree as I climbed steps leading to the porch. He came close and stood on his hind legs, cheeks going fast as if he had a lot to say to me.

'I bet she feeds you, doesn't she?' I said to him as I got out the key.

He stood with his front paws up, as if protesting something. 'Well, I don't have a thing except memories of a pretzel,' I said. 'I'm really very sorry.' I paused as he hopped a little closer. 'And if you're rabid I'll have to shoot you.'

I went inside, disappointed there was no burglar alarm.

'Too bad,' I said, but I wasn't going to move.

I locked the door and turned the dead bolt. No one knew I was here. I should be fine. Anna had been coming to Hilton Head for years and saw no need for a security system. Gault was in New York and I did not see how he could have followed me. I walked into the living room, with its rustic wood and windows from floor to sky. Hardwood was covered in a bright Indian rug, and furniture was bleached mahogany upholstered in practical fabrics in lovely bright shades.

I wandered from room to room, getting hungrier as the ocean turned to molten lead and a determined army of dark clouds marched in from the north. A long boardwalk led from the house, over dunes, and I carried coffee to its end. I watched people walking and riding bicycles, and an occasional jogger. Sand was hard and gray, and squadrons of brown pelicans flew in formation as if mounting an air attack on a country of unfriendly fish or perhaps the weather.

A porpoise surfaced as men drove golf balls into the sea, and then a small boy's Styrofoam surfboard blew out of his hands. It cartwheeled across the beach while he madly ran. I watched the chase for a quarter of a mile, until his prize tumbled through sea oats up my dune and leapt over my fence. I ran down steps and grabbed it before the wind could abduct it again, and the boy's gait faltered as he watched me watching him.

He could not have been older than eight or nine, dressed in jeans and sweatshirt. Down the beach his mother was trying to catch up with him.

'May I have my surfboard, please?' he said, staring at the sand.

'Would you like me to help you get it back to your mother?' I asked kindly. 'In this wind it will be hard for one person to carry.'

'No, thank you,' he shyly mumbled with outstretched hands.

I felt rejected as I stood on Anna's boardwalk, watching him fight the wind. He finally flattened the surfboard against himself like an ironing board and trudged across damp sand. I watched him with his mother until they were scratches on a horizon I eventually could not see. I tried to imagine where they went. Was it a hotel or a house? Where did little boys and mothers stay on stormy nights out here?

I had not taken one vacation when I was growing up because we had no money, and now I had no children. I thought of Wesley and wanted to call him as I listened to the loud wash of surf rushing to shore. Stars showed through cloudy veils and voices carried on the wind and I could not decipher a word. I may as well have been hearing frogs scream or birds crying. I carried my empty coffee cup inside and did not feel afraid for once.

It occurred to me that there was probably nothing to eat in this house and all I'd had today was that pretzel.

'Thank you, Anna,' I said when I found a stack of Lean Cuisines.

I heated turkey and mixed vegetables, turned on the gas fire and fell asleep on a white couch, my Browning not too far away. I was too tired to dream. The sun and I rose together, and the reality of my mission did not seem real until I spied my briefcase and thought about what was in it. It was too early to leave, and I put on sweater and jeans and went out for a walk.

The sand was firm and flat toward Sea Pines, the sun white gold on water. Birds embroidered the noisy surf with their songs. Willets wandered for mole crabs and worms, gulls glided on the wind, and crows loitered like black-hooded highwaymen.

Older people were out now while the sun was weak, and as I walked I concentrated on the sea air blowing through me. I felt I could breathe. I warmed to the smiles of strangers strolling past, hand in hand, and I waved if they did. Lovers had arms around each other, and solitary people drank coffee on boardwalks and looked out at the water.

Back in Anna's house, I toasted a bagel I found in the freezer and took a long shower. Then I put on my same black blazer and slacks. I packed and closed up the house as if I would not be back. I had no sense of being watched until the squirrel reappeared.

'Oh no,' I said, unlocking the car door. 'Not you again.'

He stood on his hind legs, giving me a lecture.

'Listen, Anna said I could stay here. I am her very good friend.'

His whiskers twitched as he showed me his small white belly.

'If you're telling me your problems, don't bother.' I threw my bag in the backseat. 'Anna's the psychiatrist. Not me.'

I opened the driver's door. He hopped a few steps closer. I couldn't stand it any longer and dug inside my briefcase, where I found a pack of peanuts from the plane. The squirrel was on his hind legs chewing furiously as I backed out of the drive beneath the shade of trees. He watched me leave.

I took 278 West and drove through a landscape lush with cattails, marsh lace, spartina grass and rushes. Ponds were tiled in lotus and lily pads, and at almost every turn, hawks hovered. Away from the islands it seemed most people were poor except in land. Narrow roads offered tiny white painted churches and mobile homes still strung with Christmas lights. Closer to Beaufort, I found auto repairs, small motels on barren plots, and a barbershop flying a Confederate flag. Twice I stopped to read my map.

On St. Helena Island I crept around a tractor on the roadside stirring up dust and began looking for a place to stop for directions. I found abandoned cinder block buildings that once had been stores. There were tomato packers, farmhouses and funeral homes along streets lined with dense live oaks and gardens guarded by scarecrows. I did not stop until I was on Tripp Island and found a place where I could have lunch.

The restaurant was the Gullah House, the woman who seated me big and dark black. She was brilliant in a flowing dress of tropical colors, and when she spoke over a counter to a waiter their language was musical and filled with strange words. The Gullah dialect is supposed to be a blend of West Indian and Elizabethan English. It was the spoken language of slaves.

I waited at my wooden table for iced tea and worried that no one who worked here could communicate to me where the Gaults lived.

'What else I get for you, honey?' My waitress returned with a glass jar of tea full of ice and lemons.

I pointed to *Biddy een de Fiel* because I could not say it. The translation promised a grilled chicken breast on Romaine lettuce.

'You want sweet-potato chips or maybe some crab frittas to start?' Her eyes roamed around the restaurant as she talked.

'No, thank you.'

Determined her customer would have more than a diet lunch, she showed me fried low-country shrimp on the back of the menu. 'We also got fresh fried shrimp today. It so good it'll make you tongue slap you brains out.'

I looked at her. 'Well, then I guess I'd better try a small side dish.'

'So you want all two of 'em.'

'Please.'

The service maintained its languid pace, and it was almost one o'clock when I paid my bill. The lady in the bright dress, who I decided was the manager, was outside in the parking lot talking to another dark woman who drove a van. The side of it read *Gullah Tours*.

'Excuse me,' I said to the manager.

Her eyes were like volcanic glass, suspicious but not unfriendly. 'You want a tour of the island?' she asked.

'Actually, I need directions,' I said. 'Are you familiar with Live Oaks Plantation?'

'It's not on no tour. Not no more.'

'So I can't get there?' I asked.

The manager turned her face and looked askance at me. 'Some new folks is moved there. They don't take kindly to tours, you hear my meaning?'

'I hear you,' I said. 'But I need to get there. I don't want a tour. I just want directions.'

It occurred to me that the dialect I was speaking wasn't the one the manager – who no doubt owned Gullah Tours – wanted to hear.

'How about if I pay for a tour,' I said, 'and you get your van driver to lead me to Live Oaks?'

That seemed a good plan. I handed over twenty dollars and was on my way. The distance was not far, and soon the van slowed and an arm in a wildly colorful sleeve pointed out the window at acres of pecan trees behind a neat white fence. The gate was open at the end of a long, unpaved drive, and about half a mile back I caught a glimpse of white wood and an old copper roof. There was no sign to indicate the owner's name and not a clue that this was Live Oaks Plantation.

I turned left into the drive and scanned spaces between old pecan trees that had already been harvested. I passed a pond covered with duckweed where a blue heron walked at the water's edge. I did not see anyone, but when I got close to what was a magnificent antebellum house, I found a car and a pickup truck. An old barn with a tin roof was in back next to a silo built of tabby. The day had gotten dark and my jacket felt too thin as I climbed steep porch steps and rang the bell.

I could tell instantly by the expression on the man's face that the gate at the end of the driveway was not supposed to have been left open.

'This is private property,' he flatly stated.

If Temple Gault was his son, I saw no resemblance. This man was wiry with graying hair, and his face was long and weathered. He wore Top-Siders, khaki slacks and a plain gray sweatshirt with a hood.

'I'm looking for Peyton Gault,' I said, meeting his gaze as I gripped my briefcase.

'The gate's suppose to be shut. Didn't you see the *No Trespassing* signs? I've only got them nailed up every other fence post. What do you want Peyton Gault for?'

'I can only tell Peyton Gault what I want him for,' I said.

He studied me carefully, indecision in his eyes. 'You aren't some kind of reporter, are you?'

'No, sir, I most certainly am not. I'm the chief medical examiner of Virginia.' I handed him my card.

He leaned against the door frame as if he felt sick. 'Good God have mercy,' he muttered. 'Why can't you people leave us be?'

I could not imagine his private punishment for what he had created, for somewhere in his father's heart he still loved his son.

'Mr. Gault,' I said. 'Please let me talk to you.'

He dug his thumb and index fingers into the corners of his eyes to stop from crying. Wrinkles deepened in his tan brow, and a sudden blaze of sunlight through clouds turned stubble to sand.

'I'm not here out of curiosity,' I said. 'I'm not here doing research. Please.'

'He's never been right from the day he was born,' Peyton Gault said, wiping his eyes.

'I know this is awful for you. It is an unapproachable horror. But I understand.'

'No one can understand,' he said.

'Please let me try.'

'There's no good to come of it.'

'There is only good to come of it,' I said. 'I am here to do the right thing.'

He looked at me with uncertainty. 'Who sent you?'

'Nobody. I came on my own.'

'Then how'd you find us?'

'I asked directions,' I said, and I told him where.

'You don't look too warm in that jacket.'

'I'm warm enough.'

'All right,' he said. 'We'll go out on the pier.'

His dock cut through marshlands that spread as far as I could see, the Barrier Islands an infrequent water tower on the horizon. We leaned against rails, watching fiddler crabs rustle across dark mud. Now and then an oyster spat.

'During Civil War times there were as many as two hundred and fifty slaves here,' he was saying as if we were here to have a friendly chat. 'Before you leave you should stop by the Chapel of Ease. It's just a tabby shell now, with rusting wrought iron around a tiny graveyard.'

I let him talk.

'Of course, the graves have been robbed for as long as anyone remembers. I guess the chapel was built around 1740.'

I was silent.

He sighed, looking out toward the ocean.

'I have photographs I want to show you,' I quietly said.

'You know' – his voice got emotional again – 'it's almost like that flood was punishment for something I did. I was born on that plantation in Albany.' He looked over at me. 'It withstood almost two centuries of war and bad weather.

Then that storm hit and the Flint River rose more than twenty feet.

'We had state police, military police barricading everything. The water reached the damn ceiling of what had been my family home, and forget the trees. Not that we've ever depended on pecans to keep food on the table. But for a while my wife and I were living like the homeless in a center with about three hundred other people.'

'Your son did not cause that flood,' I gently said. 'Even he can't bring about a natural disaster.'

'Well, it's probably just as well we moved. People were coming around all the time trying to see where he grew up. It's had a bad effect on Rachael's nerves.'

'Rachael is your wife?'

He nodded.

'What about your daughter?'

'That's another sorry story. We had to send Jayne west when she was eleven.'

'That's her name?' I said, astonished.

'Actually, it's Rachael. But her middle name's Jayne with a *y*. I don't know if you knew this, but Temple and Jayne are twins.'

'I had no idea,' I said.

'And he was always jealous of her. It was a terrible sight to behold, because she was just crazy about him. They were the cutest little blond things you'd ever want to see, and it's like from day one Temple wanted to squash her like a bug. He was cruel.' He paused.

A herring gull flew by, screaming, and troops of fiddler crabs charged a clump of cattails.

Peyton Gault smoothed back his hair and propped one foot on a lower rail. He said, 'I guess I knew the worst when he was five and Jayne had a puppy. Just the nicest little dog, a mutt.' He paused again. 'Well' – his voice caught – 'the puppy disappeared and that night Jayne woke up to find it dead in her bed. Temple probably strangled it.'

'You said Jayne eventually lived on the West Coast?' I asked.

'Rachael and I didn't know what else to do. We knew it was a matter of time before he killed her – which he almost succeeded in doing later on, it's my belief. You see, I had a brother in Seattle. Luther.'

'The general,' I said.

He continued staring straight ahead. 'I guess you folks do know a lot about us. Temple's made damn sure of that. And next thing I'll be reading about it in books and seeing it on movies.' He pounded his fist softly on the rail.

'Jayne moved in with your brother and his wife?'

'And we kept Temple in Albany. Believe me, if I could have sent him off and held on to her, that's what I would have done. She was a sweet, sensitive child. Real dreamy and kind.' Tears rolled down his cheeks. 'She could play the piano and the saxophone, and Luther loved her like one of his. He had sons.

'All went as well as could be expected, in light of the trouble we had on our hands. Rachael and I went out to Seattle several times a year. I'm telling you, it was hard on me, but it nearly broke her heart. Then we made a big mistake.'

He paused until he could talk again, clearing his throat several times. 'Jayne insisted she wanted to come home one summer. And I guess this was when she was about to turn twenty-five, and she wanted to spend her birthday with everyone. So she, Luther and his wife, Sara, flew to Albany from Seattle. Temple acted like he wasn't fazed a bit, and I remember . . .'

He cleared his throat. 'I remember so clearly thinking that maybe everything would be okay. Maybe he'd finally outgrown whatever it was that possessed him. Jayne had a grand time at her party, and she decided to take our old hound dog, Snaggletooth, out for a walk. She wanted her picture taken, and we did that. Among the pecan trees. Then we all went back into the house except her and Temple.

'He came in around suppertime and I said to him, "Where's your sister?"

'He replied, "She said she was going horseback riding."

'Well, we waited and we waited, and she didn't come back. So Luther and I went out to hunt for her. We found her horse still saddled up and wandering about the stable, and she was there on the ground with all this blood everywhere.'

He wiped his face with his hands, and I could not describe the pity I felt for this man or for his daughter, Jayne. I dreaded telling him his story had an ending.

'The doctor,' he struggled on, 'figured she just got kicked by the horse, but I was suspicious. I thought Luther would kill the boy. You know, he didn't win a Medal of Honor for handing out mess kits. So after Jayne recovered enough to leave the hospital, Luther took her back home. But she was never right.'

'Mr. Gault,' I said. 'Do you have any idea where your daughter is now?'

'Well, she eventually went out on her own four or five years ago when Luther passed on. We usually hear from her at birthdays, Christmas, whenever the mood strikes.'

'Did you hear from her this Christmas?' I asked.

'Not directly on Christmas Day, but a week or two before.' He thought hard, an odd expression on his face.

'Where was she?'

'She called from New York City.'

'Do you know what she was doing there, Mr. Gault?'

'I never know what she's doing. I think she just wanders around and calls when she needs money, to tell you the truth.' He stared out at a snowy egret standing on a stump.

'When she called from New York,' I persisted, 'did she ask for money?'

'Do you mind if I smoke?'

'Of course not.'

He fished a pack of Merits from his breast pocket and fought to light one in the wind. He turned this way and that, and

293

finally I cupped a hand on top of his and held the match. He was shaking.

'It's very important you tell me about the money,' I said. 'How much and how did she get it?'

He paused. 'You see, Rachael does all that.'

'Did your wife wire the money? Did she send a check?'

'I guess you don't know my daughter. No way anybody is going to cash a check for her. Rachael wires money to her on a regular basis. You see, Jayne has to be on medicine to prevent seizures. Because of what happened to her head.'

'Where is the money wired?' I asked.

'A Western Union office. Rachael could tell you which one.'

'What about your son? Do you communicate with him?'

His face got hard. 'Not a bit.'

'He's never tried to come home?'

'Nope.'

'What about here? Does he know you're here?'

'About the only communicating I intend to do with Temple is with a double-barrel shotgun.' His jaw muscles bunched. 'I don't give a damn if he is my son.'

'Are you aware that he is using your AT&T charge card?'

Mr. Gault stood up straight and tapped an ash that scattered in the wind. 'That can't be.'

'Your wife pays the bills?'

'Well, those kind she does.'

'I see,' I said.

He flicked the cigarette into the mud and a crab went after it.

He said, 'Jayne's dead, isn't she? You're a coroner and that's why you're here.'

'Yes, Mr. Gault. I'm so sorry.'

'I had a feeling when you told me who you are. My little girl's that lady they think Temple murdered in Central Park.'

'That's why I'm here,' I said. 'But I need your help if I'm going to prove she is your daughter.'

He looked me in the eye, and I sensed bone-weary relief. He drew himself up and I felt his pride. 'Ma'am, I don't want her in some godforsaken pauper's grave. I want her here with Rachael and me. For once she can live with us because it's too late for him to hurt her.'

We walked along the pier.

'I can make certain that happens,' I said as wind flattened the grass and tore through our hair. 'All I need is your blood.'

18

Before we went inside his house, Mr. Gault warned me that his wife did not have good coping skills. He explained as delicately as he could that Rachael Gault had never faced the reality of her offsprings' blighted destinies.

'It's not that she's going to pitch a fit,' he explained in a soft voice as we climbed the porch steps. 'She just won't accept it, if you know what I mean.'

'You may want to look at the pictures out here,' I said.

'Of Jayne.' He got very tired again.

'Of her and of footprints.'

'Footprints?' He ran callused fingers through his hair.

'Do you remember her owning a pair of army jungle boots?' I then asked.

'No.' He slowly shook his head. 'But Luther had all kinds of things like that.'

'Do you know what size shoe he wore?'

'His foot was smaller than mine. I guess he wore a seven and a half or an eight.'

'Did he ever give a pair of his boots to Temple?'

'Huh,' he said shortly. 'The only way Luther would have

297

given that boy boots would be if Luther still had 'em on and was kicking Temple's butt.'

'The boots could have belonged to Jayne.'

'Oh sure. She and Luther probably wore close to the same size. She was a big girl. In fact, she was about the size of Temple. And I always suspected that was part of his problem.'

Mr. Gault would have stood out in prevailing winds and talked all day. He did not want me opening my briefcase because he knew what was inside.

'We don't have to do this. You don't have to look at anything,' I said. 'We can use DNA.'

'If it's all the same to you,' he said, eyes bright as he reached for the door. 'I guess I'd better tell Rachael.'

The entrance of the Gault house was whitewashed and bordered in a pale shade of gray. An old brass chandelier hung from the high ceiling, and a graceful spiral stairway led to the second floor. In the living room were English antiques, oriental rugs and formidable oil portraits of people from lives past. Rachael Gault sat on a prim sofa, needlepoint in her lap. I could see through a spacious archway that needlepoint covered the dining room chairs.

'Rachael?' Mr. Gault stood before her like a bashful bachelor with hat in hand. 'We have company.'

She dipped her needle in and out. 'Oh, how nice.' She smiled and put down her work.

Rachael Gault once had been a fair beauty with light skin, eyes and hair. I was fascinated that Temple and Jayne had gotten their looks from their mother and their uncle, and I chose not to speculate but to attribute this to Mendel's law of dominance or his statistics of genetic chance.

Mr. Gault sat on the sofa and offered me the high-back chair.

'What's the weather doing out there?' Mrs. Gault asked with her son's thin smile and the hypnotic cadences of a Deep South drawl. 'I wonder if there are any shrimp left.' She looked directly at me. 'You know, I don't know your name. Now, Peyton, let's not be rude. Introduce me to this new friend you've made.'

'Rachael,' Mr. Gault tried again. Hands on his knees, he hung his head. 'She's a doctor from Virginia.'

'Oh?' Her delicate hands plucked at the canvas in her lap.

'I guess you'd call her a coroner.' He looked over at his wife. 'Honey, Jayne's dead.'

Mrs. Gault resumed her needlework with nimble fingers. 'You know, we had a magnolia out there that lasted nearly a hundred years before lightning struck it in the spring. Can you imagine?' She sewed on. 'We do get storms here. What's it like where you're from?'

'I live in Richmond,' I replied.

'Oh yes,' she said, the needle dipping faster. 'Now see, we were lucky we didn't get all burned up in the war. I bet you had a great-granddaddy who fought in it?'

'I'm Italian,' I said. 'I'm from Miami, originally.'

'Well, it certainly gets hot down there.'

Mr. Gault sat helpless on the couch. He gave up looking at anyone.

'Mrs. Gault,' I said, 'I saw Jayne in New York.'

'You did?' She seemed genuinely pleased. 'Why, tell me all about it.' Her hands were like hummingbirds.

'When I saw her she was awfully thin and she'd cut her hair.'

'She never is satisfied with her hair. When she wore it short she looked like Temple. They're twins and people used to confuse them and think she was a boy. So she's always worn it long, which is why I'm surprised you would say she's cut it short.'

'Do you talk to your son?' I asked.

'He doesn't call as often as he should, that bad boy. But he knows he can.'

'Jayne called here a couple weeks before Christmas,' I said.

She said nothing as she sewed.

'Did she say anything to you about seeing her brother?'

She was silent.

'I'm wondering because he was in New York, too.'

'Certainly, I told him he ought to look up his sister and wish her a Merry Christmas,' Mrs. Gault said as her husband winced.

'You sent her money?' I went on.

She looked up at me. 'Now I believe you're getting a bit personal.'

'Yes, ma'am. I'm afraid I have to get personal.'

She threaded a needle with bright blue yarn.

'Doctors get personal.' I tried a different tack. 'That's part of our job.'

She laughed a little. 'Well now, they do. I suppose that's why I hate going to them. They think they can cure everything with milk of magnesia. It's like drinking white paint. Peyton? Would you mind getting me a glass of water with a little ice? And see what our guest would like.'

'Nothing,' I told him quietly as he reluctantly got up and left the room.

'That was very thoughtful of you to send your daughter money,' I said. 'Please tell me how you did it in a city as big and busy as New York.'

'I had Western Union wire it, same as I always do.'

'Where exactly did you wire it?'

'New York, where Jayne is.'

'Where in New York, Mrs. Gault? And have you done this more than once?'

'A drugstore up there. Because she has to get her medicine.'

'For her seizures. Her diphenylhydantoin.'

'Jayne said it wasn't a very good part of town.' She sewed some more. 'It was called Houston. Only it's not pronounced like the city in Texas.'

'Houston and what?' I asked.

'Why, I don't know what you mean.' She was getting agitated.

'A cross street. I need an address.'

'Why in the world?'

'Because that may be where your daughter went right before she died.'

She sewed faster, her lips a thin line.

'Please help me, Mrs. Gault.'

'She rides the bus a lot. She says she can see America flow by like a movie when she's on the bus.'

'I know you don't want anyone else to die.'

She squeezed her eyes shut.

'Please.'

'Now I lay me.'

'What?' I said.

'Rachael.' Mr. Gault returned to the room. 'There isn't any ice. I don't know what happened.'

'Down to sleep,' she said.

Dumbfounded, I looked at her husband.

'Now I lay me down to sleep, I pray the Lord my soul to keep,' he said, looking at her. 'We prayed that with the kids every night when they were small. Is that what you're thinking of, honey?'

'Test question for Western Union,' she said.

'Because Jayne had no identification,' I said. 'Of course. So they made her answer a test question to pick up the money and her prescription.'

'Oh yes. It was what we always used. For years now.'

'And what about Temple?'

'For him, too.'

Mr. Gault rubbed his face. 'Rachael, you haven't been giving him money, too. Please don't tell me . . .'

'It's my money. I have my own from my family just like you do.' She resumed sewing, turning the canvas this way and that.

301

'Mrs. Gault,' I said, 'did Temple know Jayne was due money from you at Western Union?'

'Of course he knew. He is her brother. He said he'd pick it up for her because she hasn't been well. When that horse threw her off. She's never been as clearheaded as Temple is. And I was sending him a little, too.'

'How often have you been sending money?' I asked again.

She tied a knot and cast about as if she had lost something.

'Mrs. Gault, I will not leave your house until you answer my question or throw me out.'

'After Luther died there wasn't anyone to care about Jayne, and she didn't want to come here,' she said. 'Jayne didn't want to be in one of those homes. So wherever she went she let me know, and I helped when I could.'

'You never told me.' Her husband was crushed.

'How long had she been in New York?' I asked.

'Since the first of December. I've been sending money regularly, just a little at a time. Fifty dollars here, a hundred dollars there. I wired some last Saturday, as usual. That's why I know she's fine. She passed the test. So she was standing right there in line.'

I wondered how long Gault had been intercepting his poor sister's money. I despised him with a zeal that was scary.

'She didn't like Philadelphia,' Mrs. Gault went on, talking faster. 'That's where she was before New York. Some city of brotherly love that is. Someone stole her flute there. Stole it right out of her hand.'

'Her tin whistle?' I asked.

'Her saxophone. You know, my father played the violin.'

Mr. Gault and I stared at her.

'Maybe it was her saxophone that got taken. Lawww, I don't know where all she's been. Honey? Remember when she came here for her birthday and went out in the pecan trees with the dog?' Her hands went still.

'That was Albany. That's not where we are now.'

She shut her eyes. 'Why, she was twenty-five and had never been kissed.' She laughed. 'I remember her at the piano playing up a storm, singing "Happy Birthday" to beat the band. Then Temple took her to the barn. She'd go anywhere with him. I never understood why. But Temple can be charming.'

A tear slipped between her lashes.

'She went out to ride that darn horse Priss and never came back.' More tears spilled. 'Oh Peyton, I never saw my little girl again.'

He said in a voice that shook, 'Temple killed her, Rachael. This can't go on.'

I drove back to Hilton Head and got an early evening flight to Charlotte. From there I flew to Richmond and retrieved my car. I did not go home. I felt a sense of urgency that set me on fire. I could not reach Wesley at Quantico, and Lucy had returned none of my calls.

It was almost nine o'clock when I drove past pitch-black artillery ranges and barracks, trees hulking shadows on either side of the narrow road. I was rattled and exhausted as I watched for signs and deer crossing, then blue lights flashed in my rearview mirror. I tried to see what was behind me. I could not tell, but I knew it was not a patrol car because those had light bars in addition to lights in the grille.

I drove on. I thought of cases I had worked in which a woman alone stopped for what she thought was a cop. Many times over the years I had warned Lucy never to stop for an unmarked car, not for any reason, especially not at night. The car was dogged, but I did not pull over until I reached the Academy guard booth.

The unmarked car halted at my rear, and instantly an MP in uniform was at my driver's door with pistol drawn. My heart seemed to stop.

'Get out and put your hands up in the air!' he ordered.

I sat perfectly still.

303

He stepped back and I realized the guard was saying something to him. Then the guard emerged from his booth and the MP tapped on my glass. I rolled down my window while the MP lowered his gun, his eyes not leaving me. He did not look a day over nineteen.

'You're going to have to get out, ma'am.' The MP was hateful because he was embarrassed.

'I will if you'll holster your weapon and move out of my way,' I said as the Academy guard stepped back. 'And I have a pistol on the console between the front seats. I'm just telling you so you aren't startled.'

'Are you DEA?' he demanded as he surveyed my Mercedes.

He had what looked like gray adhesive residue for a mustache. My blood was roaring. I knew he was going to put on a manly show because the Academy guard was watching.

I was out of my car now, blue lights throbbing on our faces.

'Am I DEA?' I glared at him.

'Yes.'

'No.'

'Are you FBI?'

'No.'

He was getting more disconcerted. 'Then what are you, ma'am?'

'I am a forensic pathologist,' I said.

'Who is your supervisor?'

'I don't have a supervisor.'

'Ma'am, you have to have a supervisor.'

'The governor of Virginia is my supervisor.'

'I'll have to see your driver's license,' he said.

'Not until you tell me what I am being charged with.'

'You were going forty-five in a thirty-five-mile-an-hour zone. And you attempted to elude.'

'Do all people who attempt to elude military police drive straight to a guard booth?'

'I must have your driver's license.'

'And let me ask you, Private,' I said, 'just why do you imagine I didn't pull over on this godforsaken road after dark?'

'I really don't know, ma'am.'

'Unmarked cars rarely make traffic stops, but psychopaths often do.'

Bright blue pulsed on his pathetically young face. He probably did not know what a psychopath was.

'I will never stop for your unmarked Chevrolet if you and I repeat this misadventure for the rest of our lives. Do you understand?' I said.

A car sped from the direction of the Academy and halted on the other side of the guard booth.

'You drew down on me,' I said, outraged, as a car door shut. 'You pulled a goddam nine-millimeter pistol and pointed it at me. Has no one in the Marine Corps taught you the meaning of *unnecessary force*?'

'Kay?' Benton Wesley appeared in the pulsing dark.

I realized the guard must have called him, but I did not understand why Wesley would be here at this hour. He could not have come from home. He lived almost in Fredericksburg.

'Good evening,' he sternly said to the MP.

They stepped aside and I could not hear what they said. But the MP walked back to his small, bland car. Blue lights quit and he drove away.

'Thanks,' Wesley said to the guard. 'Come on,' he said to me. 'Follow me.'

He did not drive into the parking lot I usually used but to reserved spaces behind Jefferson. There was no other car in the lot but a big pickup truck I recognized as Marino's. I got out.

'What is going on?' I asked, my breath smoky in the cold.

'Marino's down in the unit.' Wesley was dressed in a dark sweater and dark slacks, and I sensed something had happened.

'Where's Lucy?' I quickly said.

He did not answer as he inserted his security card into a slot, opening a back door.

'You and I need to talk,' he said.

'No.' I knew what he meant. 'I am too worried.'

'Kay, I am not your enemy.'

'You have seemed like it at times.'

We walked quickly and did not bother with the elevator.

'I'm sorry,' he said. 'I love you and don't know what to do.'

'I know.' I was shaken. 'I don't know what to do, either. I keep wanting someone to tell me. But I don't want this, Benton. I want what we've had and I don't want it ever.'

For a while he did not speak.

'Lucy got a hit on CAIN,' he eventually said. 'We've deployed HRT.'

'Then she's here,' I said, relieved.

'She's in New York. We're on our way there.' He looked at his watch.

'I don't understand,' I said as our feet sounded on stairs.

We moved swiftly down a long corridor where hostage negotiators spent their days when they weren't abroad talking terrorists out of buildings and hijackers out of planes.

'I don't understand why she's in New York,' I said, unnerved. 'Why does she need to be there?'

We walked into his office, where Marino was squatting by a tote bag. It was unzipped, and next to it on the carpet were a shaving kit and three loaded magazines for his Sig Sauer. He was looking for something else and glanced up at me.

He said to Wesley, 'Can you believe it? I forgot my razor.'

'They have them in New York,' Wesley said, his mouth grim.

'I've been in South Carolina,' I said. 'I talked to the Gaults.'

Marino stopped digging and stared up at me. Wesley sat behind his desk.

'I hope they don't know where their son is staying,' he said oddly.

'I have no indication that they do.' I looked curiously at him.

'Well, maybe it doesn't matter.' He rubbed his eyes. 'I just don't want anyone tipping him off.'

'Lucy kept him on CAIN long enough for the call to be traced,' I assumed.

Marino got up and sat in a chair. He said, 'The squirrel's got a crib right on Central Park.'

'Where?' I asked.

'The Dakota.'

I thought of Christmas Eve when we were at the fountain in Cherry Hill. Gault could have been watching. He could have seen our lights from his room.

'He can't afford the Dakota,' I said.

'You remember his fake ID?' Marino asked. 'The Italian guy named Benelli?'

'It's his apartment?'

'Yes,' Wesley answered. 'Mr. Benelli apparently is a flamboyant heir to a considerable family fortune. Management has assumed the current occupant – Gault – is an Italian relative. At any rate, they don't ask many questions there, and he's been speaking with an accent. It also is very convenient because Mr. Benelli does not pay his rent. His father in Verona does.'

'Why can't you go into the Dakota and get Gault?' I asked. 'Why can't HRT do that?'

'We could, but I'd rather not. It's too risky,' Wesley said. 'This isn't war, Kay. We don't want any casualties, and we are bound by law. There are people inside the Dakota who could get hurt. We don't know where Benelli is. He could be in the room.'

'Yeah, in a plastic bag in a steamer trunk,' Marino said.

'We know where Gault is and we have the building under surveillance. But Manhattan is not where I would have chosen to catch this guy. It's too damn crowded. You get in an exchange of firepower – I don't care how good you are – and someone's going to get hit. Someone else is going to die. A woman, a man, a child who just happens to walk out at the wrong time.'

'I understand,' I said. 'I'm not disagreeing with you. Is Gault in the apartment now? And what about Carrie?'

Wesley said, 'Neither has been sighted, and we have no reason to suspect Carrie travels with him.'

'He hasn't used my charge card to buy her plane tickets,' I considered. 'That much I can tell.'

'We do know Gault was in the apartment as recently as eight o'clock this evening,' Wesley said. 'That's when he got on the line and Lucy trapped him.'

'She trapped him?' I looked at both men. 'She trapped him from here and now she's gone? Did she get deployed with HRT?'

I had a bizarre image of Lucy in black boots and fatigues being loaded on a plane at Andrews Air Force Base. I imagined her with a group of supremely fit helicopter pilots, snipers and experts in explosives, and my incredulity grew.

Wesley met my eyes. 'She's been in New York for the past couple of days. She's working on the Transit Police computer. She got the hit in New York.'

'Why not work here where CAIN is located?' I wanted to know, because I did not want Lucy in New York. I did not want her in the same state where Temple Gault was.

'Transit's got an extremely sophisticated system,' he said.

Marino spoke. 'It's got things we don't have, Doc.'

'Like what?'

'Like a computerized map of the entire subway system.' Marino leaned closer to me, forearms resting on his knees. He understood what I was feeling. I could see it in his eyes. 'We think that's how Gault's been getting around.'

Wesley explained, 'We think Carrie Grethen somehow got Gault into the Transit Police computer, through CAIN. He was able to map out for himself a way to move around the city through the tunnels, so he could get his drugs and commit his crimes. He has had access to detailed diagrams that include stations, catwalks, tunnels and escape hatches.'

'What escape hatches?' I asked.

'The subway system has emergency exits that lead out of the tunnels, in the event a train should have to stop for some reason down there. Passengers can be routed through an emergency exit that will bring them back above ground. Central Park has a number of them.'

Wesley got up and went to his suitcase. He opened it and pulled out a thick roll of white paper. Removing the rubber band, he spread open very long drawings of New York's subway system that included all tracks and structures, every manhole, trash can, car marker, platform edge. The diagrams covered most of his office floor, some more than six feet long. I studied them, fascinated.

'This is from Commander Penn,' I said.

'Right,' Wesley replied. 'And what's on her computer is even more detailed. For example' – he squatted, pointing and moving his tie out of the way – 'in March of 1979, turnstiles at CB number 300 were removed. That's right here.' He showed me on a drawing of the 110th Street station at Lenox Avenue and 112th Street.

'And a change like that now,' he went on, 'goes directly into the Transit Police computer system.'

'Meaning that any changes are instantly reflected on the computerized maps,' I said.

'Right.' He pulled another drawing closer, this one of the Eighty-first Street Museum of Natural History station. 'Now the reason we think Gault is using these maps is right here.' He tapped an area on the field survey that indicated an emergency exit very near Cherry Hill.

'If Gault was looking at this drawing,' Wesley went on, 'he most likely would choose this emergency exit as the one to come in and out of when he committed the murder in Central Park. That way he and his victim could travel unseen through the tunnels after leaving the museum, and when they surfaced in the park they would be very close to the fountain where he planned to display the body.

'But what you don't know from looking at this three-month-old printout is the day before the murder, the Maintenance of Way Department bolted that escape door shut for repairs. We think that might be why Gault and his victim started out closer to the Ramble,' he said. 'Some footwear impressions recovered in that area, as it turns out, are consistent with theirs. And the tracks were found near an emergency exit.'

'So you have to ask how he knew that exit in Cherry Hill was bolted shut,' Marino said.

'I suppose he could have checked it first,' I said.

'You can't do that above ground because the doors don't open except from inside the tunnels,' Marino said.

'Maybe he was down in the tunnel and saw from the inside that the door was bolted,' I argued, because I sensed where this was leading and did not like it.

'Of course that's possible,' Wesley reasonably said. 'But Transit cops go down into the tunnels a lot. They're all over the platforms and the stations, and none of them remembers seeing Gault. I believe he travels down there by computer until it suits his purposes to make an appearance.'

'What is Lucy's role?' I asked.

'To manipulate,' Marino said.

'I'm not a computer person,' Wesley added. 'But as best I can understand, she has worked it so when he logs on to this computerized map, he's really seeing one she is altering.'

'Altering for what purpose?'

'We're hoping to come up with a way of trapping him like a rat in a maze.'

'I thought HRT had been deployed.'

'We are going to try whatever it takes.'

'Well then, let me suggest you consider one other plan,' I said. 'Gault goes to Houston Professional Pharmacy when he wants money.'

They looked at me as if I were crazy.

'That's where his mother has been wiring money to Temple's sister, Jayne—'

'Wait a minute,' Marino interrupted

But I went on, 'I tried to call earlier to tell you. I know that Temple has been intercepting the money because Mrs. Gault wired money after Jayne was already dead. And someone signed for it. This person knew the test question.'

'Hold on,' Marino said. 'Hold on one damn minute. Are you telling me that son of a bitch murdered his own sister?'

'Yes,' I answered. 'She was his twin.'

'Jesus. No one told me.' He looked accusingly at Wesley.

'You just got here two minutes before Kay got arrested,' Wesley said to him.

'I didn't get arrested,' I said. 'Her middle name actually is Jayne, with a *y*,' I added, and then I filled them in.

'This changes everything,' Wesley said, and he called New York.

It was almost eleven when he got off the phone. He stood and picked up his briefcase and his bag and a portable radio that was on his desk. Marino rose from his chair, too.

'Unit three to unit seventeen,' Wesley spoke into the radio.

'Seventeen.'

'We're heading your way.'

'Yes, sir.'

'I'm coming with you,' I said to Wesley.

He looked at me. I was not on the original passenger list.

'All right,' he said. 'Let's go.'

19

We discussed the plan in the air as our pilot flew toward Manhattan. The Bureau's New York field office would assign an undercover agent to the pharmacy at Houston and Second Avenue, while a pair of agents from Atlanta would be dispatched to Live Oaks Plantation. This was happening even as we talked into our voice-activated microphones.

If Mrs. Gault maintained the usual schedule, money was due to be wired again tomorrow. Since Gault had no way of knowing his parents had been told their daughter was dead, he would assume the money would arrive as usual.

'What he's not going to do is just take a taxi to the pharmacy.' Wesley's voice filled my headset as I looked out at plains of darkness.

'Naw,' Marino said. 'I doubt it. He knows everybody but the queen of England is out looking for him.'

'We want him to go underground.'

'It seems riskier down there,' I said, thinking of Davila. 'No lights. And the third rails and the trains.'

'I know,' said Wesley. 'But he has the mentality of a terrorist. He doesn't care who he kills. We can't have a shoot-out in

Manhattan in the middle of the day.'

I understood his point.

'So how do you make certain he travels through the tunnels to get to the pharmacy?' I asked.

'We turn up the heat without scaring him off.'

'How?'

'Apparently, there's a March Against Crime parade tomorrow.'

'That's appropriate,' I said ironically. 'It's through the Bowery?'

'Yes. The route can easily be changed to go along Houston and Second Avenue.'

Marino cut in. 'All you do is move traffic cones.'

'Transit PD can send out a computerized communication notifying police in the Bowery that there is a parade at such and such a time. Gault will see on the computer that the parade is supposed to go through the area at the exact time he is supposed to pick up the money. He'll see that the subway station at Second Avenue has been temporarily closed.'

A nuclear power plant in Delaware glowed like a heating element on high, and cold air seeped in.

I said, 'So he'll know it's not a good time to be traveling above ground.'

'Exactly. When there's a parade, there are cops.'

'I worry about him deciding not to go for the money,' Marino said.

'He'll go for it,' Wesley said as if he knew.

'Yes,' I said. 'He's addicted to crack. That is a more powerful motivator than any fear he might have.'

'Do you think he killed his sister for money?' Marino asked.

'No,' Wesley said. 'But the small sums her mother sent her were just one more thing he appropriated. In the end, he took everything his sister ever had.'

'No, he didn't,' I said. 'She was never evil like him. That's the best thing she had, and Gault couldn't take it.'

'We're arriving in the Big Apple with guns,' Marino's voice blurted over the air.

314

'My bag,' I said. 'I forgot.'

'I'll talk to the commissioner first thing in the morning.'

'It is first thing in the morning,' Marino said.

We landed at the helipad on the Hudson near the *Intrepid* aircraft carrier, which was strung with Christmas lights. A Transit Police cruiser was waiting, and I remembered arriving here not that long ago and meeting Commander Penn for the first time. I remembered seeing Jayne's blood in the snow when I did not know the unbearable truth about her.

We arrived at the New York Athletic Club again.

'Which room is Lucy in?' I asked Wesley as we checked in with an old man who looked as if he had always worked unearthly hours.

'She isn't.' He handed out keys.

We walked away from the desk.

'Okay,' I said. 'Now tell me.'

Marino yawned. 'We sold her to a small factory in the Garment District.'

'She's in protective custody, sort of.' Wesley smiled a little as brass elevator doors opened. 'She's staying with Commander Penn.'

In my room I took my suit off and hung it in the shower. I steamed it as I had the last two nights and considered throwing it out should I ever get a chance to change my clothes again. I slept under several blankets and with windows open wide. At six I got up before the alarm. I showered and ordered a bagel and coffee.

At seven, Wesley called and then he and Marino were at my door. We went down to the lobby and on to an awaiting police car. My Browning was in my briefcase, and I hoped Wesley got special permits and did it fast, because I did not wish to be in violation of New York gun laws. I thought of Bernhard Goetz.

'Here's what we're going to do,' Wesley said as we drove toward lower Manhattan. 'I'm going to spend the morning on the phone. Marino, I want you out on the street with Transit cops. Make damn sure those traffic cones are exactly where they ought to be.'

'Got it.'

'Kay, I want you with Commander Penn and Lucy. They'll be in direct contact with the agents in South Carolina and the one at the pharmacy.' Wesley looked at his watch. 'The agents in South Carolina, as a matter of fact, should be reaching the plantation within the hour.'

'Let's just hope the Gaults don't screw this up,' said Marino, who was riding shotgun.

Wesley looked over at me.

'When I left the Gaults they seemed willing to help,' I said. 'But can't we just wire the money in her name and keep her out of it?'

Wesley said, 'We could. But the less attention we draw to what we're doing, the better. Mrs. Gault lives in a small town. If agents go in and wire the money, someone might talk.'

'And what someone might say might get back to Gault?' I asked skeptically.

'If the Western Union agent in Beaufort somehow tips his hand to the one here in New York, you just never know what might happen to scare off Gault. We don't want to take the chance, and the fewer people we involve, the better.'

'I understand,' I said.

'That's another reason I want you with the commander,' Wesley went on. 'Should Mrs. Gault decide to interfere in any way, I'm going to need you to talk to her and get her back in the right frame of mind.'

'Gault just might show up at the pharmacy anyway,' Marino said. 'He might not know until he gets to the counter that the money's not coming, if that's what happens because his old lady wimps out on us.'

'We don't know what he'll do,' Wesley said. 'But I would suspect he'd call first.'

'She's got to wire the money,' I agreed. 'She absolutely must go through with it. And that's hard.'

'Right, it's her son,' Wesley said.

'Then what happens?' I asked.

'We've arranged it so the parade starts at two, which is about the time the money has been wired in the past. We'll have HRT out – some of them will actually be in the parade. And there will be other agents as well. Plus plainclothes police. These will be mostly positioned in the subway and in areas where there are emergency exits.'

'What about in the pharmacy?' I asked.

Wesley paused. 'Of course, we'll have a couple agents in there. But we don't want to grab Gault in the store or near it. He might start spraying bullets. If there are to be any casualties, it will be just one.'

'All I ask is let me be the lucky guy who does him,' Marino said. 'After that I could retire.'

'We absolutely must get him underground.' Wesley was emphatic. 'We don't know what weapons he has at present. We don't know how many people he could take out with karate. There's so much we don't know. But I believe he's fired up on coke and rapidly decompensating. And he's not afraid. That's why he's so dangerous.'

'Where are we going?' I asked, watching dreary buildings flow by as a light rain fell. It was not a good day for a parade.

'Penn's set up a command post at Bleecker Street, which is close to Houston Pharmacy but a safe distance, too,' Wesley said. 'Her team's been at it all night, bringing in computer equipment and so on. Lucy's with them.'

'This is inside the actual subway station?'

The officer driving answered, 'Yes, ma'am. It's a local stop that operates only during the week. Trains don't stop here on the weekends, so it should be quiet. Transit PD's got a miniprecinct here that covers the Bowery.'

He was parking in front of the stairs going down into a station.

Sidewalks and streets were busy with people carrying umbrellas and holding newspapers over their heads.

'You just go down and you'll see the wooden door to the left of the turnstiles. It's next to the information window,' the officer said.

He unhooked his mike. 'Unit one-eleven.'

'Unit one-eleven,' the dispatcher came back.

'Ten-five unit three.'

The dispatcher contacted unit three and I recognized Commander Penn's voice. She knew we had arrived. Wesley, Marino and I carefully descended slick steps as rain fell harder. The tile floor inside was wet and dirty, but no one was around. I was getting increasingly anxious.

We passed the information window, and Wesley knocked on a wooden door. It opened and Detective Maier, whom I had first met at the morgue after Davila's death, let us into a space that had been turned, essentially, into a control room. Closed-circuit television monitors were on a long table, and my niece sat at a console equipped with telephones, radio equipment and computers.

Frances Penn, wearing the dark commando sweater and pants of the troops she commanded, came straight to me and warmly grasped my hand.

'Kay, I'm so happy you're here,' she said, and she was full of nervous energy.

Lucy was absorbed in a row of four monitors. Each showed a blueprint of a different section of the subway system.

Wesley said to Commander Penn, 'I've got to go on to the field office. Marino will be out with your guys, as we discussed.'

She nodded.

'So I'll leave Dr. Scarpetta here.'

'Very good.'

'Where is this going down, exactly?' I inquired.

'Well, we're closing Second Avenue station, which is right there at the pharmacy,' Commander Penn answered me. 'We'll block the entrance with traffic cones and sawhorses. We can't risk a confrontation when civilians are in the area. We expect him to come up through the tunnel along the northbound track or leave that way, and he's more likely to be enticed by Second Avenue if it's not open.' She paused, looking over at Lucy. 'It will make more sense when your niece shows you on the screen.'

'Then you hope to grab him somewhere inside that station,' I said.

'That's what we hope,' Wesley said. 'We'll have guys out there in the dark. HRT will be out there and all around. The bottom line is we want to grab him away from people.'

'Of course,' I said.

Maier was watching us closely. 'How did you figure out the lady from the park was his sister?' he asked, looking straight at me.

I gave him a quick summary, adding, 'We'll use DNA to verify it.'

'Not from what I heard,' he said. 'I heard they lost her blood and shit at the morgue.'

'Where did you hear that?' I asked.

'I know a bunch of guys who work over there. You know, detectives in the Missing Persons Division for NYPD.'

'We will get her identified,' I said, watching him closely.

'Well, you ask me, it's a shame if they figure it out.'

Commander Penn was listening carefully. I sensed she and I were arriving at the same conclusion.

'Why would you say that?' she asked him.

Maier was getting angry. 'Because the way the stinking system works in this stinking city is we nab the asshole here, right? So he gets charged with killing that lady because there isn't enough evidence to convict him of killing Jimmy Davila. And we don't have capital punishment in New York. And the case just gets weaker if the lady's got no name – if no one knows who she is.'

'It sounds as if you're saying you want the case to be weak,' Wesley said.

'Yeah. It sounds that way because I do.'

Marino was staring at him with no expression. He said, 'The toad whacked Davila with his own service revolver. The way it ought to work is Gault ought to fry.'

'You're damn right he should.' Maier's jaw muscles clenched. 'He wasted a cop. A goddam good cop who's getting accused of a bunch of bullshit because that's what happens when you get killed in the line of duty. People, politicians, internal affairs – they speculate. Everybody's got an agenda. The whole world does. We'd all be better off if Gault gets tried in Virginia, not here.'

He looked at me again. I knew what had happened to Jayne's biological samples. Detective Maier had gotten his friends at the morgue to do him a favor in honor of their slain comrade. Though what they had done was terribly wrong, I almost could not blame them.

'You got the electric chair in Virginia, where Gault's also committed murders,' he said. 'And word has it that the Doc here breaks the record for getting these animals convicted of capital murder. Only if the bastard gets tried in New York, you probably won't be testifying, right?'

'I don't know,' I said.

'See. She don't know. That means forget it.' He looked around at everyone as if he'd argued his case and there could be no rebuttal. 'The asshole needs to go to Virginia and get cooked, if he don't get nailed here first by one of us.'

'Detective Maier,' Commander Penn quietly said, 'I need to see you in private. Let's go back to my office.'

They left and went through a door in back. She would pull him from the assignment because he could not be controlled. She would give him a Complaint and he would probably be suspended.

'We're out of here,' Wesley said.

'Yeah,' Marino said. 'Next time you see us it will be on TV.' He referred to the monitors around the control room.

I was taking off my coat and gloves and about to talk to Lucy when the door in back opened and Maier emerged. He walked with quick, angry strides until he got to me.

'Do it for Jimbo,' he said with emotion. 'Don't let that asshole get away with it.'

The veins were standing out in his neck and he looked up at the ceiling. 'I'm sorry.' He blinked back tears and almost could not talk as he flung open the door and left.

'Lucy?' I said, and we were alone.

She was typing and concentrating intensely. 'Hi,' she said.

I went to her and kissed the top of her head.

'Have a seat,' she said without looking away from what she was doing.

I scanned monitors. There were arrows for Manhattan-bound, Brooklyn-, Bronx- and Queens-bound trains and an intricate grid showing streets, schools and medical centers. All were numbered. I sat beside her and got my glasses out of my briefcase as Commander Penn reappeared, her face stressed.

'That was no fun to do,' she said, standing behind us, the pistol on her belt almost touching my ear.

'What are these flashing symbols that look like twisted ladders?' I asked, pointing out several on the screen.

'They're the emergency exits,' Commander Penn said.

'Can you explain what you're doing here?' I asked.

'Lucy, I'll let you do that,' the commander said.

'It's really pretty simple,' Lucy said, and I never believed her when she said that. 'I'm supposing that Gault is looking at these maps, too. So I'm letting him see what I want him to see.'

She hit several keys and another part of the subway was there before me, with its symbols and long linear depictions of tracks. She typed and a hatchwork appeared in red.

'This is the route we believe he'll take,' she said. 'Logic would tell you that he'll penetrate the subway here.'

Lucy pointed to the monitor left of the one directly in front of her. 'This is for the Museum of Natural History station. And as you can see there are three emergency exits right here near Hayden Planetarium and one up by Beresford Apartments. He also could go southbound closer to Kenilworth Apartments and get into the tunnels that way and then pick any platform he wants when it's time to get on a train.

'I haven't altered anything on these field surveys,' Lucy went on. 'It's more important to confuse him at the other end, when he gets to the Bowery.'

She rapidly typed and one after another images appeared on each monitor. She was able to tilt, move and manipulate them as if they were models she was turning in her hands. On the center screen in front of her the symbol for an emergency exit was lit up and a square had been drawn around it.

'We think this is his snake hole,' Lucy resumed. 'It is an emergency exit where Fourth and Third merge into the Bowery.' She pointed. 'Here behind this big brownstone. The Cooper Union Foundation Building.'

Commander Penn spoke. 'The reason we think he has been using this exit is we've discovered it has been tampered with. A folded strip of aluminum foil has been wedged between the door and its frame so someone could access the exit from above ground.

'It's also the closest exit to the pharmacy,' Commander Penn continued. 'It's remote, back here behind this building, basically in an alleyway between Dumpsters. Gault could go in and out whenever he pleased, and it's unlikely anyone would see him, even in broad daylight.'

'And there's another thing,' Lucy said. 'At Cooper Square there's a famous music store. The Carl Fischer Music Store.'

'Right,' Commander Penn said. 'Someone who works there recalls Jayne. Now and then she wandered in and browsed. This would have been during December.'

'Did anyone talk to her?' I asked, and the image made me sad.

'All they recalled was that she was interested in jazz sheet music. My point is, we don't know what Gault's connections to this area are. But they could be more involved than we think.'

'What we've done,' Lucy said, 'is take away this emergency exit. The police have bolted it shut, and boom.'

She hit more keys. The symbol was no longer lit up and a message next to it said *Disabled*.

'It seems that might be a good location to catch him,' I said. 'Why don't we want him there behind the Cooper Union Building?'

'Again,' the commander said, 'it's too close to a crowded area, and should Gault duck back into the tunnel, he would be very deep inside it. Literally, in the bowels of the Bowery. A pursuit would be terribly dangerous and we might not catch him. My guess is he knows his way around down there even better than we do.'

'All right,' I said. 'Then what happens?'

'What happens is, since he can't use his favorite emergency exit, he has two choices. He can pick another exit that's farther north along the tracks. Or he can continue walking through the tunnels and surface at the Second Avenue platform.'

'We don't think he'll pick another emergency exit,' Commander Penn said. 'It would place him above ground too long. And with a parade in progress, he's going to know there will be a lot of cops out. So our theory is he will stay in the tunnels for as long as he can.'

'Right,' Lucy said. 'It's perfect. He knows the station has been temporarily closed. No one's going to see him when he comes up from the tracks. And then he's right there at the pharmacy – practically next door to it. He gets his money and goes back the same way he came.'

'Maybe he will,' I said. 'And maybe he won't.'

'He knows about the parade,' Lucy said adamantly. 'He knows the Second Avenue station is closed. He knows the emergency exit he's tampered with has been disabled. He

323

knows everything we want him to know.'

I looked skeptically at her. 'Please tell me how you can be so sure.'

'I've worked it so I get a message the minute those files are accessed. I know all of them were and I know when.' Anger flashed in her eyes.

'Someone else couldn't have?'

'Not the way I rigged it.'

'Kay,' Commander Penn said. 'There's another big part of all this. Look over here.' She directed my attention to the closed-circuit TV monitors set up on a long, high table. 'Lucy, show her.'

Lucy typed, and the televisions came on, each showing a different subway station. I could see people walking past. Umbrellas were closed and tucked under arms, and I recognized shopping bags from Bloomingdale's, Dean & DeLuca food market and the Second Avenue Deli.

'It's stopped raining,' I said.

'Now watch this,' Lucy said.

She typed more commands, synchronizing closed-circuit TV with the computerized diagrams. When one was on-screen, so was the other.

'What I can do,' she explained, 'is act as an air traffic controller, in a sense. If Gault does something unexpected, I will be in constant contact with the cops, the feds, via radio.'

'For example, if, God forbid, he should break free and head deep into the system, along these tracks here' – Commander Penn pointed to a map on screen – 'then Lucy can apprise police by radio that there is a wooden barricade coming up on the right. Or a platform edge, express train tracks, an emergency exit, a passageway, a signal tower.'

'This is if he escapes and we must chase him through the hell where he killed Davila,' I said. 'This is if the worst happens.'

Frances Penn looked at me. 'What is the worst when you're dealing with him?'

'I pray we have already seen it,' I said.

'You know that Transit's got a touch screen telephone system.' Lucy showed me. 'If the numbers are in the computer, you can dial anywhere in the world. And what's really cool is 911. If it's dialed above ground, the call goes to NYPD. If it's dialed in the subway, it comes to Transit Police.'

'When do you close Second Avenue station?' I got up and said to Commander Penn.

She looked at her watch. 'In a little less than an hour.'

'Will the trains run?'

'Of course,' she said, 'but they won't stop there.'

20

The March Against Crime began on time with fifteen church groups and a miscellaneous contingent of men, women and children who wanted to take their neighborhoods back. The weather had worsened and snow blew on frigid winds that drove more people into taxis and the subways because it was too cold to walk.

At two-fifteen, Lucy, Commander Penn and I were in the control room, every monitor, television and radio turned on. Wesley was in one of several Bureau cars that ERF had painted to look like yellow cabs and equipped with radios, scanners, and other surveillance devices. Marino was on the street with Transit cops and plainclothes FBI. HRT was divided among the Dakota, the drugstore and Bleecker Street. We were unclear on the precise location of anyone because no one on the outside was standing still, and we were in here, not moving.

'Why hasn't anyone called?' Lucy complained.

'He hasn't been sighted,' said Commander Penn, and she was steady but uptight.

'I assume the parade has started,' I said.

Commander Penn said, 'It's on Lafayette, headed this way.'

She and Lucy were wearing headphones that plugged into the base station on the console. They were on different channels.

'All right, all right,' Commander Penn said, sitting up straighter. 'We've spotted him. The number seven platform,' she exclaimed to Lucy, whose fingers flew. 'He's just come in from a cat-walk. He's entered the system from a tunnel that runs under the park.'

Then the number seven platform was on black-and-white TV. We watched a figure in a long dark coat. He wore boots, a hat and dark glasses, and stood back from other passengers at the platform's edge. Lucy brought up another subway survey on the screen as Commander Penn stayed on the radio. I watched passengers walking, sitting, reading maps and standing. A train screamed by and got slower as it stopped. Doors opened and he got on.

'Which way is he bound?' I asked.

'South. He's coming this way,' Commander Penn said, excited.

'He's on the A line,' Lucy said, studying her monitors.

'Right.' Commander Penn got on the air. 'He can only go as far as Washington Square,' she told someone. 'Then he can transfer and take the F line straight to Second Avenue.'

Lucy said, 'We'll check one station after another. We don't know where he might get off. But he's got to get off somewhere so he can go back into the tunnels.'

'He has to do that if he comes in the Second Avenue way,' Commander Penn relayed to the radio. 'He can't take the train in there because it's not stopping there.'

Lucy manipulated the closed-circuit television monitors. At rapid intervals they showed a different station as a train we could not see headed toward us.

'He's not at Forty-second,' she said. 'We don't see him at Penn Station or Twenty-third.'

Monitors blinked on and off, showing platforms and people who did not know they were being watched.

'If he stayed on that train he should be at Fourteenth Street,' Commander Penn said.

But if he was, he did not disembark, or at least we did not see him. Then our luck suddenly changed in an unexpected way.

'My God,' Lucy said. 'He's at Grand Central Station. How the hell did he get there?'

'He must have turned east before we thought he would and cut through Times Square,' Commander Penn said.

'But why?' Lucy said. 'That doesn't make sense.'

Commander Penn radioed unit two, which was Benton Wesley. She asked him if Gault had called the pharmacy yet. She took her headphones off and set the microphone so we could hear what was said.

'No, there's been no call,' came Wesley's reply.

'Our monitors have just picked him up at Grand Central,' she explained.

'What?'

'I don't know why he's gone that way. But there are so many alternative routes he could take. He could get off anywhere for any reason.'

'I'm afraid so,' Wesley said.

'What about in South Carolina?' Commander Penn then asked.

'Everything's ten-four. The bird has flown and landed,' Wesley said.

Mrs. Gault had wired the money, or the Bureau had. We watched while her only son casually rode with other people who did not know he was a monster.

'Wait a minute,' Commander Penn continued to broadcast information. 'He's at Fourteenth Street and Union Square, going south right at you.'

It drove me crazy that we could not stop him. We could see him and yet it did no good.

'It sounds like he's changing trains a lot,' Wesley said.

Commander Penn said, 'He's gone again. The train's left.

We've got Astor Place on-screen. That's the last stop unless he goes past us and gets out at the Bowery.'

'The train's stopping,' Lucy announced.

We watched people in the monitors and did not see Gault.

'All right, he must be staying on,' Commander Penn said into the microphone.

'We've lost him,' Lucy said.

She changed pictures like a frustrated person flipping television channels. We did not see him.

'Shit,' she muttered.

'Where could he be?' The commander was baffled. 'He's got to get out somewhere. If he's going into the pharmacy, he can't use the exit at Cooper Union.' She looked at Lucy. 'That's it. Maybe he's going to try. But he won't get out. It's bolted. But he might not know.'

She said. 'He's got to know. He read the electronic messages we sent.'

She scanned some more. Still, we did not see him and the radio remained tensely silent.

'Damn,' Lucy said. 'He should be on the number six line. Let's look at Astor Place and Lafayette again.'

It did no good.

We sat without talking for a while, looking at the shut wooden door that led into our empty station. Above us, hundreds of people were walking sodden streets to demonstrate they were fed up with crime. I began looking at a subway map.

Commander Penn said, 'He should be at Second Avenue now. He should have gotten off at an earlier or later stop and walked the rest of the way through the tunnel.'

A terrible thought occurred to me. 'He could do the same thing here. We're not as close to the pharmacy, but we're on the number six line too.'

'Yeah,' Lucy said, turning around to look at me. 'The walk from here to Houston is nothing.'

'But we're closed,' I said.

Lucy was typing again.

I got up out of my chair and looked at Commander Penn. 'We're here alone. It's just the three of us. The trains don't stop here on the weekends. There is no one. Everyone is at Second Avenue and the pharmacy.'

'Base station to unit two,' Lucy was saying into the radio.

'Unit two,' Wesley said.

'Everything ten-four? Because we've lost him.'

'Stand by.'

I opened my briefcase and got out my gun. I cocked it and pushed on the safety.

'What's your ten-twenty?' Commander Penn got on the air to ask for their location.

'Holding steady at the pharmacy.'

Screens were flashing by crazily as Lucy tried to locate Gault.

'Hold on. Hold on,' Wesley's voice came over the air.

Then we heard Marino. 'It looks like we've got him.'

'You've got him?' Commander Penn, incredulous, asked the radio. 'What is the location?'

'He's walking into the pharmacy.' Wesley was back. 'Wait a minute. Wait a minute.'

There was silence. Then Wesley said, 'He's at the counter getting the money. Stand by.'

We waited in frantic silence.

Three minutes passed. Wesley was back on the air. 'He's leaving. We're going to close in once he gets inside the terminal. Stand by.'

'What's he wearing?' I asked. 'Are we sure it's the person who got on at the museum?'

Nobody paid me any mind.

'Oh Christ,' Lucy suddenly exclaimed, and we looked at the monitors.

We could see the platforms of Second Avenue station, and HRT exploding out of the darkness of the tracks. Dressed in black fatigues and combat boots, they ran across the platform and up steps leading to the street.

'Something's gone wrong,' Commander Penn said. 'They're grabbing him above ground!'

Voices ricocheted on the radio.

'We've got him.'

'He's trying to run.'

'Okay, okay, we've got his gun. He's down.'

'Have you got him cuffed?'

A siren went off inside the control room. Lights along the ceiling began flashing blood red, and a red code 429 began flashing on a computer screen.

'Mayday!' Commander Penn exclaimed. 'An officer is down! He's hit the emergency button on his radio!' She stared at the computer screen in stunned disbelief.

'What's happening?' Lucy demanded into the radio.

'I don't know,' Wesley's voice crackled. 'Something's wrong. Stand by.'

'That's not where it is. The Mayday isn't at Second Avenue station,' Commander Penn said, awed. 'This code on the screen is Davila's.'

'Davila?' I said numbly. 'Jimmy Davila?'

'He was unit four twenty-nine. That's his code. It hasn't been reassigned. It's right here.'

We stared at the screen. The flashing red code was changing locations along a computerized grid. I was shocked no one had thought of it before.

'Was Davila's radio with him when his body was found?' I asked.

Commander Penn didn't react.

'Gault's got it,' I said. 'He's got Davila's radio.'

Wesley's voice came back, and he could not know of our difficulty. He could not know about the Mayday.

'We're not sure we have him,' Wesley said. 'We're not sure who we have.'

Lucy intensely looked over at me. 'Carrie,' she said. 'They're not sure if they have her or Gault. She and Gault are probably dressed alike again.'

Inside our small control room with no windows and no people nearby, we watched the flashing red Mayday code move along the computer screen, getting closer to where we sat.

'It's in the southbound tunnel heading straight at us,' Commander Penn said with growing urgency.

'She didn't get the messages we sent.' Lucy had it figured out.

'She?' Commander Penn asked, looking oddly at her.

'She doesn't know about the parade or that Second Avenue is closed,' Lucy went on. 'She may have tried the emergency exit in the alleyway and couldn't get out because it's been bolted. So she just stayed under and has been moving around since we sighted her at Grand Central Station.'

'We didn't see Gault or Carrie on the platforms of the stations closer to us,' I said. 'And you don't know it's her.'

'There are so many stations,' Commander Penn said. 'Someone could have gotten out and we just didn't see them.'

'Gault sent her to the pharmacy for him,' I said, more unnerved by the minute. 'He somehow knows every goddam thing we're doing.'

'CAIN,' Lucy muttered.

'Yes. That and he's probably been watching.'

Lucy had our location, the Bleecker Street local stop, on closed-circuit TV. Three of the monitors showed the platform and turnstiles from different angles, but one monitor was dark.

'Something's blocking one of the cameras,' she said.

'Was it blocked earlier?' I asked.

'Not when we first got here,' she said. 'But we haven't been monitoring this station where we are. There didn't seem to be a reason to check here.'

We watched the red code slowly move across the grid.

'We've got to stay off the air,' I told Commander Penn. 'He has a radio,' I added, because I knew Gault was the red code on our screen. I had no doubt. 'You know it's on and he's hearing every word we say.'

'Why's the Mayday light still on?' Lucy asked. 'Does she want us to know where she is?'

I stared at her. It was as if Lucy were in a trance.

'The button may have been hit inadvertently,' Commander Penn said. 'If you don't know about the button, you wouldn't realize it's for Maydays. And since it's a silent alarm, you could have it on and not know it.'

But I did not believe anything happening was inadvertent. Gault was coming to us because this was where he wanted to be. He was a shark swimming through the blackness of the tunnel, and I thought of what Anna had said about his hideous gifts to me.

'It's almost at the signal tower.' Lucy was pointing at the screen. 'Goddam that's close.'

We did not know what to do. If we radioed Wesley, Gault would overhear and disappear back through the tunnels. If we did not make contact, the troops would not know what was happening here. Lucy was at the door, and she opened it a little.

'What are you doing?' I almost screamed at her.

She quickly shut the door. 'It's the ladies' room. I guess a janitor propped open the door while cleaning and left it that way. The door's blocking the camera.'

'Did you see anybody out there?' I asked.

'No,' she said, hatred in her eyes. 'They think they have her. How do they know it's not Gault? It may be her who's got Davila's radio. I know her. She probably knows I'm in here.'

Commander Penn was tense when she said to me, 'There's some gear in the office.'

'Yes,' I said.

We hurried back to a cramped space with a beat-up wooden

desk and chair. She opened a cabinet and we grabbed shotguns, boxes of shells, and Kevlar vests. We were gone minutes, and when we returned to the control room Lucy was not there.

I looked at the closed-circuit TV monitors and saw a picture blink onto the fourth screen as someone shut the ladies' room door. The flashing red code on the survey grid was deeper inside the station now. It was on a catwalk. At any second it would be on the platform. I looked for my Browning pistol, but it was not on the console where I had left it.

'She took my gun,' I said in amazement. 'She's gone out there. She's gone after Carrie!'

We loaded shotguns as fast as we could but did not take the time for vests. My hands were clumsy and cold.

'You've got to radio Wesley,' I said, frantic. 'You've got to do something to get them here.'

'You can't go out there alone,' Commander Penn said.

'I can't leave Lucy out there alone.'

'We'll both go. Here. Take a flashlight.'

'No. You get help. Get someone here.'

I ran out not knowing what I would find. But the station was deserted. I stood perfectly still with the shotgun ready. I noticed the fixed camera bracketed to the green tile wall near the restrooms. The platform was empty, and I heard a train in the distance. It rushed by without pause because it did not have to stop at this station on Saturdays. Through windows I saw commuters sleeping, reading. Few seemed to notice the woman with a shotgun or even think it odd.

I wondered if Lucy could be in the bathroom, but that didn't make sense. There was a toilet just off the control room, inside our shelter where we had been all day. I walked closer to the platform as my heart pounded. The temperature was biting and I did not have my coat. My fingers were getting stiff around the stock of the gun.

It occurred to me with some relief that Lucy might have gone for help. Perhaps she shut the bathroom door and ran toward

Second Avenue. But what if she hadn't? I stared at that shut door and did not want to go through it.

I walked closer, one slow step at a time, and wished I had a pistol. A shotgun was awkward in confined spaces and around corners. When I reached the door my heart was pounding in my throat. I grabbed the handle, yanked hard and thrust myself inside with the shotgun aimed. The area around the sink was blank. I did not hear a sound. I looked under the stalls and stopped breathing when I saw blue trousers and a pair of brown leather work boots that were too big to be a woman's. Metal clanked.

I racked the shotgun, shaking as I demanded, 'Come out with your hands in the air!'

A big wrench clanged to the tile floor. The maintenance man in his coveralls and coat looked as if he might have a heart attack when he emerged from the stall. His eyes bulged from his head as he stared at me and the shotgun.

'I'm just fixing the toilet in here. I don't have any money,' he said in terror, hands straight up as if someone had just scored a touchdown.

'You're in the middle of a police operation,' I exclaimed, pointing the shotgun at the ceiling and pushing the safety on. 'You must get out of here now!'

He did not need the suggestion twice. He did not collect his tools or put the padlock back on the bathroom door. He fled up steps to the street as I began walking around the platform again. I located each of the cameras, wondering if Commander Penn saw me on the monitors. I was about to return to the control room when I looked down dark tracks and thought I heard voices. Suddenly there was scuffling and what sounded like a grunt. Lucy began to scream.

'No! No! Don't!'

A loud pop sounded like an explosion inside a metal drum. Sparks showered the darkness where the sound came from as the lights inside Bleecker Street station flickered.

*　　*　　*

Along the tracks there was no light, and I could not see because I did not dare turn on the one in my hand. I felt my way to a metal catwalk and carefully descended narrow stairs that led into the tunnel.

As I inched my way along, breathing rapid, shallow breaths, my eyes began to adjust. I could barely see the shapes of arches, rails and concrete places where the homeless made their beds. My feet hit trash and were loud when they knocked objects made of metal or glass.

I held the shotgun out in front to shield my head from any projection I might not see. I smelled filth and human waste, and flesh burning. The farther I walked, the more intense the stench, and then a strong light rose loudly like a moon as a train appeared on northbound tracks. Temple Gault was no more than fifteen feet ahead of me.

He held Lucy in a choke hold, a knife at her throat. Not far from them Detective Maier was welded to the third rail of southbound tracks, hands and teeth clenched as electricity flowed through his dead body. The train screamed past, returning the darkness.

'Let her go,' my voice quavered as I turned on the flashlight.

Squinting, Gault shielded his face from the light. He was so pale he looked like an albino, and I could see small muscles and tendons in his bare hands as he held the steel dissecting knife he had stolen from me. In one quick motion he could cut Lucy's throat to her spine. She stared at me in frozen terror.

'It's not her you want.' I stepped closer.

'Don't shine that light in my face,' he said. 'Set it down.'

I did not turn the flashlight off but slowly set it on a concrete ledge, where it cast an irregular light and shone directly on Detective Maier's burned, bloody head. I wondered why Gault did not tell me to put the shotgun down. Maybe he couldn't see it. I held it pointed up. I was no more than six feet from them now.

Gault's lips were chapped and he sniffed loudly. He was emaciated and disheveled, and I wondered if he were high on crack or on his way down. He wore jeans and jungle boots and a black leather jacket that was scraped and ripped. In a lapel was the caduceus pin I imagined he had bought in Richmond several days before Christmas.

'She's no fun.' I could not stop my voice from trembling.

His terrible eyes seemed to focus as a thread of blood ran down Lucy's neck. I tightened my grip on the gun.

'Let her go. Then it's just you and me. I'm who you want.'

Light sparked in his eyes, and I could almost see their weird blue color in the incomplete dark. His hands suddenly moved, violently shoving Lucy toward the third rail, and I lunged for her. I grabbed her sweater, yanking her on top of me, and together we fell to the ground and the shotgun clattered. Fire popped and sparks flew as the greedy rail grabbed it.

Gault smiled, my Browning in hand as he tossed the knife out of his way for now. He snapped the slide back, gripping the pistol with both hands, pointing the barrel at Lucy's head. He was used to his Glock and did not seem to know that my Browning had a safety. He squeezed the trigger and nothing happened. He did not understand.

'Run!' I yelled to Lucy, pushing her. 'RUN!'

Gault cocked the gun, but it was already cocked, and no cartridge ejected, so now he had a double-feed. Enraged, he squeezed the trigger, but the pistol was jammed.

'RUN!' I screamed.

I was on the ground and did not try to get away because I did not believe he would go after Lucy if I stayed here. He was forcing the slide open, shaking the gun as Lucy began to cry, stumbling through the dark. The knife was close to the third rail, and I groped for it as a rat ran over my legs and I cut myself on broken glass. My head was dangerously close to Gault's boots.

He could not seem to fix the gun and then I saw him tense as he looked at me. I could feel his thought as I tightened my grip on the cold steel handle. I knew what he could do with his feet, and I could not reach his chest or a major vessel in his neck because there was not time. I was on my knees. I raised the knife as he got in position to kick and plunged the surgical blade into his upper thigh. With both hands I cut as much as I could as he shrieked.

Arterial blood squirted across my face as I pulled the knife out and his transected femoral artery hemorrhaged to the rhythm of his horrible heart. I ducked out of the way because I knew HRT would have him in their sights and were waiting.

'You stabbed me,' Gault said with childlike disbelief. Hunched over, he stared with shocked fascination at blood spurting between his fingers clutching his leg. 'It won't stop. You're a doctor. Make it stop.'

I looked at him. His head was shaved beneath his cap. I thought of his dead twin, of Lucy's neck. A sniper rifle cracked twice from inside the tunnel in the direction of the station, bullets pinged, and Gault fell close to the rail he had almost thrown Lucy on. A train was coming and I did not move him free of the tracks. I walked away and did not look back.

Lucy, Wesley and I left New York on Monday, and first the helicopter flew due east. We passed over cliffs and the mansions of Westchester, finally reaching that ragged, wretched island not found on any tourist map. A crumbling smokestack rose from the ruins of an old brick penitentiary. We circled Potter's Field while prisoners and their guards gazed up into an overcast morning.

The BellJet Ranger went as low as it could go, and I hoped nothing would force us to land. I did not want to be near the men from Rikers Island. Grave markers looked like white teeth protruding from patchy grass, and someone had fashioned a cross from rocks. A flatbed truck was parked near the open grave, and men were lifting out the new pine box.

They stopped to look up as we churned air with more force than the harsh winds they knew. Lucy and I were in the helicopter's backseat, holding hands. Prisoners, bundled for winter, did not wave. A rusting ferry swayed on the water, waiting to take the coffin into Manhattan for one last test. Gault's twin sister would cross the river today. Jayne, at last, would go home.